THE MARTYR OF AUSCHWITZ

DAVID LAWS

BLOODHOUND
— BOOKS —

www.bloodhoundbooks.com

Print ISBN 978-1-914614-95-8

ALSO BY DAVID LAWS

The Fuhrer's Orphans

To Eleanor and Richard and all the grandchildren

PREFACE

In September 1938 Neville Chamberlain, the British Prime Minister, flew home from Munich waving a piece of paper containing Adolf Hitler's promise not to go to war. Later he proclaimed from 10 Downing Street: 'Peace with honour; peace for our time.'

Less than a year later war was declared, Britain having given the Führer what he wanted at Munich, an important part of Czechoslovakia, which led directly, by a series of German aggressions, to the Second World War.

Verdict from veteran German watcher, US radio correspondent William Shirer: 'The prime minister's stubborn, fanatical insistence on giving Hitler what he wanted... added immeasurably to the power of the Third Reich. The calamitous consequences of the surrender were scarcely comprehended by Chamberlain but, strategically, France and Great Britain were worse off when war was declared in September 1939 than at the time of Munich in 1938.'

Question: Why didn't someone stop the arch-appeaser?

Answer: Someone tried...

CHAPTER ONE

L imp, windless and shameful. A giant swastika flag and the Union Jack drape side by side over a portico in ignominious unison, below a bronze eagle sitting on a ledge clutching another swastika set in stone.

Enough to make me scream in dismay – but, of course, I don't. Tonight I'm playing the game, the foreign correspondent game, and I'm one of a crowd. These are my colleagues and friends, veterans of five turbulent years of reporting on the rise of Nazi Germany. The time is well past midnight and our little group is standing in the glare of a lamp on the bottom step of the grandiose entrance to the Führerbau.

We're waiting. Everyone is waiting. The three-storey building, designed on a scale to intimidate and belittle the human frame, squats like a skulking predator, exuding granite menace, illuminated in a ghostly glow. I listen to my heartbeat, trying to repress all thought of danger.

On the other side of the wide boulevard of Arcis Strasse, just around the corner from the Königsplatz parade ground, clusters of people gather beneath the lamp standards, casting spectral shadows into the roadway.

1

The correspondents are expecting that, when the conference ends, Joseph Goebbels, the Reich Minister of Propaganda, will shuffle down these eight fateful steps to announce to us and to the world the result of the deliberations of the four national leaders, probably insisting we use only the official communiqué, to be read over the airwaves and typed on to teleprinters. Straying from the official line will get my radio broadcast back to America cut off in mid-sentence – plus a ticket on the next plane home.

We've been here most of the day. We're tensed in anticipation but so too is the world. Everyone is on edge. War feels very close.

'Hey, Brad!' My colleague Bill Morrel, a veteran of the London *Daily Express*, is tugging open my big loden coat. Munich in late September is no place for shirtsleeves. 'What's all this?' he demands, peering at my dark-blue pinstripe and red pocket square beneath the coat. 'Why so dressed up all of a sudden? You been visiting Savile Row on the quiet?'

Forced grin, sweaty palms, bile in the mouth. 'For the big occasion,' is the best response I can manage. Humour this night is in short supply. Once again I scan the faces of the crowd. The English correspondents are ready to make a dash for the Swiss border to escape internment should the conference fail and war be declared, their cars loaded and ready, hoping to make it to Constance before the crossing barriers slam shut. However, Packard and Beattie of United Press, Alex Small of the *Chicago Tribune* and the others from New York's *Herald Tribune* and *Times* are all counting on American neutrality to keep them in favour with the Propaganda Minister.

And the crowds, patient, silent, respectful and running to several hundred, have been kept anxiously from their beds, ready at any minute to head for the bomb shelters should the worst occur. Queueing on the opposite side of the street, they stand behind a line of scrawny, leafless alder trees, staring up at the first-floor windows.

We've all seen the glossy pictures of the Führer's private office; we all know what's going on up there amid the splendour of the marble floor, the heavy Bavarian wood desk and the fireplace topped by a portrait of Frederick the Great, and no one in our little group of professional German watchers is glad about it. Neville Chamberlain, leader of the world's foremost Great Power, has arrived in this city on bended knee to give Adolf Hitler what he wants: the Sudetenland, Czechoslovakia's key fortified zone, thus rendering the rest of that country completely defenceless. No doubt the fool intends to go back to London waving victoriously and proclaiming 'peace in our time' – or some such nonsense. Certainly not peace with honour. This fix is nothing short of a launch pad for another world war – that's clear to anyone with an iota of common sense. Someone has got to stop him signing up to this disgraceful agreement. Several have already tried but so far all have failed.

So can I remain a passive spectator? A reporter content merely to write an obituary to peace?

No, I cannot. I turn and dig in the pocket of the big loden, fumbling out my soft pack of Camels, hands trembling.

'Nervous?' Bill Morrel asks.

'Look,' I say quietly so that we're in a little bubble of our own, 'you should be prepared for an even bigger story than the one you're expecting.'

He rolls his eyes to the sky. 'Yeah, yeah! Not like you to shoot a line, Brad.'

I lick my lips. I can't say much. Any prior knowledge would destroy my chances and the press corps is just one great leaky colander, so I hush my voice to a mere whisper, hoping the others won't be attracted. 'Look, I've got an exclusive and it's not for you, not yet anyway.'

I have his complete attention.

'Been to Leipzig to see Carl G.' He raises an eyebrow. He knows who I mean. Carl Goerdeler, one-time mayor of that city and just about the most prominent anti-Nazi politician still alive.

'Given me an explosive piece of news. There's a backgrounder in your pigeonhole back at the hotel, plus a copy of his letter. Guard it well. In case I don't come back.'

'Don't be so damned mysterious,' he hisses. 'Tell me now.'

'Tell you later.'

What he doesn't yet know, and what I won't tell because wagging ears are turning our way, is the rest of my note to him, sitting back at the hotel: 'Bill, If I'm not around to write this story in the next day or so, it's down to you. Don't risk your neck – fly out of the country to file it to avoid the reprisals. When you read the attached letter you'll know it transforms the whole war-or-peace situation. Now I'm off to put my neck on the line. Wish me luck.'

I turn away, mumbling the brand slogan: 'I'd walk a mile for a Camel.' The cigarette break is my ploy for edging from the group. Bill Morrel knows the feeling. He too is a four-pack-a-day man and returns to other conversations as I drift casually along the wide frontage, careful to give the impression to anyone observing from the windows that everything is normal. This is just one Bradley C Wilkes, European correspondent of the North American Broadcasting Company, indulging his craving for tobacco. Glancing up, I see human shapes crouched at the roof rim and a glint of steel. Once a hunter myself, I now experience the feeling of being at the wrong end of a rifle scope.

My movement is not a random act. The minute hand on my watch has reached the half hour. Time for the signal. It comes from a figure in a trilby and macintosh, standing next to a small concrete bollard on the other side of the street, a point where the crowd has thinned, his only badge a deep ivy-green shopping bag from Oberpollinger, the big department store down by the Karlsplatz. Out across the expanse of the boulevard, beneath those trees, a newspaper is being transferred from the left hand to the right.

My answering gesture is a tip of the hat.

The figure with the bag and the newspaper is Emil Jarek. Without greeting we stroll unhurriedly along to the end of the street which is given over to a building site, the first stage of a massive new Reich Chancellery for the area behind the Führerbau, now shuttered and hidden from view by tall blue fencing. There's not a crack anywhere to peer through. Just a flush-fitting door, for which Jarek has the key.

Don't ask how, I tell myself, quaking with anxiety, marvelling at this man's ingenuity and network of secret contacts. *Just pray the key fits.*

I'm behind him. I hear him grunting. I can hear the twisting of the key. How long can I linger without being noticed? Finally the door opens and I inch warily forward, following Jarek inside, heart thumping like a paratrooper on his first jump.

Jarek whispers that it's early days, they haven't yet put in a nightwatchman, as we skirt piles of prestressed concrete segments for a tunnel and a maze of trenches, now slopping with rainwater. I'm cursing the foolish inadequacy of my shoes which are beginning to leak; the temperature is dropping; there will be a frost in the morning. Jarek points a warning finger to avoid stumbling into a line of ladders. I'm lucky to have this man. I can only guess at the raft of shadowy opposition groups in Prague, Munich and elsewhere that have got us this far. I know Jarek is a determined opponent of Hitler. Last summer I hunted with him in the forests outside

Prague; like me, he's a marksman of some merit and I sense his capacity for ruthlessness, but I have insisted we cannot talk through the barrel of a gun. Ours must be a peaceful demonstration. When he looks askance I explain: 'Chamberlain has been cocooned by yes-men, impervious to counterarguments, untouched by over-polite critics in the British Parliament, so now I'm banking everything on the shock value of a noisy intervention. Today the Prime Minister is outside his normal comfort zone. He won't ever have had to face anything like us before. We'll be in his face. Raucous. With our logic to blow away his pretensions. Shatter the absurd delusion that he can negotiate with a gangster like Hitler. Our message will stop him dead, will transform everything.'

'But he hasn't listened so far, damn him,' objects Jarek. 'The fool is all set to sell out Czechoslovakia and betray us all to the Nazis.'

'Then it's up to us,' I say.

A grey metal door set in a flat wall opens and we step inside, to be greeted by stone steps leading down to a basement. Behind the door is a man introduced to me only as Helmut. He has sad green eyes and a vague manner and is dressed in the field grey of a Wehrmacht lieutenant. And now, as if to increase my already racing pulse, he issues an urgent imperative.

'You must hurry. The signing ceremony... it's only minutes away.'

We speed through a labyrinth of underground passages, supposedly a bomb shelter but now being used by a dissident section of the Abwehr, the army's intelligence arm. At the bottom of some stairs I discard the loden coat to reveal the wide-set pinstripe and waistcoat in all its glory – strikingly blue with a contrasting white shirt, gold cufflinks, gold tiepin and a one-point fold to a red pocket square. I've even added a tiny Pall

Mall Club badge, a sartorial flourish designed to convince the uninitiated that this is the uniform of a London diplomat.

Helmut is the ultimate well-prepared prop man; he has rags to wipe the mud from our shoes and for me, a large black file and a long teleprinter message printout. Jarek is given a briefcase and clipboard. Both of us fix to our lapels Union Jack name tags. Mine announces: *Theodore Dalrymple, Second Secretary Political, HM Government delegation, Foreign Office, United Kingdom of Great Britain and Northern Ireland.*

Jarek's is equally inventive: *Peregrine Simon, Third Secretary.*

Helmut's on the top step with his hand on the doorknob. Nervy and speaking almost in a whisper. 'Once through here,' he says, 'you're on your own.'

I look at Jarek and he nods his encouragement. I've already extracted from him a promise of non-violence. 'Today, just words,' he reassures. 'No action against Hitler.' It's a pact and we shake on it.

Helmut is waiting. He shrugs – like he thinks we're both doomed.

We can expect arrest – and that's the best we can hope for. I breathe in deeply, clench my teeth, ball my fists and again touch my inside pocket where the Goerdeler letter had been. How I would love to flourish it publicly as a challenge but such a document cannot be taken into the Führerbau for fear of compromising my sources and revealing identities. Instead I've delivered it as a matter of urgency to my contact in the British delegation, Vaughan, a young Foreign Office eagle stationed at the Regina-Palast-Hotel on Maximiliansplatz to guard his government's confidential papers.

Vaughan has explained to me the agonised diplomatic exchanges that have taken place in London over the last few months: a succession of prominent anti-Nazis – Kleist, Halder,

Kordt – warning the British Government of Hitler's war plans, counselling against appeasement, giving notice of their intention to resist Nazi aggression.

Chamberlain has ignored them all.

But surely he will have to listen now. The solemn pledge I have brought back from Leipzig transforms the situation. Now it's down to me and my determination to administer a shock tactic on the British Prime Minister.

Emil nods. No more time for contemplation; we're both ready. Up and out we go.

The corridor is all gloomy marble and heavy with Germanic symbolism. It's awash with all manner of uniforms, suits and occasional dashes of female dress. We put on our act: harassed officials of the delegation with an urgent message to deliver. I flourish a flimsy printout while in muted conversation with Jarek, murmuring phrases about it only just coming over the wires, hoping no one will see through my attempt at a British accent.

Disaster threatens as we begin to climb the stairs to the ground floor. A braying English voice, the accent unmistakably cut-glass, stuns me into silence.

'It's too bad, it really is. I ask myself, will we ever see our beds tonight?'

I keep my gaze low but risk a sideways glance. Descending is a man in a Harris tweed jacket, red-spotted cravat and grey flannels, the whole ensemble shouting Jermyn Street. His attention is all on his female companion but if he looks to his right and spots me through the others on the stairway, will the genuine diplomat see through the fake?

'Really, Celia, I have to say, you'd think they'd try to settle matters at a civilised hour.'

Celia says something in response but the words are inaudible. I dare to breathe out as their voices trail behind me.

Ruffled feathers, the brittle tones of annoyance at a disturbed routine, have saved us – for the moment.

Emerging on the ground floor my sense of relief is short-lived. Black uniforms line the stairwell, the stairs and the gangways. Their caps are off, the sides of their heads close-shaved like shorn sheep just out of the dip. Tiny outcrops of hair are permitted only at the crown. As we approach the main staircase it seems a thousand eyes are stripping bare our pretence, that it's just a matter of seconds before pistols are drawn.

But then I take heart. The hubbub of conversation does not die. This is a four-power conference – Italy, Britain, France and Germany – with delegates and hangers-on far too numerous for tight security, and we start to climb unhindered up the vast marble steps to the first floor.

Heavy columns and stretched rectangular balusters define the pomposity of this place. Our goal is the Führer's private room at the front of the building where even now the signing ceremony may have begun. So this is hardly the time to drop a pencil. But I do.

It clatters noisily on the marble and rolls down a step. I stoop to retrieve it but a black-clad figure, complete with SS police runic insignia on the left breast, gets there first, hands me the pencil and looks searchingly into my face. He's familiar. I struggle for a name. Then I remember: Kruger, one of my inquisitors at the Prinz-Albrecht-Strasse all those years ago in Berlin.

'I know you,' he says, peering at the British name tag. 'I know that face, sure I do. You're...' He's scowling but looking away, searching his memory, not quite as fast as mine.

'Sorry,' I say, thrusting my clipboard and message pad high into his vision, 'can't help you. A mistake.'

I grab the pencil and carry on climbing, counting on his

uncertainty to keep him from making a scene but a pain in my left leg is slowing me down. It's an old crag-hopping injury from happier times – carefree times back home, of drawing a bead on a stag among the outcrops of Snake River. Trouble is, the wound tends to re-announce itself under stress. Will it mark me out from the crowd? Is Kruger following? I fear to look behind but I must know my colleague Jarek is keeping up. Separation would spell disaster. I need him for his inside knowledge of the building; I need him for his moral support. We are fused together in this endeavour, feeding off each other's courage.

Finally, at the top step, he draws level. Massive relief, and I feel a sense of great achievement in reaching within a dozen steps of our goal. So near yet so far. The crowd is even thicker. How to find the right door? It's Room 105, but will it be numbered?

I can't see any markings. I push my way through the crush towards the far wall and glancing down at my painful leg once again, I do not see the hand across my chest that bars the way.

'Brad! Darling! What are you doing in here? I thought you said you were a reporter.'

I stop in alarm. It's Anasztaizia Nemet, the girl I flirted with at last week's British Embassy party to mark the ambassador's birthday, all bright eyes, wafts of perfume and hanging on the arm of a glowering party apparatchik, plain-clothed, heavy-lidded and with a set of hideously bulbous lips.

'What's this?' she says, picking up my name tag on its chain and drawing it close to read the bogus details.

I quickly grab it back before she can blurt the name Dalrymple. 'Please,' I say from the corner of my mouth, 'I don't know you and you don't know me.'

Her head jerks back. 'But of course I know you, darling. It's Brad, isn't it? Bradley Wilkes.' Then, with a mischievous smile, she bends forward to deliver a stage whisper: 'Do you forget all your lady friends so quickly?'

I do remember the party and I do remember Anasztaizia, an impish Hungarian with silver-blonde hair falling over slender shoulders and with a propensity to tease.

'Of course!' I flick a hand in sudden recall. Time for a response in kind. 'How could I forget? Swimming naked in Lake Starnberg. What a summer. What fantastic fun. We must do it again. The sheer pleasure of nudity, so exhilarating, so natural – next week perhaps?'

'Don't be ridiculous, I never–'

'September not too cold for you, is it?'

She looks round in alarm to gauge the reaction of Pouty Lips who's sporting a tiny swastika lapel badge and I seize the chance to push on into the crowd. Behind me I can hear a voice, an alarmingly familiar voice, Kruger's voice, calling through the crowd: 'Fraulein, fraulein, what was that name? That man you just spoke to; who was he?'

Jarek is propelling me from behind to the curving rim of the first-floor landing, then he pulls me leftwards and suddenly I see it: the marble lip over the doorway, the big oak doors folded open and the security desk just inside.

We have a matter of seconds, perhaps a minute or two at most, before Kruger realises our deception and raises the alarm. We have just one chance at this. My leg is aching and I'm breathless with anxiety but bravado makes a timely return. We rattle our name tags, flash our bogus passes and say: 'Urgent message for the Prime Minister.'

A scharführer with the ominous zigzag collar flashes is seated at the desk and looks as if he might issue a challenge, but then he looks away, sighing at the brass neck of yet another group of oddball foreigners. We press on into a large empty space of the private office. At the far end, by a big conference table, is a huddle of figures with backs turned.

I recognise no one.

'Can you see The Bird?' I whisper.

My name for the British Prime Minister. The Bird. The Owl. The Old Crow. The Black Vulture. Just like the carrion eating the dead I've seen out in India. By now Jarek has become used to my ways and my mannerisms, as I with his.

'There!'

Finally, I see him: the pursed lips, the protruding eyes, the winged collar, the all-black outfit.

Jarek and I stride towards him.

He turns. So do the figures around him. I recognise the cocky figure of the Duce, the beaten look of the French Premier Daladier, and then the staring gaze of the grey-suited figure with the tiny black moustache. A chill goes down my spine when I'm fixed by those eyes. Warning voices scream in my head – but, surprisingly, the Führer's not looking victorious. More startled. He takes a couple of steps in my direction and cocks his right shoulder. Then his left leg snaps up. The nervous tic I've seen so often all through these years; what my party contacts openly call the *teppichfresser*, a man who chews carpets in a rage.

He barks: 'Was nun?'

I pretend not to hear.

He erupts: 'Ich bin fertig mit all dem Gerede. Es ist Zeit zu unterschreiben!' One frustrated dictator who's all done talking and thinks our appearance is just another diplomatic ploy to delay the signing.

I look away, feigning incomprehension, turning all my attention to Chamberlain. This is my moment. Whatever happens, I must not botch it. Across the few remaining steps of highly polished parquet still between us I summon a loud voice and say: 'Mr Prime Minister, you can't do business with this man. He's a gangster. He won't keep his promises.'

Chamberlain's eyes register surprise and the mouth goes slack. With peripheral vision I register other figures recovering from their surprise and moving closer. I'm desperate to deliver the message. I have to believe in it. I can do this. I can deliver the message that will make the difference.

'Mr Chamberlain, there's been a major new political development. Everything about today's situation has changed.'

Figures are almost on me. I have only a second or two left.

'Don't sign,' I shout, 'until you've read the Vaughan Memorandum.'

I'm conscious of a collective gasp, and those rushing to close in on me suddenly stop dead and draw back. They're in shock and I sense a movement to my right. It's Jarek.

The next few seconds seem so stark, as if they're being played out in slow motion. Three images are imprinted on my mind, will stay with me forever. Jarek's face no longer the cultured man I met so long ago on the Charles Bridge in Prague. Now a mask of hatred. In his hand a pistol. A Czech 9mm. Pointing at the Führer.

'No, Emil,' I shout, 'no violence!'

He waves a dismissive hand and I feel aggrieved, duped, cheated. Despite our agreement, the man reveals himself to be an assassin, plain and simple.

Then, the second image. Jarek switches aim from Hitler to Chamberlain. 'I keep my promises,' he says, almost a snarl, levelling at the Prime Minister, taking up finger pressure on the trigger. 'No Hitler! But this man, this betrayer...'

I cringe, expecting a shot.

Third image: the gun flies up in the air, as if propelled by some clever conjuring trick, and Jarek goes down in a sprawling heap, tackled from behind by an unseen assailant.

Then the assailant turns and I recognise him: Kruger.

Before I can take this in, or react, or tell my stricken colleague he should never have descended to gangster tactics, I feel a strange force propelling me forward, a deadening blackness, an odd anaesthetising feeling at the back of my head, followed by a fading, slipping, slowly releasing hold on consciousness.

CHAPTER TWO

'My biggest challenge right now is to rescue a certain lady from herself.'

It was late on Friday and the big oak-panelled hall at St James's College was almost empty of undergraduates who had long gone about their weekend business of carousing and copulation. However, high table remained in seriously extended session and Professor Chadwick was formally attired in a seedy dinner jacket, fluffy red tie and an ancient black gown, seemingly oblivious of the effect it had on students and fellows. His colleagues looked out in amusement from their high perch at right angles to the student benches, flanked on one side by a galaxy of portraits of old bursars and old masters. They had reason to linger after the meal had been cleared away, for tonight the American was their special guest.

'Cedric, old pal,' the man from Washington was saying, 'I expect soon to see you on the small screen, fronting up a new pop history series, or making a documentary on medieval monks, or mixing it with some passion in a fractious studio debate with the latest crop of revisionists.'

They all laughed – including Chadwick.

'Must get your name in the public eye,' the American persisted. 'That's the thing. Public profile. Ditch that gown, Cedric, dump the tie. What you need is designer jeans and sturdy big brown boots. Then stride up and down the TV studio, waving your arms in elaborate gestures and pointing at the latest digital graphics. Bring history into the 21st century.'

Chadwick didn't take offence at his public ribbing. It was an annual event. The American came every year on a scouting mission.

'No, no, Lance, I think not; not me at all.' Chadwick chuckled good-naturedly. 'My big thing right now is a lot nearer home. In fact, a mission to save my research assistant from herself.'

Canadine, a specialist in early Victorian crime, raised an eyebrow. 'You mean, the girl with the very smart Porsche sports car? Classy bodywork all round, eh?'

The woman at the end of the row gave him a glare.

'The thing is, Chadders old horse, how on earth does she afford it on a researcher's money? That's what I want to know. You'll be able to tell us, won't you, you being her mentor.'

Chadwick made a vague gesture with his right hand. 'Private money,' he said. 'A modest legacy, I believe, affording her creature comforts out of reach of her less fortunate peers.'

'I think you'd better tell us all about her,' Lance said.

'Later, in detail, when we're all finished here.'

It was some time, and several bulbous-bottomed Glencairn whisky glasses later, when Chadwick and Lance Scranton were perched in the professor's cramped and crowded room. Chadwick's choice was Glenmorangie, Scranton's Tullamore Dew. The two of them went back a long way. Ever since they met at Berkeley, or so it was said. The American was generally supposed by the fellows at high table to be a good thing – a lobbyist, a financier or a fixer of some kind, useful for finding promising postgrads high-profile jobs in the US.

'Something wonderful has just dropped into my lap,' Chadwick said. 'Lots of fascinating new information on my pet subject.'

'Yeah,' Scranton interrupted, 'you're obsessing about Appeasement, I know that – Munich, Chamberlain, Hitler, Peace In Our Time and all that – but let's be honest, Cedric, you're getting nowhere with it. There's already been umpteen books out on the subject. How can you take it any further?'

Chadwick grinned. 'But now, at last, I can.'

'Okay!' Scranton seemed eager to cut the subject short. 'But I thought we came here to talk about your girl. You know my thing, not really history but talent, talent that can be developed, that's what I'm interested in. There are great opportunities over the water for talent.'

'Yes, Lance, I know that, but I'm putting the two together – history and talent.'

'The girl, Cedric.'

Chadwick took a deep breath. 'She's my best by far. Best for years. A bright young woman with a great brain and a bright future but she's suffered something of a reverse, a professional setback. Don't need to go into details. Could have happened to anyone, but she's taken it rather hard. And the one thing I don't want to happen is to lose her to the indulgent lifestyle.'

'Indulgent?'

'Fast cars, yachts, the odd casino here and there, the idle set in the South of France, people wasting her time and distracting her with the specious glamour of the high life. She's in danger of losing focus. Something's got to be done with her. I can't protect her forever.'

Chadwick was distracted for a moment by a bowler-hatted

porter spiking a single piece of offending litter from the perfect St James's greensward under the shadow of the bell tower that called them all to dinner at 7.30 of an evening. He returned his gaze to Scranton. 'However...' he said, eyes glinting in the electric light.

'Out with it!'

'A little secret I've been keeping all to myself but now I can share it with you.' The gestures, arms akimbo, fingers pointing, had become even more animated. 'She needs a new challenge. A new direction. And something's come up that is a perfect fit for her.'

'What I like about you, Cedric, is the big, big build-up.'

'Well, here's the nub of it. Our clever girl is the granddaughter of an American radio correspondent who vanished in the middle of the Appeasement Crisis.'

'Now... you don't say. A real live genuine Yankie connection.'

'And what's more,' Chadwick said, 'she's always had a thing about what happened to her grandpa.'

'Sure.'

'She'd really like to know how he simply vanished off the face of the earth after a distinguished career commentating on the rise of the Nazis. Suddenly he isn't there anymore and no one – but no one – ever hears of him again.'

Scranton looked interested. He had been riffling through a book without paying much attention. Now he replaced it on the shelf. 'Intriguing, I'll grant you, but how are you going to take it forward?'

Chadwick disappeared behind his desk for some minutes, scrabbling on the floor at a recalcitrant pile of papers, until at last he emerged triumphant with a slim brochure in his hand. He slipped it across to Scranton.

'Take a look at that. Some kind soul thought I'd be

interested. A booklet to celebrate the 80th anniversary of the founding of the North American Broadcasting Company.'

'Aha! The NABC. Great station. Can't beat it for sport.'

'Right now, it's not the sport I'm interested in.' Chadwick leaned over, flicked to page four and pointed. 'What I want you to look at is down that page.'

'Which part?'

'Where it talks about radio news broadcasts being a breakthrough in the thirties.' Chadwick sat back in his chair and stayed silent while his friend soaked up the details: the first international radio hook-up and then, at the foot of the next page, the mystery of how NABC's distinguished correspondent in Germany disappeared in the middle of the Munich crisis, right at the point where he was supposed to be broadcasting the result of the Hitler talks.

Scranton looked up. 'I get it. The mystery of the missing correspondent... but the problem is, every goddamned historian in the English-speaking world has crawled all over Munich.'

'Ah!' interrupted Chadwick, 'but they haven't solved the mystery of the missing correspondent. And so much more. This is why I'm so buoyed up. New facts, Lance, new facts.'

Scranton laughed. 'And by the look in your eye, I guess you've just struck an academic pot of gold.'

Chadwick had the Irish whiskey bottle in his right hand. 'Refill?' Then, the duties of a host fulfilled, he said: 'I admit it, there's no doubting it. A treasure-trove archive. It's significant, a game-changer and it'll transform our understanding of the period.'

'Which might just end up having your name attached to it?'

Chadwick grinned. 'Possibly.'

'And where did you uncover this treasure?'

'Former student of mine. Remembers me well. Knows my

obsessive interest.' He stressed the word with a grin. What Chadwick didn't say was that a bundle of notes, reports and files, many of them overlaid with the smudged and fading red stamp 'Most Secret' and almost all relating to the Munich crisis, had been found in a loft, stuffed inside a briefcase once owned by an air marshal, now deceased. He could imagine Scranton's reaction: 'Call that security? They'd toast any American doing that.'

What Scranton *did* say was: 'Okay, okay, but let's get back to your girl. Despite all the excitement, you still have a problem. One young lady who is apparently rather too busy having a good time with her rich friends.'

From somewhere on the floor above them came the sound of raucous laughter. Not all the students had vacated the premises, it seemed, but Chadwick was not distracted. He was nodding vigorously. 'Her big opportunity. The best she's going to get. How can she fail to be impressed? To be persuaded? We'll have to talk. I have every confidence in her, every confidence that as soon as she sees what a big opportunity this is – and it is – she'll be anxious to come aboard.'

'Is she the only candidate?'

'The best by far. By a country mile. By a long American country mile. And with the mystery of her grandfather as bait, who better?' Then he lowered his voice. 'Especially if there is a certain proposal on the table.'

Scranton laughed. 'You old fox.'

Chadwick grinned. 'Talent. That's what you're about, is it not?'

'Indeed.' The American folded his arms, rocking in his chair, a knowing smile in place. 'Then perhaps you'd better tell me the rest. Let's start at the beginning, shall we? With the name.'

'The name,' Chadwick said slowly, so that it could be spelled out in Scranton's notebook, 'is E-m-m-a D-r-a-k-e.'

From the sun terrace it could be heard quite distinctly. The front door crashing open, something heavy being dumped on the hallway floor, a loud swoosh of air escaping in a flatulent burst from the sofa, followed by a stream of uninhibited expletives.

'I'm out here,' the girl on the lounger called, looking up from her prone position.

Thirty seconds later Emma Drake was framed in the doorway.

'Oh dear, you look fit to kill,' Angie said, propping herself up on one elbow. 'Don't tell me! Someone's cut you up on the A1? Dented that precious Porsche?'

Emma shook her head. The face was flushed, the mouth a tight line.

'Had a row with your professor? Criticised your appearance? Got the better of you in an argument?'

'As if!'

'The *History* mag's just rejected your latest article?'

'Nope.'

A sigh from Angie. 'Really serious then. You've got the sack?'

Emma shook her head. 'No; not yet anyway, though it may come to that.' She turned away then, reappearing a moment later dragging a large, bulging shoulder bag across the carpet, bumping over a step and scraping it noisily along the patio flagstones.

'Why vandalise a perfectly serviceable bag?' Angie demanded. 'A Christmas pressie from me, as I recall.'

Emma was unloading on to a low coffee table papers, files, bundles of documents until there was not an inch of space remaining. She said: 'A professional disaster unheard of in the history of the university. I've fallen into a chasm so deep I doubt I'll ever be able to climb out.'

A snort came from the sunlounger, angled to the west and placed precisely to catch the best of the afternoon rays. 'Oh don't be so damned melodramatic!' Angie gathered herself and sat up. This was her rooftop terrace; her Chelsea apartment on the ninth floor. 'For God's sake, fix yourself a drink, then come and tell me.'

But Emma made no move to the drinks cabinet. Instead, she looked her friend in the eye. 'You were once a dancer, right?'

'In a past life.'

'How would you feel if the person you thought was your best friend, your understudy, kicked you in the shins and then took your place on the stage, glorying in the spotlight while you limped off to A&E?'

'This is your co-researcher, yes?'

Emma nodded. 'One Shelley Squires, otherwise known as Madam Judas.' Her fist clenched, her jaw tightened, then she leaned into the voluminous bag once more and threw a fat notebook onto the floor space between them. It was clamped together with elastic bands, coloured tabs and bulldog clips. 'All this wasted effort!' Then the details came flooding out in a fast-flowing tide of bitterness: how Emma, in her role of a post-doctoral history researcher at St James's College, had persuaded her departmental head to put up £11,000 to acquire at auction a treasure trove of historical documents; how excited they had all been with the newly discovered love letters written by the secret wife of the French king Louis XIV; and how, once the money had changed hands, the letters were exposed as the work of a forger.

'Now my reputation's in the gloop,' Emma said. 'Deep in the swamp! I doubt there's any future in academia after this. No chance of fresh funding! I'm the one who blew all that money!

Made a fool of myself and my department. They're going to steer well clear in future.'

'Oh dear, oh dear.' Angie was sympathetic, then her brow furrowed. 'But why blame your friend?'

'Got away Persil clean, didn't she? No fallout of blame on her. Made out she had nothing to do with the auction disaster. Even capitalised on it by burgling my idea for a book on queens and consorts.' She kicked the big notebook. 'And now she's won herself new funding to write it.'

Angie snorted. 'The academic jungle! Sounds every bit as cut-throat as business. But at least occasionally I can do some good.' Angie worked at her mother's ceramics gallery in Knightsbridge and was known for tapping up customers for contributions to the Red Cross. 'Got a fifty out of an American who bought two Meissen figurines today,' she said.

Emma's mood of angry despondency lifted momentarily. 'He could probably afford it.'

'Even better last week. Persuaded Daddy to put in a grand.' Angie drew in a long breath. 'Mind you, in your shoes, I reckon I'd have killed that Squires woman.' There was a silence for some seconds, before she added: 'You know, don't you, that whatever happens, your friends are around you.'

Emma's eyelids flickered.

'I mean, whatever problems you run into at Cambridge, there's plenty of compensations here.' She swirled her drink around her glass without sipping. 'Join us in June. A great way to bury your troubles. Father's getting a new boat. I could persuade him to put in at Paphos and visit that place you're enthused about... What was it? The latest dig for pre-pottery Neolithic?'

Emma let out a sigh. 'June? I'll never survive that far. I'll be a pauper long before then.'

'Oh, forget money!'

Emma sat up, glancing around sharply. 'You know I always insist. Pay my own way. Always have.'

A long sigh. 'I know, I know. Quite tiresome you are about it sometimes.'

'I won't play the sponge.'

But Angie's attention had wandered to the coming summer. 'Or perhaps we could drive down to the Loire and visit this fantastic vineyard.' She picked up a long glass of Didier Dagueneau. Then a giggle. 'Remember the South of France? That glorious beach?'

'Don't remind me.' But remind Emma it did. From now on Cannes was off any foreseeable itinerary. Angie's fun chest might be infinite – Mother was a successful dealer with an international clientele and Father was in pharmaceuticals – but Emma's didn't enjoy that sort of backup. Selling Granny's legacy, an Augustus John watercolour, had given her a life-enhancing release from the constraints of a researcher's budget. She liked the good things of life but the ten grand she'd made two years back was diminishing fast.

Her expression must have betrayed her because Angie said: 'Okay, okay, let's talk disaster then, if we really must.' She chuckled. 'But I must say I'm intrigued. You haven't actually got any of these love letters I could read, have you?'

Emma retrieved several items from her briefcase. There was a catalogue from Maxims, auctioneers of historic documents and ephemera with 'Lot 54, Letters of Marquise de Maintenon' ringed in red; a black-and-white drawing of a medieval beauty with long hair tumbling down bare shoulders adorned the front dustcover of *Life and Love With The King*; attached to it was a newspaper cutting with the headline: '£11,000 price tag for "sexy queen" sting'. Emma passed over a transparent folder containing spidery handwriting on items of yellowing paper.

Emma sighed, closed her eyes and allowed herself to feel

the sun on her legs and arms while pages were turned. Several chuckles later, 'Juicy stuff' was the considered verdict. 'Raunchy old bunch. Don't think I'd tell my man this sort of thing.'

Emma drew in a long breath. 'I should have been more suspicious, more on my guard... but really, it seemed so genuine. So very real. Dovetailed with everything we knew, the references to events, people and places, they were all spot on. The faker – he's a clever bastard – made his packet and destroyed me with it.'

Angie picked up a letter of authentication from Dr Dorsey Paxton, Professor of English and Medieval Literature at Beaufort College. 'What about him – doesn't he take the blame?'

'Reckoned I'd rushed him into it,' Emma said. 'Complained I hadn't given him enough time. Busy trying to wriggle out of responsibility by saying he'd had insufficient samples to make a proper judgement.'

'What about your professor? Is he on your back?'

'Strangely, no. If I was in his position, I'd be kicking butt, but he just paid up and looked cheerful. In a way, that's worse – makes me feel guilty. How do I make it up to him?'

'You could always invite him to France.'

Emma laughed but couldn't keep the bitterness out of her tone. 'He'd be the Quaker at a beer festival.' She picked up the news report. 'That was the killer,' she said, pointing out the statement from the country's foremost manuscript expert, Dr Sybil Williams, head of Scotland Yard's Questioned Documents Unit, trashing the love letters as 'forgeries sufficient only to entrap the unwary'.

Emma looked away. 'That's me. The unwary. The sap. The swindler's dream. The guileless dupe. Will I ever live that down?'

Angie was still scanning the yellowing letters and tittering at some of the phrases when Emma's phone squawked.

'Don't answer that,' Angie instructed, 'bound to be something tedious.' She rummaged around in her own bag. 'Just remembered! You must come down on Thursday. Somewhere in here... I've got two tickets for a show.'

Emma was shaking her head. 'Mud sticks. You know my plan. Career path leading to a position of prominence from where I can open up the big Grandfather mystery.'

'Oh, him again, yes, your obsession with dear old Grando; yes, I do remember.'

'What chance now? I'll need serious credibility to access all those closed archives. That presupposes funds but above all, reputation. Reputation as an historian is what it's all about and I've just zonked mine.'

Emma's phone buzzed again. 'Oh my God, it's him. Professor Chadwick. He's gone on to answerphone.'

'On a Friday? Really? Not at the weekend, surely?'

Emma took a deep breath. 'He wants to see me on Monday morning. At nine o'clock!'

'So early. How dreadful.'

'Probably changed his tune. Going to dump me big time.'

'Can he do that? I mean, aren't you funded until some date in the future?'

'Maybe Mr Moneybags at the funding institute has decided to cut me short and poor old Chadwick has got the job of breaking it gently.'

Angie carefully tucked the letters away then waved her arms in an expansive gesture. 'Then let's forget all about this for now. You need some serious stroking. Let's make it a wonderful weekend. Have a great time and to hell with promiscuous royals and peevish professors.'

'A great time, yes,' Emma echoed sourly. 'Until the early train on Monday morning.'

It was ridiculously early. King's Cross loomed up like a phantom ship blanketed in a night fog – or was it simply Emma's dour perspective at six o'clock? Who, she demanded of no one in particular, would travel at this hour?

In the ticket hall she looked about her. She expected to see tramps and cleaners and men in donkey jackets carrying hurricane lamps. She did not. Instead, businessmen with briefcases, smartly dressed women and families.

She puffed out her cheeks and took an uncomfortable plastic bucket seat on the concourse. The 6.52 had not even appeared on the indicator board and she silently cursed the broken camshaft that had kept the Porsche in her brother's garage. She cupped a muzzy head in a weary hand and felt the weight of a great depression. Then she cursed Professor Chadwick for insisting on a nine o'clock meeting. When she'd finished calling him all the derogatory names she could think of, a silent voice of conscience interrupted her catalogue of self-pity. Even as she had maligned the man, she knew she was simply using him as a foil to deflect the blame from where it truly lay: herself.

In reality, she had to concede, Chadwick had been an heroic example of forbearance and loyalty. He had stood by her, had issued not a word of criticism. Before the auction disaster she had regarded her career as being on an ever-upward trajectory; now, by a catastrophic lapse of judgement, she had cast it into a deep chasm. The fault was all hers; she needed to admit it to herself. It made her angry but it did not make her ashamed.

The regal tones of an elocution-perfect announcer had the

Cambridge crowd on their feet and running for Platform 13. It was only when she was comfortably settled in a corner seat that Emma pulled out her latest purchase, *The Life of Basil Liddell Hart*. Certainly not her period – the man who'd tried to tell the generals how to fight the last war – but the book nicely complemented an article she'd read about the chaos of sorting and cataloguing the paper mountain Liddell Hart's widow bequeathed to King's College. So, she decided, despite everything, despite all her travails, she was still captivated by the role of the historian.

As she thumbed through the contents list and sources, she thought of her peers back at Cambridge and how they had spent their weekends: noses glued to screens, locked in libraries or cupboard-sized studies. She knew from their disapproving looks how they expected twenty-four-hour, seven-day dedication from a serious historian. She contrasted their spartan weekends with her own: good food, fine wine, tickets to the opera, shopping at Reiss, lunch at the Oxo Tower and dinner at The Wolseley or the Oyster Bar. Who wouldn't enjoy what good fortune had brought her? She saw no point in denying herself these pleasures merely for the sake of wearing a hair shirt but she still felt sorry for her penurious peers and did her best to compensate with small tokens that might prove of practical value. She ran errands for them in the big city, as often as not trawling the bookshops along the Charing Cross Road for obscure volumes. And her bag, so heavy this day, was full of what she thought of as her Monday morning parcels: a hot water bottle for Lottie, chunky-sized bars of Toblerone for the skinny boy in the porters' office, and a sweet little pouring jug for Jane to cure her of the annoying habit of parking a carton of milk next to her teacup.

Emma fiddled distractedly with her book, looking out of the window as the train picked up speed. The bleak back gardens and tatty yards of Islington flashed past as she made up her mind how she would play the day. She determined to take on the chin whatever fate Chadwick had in store for her but she would not slink dispiritedly away, would not adopt the shame-faced mantle of the college pariah. Only one person at St James's had so far had the gall to sneer out loud. Poor little Norris, the one with the straggly beard and the spindly legs whom she consistently beat at badminton on a Tuesday, made a slighting reference to 'throwing eleven grand out of the college window'. She turned on him: 'Given the same chance to go for it, you'd never have had the balls.'

But what if it were all to finish – perhaps even today?

She jolted upright. She thought of all her past hard work. All the plans she had for the future. And no, she didn't want it to end.

Emma jammed the book back in her case and decided instead to attack the big crossword in *The Telegraph*. She looked at her watch: fifteen minutes still to go before reaching Cambridge. That was the goal she set herself, confident she could complete all the grid by the time the train pulled into the station.

CHAPTER THREE

The day he got out of jail the sun had taken a holiday and Wormwood Scrubs looked as if it was engulfed in an old-fashioned fifties' smog. But what did he care?

Gerald Erle Roper was out – legit, that is, via the front gate. And even though the other inmates had granted him a measure of tolerance as a useful letter writer (their very own in-house excuse-maker to wives, mothers and sweethearts), prison had still been the low watermark of his life. Especially so for a self-proclaimed law-abiding middle-class professional who didn't naturally fit into the prevailing criminal mindset.

But that had been his downfall: he hadn't exactly been one hundred per cent law-abiding.

He sighed. Prison changed you. It had certainly changed Roper. He'd gone inside three years before as a cocksure trickster up to every ruse known in the phone hackers' lexicon. He'd done it all – message deleting, picture snatching, eavesdropping, hassling – until the heavy hand of the law had brought his reporting career to a premature close.

Now, breathing in the glorious if murky air of freedom, he

was a changed man. Hacking was history. So was his job. And they hadn't even paid out his contract.

Roper had approached the gate with a mixture of longing, fear and uncertainty. He had a knot in his stomach. It was a moment of great trepidation as he stepped carefully through the tunnel-like exit door and out into the open space beyond. He glanced up at the big bombastic building made famous by film: two octagonal towers built by Victorian convicts to resemble a medieval gatehouse. Briefly, he noticed two terracotta figures perched aloft but he was too anxious to quit the place to wonder who they were.

Instead he walked past a notice threatening a ten-year stretch for anyone aiding and abetting a prison bust and through the gold-and-black wrought-iron gates to reach the street.

Then he stood still at the kerb, savouring his first real moment of release, deciding that whatever the weather, whatever the landscape, this unremarkable, scrappy piece of roadway with its parked cars and the Tube rattling away across a distant fence was simply the most beautiful place he had ever seen.

Finally, he turned left as he had been instructed, to reach the bus stop outside Hammersmith Hospital. In his pocket some small change, a Standard Class travel warrant to Northallerton and three crisp twenties formed the measure of his current status. Du Cane Road was an unceasing whirl of rushing traffic but there were no high brick walls, not a trace of barbed wire, not a lock nor a jangle of keys anywhere in sight or sound. Just one wonderful long walk stretching into the distance, unseen, unknown, alluring, beckoning him onwards.

He approached the bus stop with its lounging smokers and spreading rain puddles but kept on walking. On and on, simply for the sheer pleasure of putting one foot in front of the other with no object and no person to turn him back. The mist still tasted wonderful. Cars, buses, trucks, motorbikes – they all raced past him; even the passers-by wore hounded expressions. Where were they all going in such incredible haste? Such a contrast, he reflected, to the pace of studied deliberation he had known on the other side of the big wall.

He overtook a gaggle of giggling female medics from Queen Charlotte's, several jostling red-jacketed schoolboys and streams of burkaed mothers, before reaching green grass at the side of the great park that formed the Scrubs' open space.

So much openness. So much freedom. So little restriction. The greenery was a trigger; he couldn't keep it locked away inside himself any longer. He threw his arms outstretched as if welcoming the world and shouted aloud, to the great astonishment of a young woman with a pram: 'I'm free! Free, I tell you!'

A couple of hundred yards further on, however, reality began to puncture this great bubble of elation. Where was this new freedom leading? No personal possessions, no home to call his own, no job, no relationship. If ever a man was down...

'Gerald!'

He was jolted from these thoughts by a voice issuing from a little car. He looked around quickly in case he was not the one being hailed.

'Gerald!'

How many Geralds were in town today?

The car drew close and stopped. Then he recognised the old Vauxhall with the battered roof.

'Couldn't find you at the gate,' she said through an open window.

He smiled a warm glow of recognition. It was extraordinary that she had made the journey all the way to the prison, amazing that she had made any effort at all.

He stood on the pavement. 'Make a habit of propositioning strange men, do you?'

'Get in, you daft devil.'

The car smelled of a recent application of lemon-scented spray, though that couldn't disguise the worn carpets and a constant hum from a vibrating roof. For him, however, it was a limousine. He sank gratefully into its plastic embrace, looking at her, smiling, quite unable to think of anything appropriate to say. His conversational skills had gone into hibernation.

'Well, aren't you going to thank me?' she demanded. 'Lost your tongue in there, did you?'

He leaned over to kiss her gently on the cheek. A few more wisps of grey, a tiny new crease at the corner of her mouth and, looking down, a size rounder on the hips, but still here was his principal supporter – in fact, his only supporter. 'All this way...' His voice tailed off into incredulity. 'Quite, quite extraordinary.'

On the drive back she kept up an incessant stream of questions. How did he feel? Was he enjoying 'being out'? Never mind those earlier guarded responses, what was it really like in there? It seemed as if she wanted him to talk and talk and talk, not to relapse into silence, to prise his feelings out into the open, however reluctant he might be to share them.

'It's the company you keep,' he said eventually, when he could no longer hold out against her inquisitive tide. 'Not elevated. Hostility, victimisation, worse if you stand out against them. Only way to survive is to go with the flow. A constant atmosphere of threat, intimidation, a vicious brand of bullying. That's the dark heart of the prison psyche.'

'Sounds like you should write about it.'

He snorted. 'I don't think so.' His mouth turned down and he looked out at the passing streets, then turned back to her. 'You know what I want most of all? A long soak in a hot bath, just to get the stink of that place out of my pores.'

But what bath? Or rather, whose bath? That was the question. His prospects were not bright – no settled destination, in fact. 'You know Deirdre's left me?' he said.

'I know.'

'Sold up the flat and moved away and dumped everything. Absolutely everything. You know what hurt the most?'

'I know. You told me on the last visit, remember? The books.'

'She really enjoyed that bit. Wrote to me describing how she'd dumped the lot, every single one, some of them first editions, collected over the years since I was a kid. All gone. In a big wheelie bin behind Sainsbury's, apparently.'

'Some women can be very bitter.'

'Her very special sort of farewell.'

'Couldn't have helped, being cooped up in there and feeling absolutely powerless.'

'I was counting the days, I can tell you. Like some army squaddie doing his national service. How much longer? A big scribble on the wall: time to do. Thirty months, two weeks, three days and sixteen minutes. Just like them. And every night, every night at lights out, I wanted to scream out loud: Get me out of this disgusting place!'

She winced.

But then, quite suddenly, he didn't want to carry on with the subject. 'Too much about me!' he said sharply, 'self-pity does no one any good,' and switched the conversation around to her; what she'd been doing these past few years, the academic progress of her clever daughter, how she was managing the house. But at the back of his mind he couldn't repress the fear. Fear of the future. Fear of failure. What was he going to do? By now he'd be both a pariah and an embarrassing memory in what was laughingly called Fleet Street. And he'd be kidding himself if he thought he'd find a friend. Most of them would have moved on. He would represent distant history. Times would be tight, they'd feel sorry for him, buy him a drink and that would be that. Disillusion, shame and depression lay down that road. So what was it? Stacking shelves? Digging spuds? Picking apples?

He said: 'Drop me off at the station, will you?'

She rounded on him, shocked, insulted. 'What on earth for?'

He leaned to one side to extract the travel warrant from his pocket, then displayed it for her inspection. 'Next train, I guess.'

She snorted. 'To your brother's?' She glared at him. 'You can't stand the man. And more to the point, he can't stand you.'

He shrugged, made a face. 'Gotta have somewhere to hang my hat.'

'Don't be a fool, Gerald; stop pretending, will you?' For the first time, she was angry. 'We both always knew you'd wash up at my place when you came out, so why hit the taxpayer for a ticket to Northallerton?'

He squirmed. 'Yeah, but... I can't keep putting on you, keep asking you for big favours, getting you to drag me out of the mire. Don't think I don't appreciate it. Of course I do. A lot.'

'Well then?'

'You were the only one. The only one when all the others ran out on me.' He looked down, reliving the experience of being cut loose from the employer he had served for ten years, cut loose from any legal help, abandoned by colleagues and friends. She had been the only one; had spoken up for him, written to the parole board pleading his case, promised support, had been his only visitor to the gloom that was the Scrubs.

Their eyes met. He smiled faintly. 'Hitching up again; is that wise? I mean, is it going to work?'

She drew in her breath and gave a little shake to the head; a gesture he knew so well. 'Ground rules,' she said. 'You're in the spare bedroom and I'm in mine. I don't think I'm ready for anything else.'

He was recalling – and by the look of her, so too was she – how they had once shared the master bedroom. A long time before he'd met the dreadful Deirdre. 'I'm more than lucky to be allowed past your front door,' he said. 'But I'm still not sure. There's your daughter to consider. How's she going to feel about it? I don't want to be the cause of trouble between you two. Sparky, quick to take offence; that much I do recall.'

'Emma doesn't have a say over who I put in my spare bedroom.'

He nodded. 'And how is the dear girl?'

'Oh...' It was a word accompanied by a toss of the head that spoke volumes. 'Just now she's a disaster area. Wasting her talents. In danger of throwing her future away.' Then she stopped abruptly and looked determinedly ahead. Roper, sensing this was an issue too fresh and too raw to explore, settled back into a comfortable silence. The sheer exuberance of being free, the exquisite pleasure of his release, had left him drained and he half-dozed contentedly, grateful that Agnes was driving as she navigated the motorways that took them out of London and on to Newmarket and Suffolk. Eventually, the signs for Bury St Edmunds came up and they turned off the A14. It was a familiar route to Roper from an earlier period of his life. As she nosed the car past the old railway bridge and the allotments down by the River Lark he turned to her: 'Don't feel obliged. Please. Because of all the things you said back there in the past. I'm a big boy now.'

Her lips puckered into a 'I've-heard-it-all-before' gesture. They were nearly at journey's end, easing down Looms Lane. He said: 'Only if you're really sure. Really sure? Just temporary. Until I get myself fixed up.'

And there it was: the narrow gulley between the houses that was Orchard Street; the familiar blue-grey bricks of the

Victorian houses and finally the bright-blue front door and ivy-clad bay window of Number 24.

She turned off the motor and a line from Brahms's tribute to the death of Nelson came to him from a recent session in the prison library.

'England, home and beauty,' he said, ignoring the two dustbins parked on the garden path.

~

'Nice to see you, Emma.'

Professor Chadwick stood by his open door, smiling broadly.

Emma was drifting in the corridor outside the room. She would resent his summons, he knew, and would be putting on a pretence of just happening to be there by chance.

'Sorry about my message,' he said. 'Hope it didn't interrupt your weekend but this is something rather important.'

'I've a tutorial in fifteen minutes.'

He stifled a guffaw. Emma – a tutorial at 9.15? That was not her style. 'I'm sure the other aspects of your busy schedule can wait. Say, half an hour?'

Her expression asked: That long? But she gave in with only a perceptible sigh.

It was a room he knew she didn't relish entering, a normal professor's room; what else did she expect? Sure, it was stacked with books, both shelved and unshelved, papers flowing about the place, mainly in piles on the floor, but he knew where everything was; it was his kind of efficiency.

She made a little performance out of clearing a chair for herself and he affected not to notice. Then, when she was seated, he viewed her contemplatively from the other side of his desk. He noted once again the full ruby lips, the golden hair, the shapely torso cloaked in a printed silk dress. Not his idea of a typical college type: no scarf, no baggy jumper, no torn jeans, no scuffed trainers. And he could tell from the tight line of her mouth that she was keeping up her act of studied indifference, the calmest person in the midst of a storm, but he well knew she was afflicted by a worrying uncertainty.

He smiled broadly. 'I've been singing your praises,' he said and was glad of the response: surprise.

That had knocked her off course. Momentarily.

'Praised you to the rafters. To the highest point in the roof. My best student, my most talented assistant, a person of enormous potential. I expect, in fact I desire you to travel far. Yes, far.'

Her expression was still neutral but clearly she anticipated a 'but'.

However, the little word did not come. 'You were the subject of a lengthy exchange at our high table on Friday night,' he said. 'We all look to and recognise a substantial intellect at work, a formidable capacity, someone capable of great things.'

She blinked and looked at him quizzically. This time she could not hold back, clearly suspecting these words were a cloak for a hidden dagger. 'Professor, is this some form of elaborate condolence for what happened at auction?'

'Ah, that.' He shook his head. 'Such setbacks are thrown at us, I feel, as a kind of challenge, to test our will and ability to overcome.'

'I see.' She was still suspicious, still waiting for the exit, perhaps a velvet one. 'I can't imagine the bursar is feeling so phlegmatic about it.'

'You leave him to me.' Chadwick spread his hands. 'I believe in you, Emma, I really do. I want to reignite your spark, get you back to your old brilliant self. Not just fully engaged – but enthusiastic!'

This last was said with a great burst of emphasis. He knew his enthusiasms were legend. They were what made the History Department work.

She blinked surprise, a mix of emotions, then smiled.

'That's better,' he said, clapping his palms together. 'I still think your Louis XIV project has legs. You could turn it around, make a virtue out of new research and even use the notoriety of the fakes as a focus to catch public attention. There's still a project there, and probably a book.'

'Huh!' she said, erupting. 'What, with Shelley Squires stabbing me in the back and pinching my idea?'

'She has just one aspect of the story,' he said carefully, 'but there are plenty of others, as I'm sure you're aware. The whole Louis reign is fascinating – lots of religious interplay, not to mention a court heaving with intrigue – but then you know that already!' He gave her a big smile. 'But let's not think about him for a moment. Let's put him aside and consider the possibility of a fresh challenge, a new direction.'

She remained wary. 'And would this new direction still be within the auspices of the university?'

'Of course. Absolutely.' He smiled again and looked at the ceiling. 'I remember it as if it were, yes, well, almost yesterday. But it must be seven years ago. No, even longer...' A deep sigh at the fast passage of the years. 'You sitting in that chair. So eager. Showing me the family albums. Telling about your grandfather. The man who inspired you to modern history. And the big quest. To find out what happened to Grandfather.'

A reaction from Emma – a look to the ceiling. 'If only life were that simple. You know the story – hit a block, had to move on.'

Chadwick rubbed his chin, looking disappointed.

Emma wagged a finger. 'I've taken the grandfather search as far as I can, examined all the letters, read all the books, trawled the web, made myself a complete pest at Kew for a month and still hit a blank. A complete full stop. Utterly disappointing but I have to accept it.' She paused a moment. 'And besides, it's just not my period anymore.'

'Your acceptance surprises me. That once keen young woman... You seem to have gone cold on the trail.'

She shook her head. 'I'm fully immersed in the Louis period. The morganatic marriage, the influence of the secret wife, her influence on affairs of state, the Edict of Nantes, that's my focus now. Built up a head of steam...' Her voice tailed off, the pain of the auction sting once again sucking away at her enthusiasm. She swallowed and added quickly: 'The last thing I want now, on top of everything else, is to be accused of taking my eye off the ball, to allow my attention to be diverted to another subject.'

Chadwick steepled his hands. 'I see, I see. Yes, I quite understand, you wouldn't want a change.' There was a long pause before he smiled benignly at her. 'You know, my job is hugely satisfying in so many ways. So rewarding to have this network of old boys and girls who keep an eye out for me. Keeping me in mind whenever they come across items of interest.'

Emma gave him a wary look.

'I must have done something right over the years' – he thrust his hands behind his head and leaned back – 'because they keep offering me little sweeties. Loyal to a fault.'

'Where are you going with this, Professor?'

'To my latest gift. From a former student. He remembers my intense interest in Appeasement and hey, what a stroke of luck! A new archive of material has dropped into my lap. A fascinating series of documents on the run-up to the Munich Agreement. Would it surprise you if I said this does not look like a dead end at all?'

It was as if someone had just fired a shot over their heads. She jerked rigidly upright. Chadwick knew she was a shooter and the image was an immediate one. A shattering, shocking effect, like the sudden discharge of a firearm.

She had her elbows on the table and stared at him, eyes wide with that intense look from which it was impossible to break free. The stare pierced him. No deflection of question, no conversational artifice would suffice to evade it. He knew of old, anyone caught in the spotlight of that gaze simply had to answer directly, so he said: 'Only had a preliminary taster so far but at first glance, yes, lots of fine detail, the minutiae of the negotiations.'

She searched his face for many seconds – it seemed like an hour – gauging his sincerity. Then she said: 'You mean, significant new material? With some real answers?'

He nodded, beaming.

'Extensive?' she demanded. 'Enough to give us a new take on the subject?' Her earlier concern with Louis XIV appeared instantly eclipsed.

'New insights into the attitudes of those on the inside of the British delegation to Munich,' he said. 'Backbiting, snide remarks, fissures within the camp. Doubts, fears and outright opposition. Anti-appeasers writing memos, the Prime Minister putting them down. Who can say what other nuggets of gold may turn up on closer examination.'

'Any mention of him?'

Chadwick didn't need to ask about *him*; knew she was once more switched on to the subject of her grandfather. 'None of this stuff ever made it to the National Archives,' he said. 'No other historian has seen this material. Kew kept in the dark. So it needs very careful sifting. And perhaps... well, there's always a chance there may be a clue...' He looked at her and smiled. 'But I quite understand you want to stay with the 17th century. The question is, who among the many talented members of my team am I going to entrust this new task to?'

She waved a dismissive hand as if the idea was simply too absurd. 'You can't be serious about any of them; you need *me* for this. No one else fits.'

Chadwick looked out of the window, seemed not to have heard, as if he were having a conversation in another room or simply pontificating to himself. 'This isn't just about history. It's bang up to date. The issues of Munich are still the issues of today. War and peace, such an ageless theme. What a resonance to our current problems. Iran, the Middle East, Korea, China, standing up to dictators, confronting aggressors, everyone fearful of the outbreak of a new war. Does this ever go away?'

Emma stood, as if to grab his attention. 'Of course it doesn't.' Her hands were still on the desk. She was leaning forward. 'This changes everything for me. Everything for the granddaughter of Bradley Wilkes.' The stare again. 'You can forget all that stuff I said earlier.' Suddenly, she began emptying books from her briefcase on to the professor's floor – some of them were his – but this act was a ritual cleansing of subject, an offloading of Louis XIV. 'Ditch the king and his court,' she said. 'Let Miss Judas bathe in that particular spotlight. All to herself. The Appeasement archive is for me, you know it is!'

Chadwick appeared to descend from his cloud. He reached for a calendar and appeared to be deciding on dates. 'I'm hugely buoyed by my new idea.' He flicked some more pages. 'I have it in mind to organise an international conference involving historians from all the nations touched by the Second World War. Show the world why the tragedy of that terrible war really came about. New perspectives. New information. Worth emphasising to today's world, wouldn't you say? Plenty of relevance to today's troubles. Parallels? Resonance?'

That stare beamed at him again. 'Professor, I know it, you know it. Munich is for me. This is my... our... big opportunity.'

Chadwick could not repress a certain sense of mischief. 'Why not myself? After all, I did discover the archive.'

'Could you really afford to divest yourself of your duties here? Could you? Absent yourself for sufficient time to complete the process of setting up, organising, conducting, analysing and so on?'

A movement outside the room caught her attention. Chadwick followed her gaze to the window. The Master chose that moment to proceed in stately, somewhat arthritic, gait across the quad. She didn't need to say it. She made it easy for him. 'Lending your name to the conference will give it all the necessary prestige I need. Why not call it the Chadwick Archive?' She smiled at him, now playing his game. 'But probably best for you to maintain a discreet distance.'

They both knew the reason. It wasn't any concern about his position with the Master, the Proctor or the Vice Chancellor. It was in case the archive turned out to be a turkey or his proposed conference a dud. Distance would keep Chadwick's reputation safe. It would be Emma's chance – and Emma's risk. *Down to me to make it a success,* she was telling him.

He made a pretence of considering his options, weighing the various candidates, toying with the booklet containing the staff list, as if he might swat a fly. Then he put it down, slowly laid his hand over it and looked at her directly. 'Fact is, there's a deal on the table. Fresh finance. Travel. Lots of it. Involves, at least initially, going to America.'

'America?'

He nodded. 'But first, an introductory conversation in London.'

He fished around the edges of his blotter, found a note that was tucked under one triangular brown corner and passed it to her.

An address, a day, a time.

He sat back in his chair beaming a hugely benign smile.

She kept her expression blank. 'Thank you, Professor, for this vote of confidence.'

'Good, good,' he said. 'When one door might seem to be in danger of closing...' He stood up to signify the end of the interview and pointed to the note in her hand. 'Be advised. This man is expecting to be impressed. And not by Louis XIV.'

Sweat poured down his face and dripped unwiped from his chin, blood ran from bruised and swollen knuckles, lungs heaved from clouds of rock dust, and teeth were clamped manically tight – but still he swung the big pick like a man demented.

Wolf Steigel was gripped by the mania of last-day desperation.

All week his gang of excavators had shovelled and dragged, loaded and shifted, packed and carted. Tons of broken rocks and spoil had been removed – to no avail. Their licence to dig lasted just a week and it was fast running out with nothing to show for it.

A fist jabbed into Steigel's heaving shoulder.

'Move over!' the second man yelled. 'Give yourself a break. Let me...'

'Nein! I know it's here. Sure of it. I know it.'

Behind him the other ten worked in a discordant din of jackhammers, drills, picks, shovels and rakes, clearing a pathway to the last cavern.

At least they hoped it was a cavern. Steigel and the men of

the Thuringia Exploration Group had convinced the directors of the Kali Company in Germany that this particular area of the maze of tunnels that made up the Kaiserode salt and potassium mine at Merkers was a likely place to discover further items of historical interest. Nobody worked the mine these days; it was a museum. Its history as the repository for the Reichsbank gold hidden here by the Nazis at the end of the war was a star attraction drawing thousands of visitors.

And twenty-four hours from now the tourists would be back – by which time all trace of Steigel's excavation had to be removed and tidied away.

'I will not accept defeat,' Steigel shouted, exhausted, handing over to the second man. 'Keep digging.'

There was another imperative. The pristine hard hats of the museum office would be around very shortly to supervise. By supervise, they meant insisting on a raft of health and safety procedures that had slowed the men of the TEG all week. But today the diggers had nothing to lose. The pristine hats would be ignored – men despised for never themselves breaking sweat or suffering a single mark on immaculate overalls; men who had never wielded a pick or a stick of gelly in their lives. The TEG may have described themselves as historians searching for museum artefacts but in truth they were treasure hunters pure and simple. And if the cavern they desperately sought yielded hidden Nazi hoards of gold, silver, precious metals, jewels, banknotes or other valuables, as they hoped, they would be filling their pockets and barging their way out of the mine emboldened by visions of riches and dreams of untold luxury. No clipboard-wielding museum official was going to stand in the way of ten determined hardmen armed with picks and crowbars.

'Keep digging!'

But the exhortation was redundant. Already Digger No.8 was thrashing at a gap and enlarging the orifice by the minute.

In five, the mood of desperation had transformed to triumphant grins. In ten, the gang were all inside a chamber that Steigel – a man with an obsession and a passion for maps – had promised them would be there.

In fifteen, they had the five metal boxes clear of all obstruction and ready to open.

'Stop!' A pristine hat had arrived to mar their moment of victory. 'This is museum property. These boxes will be removed and opened under supervision in our workshop.'

Steigel barged the man out of the way and swung the pick at the first of the five boxes.

The lock splintered, the retaining clips came loose and the lid swung open.

Pristine Hat scrambled up from the pile of rocks where he had landed. 'You have violated the terms of your excavation licence. I insist on taking possession...'

Steigel swung his pick again on box No.2. Then 3. And 4. And 5.

The ten men of the TEG and the now silent official of the Merkers Museum stood back to look in shock at the results of this week-long excavation. Hats were pushed back on heads, hands went to hips, begrimed smiles turned to puzzlement and dismay. Steigel threw down the pick in disgust.

'What a crock of shit! Just a load of stinking paper. Tons of the stuff.'

Pristine Hat looked up cautiously, then deemed it safe to crouch and examine. 'A fine archival haul, I would say; a valuable record of the past.'

'And you're bloody well welcome to it!' Steigel kicked the pick across the littered floor. 'Welcome to all of it.' He turned away. 'After all that effort...'

Ten begrimed men threw down their tools and melted disconsolately from the chamber, leaving the museum man examining in detail a fine new historical exhibit, a vast haul of government files, all stamped on the covers with the words *Schutzpolizei des Reiches.*

On each cover was the same symbol: the German eagle, wings spread wide, a laurel wreath and a swastika symbol at the foot.

He turned the pages. He may not have had a speck of grime on his perfect blue overalls, may never have wielded a hammer or swung a crowbar, but he knew his history, knew intimately the story of Merkers, and had immersed himself in the fine detail of the disintegrating Third Reich.

'The missing Gestapo archive,' he said in an awed tone, and hurried away to inform the museum director.

CHAPTER FOUR

R oper put down the phone, pensive for the briefest of moments, then broke out into a wide, relieved smile.

'Was that wise?' she wanted to know.

They were in Agnes's tiny living room at 24 Orchard Street. The armchairs had paisley covers and plumped-up cushions and they balanced china teacups on knees: Earl Grey for her, plain Co-op brew for him. It was warm and cosy, a sanctuary from the sourness of the outside world.

'Sure, it was wise,' Roper said. 'I made up my mind some time ago and I'm sticking to it. I'm not going back.'

She shrugged. 'Did he make a definite offer?'

He was Roper's old boss at the agency.

'Just a lot of iffing and butting and maybes. I'm not having that,' Roper said. 'And anyway, I've made my mind up, I'm making a clean break. I'm the one who's going to disprove the theory that ex-cons always reoffend, always go back to their bad old ways, that bad habits always drag you down. I don't want to be subject to those temptations.'

'Leaves you out in the cold.'

'I'll find something.' He laughed, determinedly

unconcerned. 'I'll be a sheep farmer, a thatcher, odd-job gardener. Or maybe a barman, car-park attendant or a tutor at a journalism college – now that would be a good joke!'

Agnes said nothing and took a long sip of tea.

'Actually, it wasn't a complete joke,' he said. 'I mean, about gardening. I got quite good in there at beans and carrots.' The Scrubs had extensive allotment gardens to encourage prisoners to develop their skills as part of the rehabilitation process, he said; the gardens and the library became the two focal points of his incarcerated life.

'If you're that good, you can have a go at mine,' she said. Agnes had an abandoned allotment down by the River Lark, bequeathed her by her father, overgrown and derelict like most of them on the other side of the town, a less than salubrious triangle of weed-strewn territory hemmed in by the river and the huge, unwelcoming corrugated-iron sides of the football stadium.

Roper looked interested.

'Seriously though,' she said, 'haven't you got any idea of what you really might like to do?'

Roper drew in a long breath. He was warmly cloistered in this room; he was wonderfully comfortable in a high-backed farmhouse Windsor armchair. 'History,' he said at last. 'Did lots of reading inside. Indulged my passion for Napoleon. Read up on all his battles. Maybe I could earn my keep as a battlefield tour guide. A thriving business at Waterloo, so I'm told.'

Agnes waved a dismissive hand and laughed. 'Be practical, Gerald.' Their conversation meandered down a nostalgic avenue of unchallenging subjects – how the town had changed, the new tower on the cathedral – and favourite haunts from their earlier time together – walking the dog on the heath and exclaiming at the fantastic roses in the Abbey Gardens – without ever touching on anything too sensitive. Roper was beset by guilt and regret; why had he been tempted away by Deirdre? And he was still surprised at Agnes's lack of resentment, still anxious to repay her generosity in any way he could. He even tried inviting her out for a meal at an old favourite, the Café Rouge.

'You can't afford it,' she said.

'Well then, a really nice takeaway?'

'I'm doing spaghetti with Swedish meatballs tonight,' she said. 'That suit?'

Despite their easy manner Roper detected an undercurrent of unstated distraction and anxiety. And there was one subject missing from Agnes's conversation: her daughter. Emma's absence as a topic was significant in itself, he decided, but he kept that thought to himself.

For the moment.

It was the day after her trip to London; the weekend already upon them and Emma was still at home. She was in her room, laying out dresses and jeans on the bed, one finger on a querulous lip and pondering her wardrobe, when her mother entered. Emma turned and smiled. No hostility, no sarcasm, no chirpy put-downs today.

'Got something to tell you,' Emma said in an even tone.

'Good news, I hope. Found a nice man? Getting married?'

'Do me a favour, Mother, try a cat, why don't you? A lot less trouble.'

'Then let me guess. You're off on another trip? On that yacht with that crazy woman; what's her name?'

'And if I was, why not?'

There was a stark pause in this conversation while they both hesitated on the brink of reopening old wounds.

'And anyway,' Emma said eventually, 'Angela's not at all mad, she just has the good fortune to be rather rich and enjoys my company. And what's more, she's fun. Really fun. She doesn't have anyone moaning or griping at her all the time. *Her* parents are only too pleased to give her whatever she wants.'

'Gambling, yachts, clubs... What happens,' her mother asked, 'when Angela gets tired of you, finds someone else, a new social butterfly, a new friend to patronise? Or when she gets married?'

'My money. I pay my whack. I never sponge, if that's what you're getting at. And anyway, a few trips out of Poole Harbour over to France hardly count as the jet-set lifestyle.'

'Monte Carlo! You went to the casino; you frittered money you got from Granny. It's a waste, a terrible waste.'

'A token sum. Just for fun. Once.'

'Twice, to my certain knowledge, and maybe more I don't know about.'

'All right! Two occasions then, both in my summer hols between Easter term and Michaelmas. Again, hardly the stuff of millionaire decadence.'

'Yes, but is this wise? Shouldn't you be saving for a home or for your future or for children?'

Emma snorted. 'Live for today, Mother; tomorrow you may be out of luck, ill or dead.'

This was an old battleground but neither had any real appetite to reopen the fight. The subject of Granny Drake's bequest – which had skipped a generation, a wounding event for Agnes – had caused friction over the years. Augustus John's watercolour of a gypsy girl had been a treasured painting picked up in Paris by Bradley Wilkes, valued but not loved by his granddaughter who demonstrated no sentimentality over objects. It was ridiculous to load emotion onto a piece of furniture, jewellery or art, she had insisted; she had no truck with rings or keepsakes, and the painting cleared her ten grand.

The end of the skirmish was marked by a deep sigh. 'Anyway,' Emma said, 'as it happens, this has got nothing to do with Angela and everything to do with Professor Chadwick. And you should be greatly pleased about it.'

'The professor? I'm surprised you're still on speaking terms, that you've still got a job after all that's happened.'

The reference to the letter-auction fiasco quieted them both for a few moments before Emma said: 'Actually, he wants to give me a new job. A big one.'

'But, of course, you turned him down, naturally – a prior engagement with a deckchair or a nightclub.'

'As it happens, I said yes.'

'Half-hearted never won any prizes.'

Emma spluttered. 'Look, you've got this all wrong. Completely! I've never been half-hearted. What rule says I can't enjoy myself and still be a career success?' When her mother drew breath for an answer Emma cut her off: 'And you should be happy. Your favourite thing. The very same you've always wanted. What you've always dreamed about. What you wanted me to do ever since I went to university.'

For the moment her mother stood silent, nonplussed.

Emma nodded, grinning.

'Grandfather. Investigating. Finding out, among other things, what happened.'

Later, downstairs, when the mother–daughter relationship had transformed into a closeness not achieved in years, the mood was made even more mellow by a phone call from Emma's brother announcing that he would be visiting the next day. Barry's industry was relentless. He rebuilt cars. His speciality was sports models. He'd been the one to restore the old Porsche to pristine condition and present it to his sister.

'He's bringing round his latest acquisition,' Emma said. 'A 1936 Riley Kestrel.'

The mood change was complete. Her mother mumbled something about Barry's appetite for risky driving but smiles were still in evidence. 'Tell me about your new job,' she prompted, 'it is about the Munich crisis, isn't it?'

'Yes, of course.' Emma puffed herself up. 'You're now talking – or soon will be – to a Montagu-Pinckney scholar.'

'I say!'

'I'll be going over to the States shortly. Means lots of extra funding. Apparently, they've got pots of money to throw at this.' She sighed. 'Just as well, really.'

'Oh dear,' her mother said. 'Running low again?'

Emma ignored the question. 'This is going to be a symposium of historians from all over Europe and America, to discuss Munich and to be held in Munich, under the auspices of the university but funded by the scholarship.'

'And you?'

'Organising the whole thing. A great opportunity for me. Could lead to great things.'

'Ah! A professorship?'

Emma shrugged and said slowly: 'Maybe.'

Her mother became reflective. 'I must say, I'd almost given up on you,' she said. 'Thought you'd gone cold on the idea. I'll admit to being pleased... and a little amazed.'

Emma made coffee – for both of them; a significant event, but said nothing.

'But can this really be true?' her mother asked doubtfully. 'I often ask myself, where is that keen young student who went to university seven years ago vowing the mystery over Grandfather was her great motivator? Don't deny it. You told your professor that. I know you did because you rehearsed your pitch on me the night before, remember?'

Emma shrugged. 'Circumstances change. Nothing stays the same. I had to switch to other subjects. And none of us stands still, we all grow into different people, different to last year or the year before, let alone seven years back.'

Her mother snorted. 'We may move on and develop but we don't alter our core. Underneath it all, we're still the same people; we don't change that much.' She stared hard at her daughter. 'Are you the same person, Emma? Or was the grandfather story a fable – just as much for me as for your professor? Were you putting us all on, back then?'

Emma gave her mother a long look. 'I meant it then,' she said, 'and I mean it now.'

The two looked at each other in silence, one attempting to demonstrate sincerity, the other assessing the value of it, when suddenly the spell was broken by the closing of a door upstairs.

It was like a pistol shot to Emma. Mouth agape, she looked to the foot of the staircase. 'What's that? Someone's upstairs, in the house...'

Her mother swallowed, then relaxed her taut expression. She even smiled a little sheepishly.

'And now,' she said, 'I've got something to tell *you*.'

CHAPTER FIVE

They had moved to the lounge, drinks cradled, armchairs occupied, but the outbreak of warmth between them had suddenly gone cold.

'Not him?' Emma demanded. 'Not Roper? Why get back with him of all people? A disgraced jailbird?'

'I've stood by him; someone had to.'

'But why you?'

'History. We go back.'

'Well!' Eyes to the ceiling, a deep sigh. 'All I can say is, I hope he's not going to be hanging around here too long. He spooks me. Just as well I'm off shortly.'

Her mother did not react. A long pause. 'There's something else.' She swallowed. 'You're going to be away a lot, is that correct?'

'True. Lots of travel. First, America, then a long spell in Munich.'

Her mother nodded. 'I'm glad for you... but a word of warning. You'll be handling it alone in a strange city. A young woman in a den of wolves.'

'Oh please! This is the 21st century.'

'You need help. Backup so no one can take liberties.'

'Don't be ridiculous. You're out of touch, Mother.'

Silence. Then her mother said: 'I want you to accept some help.' More silence, then: 'Gerald.'

'What? Him? Are you joking? Why bring him into this? What's he got?'

'A lot. You don't speak German. He does. You don't know the country. He does. He's worked there in the past. You have no contacts over there or experience of dealing with them. He does and has.'

'Look, I've just won a scholarship from America, I'm a post-grad researcher at the university, I'm widely travelled, used to going all over, and I have all the authority I need for this job.'

'You could be the target for intimidation. There's still bad feelings left over from the war.'

'I don't need a minder.'

'Yes you do.

'No – and certainly not your boyfriend. Not an ex-con!'

'He'll stay in the background, be discreet; just a watching brief. Someone you can turn to in a crisis.'

'Why are you doing this to me?' Emma let out an exasperated yelp. 'I mean! Setting an aged watchdog on me. *This* aged watchdog! No, no, no. I don't want him.'

'He's going anyway!'

Emma threw up her hands, looked out of the window and sighed deeply, then in a resigned voice said: 'I know you. Oh God, do I know you. You'll go on and on until I give in, but I'll tell you this much, something I insist on – your darned watchdog had better stay well tucked up in his kennel and keep right out of my way.'

They were standing in the kitchen and Roper, just back from his expedition to the allotments by the River Lark, was being introduced to the rules of the house: shoes off at the door, no newspapers allowed on the breakfast table and no dirty crocks in the sink.

He grinned good-naturedly. The sour taste of Wormwood Scrubs was already beginning to fade. He felt comfortable with the routine at 24 Orchard Street: the key on a piece of string behind the letter box, Thomas the cat who needed feeding twice a day, dustbins collected on a Thursday and Agnes cycling off at six to do the night turn at the Northgate Nursing Home. He had already made a start on clipping back the ivy which crept too luxuriantly around the sill of the front bay window.

He shrugged his shoulders: 'I've got to be honest, Agnes, your allotment patch is *Mission Impossible.*'

She looked at him sharply and he noted how her expression had hardened. There was a tension about her he hadn't seen before.

'You'd need a JCB digger up there for a month,' he said, 'just to clear away the undergrowth. And did you know about that huge black swan? It's a menace!'

She didn't respond and he knew she didn't want to discuss allotments. What had earlier seemed to him to be an indulgent if vaguely anxious mood had seeped away. He was about to prompt her on this when they heard a drumming on the stairs and then the front door slam shut with a juddering crash.

He chuckled. That was Emma leaving for Cambridge. They were alone in the house and the slammed door became a signal. Agnes walked to the big old wooden table with its aged swirls and cracks and blue-patterned tablemats and beckoned him over to sit. This was her moment, Roper realised, the moment she had been waiting for. There was a charge between them.

'Something to tell you,' she announced, and without preliminary came straight out with what was on her mind – a subject which, he soon realised, had been dominating her thoughts all along – Emma; how proud she was; how happy she was; how worried she was.

For a brief, selfish moment he felt a twinge of resentment at discovering that his arrival on the scene was not, after all, the biggest item on Agnes's horizon. Soon, however, he was caught up in the fascination of Emma's news: the huge challenge of organising a history conference in Munich – and, just as intriguing to Roper, the family background and story of the grandfather's disappearance.

He absorbed all this and began to think about the events of the Chamberlain era and what he could recall of them, but in her mother, he noted, the excitement and pride was allied to fear.

'She's had so many ups and downs, that girl, so many disasters, I'm really pleased that now, at last, she's got a really great opportunity,' Agnes said. 'Really pleased for her.'

'Disasters?' Roper queried, casting his mind back with a frown to a period several years before when he had been around – fleetingly – during Emma's teenage years. Was this a reference to the girl's father, missing since she was two?

'I'm talking current disaster,' Agnes repeated emphatically, and gradually, piece by painful piece, the details emerged of the Louis XIV auction forgery that had blighted Emma's career prospects. He took a deep breath and made a face: £11,000 down the drain on a packet of bogus royal love letters... That was some trap to fall into. A cup of tea on the worktop was going cold but he ignored it, visualising the damage, the sense of utter defeat, the humiliation, perhaps even the loss of much hard work based on a falsehood. A new light was being thrown on Emma's skewed take on the world. He could imagine the fury and the humiliation – and the titanic eruption that doubtless accompanied it. He looked into the distance then summoned from memory a recently-read passage: "Betrayed by credulous innocence with falsehood and base forgery".'

Agnes, however, was clearly not in the mood for quotations. 'You spent too long in that damned library.'

'Milton.'

'Do us both a favour, Gerald, don't play the Bard of Wormwood Scrubs when Emma's around.'

He waved a contrite hand. 'Perhaps not.' But then he said: 'She isn't the first to be ambushed by a forger. Plenty of other historians with reputations far greater than hers have fallen into the trap. Just think of my namesake: Hugh Trevor-Roper and the *Hitler Diaries*. She'll survive. She'll get over it.'

His sentiments seemed to encourage Agnes. She sat forward, put her elbows on the table, clasped her hands before her and held his gaze. 'Something you said before... about history, about your love of history. It gave me an idea. This is not about Napoleon. This is much closer to home.'

Roper's imagination was in a whirl.

'This time Emma has to succeed,' she said. 'This new job is her redemption. She's had such a lot to contend with. I don't want another black hole in her life.' Her stare was unrelenting. 'That's where you come in, Gerald. I know it's a big ask but I want you to be patient with her. Very, very patient.'

Roper was nodding. 'Of course, only too pleased... Anything I can do to help.'

'She's had so many hard blows I'm desperate for her to make a success of this.' More eye contact. 'That's why I want you to help. Give her a big boost for this new task of hers.'

'Of course, I've told you, I'm on it... though not quite sure how.'

Agnes seemed to have crossed a bridge somewhere. 'Good,'

she said and sighed in evident relief. Then she gave him another challenging look. 'I want you to partner her.'

'Partner her?'

'Hold her hand.'

His quizzical reaction prompted more. She said: 'Oh, I know she can be a little difficult sometimes, but you can do it. Assistant, advisor, protector, anything and everything. Out in front, right behind, in the background, whatever! I'm putting great faith in you, Gerald, in your good sense and powers of persuasion. And protection.'

He shrugged, trying not to let his scepticism show. 'Of course, if she'll agree...' In the ensuing silence, he wondered quite what he had signed up to, but he was always going to say yes to Agnes. He owed her this; he owed her big time.

She was still staring at him, clearly willing him to give a more positive response, so he smiled widely and put a reassuring hand on hers. 'Stop worrying,' he said, leaning in close. 'If it's humanly possible, I'll do all I can to get her through this. Promise. Give it my very best.'

Emma locked the car, wondering briefly who might be using her reserved space while she was away. Then, with determined step, she strode up Trumpington Street, turning in at the college gates, leaving behind the bustle and noise of the town for the ivy-clad cloistered calm of St James's.

Her first gesture was to celebrate her new status by ignoring the gravel path around the edge of the quad. Instead, knowing there would be disapproving glances from the window of the porters' lodge, she strode across the middle of the grass.

The professor was ready for her – a white china teapot and two refectory cups perched on the corner of his cluttered desk and despite his apparent air of self-obsession he had remembered that she preferred peppermint. There was a further token of approval: he had cleared another space, the one closest to her chair, so that she could lay out pen, notebook and at least one A4 file.

'Good trip? Everything suit?'

She nodded. It wasn't her way to blubber gratitude, nor his to inquire. Instead, he made do with a knowing smile. For her part, Emma wondered just how deep his knowledge and relationship ran with Lance Scranton.

'Been in touch with Munich,' he said. His opposite number at the university there had agreed to co-sponsor the event.

The event? He was calling it The Appeasement Re-evaluation Conference and already had a list of probable participants: countries, universities, delegates. It was a planning session that was going to stretch into mid-morning. 'As I see it, you have three big pluses to set you on the right road,' Chadwick said, counting them out on his fingers.

'First, the Merkers mine.' Here he enthused about the possibility of looking into police files to discover what happened behind the scenes in 1938. Second was the voluminous archive of information from the air marshal's loft. There was a box of it by Chadwick's chair.

'What I'm also looking for,' Emma interrupted, 'is a way into tapping into the mystery of my grandfather.'

'Quite so, quite so. And that's number three. I must say the obit pages of *The Telegraph* are an absolute treasure house.'

'Obit pages?'

'Absolutely. *The Guardian* does dead poets, *The Times* scientists and *The Tele*' heroes. So many fascinating people dying off lately. The great, the good and particularly the brave. Wonderful, heroic people who did incredible – and important – things in the war. And just before...'

She screwed a face of distaste. She knew where this was leading: diaries from the dead – a sore subject with her after the Mercer auction disaster. But Chadwick, looking over his glasses, was ignoring her recent history, recalling his own past exploits. 'A good starting point for the paper chase, I've always found. Often works wonders if you get in quick before the family starts throwing things out. Collections of old documents, articles, diaries, papers they've written. Many, many unpublished books lying in bottom drawers. Conversations with friends and relatives. And they collect keepsakes. Hence our airman with gold in his loft.'

She looked down, cleared some of her own clutter on to an unoccupied place on the floor, found a fresh page in her notebook and said: 'So, do we have a specific dead hero in mind, complete with warm trail to follow?'

CHAPTER SIX

The Porsche Sport was made for the motorway. Beside her, in the deep dark burr maple passenger seat, Roper sat stiff and tense and staring silently ahead.

His presence was still a fraught subject but Emma knew she had to concede: having him ride along as protector was her mother's non-negotiable red line. For all that they argued over lifestyles, clothing and friendships, there were boundaries, certain places Emma would not go. Too much history there; too much in the past for loyalties to be trampled.

Still, that didn't mean she was going to make it easy for him. Passing a service station, she spoke for the first time since leaving Cambridge. 'I suppose you know you'll be up against some pretty dangerous customers on this trip. Some of those professors! Wow! Real scary.'

He chuckled, then turned to her: 'I'm doing this to reassure your mother that no harm will come...' He shrugged slightly. 'And because I happen to agree with her; you need some help, you can't do this all on your own.' She said nothing, so he added: 'It's more than likely you'll attract some unsavoury characters.'

This time she did react with snorting incredulity. 'Academics?'

'There'll be others.'

Silence, then she gave him a sideways glance. 'Must be strange to be on the outside... amongst normal people?'

He didn't respond; looked straight ahead.

'Still, better than writing letters for old lags, I suppose.'

He smiled slightly. 'Quite an eye-opener it was. A window into a strange subculture. Another world.'

'So, what's it like to be on the outside of the barbed wire? Don't you get agoraphobia?'

Roper looked down at his bucket seat. 'Just at the moment, more a case of claustrophobia.'

But Emma wasn't done. 'Surely you're going to find this trip deadly dull. I mean, all that peering down the throat of the past. Thought you'd be hankering after your pals in the street of shame. Excitement of the chase and all that. Aren't you anxious to get back to the fray?'

He shook his head. 'That's all in my past. Like all the ex-cons say, I'm going straight now.'

'And about as believable.'

'Honest, guv,' he said putting on a stagy cockney voice. 'Turned over a new leaf. A new page in the notebook of life. Now I'm into allotments and galleries and good food.'

'Oh yes, I heard about your new leaf down at The Dove. Amateur theatricals over a pint of the Wherry, so I hear.'

He shrugged. 'I admit it. Have been known to break into verse on the odd occasion. "Shoulder the sky, my lad, and drink your ale".' He laughed. 'Just the odd line or two of Housman. Seemed appropriate. A very decent drop of ale down at The Dove, I have to say.' He turned to her. 'Anyhow, I'm quite partial to a bit of history myself, though I have to admit to a preference for old Boney.'

For a taut moment Emma concentrated on the road ahead, twisting the two-tone steering wheel to overtake a bus and several lorries hogging the middle lane, before pointing an admonishing finger. She said: 'I want to make one thing clear from the off. I shall not be requiring you to give an opinion, right? Whatever amateur theories you may offer down at The Dove, I don't want to hear them. You're not part of my history team.'

Evidently Roper was expecting a tirade. He'd probably been preprogrammed to deal with her temper. All he said was: 'Just consider me your security consultant.' There was even a slight smile.

'I don't need a security consultant to go to a funeral in a Berkshire village.'

'You never know... who you might meet, what difficulties you might encounter. A second pair of hands might come in useful.'

She sighed, not looking at him. 'I suppose you could be handy as an extra driver.'

He chortled and slapped the dashboard. 'So, I get to drive this little beast then?'

Still not looking, she said: 'If I have to put up with you all the way down to Yardley Broadmayne, the least you can do is stand me lunch.'

Roper was never intimidated by displays of hostility. He could shrug off any amount of opposition and still turn on the charm to melt a difficult interviewee. It took a bloodhound to shake off an old newshound.

Besides, he could read her. He knew Emma was under huge pressure to succeed. A heavy responsibility clung to those handsome shoulders. This was her defence mechanism; she was gearing up to confront the many dominant personalities she could expect to meet in the US and Germany.

However, when they stopped at a chilly service station for a meal, he decided it was time to flex a little muscle, insisting he needed 'to be put in the picture' so he would know what to expect when they reached Yardley.

A shade reluctantly, the relevant details were supplied in a page torn from the previous day's paper: Sir Denis Bracewell Grainger, KGB, last surviving member of the British Government delegation to the Munich talks in 1938 when he was the most junior civil servant present.

Roper concentrated on the list of Grainger's career details: head of German Desk at the Foreign Office between 1960 and 1968 and a Permanent Undersecretary from 1968 until 1980. Died, aged ninety-three, last Thursday.

A possible witness to Emma's family drama, but now a silent one.

He looked up at the sound of Emma's voice; she was calling up someone familiar with a 'had to rush away, no time to explain' type of message. Roper tried to concentrate on the page but her voice was so penetrating he couldn't fail to hear her concluding remarks: 'Tell Terry, sorry, but I won't be making it for the next few Thursdays.'

When she cut the connection he said: 'Tell me about Thursdays.'

'You wouldn't be interested.'

He said nothing. Just looked at her.

'Shooting session, university rifle club; satisfied?'

'Many women?'

'Mostly women.'

'Attraction?'

'Doing something well, the buzz of the bullseye, bonding, camaraderie...'

'Good shot?'

But she looked away, pushing her pasta to a far corner of the table in a gesture of disgust. 'That was revolting,' she said, pointing to her plate. 'Next time, I'll choose the stopover.'

Yardley Broadmayne turned out to be a large village of thatches, high hedges, gabled houses and tall farm barns. It was the work of a few minutes to locate St Stephen's, close to the village green, and park the car. Outside, Emma smoothed out the creases of her long black coat, raided from her mother's wardrobe, while Roper worked at ignoring the discomfort of a suit – the only one he possessed and last worn when he appeared in the dock – that was now two sizes too large, the waistband clipped together with one of Agnes's large safety pins.

They began to walk towards the church. He knew she was on edge. This was a new experience for her but not for him. They had no invitation; that bothered her but he knew the routine. He said: 'This Grainger character, he's Establishment, a big noise, right? Hundreds are going to come. It's a public event. All wanting to feed off his importance. Believe me, more than half of them will be strangers.' Then, to give her encouragement, he added: 'Relax. Act restrained, sad; just look the part.'

She gave him a sharp look but said nothing and they dropped in behind two men in long grey overcoats and a woman all in black, turning right under the lychgate, following in line along a lengthy gravel path past high hedges and crumbling gravestones whose names had long been obliterated by wind and rain. At the porch they were directed without check along the rear of the last pew, then right down the centre aisle of the busy nave. The pews were packed. The size of the church, more on the scale of a small cathedral, spoke volumes about the past riches of the village. Roper looked up to gaze at memorials to the dead of two world wars; lists of traditional English names sprinkled with a few originating in Central Europe. Higher still a huge expanse of stained glass seemed to dwarf rows of bowed heads.

When the tributes began he slipped out a small notebook and started taking a shorthand note.

She nudged him. A hoarse whisper in his ear. 'What the hell are you doing?'

He cupped a reply directly to hers. 'These are the first clues, aren't they?' She didn't respond. 'The tributes, describing his great life; we need that. Are you going to remember it all? You can't ask them to repeat it later.'

She shrugged.

At the interment, they stood apart from the family mourners, keeping a discreet distance, standing close to a line of oaks and willows that ringed the churchyard. A chill wind nipped at them.

'Shorthand?' she said to him with a quizzical expression.

'Should you be surprised?'

She flicked an agitated shoulder and touched her neck. He noticed the birthmark. 'So far, I feel more like a snooping journalist than a history researcher.'

'A crossover. Making use of the skills of one to help the other.'

She sniffed.

He persisted: 'You won't find everything you need in some dusty archive.'

'I'll drink to that,' she said.

There was no more conversation until they judged the timing right to enter the wake at the Grainger home, a large sprawling house on the edge of the village. They walked up a path, noting a once-loved garden, now a neglected tangle of unpruned roses, straggly bushes and unkempt lawns.

Inside, the crowd was dense. A room had been cleared of furniture except for a table laden with best china and delicately cut finger sandwiches. Roper picked up on the décor. Dowdy, as one might expect in the home of a very old man who had lived on his own for a very long time. The rose petal wallpaper was fading and the picture rail and dado shouted early post-war. No one in the crowd had removed their outer clothing and a fug was building. He followed Emma, squeezing between several groups engaged in hushed conversations, before they spotted the surviving son of the great Foreign Office mandarin. But this was not the moment. The young Mr Grainger, now well past retiring age, cleared his throat and embarked on a speech.

'I want to thank you all for coming,' he said.

The throng hushed in respectful silence.

'So many people,' he said. 'So many people my dear father knew – family, work, societies, clubs. The result of all the different strands of his long and busy life. I never knew the full extent of it. Quite a revelation, I have to say. Once again, many thanks.'

Nodded heads and a small silence.

Roper assessed the son as a benign character; a little overwhelmed by the occasion but not visibly stricken with grief. The father had clung to life a lot longer than most and the son might well be welcoming a much delayed bequest. And Emma, he noticed, was quick to grasp her chance. 'Mr Grainger, may we introduce ourselves?' Her pitch was just right: smooth, respectful, engaging. She didn't have the privilege of knowing Sir Denis personally, she told him, but her university was keen to pay proper tribute to a man who'd played such a distinguished part in the history of the nation. And history was so important, didn't he agree?

Roper repressed a smile. She might make disparaging references to his snooping but she could lay on the charm when needed.

Grainger made some vaguely neutral response but she pressed him; at a later date the university's History Department was keen to talk to him.

'About what, precisely?'

Any memoranda, historic materials or memories which might throw a new light on, and increase our understanding of, the difficult times in which his father had played such a pivotal role.

The younger Grainger seemed unsure on this point. 'I don't know about any of that,' he said mildly. 'I very much think that you'll have to talk to one of these gentlemen...'

They turned to see a semicircle of Crombie-clad figures. Looking much like a ring of well-dressed sheepdogs. All men, all glassy-eyed. The tallest, thin-lipped with a pale face, receding hairline and dressed in an immaculate fur-collared coat, flicked an eyebrow and took a pace forward.

'Have you a moment, please? I think we should move into that corner.'

Emma and Roper were both being corralled, shepherded to a place where conversations were unlikely to be overheard.

The tall man said: 'I shall have to talk to your Vice Chancellor. This is highly sensitive. I really do think the university authorities ought to have been in touch with us before.'

'Us?' queried Roper, but he was ignored.

'Actually, we do not welcome inquiries of this sort. You see, we are part of this great family. We are here today to venerate a great member of our service. A tower, an inspiration, one of us.'

Emma looked at Roper and Roper looked at her. He noticed again how she touched her neck. The tall man in the fur collar had clearly spent a lifetime pronouncing judgements; his sheepdogs – or were they watchdogs? – listened attentively.

Roper said: 'That's the point, surely, to pay tribute to this man's good works...'

'I have to advise you that the details of Sir Denis's good works will remain a secret. Certainly not the stuff of any diaries or recollections or papers, or anything at all, in fact. I have to tell you, completely off the record and not to be repeated under any circumstances with the exception of your Vice Chancellor, that all the papers and information relating to this man's activities have been marked secret, not to be released for a hundred years. Does that make it clear to you?'

'A hundred years?' Emma spluttered. 'That's ridiculous.'

'I shall, of course, and for the avoidance of doubt, have to make this crystal clear to the university authorities.' He turned to go but paused long enough to add over a stooped shoulder: 'I'm very much afraid you've been wasting your time here today. Completely.'

But he did not make his escape. Emma moved quickly to block his path. 'On whose authority is this decision made? I wish to challenge it.'

'Challenge?' The word seemed an affront. 'Challenge? This is a matter of government policy. At the highest level. Not a matter for public debate.'

She was still blocking his retreat. 'You serve the public, right? Not the other way round.'

'Madam, I advise you to be very careful. These are security concerns; you are straying into the area of national security.'

'What? Seventy-five years on? Rubbish; it's a cover-up.'

A deep breath was drawn. Self-control visibly retained. 'I hardly think this the appropriate place or occasion in which to have a discussion of this kind.'

'Then let's have a discussion of this kind outside.'

'I think not.'

Two bulldogs eye to eye. *What's going to happen next?* Roper asked himself.

Emma flicked her gaze away and announced: 'I think we're done here.' Then, without waiting for any reply, she stalked from the house and didn't stop until they were in the lane outside.

There she turned and demanded of Roper: 'Who does he think he is? God?'

'Judging by the expressions of his friends, yes, he thinks he is and they think so too. Obviously the sort who's spent a lifetime giving orders and expecting them to be obeyed.'

'Well, he's hit a brick wall this time.'

Roper grinned. 'I rather think I'm going to enjoy this trip.'

'Did you get that one-hundred-year rule? Ridiculous! Surely they can't classify stuff like that without substantial justification? There must be rules; it can't be arbitrary.'

'He seems pretty sure of himself.'

'I'll appeal against it.'

Roper chose his words carefully in view of her fiery mood. 'Have you thought about the repercussions? Aren't you concerned about what your professor will say... when word gets back?'

She snorted. 'They won't get far with him; he'll smother them with a great bubble of enthusiasm. Like trying to stir a rice pudding with a bent spoon.'

'I was rather thinking of the Vice Chancellor's reaction.'

'I'll get in first and demand our local MP put down a Parliamentary Question. Or maybe hit 'em with a Freedom of Information request – and get the local rag in on it.'

They continued to loiter in the little lane outside the house, close to the straggly hedge, disappointed but not yet ready to admit defeat.

'Not sure standing here is a wise move,' Roper said. 'Storing up trouble if those stiffs see us sniffing around.'

'Excuse me.'

They turned to see a small woman with a worried expression. 'I couldn't help hearing what was said to you in there.' She shook her head in a gesture of disapproval. 'Not a nice thing to say or do.'

'No,' Emma agreed.

'May I make a suggestion?'

Roper eyed her keenly. 'Suggest away.'

'I think the university has a right to ask for historic information. The public has a right to know.'

'Glad you feel that way,' Roper said.

'The old man, Grainger, he had a friend. Another diplomatic gentleman. Quite close they were. Worked together, so I understand.'

'Oh?'

'You might get something out of the friend's daughter. I know the two old chaps talked a lot. About the old days.'

Roper gave the woman a grateful smile. 'The name? Do you have that?'

The little woman nodded. 'Latimer,' she said. 'Or Latemoor. Something like that.'

Roper repressed a sigh. 'You have an address?'

'Over Backton way,' the woman said, with a sweep of a hand.

Roper demonstrated all the old abilities that had lain unused since entering Wormwood Scrubs three years earlier.

'We have a day,' he said, anxious to earn his keep by locating the relative of Sir Denis Grainger's friend. The two of them were booked on a flight to New York in forty-eight hours. Emma, he knew, had again argued against including him on the America trip but had lost out to an insistent mother.

Roper stayed over in Yardley, next day touring the villages in the direction the woman at the funeral had indicated, and drew several blanks before locating an inn where the two old men were remembered. They'd had frequent meetings there and a barman recalled ordering a taxi for one of them to take him home to Backton. At Backton, Roper toured the post office, the pub, shops and a park. Finally he found a dog walker who pointed him towards the vicar who in turn directed him to an undertaker, the old man having gone to his maker some three or four years earlier.

By five in the evening Roper was in Studholme, at the bungalow occupied by the daughter, but here his sense of triumph was short-lived: all locked up and silent. From a neighbour, he established that Miss Louise Latimer was away on holiday and would not be back until the end of the week.

A day later he and Emma were high above the clouds somewhere over the Atlantic.

CHAPTER SEVEN

E mma hid her acute sense of anticipation and excitement behind a mask of irritability. It was important to look cool, to maintain her normal air of self-control. She would not elaborate her true feelings; she would stick rigidly to the stated purpose of the trip, discouraging any discussion beyond it. Roper, meanwhile, seemed unable to contain himself. He was clearly not going to spend the eight hours to New York in monkish silence staring at a TV screen. Despite her silence, he seemed determined to engage in a conversation.

'We've made a start,' he said, handing her breakfast from the hostess trolley. 'Though I say it myself, I'm quite bucked at locating Louise Latimer's bungalow.'

'Didn't you do well?' It was a mocking reply, then: 'Don't get too cocky, there's a long way to go yet, and anyway Louise Latimer's nothing but a long shot; she could well turn out to be a dud – a complete irrelevance.'

'Never give praise where it's due, eh?'

'My source,' Emma said, examining minutely her bacon and eggs and wishing they had upgraded to business class, 'could well turn out to be everything I need. The old lady, she must know plenty.'

Roper shrugged. 'If she does, she's been keeping pretty quiet about it.'

Emma was still extracting the contents of her breakfast pack. She wasn't impressed.

Roper persisted: 'The old lady... I'm not sure I quite get the family picture here. What's your connection?'

'Great aunt, third cousin to her grandsons.'

'Draw me a picture. The family tree.'

Emma frowned but with a weary expression, relented: 'Two Wilkes brothers, one born 1910, that's Bradley, my grandfather. He marries in the States but has an affair with my grandmother in this country. She has my father and here I am.'

'But what about the others? Where does the old lady fit in?'

'Second Wilkes brother, he's born ten years earlier, has a son who marries the old lady. She has a son who in turn produces two more, Cyrus and Wendell, also very much alive.'

'So you're the... how shall we put it?'

'The illegitimate British branch of the family, right, and resented by the other lot because of it.' Emma left it at that. An old sore that still rankled. She sighed, had little appetite for the food on offer and looked out of the porthole window. Nothing but clouds. The subject was closed, she thought – but Roper wasn't done.

'Didn't I read somewhere that one of the cousins was about to announce he's standing for President?'

She nodded. 'Wendell.'

'Won't that be a problem? I mean, getting access. So many other people dancing around, bodyguards and all?'

'I'll get there,' she said in the tone of complete certainty he was beginning to know. He grinned. 'Tell me,' he said in a confidential tone, 'indulge my curiosity. Something I can't get to grips with. Why you're so focused on this job. Why suddenly so manic about it? Be honest! You see, I know, your mother told me. Only a short time ago you'd gone quite soft on the subject. Why the sudden change?'

She turned to give him an icy stare. 'You don't have to understand, Roper, you just have to do your job.'

'Oh, I don't get put off that easily.'

Persistent. He was certainly that. She shook her head. 'If you really must know, it's a well-funded scholarship and I was advised to take an assistant... and since this seems to be the truth game we're playing here, you were the third choice, okay? And don't go getting all uptight about it. You're a big boy now and you can handle it.'

'Third choice?'

'Chadwick wanted an academic but, looking at the state of them, I said no. I wanted someone with gumption, with a bit of practical nous. In fact, I wanted my brother – but he's in hock to that damned workshop of his and can't get away.'

'And Chadwick went along with all this?'

'You don't have to know who went along with what. All you need to know is that I'm number one, this is my territory and don't trespass on it, right?'

Roper leaned back with a grin and got on with breakfast. It was an irritating response, this duck's-back style of his; the man just would not be put down. Even before the detritus of breakfast was cleared away, she had to put up with another bout of inquisition.

'I was thinking about your mother,' he said. 'Lovely, lovely woman. So why are you two at such loggerheads?'

Emma snorted. *Was it really so difficult?* 'Don't tell me you haven't heard her on the subject of her wayward daughter,' she said.

'She has your best interests at heart. She's concerned.'

'I know that!' Emma sighed. Her snappy responses were not having the desired effect. 'Here, do you want this?' She held up a plastic-encased bread roll. Roper nodded and added it to his plate. 'We're worlds apart. Differ on all sorts of issues,' Emma said, 'different generation.' She shrugged and softened her tone. 'But we're not really out of sorts with each other.'

'No?' Roper's expression was sceptical.

'No, there are boundaries. I'd never do anything absolutely beyond awful. Never defy her on something really important.' She paused and felt a twinge of discomfort. Roper was watching her intently. 'Let's just say, if it wasn't for her, I wouldn't still be here. Some fairly traumatic moments in my past.'

'Oh?' he said, expression quizzical.

'Don't expect explanations. It's just... I won't let her interfere with my everyday life. Who I see, my friends, where I go. You can't let your mother run your life. But there are some things, some lines, I will not cross.'

'Oh?' he said again.

She shook her head. The man was relentless. 'You're not a priest; this is not a confessional.'

He grinned back at her. 'You know,' he said, 'you might just as well give in gracefully. I'll get it out of you. Eventually. I always do. I'm very good at extracting secrets. It's why I'm here.'

She couldn't help it. She laughed. 'You nosy, prying, snooping bastard,' she said, and gave him a slap on the shoulder.

He returned a smile. 'You'll tell me in your own time.'

She shook her head.

'Most people can't wait,' he said. 'Whatever they may say to the contrary, most are simply itching to tell.'

Irritating man! Emma shrank back into her shell. She wasn't going to open up to him. She wasn't going to share with anyone her darkest moments. She tensed at the memories: the awful spectre of the maternity ward, the adoption clinic, the stomach pump and the humiliation of A&E. Saved from herself, by her mother, at the very brink of extinction.

She wasn't going to share her guilt feelings for her brother, either. How they had fought as children, taken rivalry right to the cliff edge; how they had raced car against motorbike; how she had driven him off the road; how she was stricken with remorse at the sight of him in hospital.

She had debts to repay: friendship to her brother; loyalty to her mother.

Silently, staring but not seeing through the little porthole, she faced another uncomfortable fact: the Great Grandfather Mystery, even if she was able to solve it, might have a brutally short conclusion. Roper had already suggested as much; that the man simply disappeared because he was a thorn in the side of the Nazis and was murdered by them. She hoped not. Nevertheless, she needed to know. All the grisly details: when, where, how.

She stared even harder into the tiny circular void to re-examine her motivation. She may have lost her teenage enthusiasm for the subject but it was all turned around now, it had come full circle. Everything was different. Now there was ambition to serve: a scholarship, a conference and an irresistible goal to strive for, plus the added attraction of danger: the peril of the ghosts from the past, the stuff that Chadwick had warned her about; the waft and web of evil from the Gestapo archive. Who knew what would come from that?

That's what she was about. That's what Roper was for.

～

The studio building was nothing like Roper had ever seen before: all glass from elevated top to basement bottom, with the interior and its inhabitants on public display, going about their daily business like someone forgot to shut the bathroom door.

He stood on Seventh Avenue ignoring the trucks and the stretched yellow buses cruising inches away and gawped at all this exposed interior activity. A secretary appeared to be haranguing her boss; a despatch rider was scooping up the mail; three young women were drinking coffee and laughing uproariously.

Finally there was a small break in the traffic. He crossed the road, barged through the revolving glass door, weaved around a straggling queue of parents and children waiting for a studio tour, and presented himself at Reception.

When it was his turn, he fluttered open his letter of authorisation, hard won from Emma and Professor Chadwick, proffered his press card, the one with the date sufficiently smudged to obscure the year, and announced that he wanted to see someone from Public Relations to discuss the history of the North American Broadcasting Company and in particular its European correspondents of the thirties.

That's what he liked about the Americans. Nothing phased them. They were so endlessly polite and helpful. Invited to take a seat, he opted instead to view the one wall that wasn't all glass, a wall nicely filled with photographs of all the old greats of the airwaves. And hey! There he was. Bradley C Wilkes himself in front of a microphone; Wilkes typing up one of his despatches in the field, watched over by a grinning German general; and Wilkes in the middle of a crowd of correspondents being briefed by a stern-looking gentleman with a tiny swastika on his lapel. All shot in the days before America became embroiled in the war.

'Mr Roper?'

A clean-cut young figure in button-down shirt, slick black hair and with at least twenty years under his belt was smiling politely at his elbow. Roper expected obstruction or at least a little opposition – perhaps not a fight but a touch of reluctance – but he didn't get any of those.

'Would you like to come this way?'

He concealed his surprise and followed the man through a plastic gate, around an elaborate atrium and past a dramatic fountain-cum-waterfall that zoomed high into the internal sky. Roper counted off three floors. What the hell was this place? Like no other newspaper office he'd ever visited – but then, he reminded himself, this was a radio studio. They might employ journos but these were the talking kind, not the key-tapping variety.

Mr Clean-Cut was pointing out the facilities, like he was conducting a tour party. Meal room, mail room and unisex toilets.

Suddenly, they were in the basement and he was being introduced to a Mr Algernon Jenks, the company's chief librarian, a man with hideously large spectacles, a blue multi-check shirt and a gold fleur-de-lys tie. Roper once again presented his accreditation letter from St James's College at Cambridge authorising him to act on behalf of this great historical quest... but Jenks didn't bother to read Professor Chadwick's elaborately honeyed words.

Instead, he gave the letter the most cursory of cursory glances and seemed to know exactly what was required. Roper was mystified. He was being given open house to studio archives without ever meriting a serious explanation. As a journalist he anticipated resistance, on occasions savoured the fight. But no, it was as if they were expecting all this. He had the distinct impression his path was being smoothed – had been smoothed – that someone else was pulling the strings. It was all too easy.

It made him feel like a marionette.

It made him angry.

The house was an architectural muddle, a jumble of gables, windows, verandahs and protruding roofs, a layer cake of bits and pieces seemingly put together by some sort of crazed eccentric. It didn't seem to have a focal point. And where was the entrance?

Emma peered from the car window, hand on the door catch, almost reluctant to open it, even a little scared to step out. After all the travelling, this was it. She had arrived. It had taken a transatlantic flight, an overnight stay at the Bowery, a shuttle from LaGuardia to Boston and now the car that had delivered her from the airport.

The driver, who had met her at Logan holding up a board on which he had misspelled her name ('Ms Drak') in blue felt tip, now turned in his seat. 'You've made it, Missy. Liberty Point.' Then, seeing her confusion, added with a chuckle: 'White-frame clapboard. Traditional in these parts.'

She got out and the driver pointed to a verandah a little wider than the others. 'Over there,' he said. 'Sure as hell it was a crazy guy who put that one together.' Then he engaged gear and drove away.

She had expected to see a jostling mass of vehicles covered in election stickers for Cousin Wendell but the drive was silent and empty. Clearly he was running his campaign elsewhere. As she crossed the gravel drive, she glanced briefly at the vast rolling lawns to her left and the grey Atlantic beyond but she had little inclination to pause. Nor, despite her interest in stylish cars, did she give much attention to the ancient

Chevrolet, gleaming and at least fifty years to the good, standing motionless in one corner.

Emma didn't know what to expect. The appointment at Boston had been made for her by Lance Scranton and she had no idea how he had overcome the opposition she had faced years before when trying to fix a meeting with the old lady. Back in her teens, Emma had been mortified to be refused, even though they were distantly related. In the intervening years she had grown resentful at the rejection. Had things really changed? Did she in any real sense belong to these people? The snub still rankled.

She was met at the door by a tall, stooping male figure of indeterminate age who provided her with no introduction of himself or of his role but curtly informed her that she was inordinately lucky to have an appointment, that The Lady did not entertain visitors, that requests were many and few were granted. 'You have ten minutes, fifteen at most, because we do not wish to tire her.'

With that she was conducted along passages both light and airy. Through picture windows on the ocean side of the house she was able to get a better view of the chauffeur at work: he wore riding breeches and a peaked cap and had a face as leathery as the cloth he used to shine his already gleaming cellulose. Emma had a picture in mind of afternoon drives with The Lady, each route precisely planned, timed and strictly adhered to, as predictable as the calendar itself.

She glanced through open doorways at a spacious living room and another with a wall-mounted TV, before passing extensive kitchens where she could hear a man laughing, the clatter of pots and the whirr of fans. Some sort of beef dish was bubbling on an unseen stove and a tantalising aroma of freshly brewed coffee made her realise what she had missed since leaving the hotel that morning. As they walked, she trailed a finger along windowsills to check the result: clear of any stains, clear of dust. A pristine household, as her mother would say.

Finally, they arrived in an enormous sunroom with space enough to accommodate the extensive Wilkes clan with all their many grandchildren and great grandchildren. Or perhaps an entire government team. The nameless escort, a small red diary tucked under one arm, doubtless to organise with precision the events of The Lady's day, proceeded ahead of her and approached a huge armchair by the window. He stooped low to whisper.

What was said Emma could not follow, so she stood apart and looked around: many armchairs, tables, even a billiard table, and cupboards. She imagined drinks being served on social occasions. She was conscious that not so long ago presidents, prime ministers, kings and queens had passed this way; great events in America's recent past had been played out here.

Emma tried to stop but she could not control her hand; it began to scratch her neck. Surely this woman, the matriarch of the great family of Wilkes in the evening of an eventful life, should be prepared to share with an avid listener her vast storehouse of memories and anecdotes. Emma was acutely aware she was about to meet the person best placed to provide the missing elements of the Bradley Wilkes story, perhaps even the clues that would unlock its final mystery.

Now the tall man was beckoning her forward and she resolved not to let the opportunity pass. She would work this opening for all it was worth, with persistence and charm, with anything it took.

The table where Roper sat was smooth, stain-free, crumb-free and shiny. The remorselessly helpful Algernon Jenks was opposite and seemed to sense exactly what Roper was after. 'Bradley Wilkes was one of our star operators back in the thirties,' he said, 'we're very familiar with him and his work. There's a lot of material about him.'

This was a digitised archive and Roper was allowed to put on headphones and listen to several of the more notable Bradley broadcasts while Jenks searched the archive for the typescripts that went with them.

Roper's earlier irritation began to fade. Now he felt useful. He was doing something constructive. He'd insisted on making a contribution, promising Emma research was his area of expertise, that he'd spent hours in newspaper libraries – hours even at the British Museum's news library at Colindale. Reluctantly, she had provided Chadwick's letter of authorisation. Roper, despite Emma's chagrin, was on the team.

And there was something else. Something about the voice that came at him through the headphones with an immediacy that made him feel as if this crisis was today's crisis: a strong, determined, uncompromising voice. It wasn't difficult to pick up on the leaden atmosphere of fear and intimidation in Nazified Berlin; from the thugs in the street to the pressure to toe the party line. All Roper's frustrations evaporated, drawn in as he was by the excitement of events viewed from close up.

Like this broadcast from London about a Hitler rally: *'For the first time in all the years I've observed him, he seemed to have completely lost control of himself. A wild, eager expression; a fanatical fire in his eyes I shall never forget.'*

Roper switched discs, drawn into events described by a man talking his listeners through crisis after crisis from a front-line seat. These were the fraught days of Munich, shortly before Chamberlain's arrival, when the world held its breath. The Führer was addressing his adoring masses at the Sportspalast, widely expected to amount to a proclamation of war: *'I'm broadcasting from a seat in the balcony just above Hitler. He's still got his nervous tic. All during his speech he keeps cocking his shoulder and the opposite leg bounces up. The audience can't see it. But I can...'*

By now Roper's journalistic juices were fully flowing. Bradley was no armchair pundit floating around the world's capitals, an opinion on everything, delivered from the comfort of five-star luxury. This reporter got up close, looked Lucifer in the eye and told you what he saw.

Roper would have stayed longer, playing disc after disc, but he reluctantly hit the stop button and took off the headphones when Jenks arrived back with the original typescripts. These were contained in shiny bright-blue box files, a slightly surreal picture for Roper. This place was like no news library he'd ever known: all plastic, glass and aluminium, bright and airy with plentiful daylight, with bright pastel chairs and coloured mosaics on the floor. Even the extensive banks of shelving screamed arty.

Normality was restored, however, when the boxes were opened. What came out when the lids were thrown back was a waft of dust from the past. He took out a bundle and immediately recognised the old-fashioned typewriter script and the uneven punching where different characters had received an uneven finger pressure from the typist – presumably, the correspondent himself. Some of the letters had jumped out of line, leaving an inky smudge, and there was an ancient cloth-and-ink smell from typewriter ribbons. Roper grinned to himself when he thought back to the early days of some of his colleagues, punching out stories on the office Underwood, or lugging an Olivetti portable around in a heavy wooden box with a creaking handle. Back then, they all prided themselves on their shorthand. Shorthand! There was that blast from the past again – but it worked well and he still used it.

Jenks, his tie bobbing in time to the man's pronounced Adam's apple, was hovering at his elbow, anxious to inquire if he had everything he needed, almost as if he sought some kind of approval rating.

'I've managed to locate the definitive company memo on the subject of Wilkes's disappearance in Munich,' Jenks said. 'What they did, what they found out and what they thought about it.'

Roper was impressed. 'Good man. Could be the key. I still can't understand how a star correspondent could suddenly vanish off the face of the earth.'

Jenks made a face. 'I'll give you this to read,' he said, handing over another dusty document. 'It's a subject that's always fascinated me. The fact that there has never been any resolution. That nothing ever came out about it. I'll be enormously intrigued if you do manage to succeed where everyone else has failed.'

Roper pointed. 'So, what does this memo tell us?'

'Nothing concrete. Just lots of rumours at the time. People thinking they heard an enormous commotion, some kind of crisis; lots of activity at the rear of the Führer building. Fenced off from public view. Neither the company man nor the inquiry agent they engaged could do anything with it. It was a dark period back then; the Nazis were well in control and no one wanted to risk talking out of turn, especially not to a foreigner. Even the inquiry agent would have been wary for his own safety.'

Roper wagged a finger. By now he was fully signed up to the quest for a solution to the Bradley Wilkes mystery. 'But what about the cops? They were supposed to look for the man. You know, a missing persons inquiry?'

'Absolutely, yes, and officially the police checked every known place where Bradley might have been – his office, the restaurant where he ate in the evenings, the pub where all the correspondents met. Nothing. They simply concluded he'd gone walkabout. Speculated. Under too much strain, mental breakdown. All highly unsatisfactory, but in those conditions the company couldn't take it further. In less than a year Europe was at war and two years later America was drawn in and everyone had to clear out quick.'

'And after the war, what then?'

'The family hoped information would emerge but nothing did. At that time Europe was awash with displaced persons. Bradley C Wilkes simply joined the millions who were missing and never found.'

Roper looked into the distance reflecting that, despite all the encouraging material he had read and heard this morning, not a single significant clue had presented itself.

Jenks said: 'All I can say is, I wish you the best of luck.' The librarian's parting gesture was to put down on the desk a package containing a compilation of Bradley's last ten radio broadcasts.

Roper nodded vaguely, pocketed the discs and made his way back through NABC's marble maze, through the plastic gate and into the revolving door. Outside, on Seventh Avenue, he hailed a cab to take him back to the Bowery where Emma and he were to meet up again the next day.

The contrast to the towering human protector could not have been more stark. Enfolded within the armchair was the diminutive figure of Martha Wilkes, matriarch of the redoubtable clan of politicians, diplomats and soldiers. Emma Drake saw the scrawny, sinewy neck below a ferret-like face, the alert expression, the eyes sharp. And the voice, when it came, was like razor wire. No concession to age here.

'I gather you describe yourself as an historian.'

Emma nodded. 'Thanks for–'

'I have to warn you I only agreed to this meeting to discover what it is you are about. And why someone from England should be in the least bit interested.'

'It's about the missing man of Munich; your missing man.'

'That was all put to bed a long time ago.' The old lips twisted into an expression of pained exasperation. 'I do not wish to have the past resurrected. Will not! There's no benefit in it. We must all look forward to tomorrow, not back to yesterday.'

'I'm an historian. The past is my business.'

This reply was received in a dead silence. Emma shifted in her chair, a hard one with no give in it, a marked contrast to the generous armchair opposite.

'Look here, young lady, you listen to me and take heed. I'll be plain. You can do us great harm. My grandson, Wendell, the youngest, will shortly announce he's standing for President. You should appreciate he's putting together a unique coalition – and I do not intend for some historian...' Here the old lady lingered in abject scorn over the word. 'For some historian to come along and ruin it. My strong advice to you is: go home and find some other mystery to solve.'

Emma recoiled. 'I really do not see–'

'You do not need to see. But for your education, here are some facts. My grandson is leading a group of modernisers; he'll go for the centre vote and he'll win because neither of the two big parties are up to solving the country's problems. For your information, coalition government is coming to America.'

'But how can I ruin anything?'

'Naive. Yes, I can see that. Very naive.' The little eyes flicked all over Emma who could feel claws and the teeth itching to strike. 'You can ruin his chances in this election by taking the focus of attention away from his message. But my boy's message and his prospects and his remedy for this country are far too important for that.'

Her boy! Recollection of a passage in Emma's interview notes came to mind. This was the woman listened to respectfully when she rang a president to advise him to get a haircut. Her sons and her grandsons! Generals, diplomats, politicians, government servants – all might be in their prime but still likely to receive similar telephone instructions. But what was the old lady afraid of? Emma again thought back to her notes: was it the ambiguity over what this branch of the Wilkes family had been doing while foreign correspondent Bradley C was blazing his trail for truth and democracy in thirties Munich? No one had been able to tie down exactly how Cousin Wilber Wilkes the First had conducted himself during those years but posing such questions would seem like treading barefoot through a forest of pine needles.

After a long pause, Emma said: 'There is another matter.'

'And what might that be?'

'My own relationship to this family.'

'Yours?'

'Yes, my relationship; I am Bradley's granddaughter.'

The little eyes darted all over Emma's form. A long and tantalising silence ensued.

Emma eventually broke it. 'There was a relationship with my grandmother during one of Bradley's many visits to the United Kingdom. Obviously, many years back. In 1937, I believe.'

'I recall hearing of this fabrication some time ago. A disgraceful piece of scandalmongering. Why, Bradley C was already married by then.'

Emma did not react. Instead, she picked up an envelope from her case. 'I thought you might take some convincing so I brought the relevant British birth certificates. Mr Wilkes was not a man to deny his responsibilities. His name appears on the birth certificate of my father in the little box marked for that purpose.'

The matriarch stayed silent and deathly still so Emma took two certificates from the envelope and proffered them. After an embarrassing pause, a claw-like hand reached out and took them.

'Never seen anything like this before!'

'The second certificate is my own. Just to establish my relationship.'

'So you're not really here about university business at all. This is some trick, a concealed attempt to establish a family connection.'

'Not at all. I am what I said I am. An historian looking into the background of the Munich meeting in 1938. Totally genuine, I assure you.'

'Then, why?'

'I simply thought you'd be interested in the point that we're related.'

The old lady handed the certificates back. 'What do you intend to do with these? Lay some legal claim to the estate, an inheritance? You wouldn't be the first; we've had all sorts of chancers trying it on.'

Emma threw up her hands. 'You mistake me. I'm interested in Munich and the family's part in it. No claims. I merely hoped to establish some kind of human connection.'

'It's money you're after, not history!'

'No. Only information. And co-operation.'

'Then go back home and stay there.'

Emma knew it was time to put down a marker. 'I have to tell you, my project is too serious and I'm too committed to it to draw back. I cannot possibly give up simply because discussion of the past is inconvenient to your family.'

'Inconvenient?' Said with a screech, an explosion of rage, which was accompanied by footsteps close by. From the corner of one eye Emma could see the approach of the towering protector. Her chances of making anything of this interview were fading fast.

'This way, Miss Drake.' The towering man was leaning over her in a most intimidating manner. 'Your time is up.'

But the matriarch had one last blast left in her locker. 'I can make you a promise, young woman. From now on, you can expect the most implacable opposition every step of your way. I can see you're trouble, persistent trouble, so I'm sending you a man you won't be able to monkey with. Believe me, you won't get anywhere with him. He's an expert at suppressing trouble.'

CHAPTER EIGHT

They had spent a depressing night at the Bowery with nothing to show for their efforts in the US. They were hardly in the mood to savour the hotel's Edwardian foppery of plush leather armchairs around an ornate fireside; instead, perched for an angry inquest at the bar, Jameson in hand, Emma swirled her glass and told Roper: 'I will not be intimidated.'

He recognised the set of her mouth.

'That damnable old crow! She's got something to hide, that's for certain, and I promise you, here and now, I'll turn over every nasty little stone to find out what it is.' She banged a fist on the polished mahogany, adding: 'She thinks she's still the power in the land – but I will defeat her.'

Roper asked, incredulously: 'And she threatened to send over a watcher?'

'Doesn't scare me. Empty rhetoric.'

'Perhaps we should wait and see.'

On the plane back to London, Emma was more analytical. She had compensated by booking business class on a Boeing Triple Seven. 'Some of that woman's venom is down to innate snobbery. Rejecting my side of the family. Done that for years. But the rest is frustration. The power of the Wilkes clan is seeping away. Her son's presidential prospects...' Emma did a thumbs down. 'He's an outsider. Whistling in the wind, hoping to regain all that status the family enjoyed years ago.'

'Interesting.' Roper nodded, impressed. 'That's a very objective, informed take on the situation for someone from our side of the Atlantic. No skewed family loyalty there! No rose-tinted family glasses. I salute your grasp.'

She said nothing and Roper sat back, stretching out his legs, savouring the unaccustomed luxury of a comfortable flight, while Emma worked at some papers. He wore a slight grin as he approached an old subject. 'Tell me again about your Thursdays.' He chuckled. 'Rifle shooting – I'm intrigued.'

'You asked me before.'

'You didn't tell before. Like, are you a good shot?'

'They didn't ask me to join a police party for my smile. Not when a puma escaped Walker's Zoo and started slaughtering sheep.'

'So?'

'Needed an extra marksman. I got the call.'

'Did you get it?'

'Another group.'

'Explain the attraction.'

She looked at him, on the point of refusal, then shrugged. 'Sounds illogical but when I look down the sights of a rifle I feel an affinity. Like I'm a little closer to my grandfather.' Another shrug. 'His obsession, my fascination.'

Roper wore a mask of puzzlement. 'I really don't get that.'

'His shooting exploits... A family legend. Lots of childhood stories. Out in real hunting territory there's a mystic bond between shooters. Among themselves, their pets, even their targets.'

'And you tap into that?'

She looked away for some seconds before saying: 'Maybe my real bond is with the past.'

Then she went back to her papers, scanning Chadwick's documents retrieved from the box in the air marshal's loft. After a while, Roper spoke again: 'Anything in those?'

She wrinkled her nose. 'So far, just a lot of detail, but what does come through strongly is how the prime minister of the day crushed any attempt to express any view diverging from his own.'

Roper called to mind the photographs and newsreels of the Appeasement period and Chamberlain's somewhat stagy mannerisms before the cameras. 'Doesn't gel with the image I have of him,' he said. 'The nice old man who did his best for peace.'

She shook her head. 'False impression. Manically egocentric and stubborn personality. His own delegation? Almost all dead scared of him,' she said.

When they touched down on a snow-dusted City airport Emma strode with a belligerent step through Customs, her mind made up. Their collective sense of disappointment gave a new impetus to the next move: a return visit to Louise Latimer's bungalow at Studholme.

It was small and chintzy, everything in its place, the nets in immaculate white lace arcs and an array of porcelain ornaments placed in symmetrical patterns on the sills. A world away from the fake Edwardian décor of New York's Bowery – or indeed the decrepit expansiveness of the late Sir Denis Grainger's household at Yardley Broadmayne.

Latimer, a small woman favouring thick, multicoloured woolly jumpers in bright reds and oranges, seemed receptive to Emma's appeal. This time there was no roundabout approach on historical truthfulness; this time it was all personal. A granddaughter in search of her grandfather and her pressing desire to know what had happened to him during the Munich conference.

Latimer nodded sympathetically. 'How much do you know already?'

'Only that he disappeared at the time of the conference and that the police could find no trace,' Emma said.

'There were rumours, never confirmed,' Roper chipped in. 'Talk of an incident at the conference.'

Emma's expression became tense. 'Can you throw any light on that?'

Both Emma and Roper were anxious, waiting for the sharp denial, the shake of the head or the shrug of the shoulders, the negative response they feared but half-expected.

Latimer said: 'I may be able to help. Put you on the right track.'

There was a perceptible easing of tension, a warm feeling of excitement.

'Tea?' the host inquired. She seemed not in the least reticent on the subject. Clearly, Emma's enemy, the Foreign Office, had not extended its forbidding tentacles this far. Emma imagined the chagrin of the obnoxious FO mandarin she and Roper had encountered at the Yardley wake if he could have heard Latimer telling her story. And while they balanced fine bone china Spode teacups with striking red, green and gold floral patterns on knees, talk Latimer certainly did: of how her father got to know Sir Denis after the war; how the diplomat was a troubled man well into retirement; and how both she and her father had been sworn to secrecy for the duration of their lifetimes.

Latimer shrugged. 'But now Sir Denis has gone to his grave, I can't see there's any reason to continue to be reticent about it, can you?'

'Certainly not.'

'My father used to talk a lot about those days and I've always found it a fascinating period of history, if a rather shaming one, from our point of view, if you know what I mean.'

'I know what you mean.' Something in Emma's expression must have prompted Latimer to dispense with any further preliminaries, for she arranged herself comfortably on the sofa. Perhaps this was the conversation she had long anticipated, savoured even, all through the years of her great reticence. The youthful Sir Denis, she said, had been a very junior civil servant at the time of Munich and was greatly buoyed to be a member of the British delegation at the conference. He had become deeply involved, even giving information to one of the protesters in the form of a copy of a memorandum to the PM entitled Situation Report. However, what had taken place in the Führer building had made a deep impression on him, troubling him greatly for many years afterwards. He felt in some way partly responsible for the protester's fate. Later in life the two old men continued to talk of the incident, still exclaiming, still incredulous, still mystified that two protesters could have succeeded in gatecrashing this high-profile closed conference attended by four heads of state.

'So what happened when the two men burst in?' Emma demanded, urgent and pensive.

'What do you think happened? A lot of shouted slogans, then pandemonium! Apparently, one of them had a gun, so it was said. A shocking breach of security. A tremendous fuss!'

'What then?'

'Violent arrests. Shouting and punching and grabbing. A lot of protests from the two who'd stormed in. Apparently, they shouted that the accords... I think that's what they called them, accords, not a treaty.'

'Yes?' Emma prompted.

'They shouted that the accords should not be signed, that it was a dreadful mistake – but were immediately dragged away. A terrible kerfuffle until some semblance of order was restored.'

'And then?'

'That's all. What happened after that is pure conjecture.'

Emma let out a long breath. 'But what about Chamberlain and the British delegation? They saw all this. They were witnesses to it all. Didn't they realise the incident was all about them? Didn't they protest? Insist on an explanation?'

Latimer sighed. 'All I know is, the whole British delegation, every member of it, was sworn to secrecy.'

'But why?'

'Chamberlain decided nothing should be allowed to imperil the conference. To spoil the moment. To prevent his triumph as the man who brought peace to Europe. What were two protesters against his supreme moment as the great peacemaker?'

'So it was all hushed up – by the Brits as well as the Germans?'

Latimer nodded. 'The entire delegation was threatened with prosecution under the Official Secrets Act and severe jail penalties if they ever spoke about it. Ever and to anyone. And you know what civil servants are like – promotion, career, pension. A threat to any of those is usually enough. Throw in jail and their lips are sealed for a lifetime.'

❧

'What do you make of that?' Emma asked Roper as they drove away from Studholme. 'Didn't I tell you there was something there? Something special, dramatic, a fantastic gesture? What a man!'

Roper looked ahead. 'Quite a step forward, although we've only got it second-hand. Actually, probably fourth-hand, but let's not quibble.'

'I think it's fantastic. Boosts my image of Bradley Wilkes no end. I always sensed he was brave, dedicated and resourceful. Now I know he was a hero. Who else would have done that?'

'What, protested at Hitler? Pulled a gun on him?' Roper shrugged. 'Suicidal, if you ask me.'

'We don't know who had the gun. Could have been the other man or just a lie.'

'True. So, to analyse then, what we've got is the gatecrashing of the conference, a protest, possibly a gun, an arrest and a cover-up.'

'Big advance,' she said. She was still brimming with the success of the visit. Still brimming with pride for an heroic ancestor.

'But,' said Roper, 'we still don't know if, or for how long, your grandfather survived after the arrest. What do you think were his chances? Realistically? In the hands of the Gestapo? With the Nazis desperate not to let the world know of any of this? Would have ruined their propaganda pitch, as well as Chamberlain's.'

She didn't answer for a long time. Did not take her eyes from the road. Did not wish to diminish her sense of triumph. Did not want to extinguish hope of a better outcome. Eventually, she managed: 'So, what next?'

'The answer, if we ever get to find it, has to be over the water.'

'Agreed; Munich next stop,' she said, then shot him a quick

glance. 'But I will find the answer. Such fantastic bravery deserves a proper place in history.'

Roper made a non-committal grunt.

Her eyes went back to the road but in the same determined voice she said: 'I'll find it. I'll tell his story; absolutely no let-up until I discover what happened.'

~

Bradley C Wilkes, the Führerbau, 11pm, Thursday 29 September, 1938

'Wilkes. Wilkes! Wach auf, du bastard!'

This is the greeting when I regain consciousness. I'm wet all over and sitting strapped to a hardback chair. Even before I open an eye I know something is wrong with my nose. It feels several sizes too large and is twisted to one side. That's not all. My left shoulder is giving me pain.

The same rough voice, out of view but close to the left ear, is staccato in its demand: 'Du musst es mir yetzt erzahlen! Wer hat Dich reingelassen?'

I part my lips, tongue investigating a monstrous swelling, its size suggesting a bee sting.

The voice wants to know who let me into the Führerbau. My silence is rewarded with a kick to the ankle, then a slap to the side of the head. I groan but begin to register my surroundings. I recognise the ugly green marble fireplace, the wide desk and the tall glass windows. Then the big portrait on the wall, Frederick the Great, clinches it. So, I'm still in Room 105, the Führer's office.

That voice again, all broken glass, and the breath hot, sour and nicotined: 'I want all your contacts.'

The crowds have gone. The Führer has departed. So have the other leaders and their hangers-on. No Mussolini, Daladier or

Chamberlain. The room appears empty of people but then someone moves forward into view: a grim individual with staring eyes, a scarred face pitted with broken veins and six-o'clock shadow. A face I recognise from my time as a correspondent in Berlin; a face no sane person should ever wish to confront up close.

Heinrich Müller.

Known throughout the security apparatus of the Reich as Gestapo Müller.

I look into the unremitting, blood-veined eyes, then manage a hoarse reply: 'You can't do this to an American citizen.'

Another slap.

'I'm a front-line radio correspondent from Chicago.' I take a deep breath. The effort is draining. 'I'm on air every night. Their voice from Europe. I have a big name back Stateside. They'll miss me.'

The battered nose takes another hit and I taste blood.

'Just as well you're not on the newsreels then.' A crooked grin. 'Not a pretty picture. Soon, no teeth!'

Without warning my chair is pitched over on its side. I hit the floor, still strapped rigidly in the sitting position. My head sings. I close my eyes tight in an effort to endure and when the ringing stops I open the right eye to examine a corner of the room close up. Strange, the left eye wants to stay shut. Stranger still, it strikes me, how the wider issues for which I have sacrificed myself seem suddenly remote, unimportant. Instead, I adopt the view of an insect, studying with a new intensity my corner of the world: the floor, the wall, a table leg. I gaze closely at the coffee stain just above the bottom tile, at a tiny speck of peeling paint, a slight unevenness in the plasterwork, and sensing without seeing the wobbly leg on my chair. I have no desire to be set upright; right now, I am content with my new perspective; will happily stay here to make the pain go dull and well away from that gruesome countenance that represents the source of fresh torment.

But it is not to be.

The chair is raised by unseen hands and I'm staring into Müller's mouth once more. 'I want your contacts, Wilkes. All of them. How you got in here.'

The throbbing in my shoulder reminds me of childhood, of terrorised visits to the dentist and my hysterical reaction to the drill, the needle and the extracting forceps. Nothing could match that terror. It's lived with me for years. Just so long as this Müller doesn't resort to that!

His mouth is close, his right hand on my ear, twisting hard. 'Who gave you the key? Who's your source?'

I feel myself floating off into that other childhood world. Another painful ordeal. Of stalking deer among the crags and slopes of Idaho's Snake River, of prowess with Grandpa's old .270 Winchester rifle, and of the hidden hole I fell into before he could save me.

Müller has some intimidating device in his hand. Looks like a cosh. 'Give me the names. The people who got you into here. I will know who they are.'

But his voice does not hold the same threat. I am now that small boy on Snake River, left in a crevice to wait in pain and terror for rescue while Grandpa goes for help. I'm too heavy for the old man to carry. All alone, with a terrible ache, fear of the wild, fear of being alone. The long, long wait for rescue – but suddenly I'm brought back to my other self with a fresh dousing of cold water. Dripping blood and water, Müller is once more in unwanted focus.

'I'll break you! Don't kid yourself, Wilkes, you can't hold out against me. They all break in the end.'

There are noises off; someone is moving something heavy and truculent words are spoken between unseen antagonists, then another person is beckoned into my view. A lean ascetic figure with the high cheekbones and flat face of an Asiatic. He takes a seat. He has a clipboard ready, no doubt, to take down the details of my confession. At the top of the page is my name in large capital letters: BRADLEY WILKES. The rest of the page is blank.

I'm determined it's going to stay that way but outright defiance is not a realistic option. A brave, thou-shall-not-pass obdurate resistance will be met by even more pain.

My first good fortune arrives in the shape of a fresh and useful memory. A police contact from way back in England, joking in a sardonic way, tells of criminals who respond, when pressed for their contacts, by citing a man in a pub; the stranger who supplies weapons, tools and information but never a name. My pub, I decide, transforms into a bridge. Specifically, Charles Bridge in the centre of Prague. That's where I met my contacts.

Müller hesitates when I tell him this, uncertain for a moment whether this revelation is progress or not. I work at the creation of a vast construct of vagueness, of just enough to sound plausible without ever being useful. Of course, the man didn't give a name or an address or explain how or where he got his key to the Führerbau building, but the idea of an entirely peaceful protest was so enticing that we all went along with it and took it on board.

This fairy story is met by a slashing, ripping, tearing pain across the thighs and legs. I don't look down. I don't want to look down. Müller is limbering up for another session with the nobbly cosh, at which point I suddenly recollect a description: a big chin, beetle brow, long nose, a moustache.

At the next application of pain a second man was bearded, spoke with a German accent and said he was a refugee, a former policeman; a third, a builder of some stripe, and yes the Charles

Bridge was my only source, definitely the best place to ask for information.

For a while the innocent, childlike naivety seems to work. No more cosh. But there's a problem: Müller is holding up a gun. 'Your friend's pistol,' he says, dangling it in front of my face. That damned gun! Why had Jarek brought it into the Führerbau? He'd ruined everything – and how can I explain it?

'A peaceful protest – with a pistol?' Müller jeers.

Just a gesture, I say, a big gesture to grab attention. Absolutely no intention to fire the damnable thing; goodness, I can't stand the noise, simply hate the things.

This is met by a mocking laugh. 'We know all about you, Wilkes; we're the most efficient police force in the world and right now I'm reading your profile. We know you're a shooter, a hunter, a man familiar with all kinds of weapons.'

'Not here,' I say, shaking my head. 'Not here. That's purely Stateside. This pistol was a mistake, designed only to make important men listen to what we had to say and persuade them to think again.'

Somewhere far off to the left, in another room, there is the sound of screaming.

'Your friend,' Müller says. 'Your Czech friend. Soon he will get the cold bath treatment. Ducking again and again until he tells us what we want to know. Then it's your turn.'

At this point I'm aware of another sound beyond the continual slamming of doors and echoing shouts and footfalls in the corridor outside. It's a departure, a new sound. Someone has entered the room and a conversation that I can't overhear is taking place but what I detect is a new tone. It's commanding, dictatorial, uncompromising – and it doesn't belong to Müller. Rough hands turn my chair and a fat barrel of a man is standing before me, feet astride, looking down, hands on hips. There's no mistaking this figure: the bulging grey uniform, the tiers of gold braid, the medals, the big black boots. I get a close-up of the full face, pouting lips and double chin. After Hitler, the most visible face of the regime: Hermann Göring.

But why is the Reichsmarschall present at my interrogation?

But before I can ask he stalks off and then the Asiatic is back, sitting opposite. One of his Cossack allies, I presume, but he addresses me in flawless English. 'We are curious,' he says, 'to know just what an American correspondent thinks he's doing. What he hopes to achieve by this shocking business.'

I take a deep breath. Müller is beyond all appeal to reason but Göring's minion is a quite different kettle of smelly fish. 'Exactly that,' I say. 'Shock. To shock Mr Chamberlain out of his agreement. To persuade him not to sign.'

'Nonsense! An attempt on the Führer's life.'

'Definitely not.'

Cossack folds his arms. 'The Reichsmarschall is considering a show trial, a great piece of propaganda for us. To show just how America is trying to sabotage our peaceful attempts to solve European questions.'

I shake my head. Time to argue, however painful. 'A trial will demonstrate to the world that there are people actively opposed to your policies. It will be that much harder for Chamberlain to sell it to his parliament. And it will be my platform. My opportunity to speak from the dock, to tell the world–'

'Tell them nothing!' Müller lashes out. 'By the time you get there, all you'll be capable of is signing your confession. And nodding when they ask you if you're guilty.'

Cossack turns to go but wags a finger at the Gestapo chief. 'Don't mess him up too bad, Müller, the Reichsmarschall doesn't want him looking like a piece of raw meat for his American friends.'

A show trial, untold retribution, a long prison sentence. I reflect on this bleak prospect and looming defeat for the very *reason I risked my neck in the first place – the attempt to scupper the Munich Agreement. Then I notice the Führer's desk. It's strewn with papers; not quite the typical German orderliness of old. I ask myself: Is this a good sign? Might chaos indicate hesitation, doubt?*

Has the Munich Agreement actually been signed? Or not?

Perhaps, after all, it might not be too late to affect events.

It's time, I decide, to play the family card.

CHAPTER NINE

S he felt she was walking in the long shadow of a malign past. With Munich map in hand and studying the street names, Emma approached this part of the city on foot, stepping with some trepidation into what had once been the heart of a sinister regime.

First, the massive square, now less than impressive as a parking place and gardens, where once, on a massive arena of paving stones, the parading, marching, banner-carrying thousands had chanted their evil slogans; past the pompous public buildings designed by the infamous architect Troost; finally, around the corner into Arcis Strasse.

And there it was, the dark heart of the beast: low, long and snake-like, the Führer building. She approached with a fluttering pulse. It was impossible to feel neutral about this place. Number 12.

On the approach a notice announced it as the Higher Music School.

She swallowed back bile. Sour, to say the least, this attempt at prosaic normality. As if to say, the world goes on; or worse still perhaps, a denial that anything untoward happened here. An attempt to say: hey look, we're normal folk now, just like you.

A few paces more and there were the eight steps up to the entrance, a massive, stark portico held aloft by four grooved square columns. She lingered, one foot on the bottom flagstone, looking up, taking in each element of the architecture she had studied so closely from photographs. The girder-like architrave from which the Union Jack had fluttered, next to the swastika; the now vacant space above where the Nazi eagle had once announced its menacing purpose; the elaborate cornice; the square windows on the top floor, curved on the lowers; the sheer length of the building which seemed to diminish its three storeys.

Such was her concentration she completely ignored the human landscape. That could be the only reason she hadn't seen the man before. But as she took two paces up the wide staircase he loomed up at her, breaking her spell of introspection, thrusting a poster into her face, grunting at her, saying something she didn't understand, bursting a bubble of beery breath into her face.

Spell broken, she looked up at his placard.

In English, written with a rough, scrawling, black felt tip, were the words: 'English historians, go home; we don't want you here.'

'Who was that madman with the placard?'

Emma, speaking with her mouth full, had resorted to peppermint to banish the cloud of bad breath. She always carried a generous supply. She reckoned any congregation of middle-aged male historians would contain fifty per cent presenting obnoxious symptoms of halitosis.

She was sitting in the Direktor's office facing, across a great slab of a desk, Frau Dr Johanna Ludwig, a middle-aged woman with clear skin, lustrous brown hair and a string of pearls. She reminded Emma a little of her mother but without the warmth. Of course, she had been prepared for this meeting; had been warned repeatedly by Roper and others of the nature of the frosty German bureaucrat. Apparently, even women were stricken with the condition when appointed to public office; the 'I'm doing you a big favour by even making eye contact' pose. It was an authority thing.

But to Emma, there was a much bigger, much more personal concern. She looked up and around at the elaborate chandelier hung from a white ceiling, the marble fireplace, the mountainous sofa, the floor-to-ceiling windows. She had already realised; this room, this very spot, had once been the Führer's private office. No picture of Frederick the Great adorned the wall now, nor any telltale insignia or badges. But there could be no mistake. She had the plan – Room 105, the balconied office just below where the big eagle had once adorned the wall outside.

Her grandfather had played out his biggest personal drama, perhaps his last, on this spot.

'You have to realise,' Frau Dr Ludwig said in an immaculate English delivery, 'that some unpleasant negative publicity has preceded your arrival.'

'Oh?'

'The Munich papers have been full of your conference.' She picked up a copy of the *Münchner Zeitung* from an otherwise empty desk space and read the headline: "English historians on the attack in Munich". Last week there was one which said, "Englanders dig up the Nazi past – again". The perception is, Miss Drake, that you're obsessed with this period. You should know, we have all moved on since then; Germany is a completely different place.'

Emma countered: 'Our whole purpose is to keep an open mind on the period.'

But Frau Direktor was having none of that. 'We do not enjoy our school being linked with this purpose. When we accepted your booking we did not anticipate these...' Here she lingered for a moment before settling on the word: 'Problems.' She cleared her throat. 'We sincerely hope you are not intending to play to any particular gallery...'

'Quite the opposite,' Emma countered. She pointed at the newspaper. 'They're the ones with the closed minds.' As she said this she once more glanced about her: at the desk that looked as if it had been uprooted from the cemetery, the marble-tiled floor and the lavish grandiosity favoured by the former regime. Snatches of Brahms and Mozart could be heard faintly in the halls and on the stairs. Despite the new purpose, it was impossible to disentangle this oppressive place from the baggage of the past. 'We thought it fitting,' Emma said, 'that the actual events of 1938 should be replayed and reanalysed in the same building.'

But Frau Dr Ludwig would have the last word, as befitted the status of Music School Direktor. 'Then I would ask you to exercise the greatest possible discretion during your stay.'

This was the building where it all happened; where her grandfather had disappeared, apparently to be arrested and dragged away, perhaps to be tortured or killed, perhaps even on these very premises.

Emma wanted a tour, a complete examination of every corner, to relive the terrifying moments of all those years ago when he'd braved the hostility of black-uniformed men given so easily to the taking of life and the inflicting of pain.

She asked to be shown round and was afforded the ungracious attention of a monosyllabic caretaker with minimal English. It didn't matter. Roper did a splendid job.

Their footsteps echoed eerily around vast hallways stretching into uncomfortable distances, huge, demonic spaces that made her shiver from a numbing coldness. They toured the first and second floors, passing rooms equipped with pianos, violas, tubas and drums accompanied by the sound of scales. There was a strong smell of floor polish. Final call was the cathedral-like Speech Hall, adorned with marble door surrounds. Once used for Nazi rallies, it had been fitted out in Bavarian baroque as a concert hall.

She had already seen the Führer's office – the next most important point on her itinerary was the cellar. She recalled reading that stone eagles had been set into the concrete of supporting pillars.

But here, at a metal door set in a wall on the lower floor, they came to a halt. Absolutely not! Expressly forbidden by Frau Direktor Ludwig, she was told. No access allowed.

Disappointed, they retraced their steps to the balconied staircase in the entrance hall. She felt the presence of Bradley Wilkes; was reminded of him at every turn. His bravery and his fate stiffened her resolve, made her quest ever more urgent. He was here; not merely battling, as she, the bad temper of a middle-aged bureaucrat, but braving the firestorm and threat of men with guns and evil purpose.

She was walking in his footsteps. She felt very small.

Emma surveyed her newly arrived flock. They were arranged in a semicircle of chairs as close as possible to the windows, leaving the formality of the stage to shadow and gloom. There was France, suited and formal, a nervous young woman from the city's university, a shaven head from Warsaw, a goatee from Budapest and a tea-drainer moustache all the way from Moscow. The stand-out, however, without any doubt, was Mimi Aschemeyer, a very stylish dresser from Vienna.

'I want to welcome you all,' Emma said, smiling widely, 'to this unique occasion. I feel privileged to be here, as I hope you do too.' She talked about a fresh perspective, the advantage of hindsight, an international consensus and a shredding of national sensibilities. In her peripheral vision she could see Roper fidgeting at the table laden with the stationery. She ignored him. This was her show. She laid out the programme: discussion sessions, submission of formal papers, a final consensus.

Eventually, she had to let him off the leash. Roper announced himself as the fixer, the man who would photocopy documents, sort technical glitches, smooth transit through the city, fix any problems at the hotel.

Dammit, she thought, *he's enjoying himself*. She frowned but then conceded that it would probably be useful to have someone batting on her side, recalling with a slight tremor of concern Professor Chadwick's warning words to her in his little box of a room back in Cambridge: 'Beware of the ghosts, Emma; they've been known to turn violent. They may come after you.'

At first she welcomed the distraction – the late arrival of two participants. Until, that is, a tall, greyish figure announced himself, without any embarrassment, as Cyrus Wilkes, representing the US.

'Wilkes?' she repeated. A frown.

'None other,' he said, grinning. 'Elder brother of Wendell,

our latest Presidential candidate; a family known to you, I believe. A recent visitor, in fact, to our home at Boston Creek.'

He was addressing Emma directly, grinning, challenging, enjoying her surprise.

'I thought we were having someone from Berkeley.' Her voice tailed off as she began flicking through the papers on her clipboard to find a list of names.

'Sorry,' he said, 'late change of plan. The professor couldn't make it. You've got me instead of him. Speaking as a member of the Wilkes family, we're banking on our storehouse of experience in dealing with Europe to give me a useful take on all this.'

Emma jerked up, abandoning her list. 'But you're not an accredited historian.'

'Ex-officio.' He grinned hugely. 'On the board at Berkeley.'

It was on the tip of her tongue to denounce him as a political appointee. And more. As the Wilkes family's snoop. Instead, she said: 'You've come to run an eye over us?'

'Sure thing.'

'So,' she said, deciding on a challenge, 'what's your take on 1938, speaking as an American historian?'

'Us getting Europe out of a jam. As usual. Yet again.'

'Specifically, Appeasement and the Munich crisis. That's three years before America came into the war. When you were still a neutral.'

'Did we have a role back then?'

'That's what we're hoping you're going to tell us. As an American. As an expert on the period.'

'A watching brief,' he said. 'Then as now.'

There was a loud throat-clearing from the body of the semicircle. 'I've got a point to make.' Tibor, from the Czech Republic, a sharp-faced seedy man given to chewing matchsticks, was definitely on Emma's list of academics. He looked at her directly. 'I gather you have a personal stake in this inquiry.'

'Where did you get that?'

'Word gets around.'

She suspected Roper. How else could this have got out? 'I'm glad you mentioned it. Time for me to declare an interest.' She stared around, smile back in place, a quick change from combatant to charmer. 'My grandfather was here in '38. Big mystery. Foreign correspondent. Disappeared in the middle of the conference.'

Tibor grunted, still chewing. Clearly an ex-smoker, she decided.

'Careful what you wish for.' It was the American, cutting in once more.

She switched back her gaze, smile fading.

'Turning over old stones,' he said. 'Never know what you'll find. The past can be a dangerous place.'

It was early November, the snows had not yet arrived but a cold wind scythed across the vast open square, direct from the icy tops of the nearby Alps, yet the tourists remained undaunted. They stood in clusters on the Marienplatz, dwarfed by the huge town hall, staring up at the clock tower, awaiting the hour: eleven o'clock and the daily spectacle of Glockenspiel.

Emma regarded it as just another facet of Munich's somewhat schmaltzy image. Ensconced inside the warm fug of the Café Dom she could view the visiting crowds through the floor-to-ceiling picture window. Her concern, however, was organising her party, clustered in a reserved corner close to the café entrance. She counted them off: the Frenchman, Jean-Francois Girolle, the Roman, Carlo Piccini, Mimi Aschemeyer from Vienna, Tibor from the Czech Republic, Imre Nyek from Budapest and Pavel Komov from Moscow. And then, of course, there was Wilkes from Washington.

None of them was in the city to see brightly-painted wooden figures revolving in lofty turrets. They had a different agenda.

Emma drew in her breath, irritated because the delegate from the tiny statelet of Nagorno-Karabakh had still not appeared. She tapped an elegant silver spoon against her coffee cup to draw attention from the flouncing waitresses and beguiling aromas of pastry, coffee and beer. Above the clatter of crockery and the hubbub of a dozen adjacent conversations, she announced: 'We begin our tour here. Now that we've taken coffee and strudel.' She smiled. 'A necessary first step... to get a sense of place, to put our discussions in the context of this modern city.'

Her voice carried above the Viennese waltz playing through the speakers and the chatter of several dozen Munich matriarchs. Tiny pork-pie hats and long swishing loden coats made a stark contrast to the nondescript anoraks and casual attire of Emma's party – with the exception of herself in a boot-hugging black coat, and Aschemeyer's flamboyant furs and vivid scarf, looking as if she'd just stepped out of an emperor's carriage.

It was Wilkes who raised the objection. It had to be Wilkes. 'Aren't we just playing at being tourists here? For God's sake, this isn't going to add anything of substance to the Appeasement Crisis now, is it?'

Emma arched her brow. 'So, you don't want to visit the relevant sites?'

Aschemeyer smiled the broad smile of the peacemaker and said in a quiet voice: 'I would quite like to take the tour.'

Emma's hostility eased. 'Good. Then that's what we shall do.'

Out in the cold the gaggle of foreign historians trailed through the streets to the places the city tourist authorities dearly wanted to forget: the flat on Prince-Regent Street where the Führer had entertained Chamberlain on the final morning of his humiliation, a vast Nazi administration building on Meiser Strasse, the field marshal's hall where Hitler's Brownshirts were defeated in a failed putsch in 1923, and the bank that replaced a bombed-out Gestapo HQ just past the obelisk on Brienner Strasse.

She grouped her party next to a tiny blue plaque on an anonymous wall. She said: 'This was once an old Wittelsbacher Palace, erected in 1843 by one of the Bavarian kings, Ludwig the First, set well back behind some chestnut trees. All that ended when the monarchy collapsed. Taken over by the Gestapo in the thirties. Became known locally as 'the house of horrors'. You'd walk past on the other side of the street if you were on the outside... but inside... Next stop was the concentration camp at Dachau.'

She turned to go and immediately became aware of an atmosphere. It was as if the normal life of the street had temporarily closed down. Passers-by had stopped to stare. There was something intimidating about these silent witnesses. Were they curious or disapproving? Some clue became evident when a man on the other side of the street began pointing and talking in an animated fashion to a companion.

Emma thought it wise to cut short her discourse and encourage the party to move on. Surely they must appear the same as any other tour party? The suspicion nevertheless grew that in some way they were recognisably different. As she approached the Music School at the old Führerbau, a group straddled the entrance stairway. At first, she assumed they were music students. Then she saw the placard. The same one as before.

The group converged on her as soon as she drew near. A different man this time, shouting: 'You're not wanted here. Why don't you go home?'

The crowd pressed around her. 'You people,' the man said in accented English, pointing an accusing finger, 'attacking Germany again. We're fed up with it; you're always attacking us. You English are obsessed with the war; why can't you forget it?'

Emma drew in a breath but before she could reply another voice accused: 'It's history; it's the past. We're a different people now; this is a different country.'

A third voice: 'You're stuck in the past; you're just a second-class nation, being left behind by the rest of us. You're not even playing catch-up.'

'Go home!' No longer single voices. 'Go home!' It was becoming a chant.

Emma was aware she was the only member of her party at the centre of a hostile crowd. Her historians were nowhere to be seen.

Then, another sound. A whistle.

Like water draining from a broken dam, the crowd gurgled rapidly away and she was left standing, bewildered and alone, on the eight portentous steps of the Music School.

She stayed motionless, a little dazed, her self-confidence momentarily dented. Again, Professor Chadwick's warning came back to her: the past can return to bite you.

Green-clad figures in peaked caps appeared on the wide pavement below, then a man in a long trenchcoat climbed slowly to the step where she stood.

'I am Police-Kommissar Kasper,' he said. 'Will you please accompany me inside?'

CHAPTER TEN

Johanna Ludwig vacated the Direktor's office with a grim expression and display of ill grace, giving Emma fierce glances as she clutched several files and a bundle of papers, disappearing into the gloom of one of her interminably long corridors. Clearly, such a humiliation to an official of her stature was an affront too far.

Kommissar Franz Kasper, however, made a show of not noticing. Water flowed easily from the back of a senior officer of the Munich police. To him, requisitioning directorial offices for an immediate interview was a matter of course. Emma realised she was now under pressure on two fronts.

Once inside, he motioned her to a seat. She looked at him and decided Kasper was not like any police officer she would have expected. He had a slouchy face running to fat, spectacles, and a gaze that was not intimidating, more of the permanently puzzled variety.

'Now, Miss Drake, we have a problem.'

She'd half-anticipated a tirade but this was an expression of almost avuncular concern. She glanced briefly behind her; his assistant, Meyer, however, was in a more predictable category: tall, upright, unsmiling and with a small brush moustache.

'I hope you're not going to hold me responsible for the actions of your citizens,' she said. Establishing a position of outraged innocence was a necessary first step. Never bow to authority, always play the rebel; it was one of her watchwords.

'We have a problem because you represent trouble,' he said, leaning forward on one elbow, displaying the same competence with language as the school's Direktor. For this generation of Germans, facility with English was normal. 'Stirring things up, digging into an unwanted past.' His lips twisted into a gesture of irritation. 'We've already had to cope with poster men, an angry press and now we have a disorderly demo on the steps of the Music School. We do not like this sort of trouble in our city. It's a quiet city. A city of culture, of good manners; a friendly place to visit. We want to keep it that way.'

'Then I suggest you police your demonstrations.'

But for all his relaxed manner Kasper was not easily contradicted. 'Now we have reports of a provocative procession through the streets of the city by a train of foreign historians.' He managed to invest the last word with a mildly scornful intonation. 'A train of foreigners which represents hostility to the peaceful nature of the citizens. Which represents the potential to stir up more trouble. It is many years since we saw violence on these streets. We don't want a repetition.'

'I'm glad you recognise the perils of the past,' she said.

'Do not attempt to get clever, Miss Drake; your position as a visitor is, shall we say, tenuous? There are certain precautions I wish you to take if you are to continue with your activities.'

Emma regarded this as a form of velvet intimidation and was about to launch into another protest when they were interrupted by a sharp rap at the door.

Kasper ignored it and leaned forward, finger wagging. 'I

want all these notices about your conference removed from any public place. I want all evidence of your presence here removed.'

The knocking continued.

Meyer went to the door and Emma heard Roper's voice in the doorway. He was argumentative. There was a pause before the man himself made it into the middle of the room, announcing himself as Emma's assistant.

Kasper ignored him and returned to his theme. 'I want all evidence of your presence here removed. No notices or agendas posted in or around the Music School. I require you to conduct yourselves in future with the maximum decorum inside this building.'

'That's ridiculous!' she said. 'You're trying to censor us. Paint us into complete anonymity.'

'Correct. And I want no more processions through the streets. No more provocative visiting. In future, you will proceed individually between your hotel and this place.'

Roper spoke up. 'Herr Kommissar, I seem to recall from my days in the Military Police in Hamburg that the Germans and the Brits always got on best when there was a spirit of co-operation and mutual respect. Each of us aware and sensitive to the other's role and needs.'

'This is not Hamburg, Herr Roper. Things are different here. And you're not a police officer now, am I correct?'

'Correct. Now I'm more in the way of a media outlet. Connected to English newspapers and television. And I presume this is what concerns you, Herr Kommissar – the media and public perception of the city, its good reputation as a tourism centre.'

Kasper said nothing.

'I would say,' Roper added thoughtfully, 'that there are two

sides to the media coin on tourism. The perception over here...
and the perception over there.'

The meaning was clear. *Over there* was Britain.

After a pause Kasper rose with a nerve-jangling squeak from
his chair. 'No more provocations,' he said. 'And no more public
notices.'

And with that he and Meyer were gone.

Emma looked up and shook her head at this sudden exit.

Roper said: 'Terribly sorry, Emma, I got waylaid by some
talkative person at the obelisk. Had no idea you were in trouble.'

She shrugged. 'And I had no idea you were a cop.'

'Long time ago. Many moons ago.'

She grinned and snorted. 'Must have been tough in
Wormwood Scrubs.'

Roper chuckled as if he quite enjoyed her repertoire of put-
downs. Perhaps he was used to that sort of humour from his
former colleagues, or from inmates at the Scrubs. But then her
mood darkened, her brow crinkling into a little delta of frowns.
She saw him staring at her, aware that he might be comparing
her physical likeness to her mother. Her one appearance
obsession was her frown. She could imagine him discussing it
with her mother during the phone calls she knew he made back
to 24 Orchard Street.

'Getting to you?' he said.

She shook her head. Defiant, disdainful. 'All this...' She
swung a dismissive hand at the Führer's old room, at the floor
and the bookcases on the end wall, wondering if they had been
present back then. 'It's nothing,' she insisted. 'Absolutely
nothing. Compared with what Grandfather had to go through.'

~

Bradley C Wilkes, the Führerbau, 3.30am, Friday 30 September, 1938

Four hours in and there's more of the same: slaps and kicks, another attack on my nose and two casually-administered cigarette burns.

Not as bad as that butcher of a dentist, I console myself, hyping up the memory of a childhood horror. Or being scalded by boiling water from a kettle knocked carelessly from old Grandpa's stove in his Idaho cabin. Oh yes, I can remember that pain all right, a big brown throbbing stain down my left thigh – and scant sympathy I received too, the old man roaring with rage at my stupidity.

Now I can see Müller unravelling a long length of electrical cable and attaching some kind of cattle prod. What's this going to do? Turn me into a vegetable? I brace for the electric shock treatment, telling myself they do this in hospitals, fearing the shame of capitulation more than the pain, but I am saved, for the moment, by another interruption. Another 'visitor'. This time it's the familiar face of Putzi Hanfstangl, the Reich foreign press liaison counsellor, everyone's fair-weather friend. He's performing a hand-wringing ritual and shaking his head. 'Brad, Brad! What have you done? How did you get involved in this? After all I've done to help you...' A sorrowful look. 'Nothing I can do to save you now.'

The interruptions are getting to Müller. He's putting away his cattle prod and I hear his voice on the telephone arranging for my transfer from the Führerbau to Gestapo headquarters on Brienner Strasse.

At this, a serious chill of fear. Everyone knows the reputation of the Brienner, of what goes on in the cellars there. Hope dies in the Brienner; your fate is either Dachau or a casket.

I make a decision. When things get tough it's time for a change of tactic. So, I talk about my family and their commercial connections, discreetly omitting my distaste for their business scruples. For a while this engages their attention – but not long enough to save me from the cattle prod, which Müller is once more unwinding. He wants more. He wants the names, so I talk again. Schmidt of the German Foreign Office; he was my source. There's some kind of rivalry going on between departments, I say, some internal squabble I took advantage of to obtain the entrance key.

Müller doesn't believe me. A jolting shock, worse than a kick or a slap. So I give him another name: Oster in Munitions. Both of these personalities are real. People I detest. Ardent Nazis already tarnished with the evil of this regime whom I am happy to compromise by implying that they have betrayed their cause.

Fingering the wrong people, of course, could come back to bite me – it's all a matter of time. How long will it take Müller to check out these lies? How thorough will he be? Given the paranoia endemic to this regime, the finger of suspicion may never be stilled. With luck I'm sewing dissension in the enemy camp.

There's another break in the interrogation. Even sadists need a rest but I'm conscious of a chaotic opening and closing of doors and the dragging of equipment. I'm grateful for the respite but fearful of what is coming. Transfer to the Brienner has to be postponed at all costs, if necessary by a new raft of lies. I can't take too much more pain – and certainly not if they get out the dental tools. What madness made Jarek and I think we could get away with this?

More footsteps approach but it's not Müller or his transport. There is a short conversation out of earshot, then Hermann Göring's Cossack factotum crosses to my chair to address me directly, pointing a skinny finger.

'You lucky man. A change of plan. There's to be no show trial. And you can thank your Mr Chamberlain for this.'

'I can?' The idea of thanks to the British Prime Minister is an odd one.

'Indeed, the Prime Minister insists no trial; in fact, no public mention of this incident at all.'

My astonishment must be written clear to see and the Cossack is at pains to explain. 'He wants no distraction to the business of peace. He wants the entire public focus to be on the signing of the accords. No silly incident in the news, no trial, just the agreement between our countries. Mr Chamberlain insists nothing should imperil the path of peace.' Cossack throws up his arms in a valedictory gesture. 'So you see, you've lost. And the accords were signed two hours ago.'

He beams down at me and I suffer the desperation of defeat. What happened to Carl Goerdeler's promise in my letter – that he and the generals would oust Hitler and seize power? I swallow and summon defiance. 'You surely can't believe this incident won't leak out.'

He glares, so I grasp the moment. 'First, they'll miss me and the papers will pursue it. Then all those people in the Führerbau... lots of them... they'll talk. And talk. The Italians, for a start! You can't stop old Giovanna from chattering. He can't keep a secret. The story will be out as quick as you like.'

But Cossack is sneering. 'Wrong. Absolutely wrong. Il Duce has taught them to do what they're told.'

'Other countries–'

'All sworn to secrecy. So you, my friend, are history. You're to be disappeared. No one will ever know you were here.' He shrugs expansively. 'Of course, our police will look for you. And a great mystery it will be. We search for the missing man here, we search for him there, we search everywhere, but never is he to be found. A drunk, a womaniser, a footloose reporter run off for some reason of his own; who can tell? A mystery, so beloved of your newspapers...'

He grins and prepares to leave.

I dare not let the moment go. 'The people outside,' I say to his retreating figure, 'my friends and colleagues…'

'Did they see you enter? That would make them complicit. Dangerous for them…'

There are snatches of muted conversation across the room but I catch enough to know Müller is being given a deadline by which time he is expected to have a full explanation of the whole affair: method of entry, contacts, underground links, the complete criminal conspiracy laid bare.

Müller's protests are loud. He needs more time; he needs to get to work in his own headquarters. But Cossack cuts him off. 'The Reichsmarschall is insistent. We need answers here and now. Ten o'clock and no later.'

I close my eyes, hiding a sigh of relief. Now I understand. I am to be handed over to some new authority. Some authority other *than the Gestapo.*

Till ten o'clock, I repeat silently to myself, licking damaged lips, wriggling burnt arms. Till ten o'clock.

CHAPTER ELEVEN

I t started with the Frenchman whingeing about the choice of hotel, it grew with the arrival of the Chinese delegate, and became a serious question mark when observing the behaviour of some of the other delegates.

'Really, Miss Drake, why here? I mean, look at it!' Several energetic shrugs from Jean-Francois Girolle. Arms spread wide. 'Why are we to be billeted in this place, all together, like a troop of poor soldiers doing their army service?'

Emma returned a puzzled frown.

'These lift gates, so old-fashioned,' he said. 'All this brass everywhere, and the wood, this enormous heavy wood, from the floor to the ceiling. I mean to say, it's so Bavarian!'

'What did you expect? In Bavaria?'

'Something a little more modern.'

'You mean, some five-star anonymous luxury. Like any town, any country?'

Girolle stood back a little, nonplussed.

'Really, Jean-Francois, I expected better. This hotel was chosen deliberately to introduce us all to some pre-war ambience. To fit the mood and theme of our deliberations.'

'But that old lift! It creaks abominably. And the jerks!'

Emma had no intention of indulging such protests. She turned and said: 'I can't believe you'd rather go for swish and anonymous,' before walking away.

It was evening and Roper was hard at work in the little room they used as an office at the Hotel Isarhof, sorting papers, working on a timetable.

'By the way,' she said, 'thanks for interceding on my behalf.'

Roper merely grinned. He'd even topped his intervention with Kasper by 'smoothing over' Frau Direktor.

Emma couldn't help it. She still resented his grandstanding, his reinventing himself as Mr Fix It, but she began to realise she would need him. The professor's warning came back to her once again; her normal self-confidence had taken a buffeting from the angry crowd on the steps of the school.

Over the next few days the conference began to bed in, the programme appeared to be working, arrangements ran more smoothly. The Russian, Pavel Komov gave his interpretation of 1938, which led subsequently to lively exchanges on the role, motives and rapid changes of direction effected by Joseph Stalin; why he made his pact with the Nazis and the hostility and coldness shown by the rest of the Western world to the communist regime. Emma began to hope for a successful outcome.

In the evenings, back at the Isarhof, named after the river that flowed nearby, she worked on recording the day's activities and working up her own notes for what she anticipated would be the key presentation at the end of the week: Great Britain and Neville Chamberlain.

Roper checked stationery, collated and stapled photocopied

documents and carried on his role as office factotum. On Tuesday he was done early, left for the bar next door for a couple of beers and returned late. Emma was still in the office listening to one of the Bradley Wilkes broadcast recordings they had obtained from the studio in the States.

When she saw him in the doorway she slipped off her headphones. 'This has really come alive for me,' she said.

'Grandfather's story?'

She nodded. 'Ever since I listened to that woman in Studholme talking about the pandemonium caused by the arrests, then walking round those big hallways at the Führerbau, it's become so vivid. And now these discs. Amazing.'

'I know,' Roper said. 'That voice; so utterly compelling.'

'Bradley Wilkes, you're a hero,' she said, as if addressing the man directly. 'So prescient. You knew what was coming. Even though you had to cope with Nazi censorship, you were warning the world. Warning of what was to come.'

She returned to the disc but was interrupted by a call from Angie. Almost a voice from the distant past, yet it could only have been a matter of days.

'Where have you been hiding yourself?' the voice from Chelsea wanted to know. 'You haven't answered my messages.'

'Totally taken up with this job.'

'All work makes a dull girl.'

'Really committed.'

'Oh, don't be so boring. Look, could you get away, at least for a couple of days? I've got tickets for the opera in Paris; how about that? Amazing, what? Next Thursday.'

Emma sighed and stole a glance at Roper who wasn't disguising his interest.

'Sorry, Angie. Can't make it; too involved here.'

'It's not every day—'

'I know, I know. Appreciate the offer. Have to be another time.'

Roper grinned when she cut the call. 'That was painful.'

She looked away, left the room, checking her other messages, regretful that she was neglecting her friends.

CHAPTER TWELVE

He was impertinent and he was inquisitive – but Roper was a necessity. Emma was reassured by his presence; she *did* need help. Her mind went to the conference participants; instinctively, she saw the pug-nosed American Wilkes and his weasel friend from Prague as a threat; she sensed their unstated menace. And in fairness she had to admit that Roper was more than just an extra pair of hands. He had investigative skills and he had instinct, a nose. He wasn't a face-value man; he could sense hidden dangers; he also had language and experience.

She sighed. She would not accord him the status of a confidant but he was a sounding board on whom she could try out ideas and get a reaction. She stood by the tiny window in their office and decided it was time to put him to work.

He was looking at her, so she waved him over and pointed. 'There's something distinctly odd about some of our new friends,' she said. 'Come and have a look at this.'

From their vantage point, they could get a direct view of the hotel lounge: the dark oak panelling, an enormous grandfather clock, a harp placed discreetly in one corner, wooden benches around the edges, the sofa dominating the centre. 'I've been standing here on and off this evening and every time I take a peek, I see those two.'

They looked. America and Nagorno-Karabakh were closeted together on the sofa in animated conversation. The latter represented a tiny republic, recognised by almost no one, sandwiched between Armenia and Azerbaijan. 'They seem to be shuffling bits of paper. Reading bits out loud,' she said.

Roper studied the scene closely. 'A submission on America's attitude to Appeasement, do you think?' he suggested.

She laughed. 'If he's capable! What is it about them that doesn't ring true? I've been watching them at the conference. They just don't contribute.'

Roper's expression was still quizzical. He rubbed the end of his nose. 'Now you mention it, neither of them look the part. They've got nothing to say. Just blank expressions, as if their presence is nothing more than a gesture.'

'But they've got plenty to say to each other now.' She jerked her head in the direction of the door. 'Time for a challenge.'

As Emma and Roper emerged on to the floor of the lounge, there was some hurried disposal of papers and closing of briefcases.

She walked directly to the sofa, stood staring down, a stern expression, saying nothing, purposely building the pressure. The American's brazen appearance as the representative of the board at Berkeley was a tangible demonstration of his family's continuing political clout but she wasn't going to give him an easy ride.

'Something wrong?' Wilkes asked eventually.

'Is there?'

A shrug. 'Not as far as I know.'

She drew in a deep breath. 'I'm most interested in your forthcoming contribution. I take it from all the paperwork going on here that you've got some great original thinking to run by us when it's your turn at the podium. Something perceptive, something penetrating, I trust?'

'Could be.'

'May we be privileged to have some indication as to its content or direction?'

'Far too early for that.'

'My contact at Berkeley does not recall any comparable contribution from you on any subject in the past.'

'On the board, as I told you.'

'A purely political appointment.' When there was no reply, nor any perceptible reaction, she said: 'I shall be watching with great interest.'

'Oh, we're all into watching with great interest.'

Next day became a study in observation: who was talking to whom in the hotel lounge, corridors, lift, dining room. The sum total of keen-eyed watches by Emma and Roper read: two long conversations between America and Nagorno; one between China and Nagorno; and another between Russia and Nagorno.

'Since the guy from the new republic seems to be so popular,' Roper suggested, 'perhaps you should have him up at the lectern next.'

When she managed to corner Nagorno's Muzalev in a corridor shortly after breakfast, his response was remarkably similar to the Chinese delegate. Cheung Jihai's line had been: keeping watching brief, hoping to learn from European rivalry; lessons for the future that might be relevant to the emerging superpower in the East, China's intentions, of course, being entirely peaceful, and so on and so on.

'Just change the geography round a bit and you have essentially the same answer,' Emma said. 'There are just too many observers at this conference and not enough people with something substantial to say.'

'Remedy that with the Czech,' suggested Roper. 'Can't go wrong with him.'

'Weasel features? And by the way, were you the leak who gave him that stuff about my grandpa?'

Roper shook his head. 'Don't be daft, Emma, he could have got that from anywhere, bits in all the papers and on the web.'

She grunted, sceptical.

'Who's to say,' he persisted, 'that the Czech and Wilkes are not in cahoots? Or, at least, in contact with each other? Perhaps before they appeared here? And if not the Czech, then Nagorno, or China or Russia.'

Abruptly, she stopped thinking about her grandfather's story. 'Are you saying,' she asked slowly, 'that you get a sense of conspiracy around here?'

His brow furrowed, then he nodded. 'They seem to spend an awful lot of time in private conversation with each other but have precious little to say in public.'

'So what do you make of that?'

'As you said yourself, half of them don't act like any academics we've ever known.'

The Weasel was at the lectern, giving his considered conclusion on Appeasement. The man from the Czech Republic, his words seemingly filtered through a vast drooping moustache, didn't hold back, but then he knew he didn't have to. Who was going to defend Appeasement?

Vincenc Tibor, despite the mildly formal nature of the occasion, could not quite rid himself of his matchstick habit. Midway through his heroic version of a far-seeing and enlightened Czech leadership, he couldn't resist a quick chew on a stick before self-consciously parking the remnants in a top pocket. Even from where she sat, Emma picked up the unmistakable aroma of Greek cigarettes, giving the lie to a professed non-smoker.

Czechoslovakia, Tibor said, was fortunate in having the ear of American president Woodrow Wilson, a talismanic world statesman who insisted on a fair deal for the small nations of Europe at the conclusion of the First World War. Without Wilson, he insisted, Britain and France would simply have carved up Germany and turned the Versailles Treaty into nothing less than a feast of empires.

Emma glanced in the direction of Wilkes. Was Tibor greasing up to the American here? Was there some other agenda at work?

The Czechs, Tibor continued, were models of moderation and tact in the interwar years, despite all provocation from the German minority in the border zone of the Sudetenland – all orchestrated by the Nazis, of course, directed from Berlin.

Unsurprisingly, Tibor concluded that his civilised, cultured and peaceful infant nation was thrown to the wolves and betrayed by the weakness of France and the egotistical brutalism of Chamberlain. In short, they allowed the Nazis to destroy his nation.

Emma sighed. A little rose-tinted, perhaps. The other delegates barely stirred. She looked across the tables. Nagorno and his friends doodled on their pads while Wilkes returned her gaze with an unblinking and remorseless watchfulness. No one spoke.

Not, that is, until Roper coughed, slipped off the stationery table where he had been perched, and said in a loud voice: 'That completely fails to take account of the tide of pacifism running through Western society at that time.'

Emma shot to her feet, turned and glared at her assistant.

Assistant. That was the key word. Assistant – not participant.

'You have to understand,' Roper added, 'the pressures both the French Premier and Chamberlain were under to prevent war from breaking out.'

Emma stayed standing, rapped: 'I'm sure the bona fide, accredited delegate from France will want to comment on that.'

But Roper seemed not to have heard. 'Public opinion,' he said, 'was running massively in favour of Chamberlain's actions.'

Emma didn't wait for Jean-Francois Girolle to stir himself. Instead, she stalked to the lectern. 'Thank you, Mr Tibor,' she said, edging the Czech to one side; 'this brings today's session to a close.'

'Just tell me,' she said, slapping the conference agenda against the corridor wall with a smack reminiscent of a school caning session, 'which part of the word *assistant* didn't you understand?'

Roper appeared completely oblivious to her mood. 'Someone had to stick up for dear old Neville,' he said, 'it was getting just too one-sided.'

'Neville? Dear old Neville? What are you? Some two-bit supporter of a pathetic old man who, apart from Hitler himself, was probably the person most responsible for the outbreak of the Second World War?'

'You're way over the top there, Emma.'

'And who gave you permission to speak? I thought I made it clear you're the conference factotum. The odd-job boy. Since when did you become an academic?'

Roper coughed and laughed, completely unfazed. 'Face it,

Emma, your conference is dying a death in there. Half of them have nothing to say. Probably because they're crooks. And the other half are asleep. I was just trying to liven it up a bit. Create a bit of controversy. See if I could wake them up. Get something going.'

'You have no right whatsoever–'

'Look, I'm doing you a big favour. Can't you see that?' He spread his hands. 'No need to have a tantrum.'

'Tantrum? Tantrum! How dare you!'

When he didn't reply, she said, loudly: 'Getting above yourself. Interfering. Poking your nose in places it shouldn't be.'

He looked at her for several long seconds. Seemed like minutes. Then he turned away from her, as if to go, before saying: 'This is where I get off the merry-go-round, Emma. Being treated like some kind of subspecies, like a servant, like someone from below stairs, is not my idea of fun.'

He turned full on to confront her.

She stared back.

He said: 'You've just lost your factotum. I'm heading home.'

She looked away, not eyeing him, posing unconcerned. 'Suit yourself,' she said over a flicked shoulder.

CHAPTER THIRTEEN

In the silence that ensued Emma quickly calmed down and considered. She hated those who tried to thwart her. She had taken Roper's passivity for granted and his interjection had caught her off guard. She was used to people wilting under her whiplash disapproval but Roper would not be put down. Instead, he had marched straight out of the building.

She breathed in deeply. She'd been told more than once that her obstinate streak was a great motivator; on occasions, however, she knew it to be a handicap. Gone was the Chelsea sun-worshipper, the casino gambler, the chirpy detractor of Professor Chadwick and his many obsessions. Now she was hooked into a serious purpose. She wouldn't let Lance Scranton down, nor her mother, nor herself. She knew what had to be done.

Steadying her nerve, she left the Führer building, took the tram back to the Isarhof and climbed the stairs to Roper's room.

A stentorian voice echoed from the interior at her knock.

'What?' A tone she hadn't heard before.

'Can we have a word?'

'And the point is?'

'Apologies, from me to you.'

The door, she noticed, was ajar but a voice, still deep in the interior, said: 'Bit late for that.'

She pushed and stood in the open doorway. 'Sorry, Roper, I was out of order back there. You were right to take offence.'

He threw an item of clothing into a suitcase lying open on the bed, then looked at her. The indulgent good humour and the placid exterior were gone. 'It's not about just now. You've been dismissive and hostile from the word go. You haven't the faintest idea how to deal with people, how to treat, how to relate. You've stretched my loyalty to your mother beyond the limit.'

She didn't answer.

He slammed in a couple of books with more than necessary force. 'You may be clever, very clever, but you've still got a lot to learn. You can't trample on everyone in your path; ultimately you have to treat people as you would like to be treated yourself.'

'Look,' she said, 'I'm doing humble pie, all right? I recognise you've contributed, helped me get this far. And now I still need help to fight these battles; you can see what I'm up against.'

He glanced up briefly from his folding.

She said: 'If you quit now, you'll be leaving me in a quagmire. I need a result – but I'm getting nowhere with these people.'

'Told you they were a peculiar bunch.'

'If I'm going to rescue any shred of credibility, I need you back on board. You're right, the whole thing's in danger of falling apart unless I – unless we – do something about it.'

He stopped to face her. 'You know, I didn't have to do this. Like a fool, I even volunteered.'

'Why?'

'Sounded like a good project, something worthwhile, something interesting. I needed something positive to do.'

'Not entirely altruistic then?'

'There you go again.'

She held up both palms in a gesture of surrender. 'Please,' she said, 'if you go, you can write failure to this whole darned project; is that what you want?'

'What I want is to see some noticeable change, what during my days in the forces we used to call attitude adjustment.'

She pursed her lips and sighed. 'You're looking at someone in transition.'

He had stopped moving, was staring at her intently. 'Interesting,' he said. Then after a long pause: 'I'll think about it.' He closed the lid of his suitcase. 'Over a drink in the bar.'

Emma gave him five minutes to get settled in the hotel bar, hopefully to simmer down, while she went off to her room to change into the wrapover-look Jersey dress in magenta she had bought on a lunchtime dash to Designer Alley. Plus matching slingbacks.

Then she went downstairs and peered through the bar window. Yes, he had his drink and, thank goodness, Wilkes and co were absent. In fact, Roper was sitting on a stool, alone at the bar, drinking what looked like whisky.

She made her entrance. The offer and ordering of a drink was always a good neutral point from which to relaunch a relationship, she thought, and asked for Helles beer. 'Developed quite a taste for it,' she said, 'a very acceptable sort of lager, don't you think?'

He made agreeable noises in response, talked about his

preference for dark beer, about the city's long history of brewing, about Germany's highly regulated recipes for beers. André Rieu and his showy, mostly female orchestra were running through one hundred years of Strauss on the loudspeaker behind the bar. 'D'you like this sort of thing?' he asked.

She nodded. 'Didn't know I could play the trumpet, did you?'

It was understood between them that trivialities were needed to cushion the harsh words spoken earlier: how her Porsche made short work of the autobahns, the hotel cuisine, an upcoming tour.

A television set mounted on a wall close by was running an English detective series; the actors and the country cottages were instantly recognisable but the sound button was on mute. Just as well. All dubbed in German.

Roper even managed a gentle joke and she laughed readily at the punchline. Perhaps it was her mood, perhaps it was the humour, or more likely the effect of alcohol; whatever it was, something was working in their favour. When he was on his fourth whisky and she her third Helles, he looked at her directly and said: 'Emma, I have to say this... in all sincerity, we need a bargain.'

'A bargain?'

'Some sort of pact, an agreement between us.'

'Getting all cuddly, you mean?'

'No, no, I'm serious. I mean, an agreement. I'm ready to stay on board but in return you have to try to be a little human occasionally.'

'Fine. I'm all human. From head to toe.'

'You have to be prepared to open up to me.'

'Oh, I see, Mr Nosey Parker finally gets his open sesame.'

'If you like.' He grinned. 'Another beer? Or will you take something stronger?'

Two new drinks later, she gave him the wide-open-arms gesture. 'Okay then, here it is, open sesame; ask me anything you like. What is it you want to know?'

He chuckled. 'So many things.' He gulped in luxurious anticipation. 'Let's start with Father.'

'Ran out on Mum and me. And wouldn't pay the university fees. Even wanted me to leave early and get a job. Dirty rat. Unforgiven.' She sighed. 'Next!'

He nodded. 'That'll do for now. For starters. Next is your brother.'

'I ran the poor little blighter off the road when he was sixteen. Him on a motorbike, me in a car. Hospital for a month. Owe him big time.'

'Lover?'

'Now you're pushing it!'

Roper sipped and waited.

'Let's just say, many regrets and the silly sod wouldn't go away; became so persistent he turned into a stalker. Had to be taught a lesson. Had to be stopped.'

'How so?'

'My brother's training... top class.'

Roper leaned back, savoured the malt and took a deep breath. 'Now for some serious inquisition. Why exactly are we here?' He leaned forward to stare at her intently but she simply eye-balled him straight back, so he said: 'Tell me truly, who is this Chadwick guy? Really?'

She did a double take. 'The professor? What do you mean, who is he?'

'I mean, I know he's a professor of history... but what else is he?'

'I don't know what you're getting at.'

'Oh but I think you do. I think you know what Chadwick's all about.'

'Well, if you think you already know, why don't you tell me?'

'You try.'

She sighed, took a deep breath and said: 'He's a passably competent professor who has a great facility for finding graduates good jobs. He has useful contacts with people who can provide high-level employment for bright and promising people.'

'And what kinds of employers are these? And what kinds of jobs?'

'Oh, for God's sake, what do you think? Academia, commerce, research, whatever.'

'And your strange man in America and this wonderful scholarship you've come up with, the Montagu-Pinckney? What's all that about?'

'Damned good luck, I'd say! Plenty of funds to invest.'

'But investment in what?'

'Oh, these big companies, they're into long-term research, always looking to the future and what it holds. How the world is going to look in so many years. Forecasts, projections, commercial applications. Charitable foundations, educational, historical...'

'And what commercially useful little discoveries or projections are you going to make, here, in little old Munich, discussing Mr Chamberlain and his ilk?'

'Look, don't knock it, okay? If he wants to put his money in, fine by me! Never argue with the gift horse, right?'

'I'd loved to have been in on your briefings.'

'Well, you weren't, so get over it. They probably didn't think an ex-jailbird qualified for inclusion.'

'Thanks for that.'

'Don't mention it.'

Roper stared back at her for some time, then subsided with the look of a disappointed man, compensated only by the drink in his hand.

Emma could hold her beer. She'd been told that, and she was confident she could out-think Roper and his display of hyperactive curiosity. And he was vulnerable. He'd been downing the malt with such relish he had failed to notice how she drained her beer into another glass.

'Tell you what!' she said. 'Let's get out of this dreary place. It's like a teak tombstone! How about we do what we've missed out on so far? A club!'

In the taxi on their way to The Bleu Lagune on Maximilian Strasse she got to thinking about the relationship with Roper. By now she regarded him less as a hurdle and more as putty in the hand. He was a good team player. She had to give him that. She enjoyed being his boss. She enjoyed having him defer to her. Then she got to thinking about Roper and her mother. How many times had she heard him declare his loyalty; about how Mother had stood by him while he was in prison and how he would repay her with the same generosity of spirit. But there was something wrong with that. Emma always regarded protestations of loyalty as suspect. In her book, if you needed to keep declaring it, there had to be a doubt about it.

The Bleu Lagune was all flashing lights, dry ice and music a little too loud for comfort. They almost had to shout even when close together. She manoeuvred him away from the bar and dragged him on to the dance floor. It was a lazy, sentimental number. She draped her arms around his neck and held him close. There might have been a gap of twenty years between them but it was time to put him to the test.

'Just how loyal are you, Roper? Eh? Really? I mean, say, just for instance, given the right circumstances, would you crave a younger woman?'

But he was not quite as woozy as she'd thought. 'And do you crave after older men?'

'Depends who they are.'

'Ah, now I see! It all adds up. Here speaks the woman with a storybook full of personal disasters.'

'You rude devil! What would you know about it?'

'I've had a little input.'

'Huh! Mother again!'

'Do I detect a little Mother envy at work?'

'What?'

'Would you be above setting out to steal your mother's other half, perhaps?'

She exploded. 'Just listen to yourself! Talk about kidology! No way, man!'

'But you do like to lead people on, don't you? Lay false trails? Enjoy the attention? I think you're an attention-seeker. Then, when they get too close, gazeek!' Roper made a gizzard-cutting gesture. 'Then they get the painful goodbye. The knuckleduster treatment.'

'Don't be ridiculous. I've only ever used it once and he was a stalker, so persistent he'd become dangerous, and he deserved it.'

'You enjoy playing the field.'

'Some people can't control their lust. Are you lusting, Roper? Can you control it? Or are you a slave to it?'

He laughed uproariously, which made her angry.

'And how are things back at Number 24?' she persisted. 'Still in the spare bedroom?'

'Your mother and I are just fine, thank you.'

The music stopped and so did they. Roper wobbled a little and she said: 'I think we'd better get back to the hotel before you make an exhibition of yourself.'

'Control freak,' he said.

CHAPTER FOURTEEN

Next up in the conference spotlight was the nervous girl from Munich University. She had a difficult brief. Putting the German viewpoint on the Appeasement Crisis was a tough one. How was she going to manage it? Fascinating though this question was, Martina Lang's coming ordeal was not uppermost in the thoughts of either Emma or Roper at the breakfast table next morning.

They were together, reconciled but still wary. Roper, ladling jam and butter on to his third croissant, said: 'I'll never get used to Continental.'

'Missing Mother's bacon and eggs?' She smiled, then lifted a coffee cup and used it as a pointer – in the direction of the other tables. 'Have you noticed anything this morning? About our fellow breakfast diners?'

He turned, counted heads and looked back at her. 'China, America, Nagorno and Russia,' he said. 'All conspicuous by their distinct lack of appetite this morning.'

She nodded. 'Precisely. Ever since I met Russia and Nagorno on the stairs yesterday. They couldn't wait to scuttle off. Now they all seem to have gone. Anxious to avoid me – in the hotel at least.'

'If you take my advice–'

'Don't count on it.'

'Stay out of this, Emma; whatever's going on between our absent friends, it's none of your damned business.'

'The hell I will! Something very peculiar is happening here. And it's got nothing to do with Munich 1938.'

'They can all do as they like in their own free time.'

Emma shook her head. 'Don't give me that. They're imposters. Not the genuine article at all. You said so yourself. A conspiracy. It's obvious, isn't it?'

He shrugged. 'Maybe.'

She said: 'Can't you see? Too many coincidences. They're all in it together. Join up the dots, man! They're using my conference as a cover.' Roper made another quizzical face. 'Suss it, Roper. This is a rank abuse and I'm not going to tolerate it.'

Roper pushed the remnants of his breakfast to one side. Gave her the full-on stare. 'Whatever it is, whatever their business is, take it from me, there will be an element of danger.'

'Dangerous?' She shrugged. 'Anyway, I don't scare easily.'

'Maybe, but you're ill-equipped to confront these people. Look at them. Laptops, briefcases full of files and papers, calculators and lots more we haven't seen. If you're right, they'll have plenty of backup. Big companies perhaps. Who knows? Crime, even the Mob, or something murkier. They'll be able to whistle up help anytime they like. And you – you're just one person pitted against them.'

She grinned. 'Not quite true.'

'Oh?'

'Us,' she said. 'We're a team, aren't we?'

He sighed. 'A team with no backing. They have all sorts of facilities we don't.'

'Ah! But you have the skills, Roper; I'm banking on your ability to defeat them.'

He looked away. 'I promised myself never to get involved again.'

'Never say never,' she said, fixing him with a slight smile. 'Nagorno's at the centre of this business, right? He's the one in the middle. He's the one they all want to talk to. So he's the key.'

'The key to what though?'

'That's what we need to find out. That's why, the minute today's session is over, I want you to tail him.'

No one saw her arrive. No one noticed she was forty-five minutes early; that she had ignored the Music School altogether; that she had gone direct to the Isarhof and entered the hotel dining hall.

Emma, halfway through her second buttered croissant, looked up to see a tall young woman in tortoiseshell glasses standing immobile by her table. Martina Lang had long tawny-brown hair, one strand of which she was twisting around the fingers of her right hand.

'Sorry to trouble you at breakfast,' she said.

Emma replied, through a mouthful of flaky pastry: 'Not at all. Come and sit. Share our coffee.'

Roper smiled broadly, as if happy to have an excuse to leave, getting to his feet. 'I'm done here anyway,' he said. 'Sorry to dash; things to do.'

Emma smiled.

Martina twiddled.

'Your turn at the lectern today,' Emma said brightly. 'All set?'

Martina's eyes watered, her mouth pensive, a deep sigh. 'I'm not looking forward to it.'

Emma was not usually tolerant of delegates stricken with lectern nerves but she bit back an instinctive sharp response. There was something altogether too vulnerable about today's participant. 'Anything I can do?' She gestured toward Martina's big bag. 'Got a script? Want me to take a look? Second opinion?'

'It's difficult...' Martina began, placing several closely-typed sheets on the breakfast table.

'A tricky brief,' Emma agreed, running a rapid eye down the first page. She swallowed the last morsel of her breakfast, turned over a page, sipped some coffee then looked up. 'Could be improved. Several important gaps. Story holes, I call them.'

Martina's eyes flickered and the hair twisting became more pronounced. 'They're going to slaughter me, aren't they?' she said, a tilt of the head toward the conference room, indicating that the 'they' in question were the other delegates. 'They'll be waiting to pounce, destroy my ideas, destroy me...'

Emma surprised herself. She put a reassuring hand on Martina's wrist, a gesture of instinctive sympathy that had her normal short fuse placed in abeyance. There was something about this person that demanded empathy. She could feel beneath her touch a quite definite tremor. 'Tell me, Martina, something's wrong; what's at the bottom of all this?' The woman's coffee cup was doing a little dance. 'Surely our conference session can't be that intimidating?'

Martina's eyelids flickered. 'But it is. It is. You can't know. Just how important that I do well. I have to make a good impression. No, no, not a good impression – a great one.'

'I see. So who is it you have to please?'

'My professor. A very difficult man. Good is not good enough. Only brilliant will do. And I didn't do well last year. This time, in this place, I have to redeem myself.'

'You don't like this man?'

Martina didn't reply immediately. She sighed, then added: 'He's my father.'

'Oh my God! You poor thing.' Emma thought about family peer pressure and suddenly Martina's nervous affliction, her palpable expression of fear, explained itself. Emma knew about academic pressure. Adding an overbearing father to the mix was a terrible burden. 'But you must have someone supportive... What about your mother?'

'A botanist.'

Emma breathed out, glimpsing the pressure cooker of a high-achieving family. 'Brothers or sisters?'

'Horst is a professor of psychology.'

Emma looked back down at the typescript and made a decision. She needed all the support she could garner from the city's university, and allowing the professor's daughter to falter was not a wise move. 'Look,' Emma said, 'I'm going to help you out here. Normally I wouldn't – this must be just between us.'

'But how?' It was almost a wail. 'There isn't time.'

'Yes there is. I'm going to reschedule. You won't be speaking today. Tomorrow instead. And in the meantime...'

Emma led Martina out of the dining room with an encouraging arm around still quivering shoulders, all the way upstairs to her room. She sat Martina down at the small table she had turned into a desk, clearing papers away, providing pens and a laptop. She had already made the dresser into a mini-library and the wardrobe into a filing cabinet. Amid this discreet landscape, away from any intrusive gaze and equipped with fresh coffee ordered from the kitchens, Emma pointed the way: books selected, pages tagged, references given.

'Remember,' she said, 'we're here for the truth, not to score points off one another. In the end your father will be pleased...'

'You don't know him.'

'Tell me.'

'Nothing I do pleases. He wants a prodigy, a genius, a son, but I don't measure up.' A gulp, a pause, then: 'I must not disgrace him – and I'm not to let anyone cast our nation in a bad light.'

'Tall order! How can you not blame the Nazis?' Emma paused, then added: 'However, there is something.'

She began to make a list, pulling books from the pile. 'You can make heroes out of the opposition to Hitler. How they were defeated at every turn, sometimes by their own failings but also by others who should have helped.'

'Like who?'

Emma was opening pages, writing rapidly on a sheet of paper, noting down numbers. 'You can make a good case,' she said, 'for blaming the British Government.'

'I can?' Martina's gaze fastened on Emma's list.

Point One: Why had Whitehall ignored all warnings coming out of Germany in the years before the war? A senior German politician risked his life to visit London in 1936 to warn of Hitler's secret preparations for war.

Point Two: Agents from the German army took similar risks to tell Chamberlain to resist Hitler's plan to annex the Sudetenland. They even declared themselves ready to topple the dictator from power the moment he gave the order to invade Czech territory.

Point Three: Why, then, did Chamberlain cut the ground from under their feet by flying to Munich to give in to Hitler?

Martina was left to rewrite her script while Emma went to the conference room to rearrange the day's schedule. On the way she asked Roper to use his press contacts: there should be a one-to-one briefing for the correspondent of the *Süddeutsche*

Zeitung, she said, to explain how expertly the German case was made and how well it was received at conference.

'Well, it will be,' she said in answer to Roper's raised eyebrow.

~

Roper had made a pledge to himself, when still inside the Scrubs, never again to become involved in any unprincipled, covert or illegal act. Only a fool would risk going back to jail after three years of the sort of misery he had endured.

Yet this was different, he reassured himself. This was Germany and this was not illegal. His mood was buoyant, a slight grin in place. After last night's bust-up with Emma, she now appeared considerably more receptive to his way of thinking. And ready to agree to ideas previously considered out of the question.

Like now. He was sitting behind the steering wheel of her Porsche.

The car was parked in Arcis Strasse, a hundred metres from the Führerbau entrance. He was to wait for the signal that Nagorno's Muzalev was on the move.

So far, nothing.

He settled more comfortably in the seat, felt the leather and ran a hand over the dash, smiling to himself, but always with an eye on the top step. The minutes ticked by. Nothing. He got to thinking about the previous night and how things had changed between them. In the early hours they'd had the sort of conversation that would have been impossible the day before. He'd learned about her father and probed more about her brother, going beyond guilt over a car crash; that her sibling had taught her the art of self-defence, specifically the use of a knuckleduster.

Roper had wagged a finger. 'Dirty fighting – and strictly illegal!'

'I'm talking a seriously unpleasant person. A stalker.'

'So, not Queensbury, then?'

'That's just for sportsmen.'

This recall was abruptly ended by the appearance on the top step of Carlo Piccini, the one delegate willing to co-operate and in whom Roper felt able to place complete trust. Emma had worked her magical powers of persuasion on the man from Italy and the consequence was that Carlo, at this very moment, was transferring a yellow folder from his left hand to his right. An outlandishly elaborate signal, Roper thought – and then he saw him, the stumpy figure of Muzalev, almost stumbling down the steps into a taxi parked at the kerb.

Roper moved off, ready to enjoy this little chore but anxious not to lose the taxi in the city traffic. He jettisoned all thought of staying well back. The black Mercedes cab moved into the crowded dual carriageway that led past the busy crossing at the Karlsplatz, and Roper needed to stay tight or risk being stranded at any of half a dozen traffic lights, keeping a wary eye out for trams, pedestrians and traffic cops. Past the Sendlinger Tor they entered a warren of little streets and Roper lost sight of the black Merc. Cursing, he was about to give up when he saw the vehicle cross his path at right angles and pull up outside the town theatre on the Gärtnerplatz. Here his quarry stopped, paid off the driver and entered the Café Klosterhof.

The Klosterhof had a glass panel above the entrance containing a line drawing of the neighbouring monastery. Inside, the walls were decorated with life-size drawings of Franciscan friars clutching large tankards, demonstrating a familiar city theme: that the gentlemen in brown brewed the best beer. Roper, equipped with a copy of that day's *Süddeutsche Zeitung*, found a distant seat from where he could observe. But if he had visions of the Russian, the American or the Chinese arriving for a secret conclave, he was disappointed. Nobody joined the man, who simply demolished a huge plate of cheese-and-tomato pizza while Roper made heavy weather of the news from South Germany.

Then his hopes took a nosedive. Muzalev rose from his table and approached Roper's with a huge grin. 'Big coincidence, eh, Mr Roper?'

Roper nodded and hoped his embarrassment didn't show.

'You can tell your lady the pizza was nice, very nice. Big, very tasty. Nothing else to report, eh?'

He turned away without waiting for the ritual pretence of innocence, waddling off, chortling.

Roper, humiliated and feeling flatter than yesterday's syrup pancake, walked disconsolately back to the parked Porsche. To complete his misery, he'd got a ticket.

Then, just as he was opening the door and berating himself for his display of rusty incompetence, he looked up and glimpsed a small consolation.

You couldn't miss him. The man had immense sticky-out ears. Roper grinned as he spotted the shaven-headed Polish delegate, Teodor Zdzislaw, striding purposefully into the café.

That afternoon Emma met Martina once again, to monitor progress, this time at a discreet alcove in the cafeteria at the Führerbau. Some brave post-war architect had managed to lift the all-encompassing Third Reich gloom from a small section of the building and introduce bright pastel fittings and stainless-steel chairs and tables. Amid this unfamiliar landscape, equipped with coffee, plum cake and Kaiserschmarrn on an elegant glass table, Emma embarked on the mentoring session.

Martina's perpetual frown was lifting. She was no longer twiddling her hair. 'I really think this might work,' she said.

Emma nodded and smiled. 'Actually, you can return the favour.' When this brought forth a puzzled look she said: 'I too have a family problem. And I'm looking for help from some of your contacts.'

'Contacts? I don't understand.'

Emma launched into the story of her family history quest: the search for the truth about her grandfather, how he'd gatecrashed the Munich conference and vanished. 'I need to know what really happened that day,' she said.

'I still don't see...'

Emma smiled encouragingly. 'I've every confidence your university has immense expertise on this subject. A Who Was Who of the Nazi period in Munich... and a Who Was Who in the German Resistance. Obviously, Grandfather had local help from opponents of the regime. Without a doubt! If anyone knows, they will know, so you see, I need to meet a surviving member. I need a contact, an old Munich resister.'

But Martina was no longer the vulnerable and grateful person of a few minutes before. She was shaking her head. 'Don't go there, Emma; far too sensitive,' she said. 'Historians seeking to reassess Munich's wartime role walk on tiptoe. Local feeling. Local hostility. Around here, a taboo subject. And the sort of people you're talking about... They're still vulnerable to recrimination, to accusations of disloyalty. They don't speak about it. They bury their past.'

But the brush-off never worked with Emma. Martina received the full-on stare. 'I really need this. Call it payback time. One good turn depends on another.'

Back at the hotel Emma was relentlessly upbeat and wouldn't hear of Roper's gloom over being confronted by the stodgy Muzalev.

'We're amateurs up against professionals,' he complained, but she waved away his depression. She had 'a very promising fishing line' out to the university, she assured him, and great news on Merkers. Roper had no idea what she was talking about and it had to be explained: all over Germany, the Gestapo destroyed their records as the war ended. All – except Würzburg and Dusseldorf and now, thanks to the manic diggers of the Thuringia Exploration Group at the Merkers mine, in Munich too. The latest find had sent an excited ripple through the historians of Europe.

Roper shrugged. 'So you think...'

'Grandpa disappeared right here in the Führerbau, so the Gestapo must have been involved. Should show up in their records.'

'Oh, come on, Emma! Face it – they probably shot him straight off. Not nice, I know, but the most likely outcome. Do you really think they'd put that in the files?'

She brushed his doubts aside. 'You know what they're like. The bureaucratic reflex. They write down absolutely everything.'

Roper sighed. 'Could take a hundred years to find it in the sort of paperwork mountain you're talking about.'

'Our good luck. An official government historian has been appointed to sift through it.'

He snorted. 'He won't let you anywhere near it. I know them. I've been here before, remember? These people, they're uptight about their history. They're really fed up at being portrayed as the world's worst bad guys. They'll sanitise your precious records before anyone else gets close. And you, you'll stand no chance.'

'We shall see.'

He looked at her closely. Saw her jaw. Saw her eyes. 'What?'

'I'm going to meet him. He's got an office over at the town hall. You worry too much. It's all fixed up. An official appointment.'

CHAPTER FIFTEEN

Next day, Roper was cloaked in black leather and a crash helmet that was a size too big. He shook his head in annoyance and the damned thing wobbled like an oversized Tommy's helmet, bouncing around on its little blobs of cork. Once again, he asked himself in a fit of overheated angst: *How does she do it? Really, how? What is it with her that you just can't say no?*

He'd vowed to plough the straight and narrow back there in the Scrubs; never to do anything that might put him back in that terrible place. Yet here he was, sitting astride a hired Honda 500, parked up in Arcis Strasse, about to perform the same foolish trick as the day before.

'Don't fret!' she'd told him. 'No one will recognise you in that gear,' then laughed herself into a fit of hysterical giggles he did not feel in the least like joining. When he had first taken the big bike out of the hire depot she had acted like a sixteen-year-old boy, listening in raptures to the tickover, herself purring like a well-fed cat, sitting astride it, revving it, loving it, riding it up and down the street even though she wasn't named on the documents.

'Remind you of the good old days, does it?' he asked. 'Or should that be the bad old *day*?'

Her answer was a sharp look.

Roper grinned at the memory and switched his attention back to the Führerbau entrance. More waiting.

Then, at last, the indispensable Carlo gave him the signal – this time, a more muted scratch of the right ear – as the podgy figure of Nagorno's Muzalev sidled down the steps to another waiting taxi.

This time, however, there was someone else with him. From his position squeezed in behind a parked car, Roper couldn't make out who.

When the taxi moved off he stayed well back. Muzalev had already demonstrated his ability to sniff out a tail. In traffic Roper kept two cars behind. Would it be the same café? And who was his companion?

Out on to the main drag, the taxi seemed to be heading away from the city centre. Roper couldn't guess at the destination and involuntarily moved closer – closer than he intended. But it was a lucky break. Because through the rear window he could see strange movements going on inside the vehicle. The two figures in the rear seats were not still, instead moving jerkily from side to side.

Roper risked easing up closer. If they were that engaged with each other, they wouldn't be looking out for him. In fact, it looked very much as if they were having an argument. Fisticuffs, even.

Suddenly the taxi swerved into the side of the road and Roper had to pull violently to the offside and overtake to avoid a collision. Straightening up, he shot a glance behind. The vehicle was stopped.

Roper stopped.

He got off the bike and was just in time to see one door open and a figure stumble out on to the pavement. The figure turned back to face the vehicle, presumably to remonstrate, and this was swiftly followed by the crack of something black and metallic, hurled from the cab. Then came the tinkling collision of other objects hitting the road.

After that, the door slammed shut and the cab moved off, passing a motionless Roper.

What to do? Chase the cab or focus on the figure stranded on the pavement?

Roper decided on the latter. He approached and quickly recognised Cheung Jihai, standing in a state of confused indecision, staring at the smashed remains of a laptop, now wedged in the gutter. Around him were pencils, sheets of paper, a calculator and a handkerchief.

Roper bent to retrieve the laptop. The screen was blank. The back was missing. Several components were scattered in the road.

'Don't think that'll work again,' Roper said, handing it over.

Cheung gaped. 'Roper?'

'What happened here, China?' Roper decided on an educated guess. This didn't look like an argument about history; more like a business deal gone sour. 'Didn't you pay him a big enough kickback?'

The other man drew in a breath and visibly pulled himself together. 'Sod off, Roper, none of your business.'

'Ah, but that's a terrible shame,' Roper said. 'Such a pity. Chinese technology these days, as good as anyone's, eh?'

Cheung was wiping a wisp of blood from his left ear and pulling at a ragged coat sleeve. 'Equal to America,' he said, tenderly examining a damaged wrist. 'Yank stuff rubbish.'

As he said this he turned a baleful gaze on the shattered state of his laptop. Which was just the distraction Roper needed. Tucked into a grass verge, unseen by the distracted delegate, were a bundle of papers and a glossy package still held together by an elastic band. By the time Cheung had examined and discarded his laptop with a visible sigh of disappointment, the papers were nestling safely in the inside pocket of Roper's anorak.

'What's he asking then, our Mr Nagorno?' Roper pressed. 'Daft prices? A couple of million bucks for his back pocket?'

But Cheung was no longer willing to talk, instead hailing a passing taxi and gathering up the detritus of his distinctly failed business meeting. All he said was: 'Him, big greedy pig.'

They had the papers spread out on the table in front of them: engineering drawings and diagrams showing the nose cone, warheads, propellant tanks, fins and control mechanism, plus a glossy photograph of the weapon on its launcher, looking sleek and menacing. The Wuhan X5 had multiple warheads, a range of 3,000 kilometres and was radar-defeatable, the blurb said. Launched from a mobile unit, it was guaranteed to strike its target.

'Looks like a good bit of kit,' Roper said. 'Proves they can make 'em like anyone else. Probably the equal of the Yanks.'

'How can you say that?' Emma demanded. She looked at the photograph again and shuddered. 'This death-dealing device?'

'From what I can see on the web,' he said, 'it's a top-of-the-range Chinese missile.' He sighed and looked at her directly. 'They're all at it, Emma; face it, we've stumbled like a couple of raw hicks into the middle of a covert arms auction here. China, America, and God knows who else... all trying to sell to Nagorno, this potty little republic sitting like a pimple on the Russians' backside.'

She drew herself up and gave him one of her stares. 'That's precisely why we've got to stop it,' she said.

He leaned back in his seat, as if she had just delivered a physical blow. 'What?'

'It's shocking,' she said. 'It's disgraceful, it's evil, it's dangerous...'

He looked at her as if she were mad. 'Dangerous, yes, very dangerous for us.'

'And it's on my patch.'

'Emma,' he said, staring back, 'we're only supposed to be holding a history conference here.'

She gave him one of her stares. 'Are you going soft on me?'

'What business is it of ours if they do a few deals on the side?'

'A few deals?' Her tone was incredulous, insulted. 'I can't believe you'd be willing to turn a blind eye.'

'You're going beyond your brief. You have no actual role in preventing—'

'I can't believe you're saying this! No role? Those people, they're betraying me. Betraying the conference. Betraying us. Abusing our trust. They're just using us as a cover for a wicked, wicked purpose. Doesn't that annoy you? Get your hackles up?'

Roper sat back. This particular eruption was unexpected. 'Didn't know you were so worked up about the arms thing,' he said quietly.

'The moral dimension, you mean? And why not?'

'I thought your focus was the conference – and your grandfather.'

'Look, I'm against illegality, against breaking trade or arms embargoes, but most of all I'm against stoking up the arms race. My grandfather fought to prevent war... and I want to think I'm treading in his footsteps to stop a build-up of dangerous weapons.'

Roper was scratching his head. 'First time I've heard you talk like this.'

She ignored this remark. 'If America or China succeed in selling missiles to Nagorno, it will stoke up Russia's fears and worries. And rightly so. Those people, in that little republic – they're a really suspect bunch. Corruption's rife.' She picked up and waved the glossy picture at him. 'Mavericks, oligarchs, nationalistic idiots – can they be trusted to understand and handle such lethal weapons?'

Roper stared at her for a long moment. 'I'm impressed,' he said. 'Such a grasp of detail.'

'Next thing,' she said, 'they'll be talking about putting nuclear tips on their missiles. Do you want that?'

There was a long silence between them until eventually she said: 'That's why we must shut them down.'

Roper went outside to get some fresh air and munch some nuts. In the old days he'd have smoked half a pack of cigarettes. He stood on the doorstep looking at the clouds and a threatening sky and thinking about Emma shutting down arms dealers. He was still surprised by her passion for the subject and her background knowledge, and he wasn't completely convinced that treading in the heroic footsteps of her grandfather offered an entirely convincing explanation.

Nothing she had said previously demonstrated such a high moral tone; nothing quite matched this campaigning fervour. All his old instincts as a copper and a scribbler came to the surface. He distrusted ideologues, campaigners. All his experience flashed up bogus, a pretence, and yet he couldn't put his finger on any flaw in her reasoning. As usual, she was utterly convincing. She always carried you along.

When he walked back into the room he decided to put to her a perfectly valid objection – the danger represented by a bunch of crooked arms dealers, plus a perfectly valid solution – hand the job over to the local police.

'No!' She was typically emphatic. 'I need to preserve this conference, make it a success. Calling the cops would kill it. A complete fiasco. The whole thing would fall apart. I won't have that. And besides, it might not even be against German law.'

Roper shrugged. 'Anyway,' he said, 'if you won't bring the police in, you can't stop them on your own. They'll just move somewhere else and do their thing, thumb their noses at you and carry on.'

She grinned. 'That's where you're wrong. They need us as their cover.'

'Need us? Why?'

'These people are normally under heavy surveillance. The Intelligence fraternity know who they are, what they do, what they're up to. Wilkes and his friends are aware their activities are monitored, so they need somewhere away from the Intelligence spotlight. So this is why they're here. We're their cover. They've reinvented themselves as historians. Pretty bland, pretty harmless. Can't be up to no good talking history, can they?'

Roper stared at her, disbelieving. 'How d'you know all this?'

'Briefings. Part of the stuff I was told about before taking on this job. It's happened in the past. Criminal elements hide inside your tent to protect themselves from the scrutiny they face outside it.'

It was that spell again. As usual, she swept him along with her conviction. He shrugged and turned his attention to practical details. He said: 'They know we're watching them. I've been rumbled. Certainly after the taxi business. They don't talk together in the open anymore. Not in the kitchens, the dining room or the lobby. Now it's all done in the hotel bedrooms. I can hear footsteps half the night, doors closing, long after everyone would be expected to be asleep.'

'Surveillance,' she suggested.

'Been there, done it, got the T-shirt. Eased open my door several times to see who's visiting who. That Yank... he must be a very poor sleeper.'

'Simple,' she said. 'Just a matter of logic. Next step, burglary.'

Roper erupted. 'Oh, no! Definitely not!'

'Look,' she said, 'what we need is documentary evidence. It's no good confronting them with what we know at this stage; they'd just deny everything and where would we be? I need something they can't deny. A document, a contract, an incriminating letter, something with their names and identities all over it.'

'No!' Roper was still adamant.

She gave him the raised eyebrow look.

In his time, back during the years with the Redcaps and the bad old days of the tabloid, Roper had made child's play out of hotel keypads. There were a dozen ways to intrude into rooms: stealing the master key, borrowing the maid's, using plastic or devious tricks with the hotel's computer.

'I know you can do it,' she said. 'That was what you did back then, wasn't it? You have the skills. The master tactician. The super interloper.'

Roper shook his head. 'I've given all that up. I told you, I'm a reformed man now. No more dodgy tactics. No more illegality. No more stinking Scrubs.'

She seemed not to hear. 'Get in there, Roper. Get me that evidence.'

CHAPTER SIXTEEN

I t was sickening but it was also amazing: the effect she had, casting her spell, bending him to her will, getting him to do things he hated. Roper pulled on the latex gloves and checked his pad of white spirit and reflected. He should have refused her, had done so several times, but still found himself doing exactly what she wanted. Perhaps it was the magic of her personality, a compelling power of persuasion.

He sighed. The stage was set. At the Führerbau she was conducting a session on Poland and attendance was complete. The key faces were all there: America, Nagorno and China. So too was Italy.

Italy was the key. Italy was the good guy, the onside man, their team player. He'd started out several sessions back as a complainant, outraged by the negligent behaviour of his fellow delegates – specifically, America and Nagorno – but Emma had turned the grumbling about their lack of academic rigour to good effect. Carlo Piccini of Italy was now their man, their ally. Carlo Piccini was the snout.

Roper knew – because he'd arranged it – that the man's

finger was poised over a mobile, ready in an instant to give warning if anyone strayed from the conference room.

When the others had left the Isarhof that morning Roper had stayed behind, citing a Delhi tummy. Now that they were all safely ensconced in conference on the other side of town, he pulled on his rubber shoes, wiped a pad over the hotel's plastic door key and grinned to himself, still thinking about Emma. Where did this inner force come from? He was no expert on academics but she didn't strike him as typical; more a dynamo suited for industry or government or even Scotland Yard. His smile widened at this idea, at the swathe he imagined her cutting through some of his erstwhile friends on the right side of the law.

Then he stopped this line of thought. Police work? He had to be joking. Here he was, 'borrowed' master key in hand, about to make an illegal entry. He contorted his face in disgust – but went ahead just the same.

Over the ensuing ten minutes he systematically examined every drawer in the wardrobe and bedside table in Wilkes's room, carefully replacing the items in what he hoped was the correct order. A woman would probably notice any tiny changes in the folds of her clothes; he hoped Wilkes would not.

Next was the suitcase, under the mattress, behind the cistern in the loo, under the rugs and inside the hem of the curtains. On the dressing table was a large tin of travel sweets, mixed fruit, still sealed in plastic. Ripping that off would be a dangerous telltale to leave behind but there was a second tin which had been opened. He took from his pocket a pair of tweezers and moved the contents to the table, examining them, then restoring each to a semblance of the original order, anxious not to leave a jumble.

He sighed.

Nothing but coloured ovals: green, red and silver.

So far, no good.

He looked doubtfully at the room safe and wondered what kind of a ruse would be necessary to obtain the key for that before fixing on a much easier target.

The fridge.

He opened and examined the contents with care.

First, the bottles. He unscrewed the caps, even the miniatures, and shook the ones with sealed tops.

Then he looked in the food compartment and frowned. Wilkes must be a strange sort of hotel guest. Why would he have a large tub of Bertolli olive oil butter? Did he make his own sandwiches?

Roper prized off the lid.

Just butter. He stuck in a finger and twirled it around. Nothing at the bottom.

Roper used a tissue to wipe his latex-enclosed finger and turned his attention to the other items. This man must be a sandwich freak. Here was a packet of cheese slices.

And then a smile lit him. The packet didn't feel right to the touch. Not soft and malleable. Not like cheese. Stiff. More like paper.

Just then the mobile vibrated in his pocket. He hesitated, then put back the packet and pressed answer. A tiny grunt served as his response.

'Roper?' It was a hushed Italian whisper. 'Wilkes is on his way. With Nagorno.'

'Why?'

'Your absence. They're suspicious. Want to know what you're doing.'

'How long?'

'I couldn't ring straight away. Sorry, too public.'

'Never mind! How long?'

'Gone over ten. Be there any minute.'

'Damn!'

Roper was behind the door of his room when footsteps sounded in the corridor and led directly to the American's door. He had an empty drinking glass up to the wall to amplify sounds from the corridor but this wasn't English plasterboard he was dealing with. The partition wall in this old hotel was more solidly built. He couldn't catch any word, only Wilkes's urgent tones and Nagorno's voluble grunts.

So far his result was nil. He had not dared to take the cheese slices and there had been no time to extract the contents.

Roper sat on the floor of his room, glass at the ready, waiting. He looked around. There was time enough for reflection. He liked this old place. The Isarhof had character. An olde worlde historic charm, right down to antediluvian lift with the concertina-style iron gates, its squeaks and its bounce. That's why they'd chosen the place.

The sound of voices alerted him once more and he pressed the glass tighter. Again no words – but Wilkes's trademark laugh was the signal. A good signal. It meant the man was relieved, relaxed, thought he was in the clear. Whatever he had checked had satisfied him, his fears allayed.

The laughing and footsteps faded. After a sustained period of silence, Roper ventured carefully into the corridor and paced to the end to look through the window which gave a view on the street.

Wilkes and Nagorno were getting into a taxi.

His search continued.

Damn! The cheese slices were gone. Removed by the laughing Wilkes, and whatever incriminating material the packet had contained was now lost to Roper.

In the bathroom he checked the tube of shaving cream. This old copper knew all the tricks. This was a favourite device for covert operations. Papers could be rolled round and round inside a false container – if this was one such – without causing telltale creasing to the document. Roper pressed the button and a stream of white emerged. He weighed it. Not heavy. It didn't rattle and the base did not appear to unscrew.

Then, another thought.

He returned to the fridge. On the top shelf was a similar tube but containing squirty whipped cream with thirty-seven per cent less fat, or so it said. What kind of a tourist had whipped cream in a hotel room?

Roper pressed the button and nothing emerged. And again. Again nothing.

This time he decided to remove the object. It was a local brand. He could, if necessary, buy another and replace it.

Back in his room he used the edge of the door as a vice while he applied both hands to the task of turning the base. It stayed rigid and he began to doubt.

Then he realised he was attacking it from the wrong end. He tried the top without success, then applied his pliers. There was a little click and the interior came away.

There was certainly no whipped cream in this canister.

Five hours later, when the conference was concluded, he was able to smooth out the document in front of Emma, finding it impossible to repress a grin of triumph, pressing the pages hard against the table to get rid of the tendency to roll back into the shape of a tube. But there was no difficulty in identifying it. It was all in English – American English – and immediately recognisable as a contract.

A contract between BSC of Jakarta and the Directorate of Financial Affairs, The Republic of Nagorno-Karabakh, with the name of Muzalev already filled in, for the delivery of a battery of ten Super Nebraska SXX2 missiles, two to each battery, to be achieved no later than one year from the date of signing, at a cost of sixty million American dollars, to be paid in three equal sums, the last on the day of delivery, at the Bank of America.

'All that's missing,' Roper said, 'is Muzalev's signature. And that will cost BSC at least another five million. Probably going up by the day.'

Emma looked up at him and smiled but there was a frown. 'Who's BSC? I was hoping it would be a corporation in the States.'

'It is!' Roper insisted. 'Stands for the Blue Star Corporation of Los Angeles. Jakarta is just to throw you. Can't put their illegality in a legal document.'

She beamed. 'Brilliant.'

'Problem is,' he said, 'if we produce this as evidence he'll know we've nicked it. He'll start hollering about us thieving from his room.'

She laughed. 'Easy,' she said. 'He carelessly left it on a chair in the dining room, where we found it.'

'But we didn't.'

'But we'll have photographic evidence of it lying there, in the dining room, an incontrovertible denial of his foolish, guilty accusations. You do have your camera with you, don't you?'

He nodded and sighed. Without ever intending it, he was being sucked little by little back into the mire he so desperately wanted to leave.

CHAPTER SEVENTEEN

Jean-Francois Girolle was in full flow, claiming that all the blame for the Appeasement Crisis rested in Whitehall; that the perfidious British were intent on humiliating France while staying safely on the sidelines behind their steep white cliffs.

'What about the French defeatists?' demanded someone from the back row of seats, but Girolle's response was obliterated by a rapid knocking at the door. It swung open to reveal the excitable face of Carlo, accompanied by energetic hand signals beckoning Emma forward. He was mouthing the word 'problem'.

She frowned. Interruptions were not to be encouraged but she responded to the evident sense of crisis, leaving Mimi Aschemeyer in the chair to keep the peace on the subject of Daladier and the defeatists.

Outside in the hallway Emma was met by a line of figures approaching fast – some glowering, some taciturn, some merely intrigued. Centre stage was Frau Direktor Ludwig with eyebrows so arched they met in the middle. Behind the line she spotted Roper jogging along, peering over the heads to attract her attention.

Frau Direktor locked on to Emma like a radar beam, the voice of authority echoing around the looming space, speaking without breaking her stride. 'Miss Drake, rules are rules and are not to be broken. Order there must be. In all my twenty years as direktor I have known nothing like this.'

She swept on past, Emma bobbing in her wake.

'Just what rules are we talking about?'

'A condition of your placement here is not to bring the Music School into disrepute.'

The tide of marching feet swept onwards, words being thrown back over a shoulder, along the wide and endless concourse that ran the length of the Führerbau. On and on, it seemed to Emma, without end.

'I have never been in favour of your activities. First, demonstrations and placards, then a visit from the Kommissar, now this.'

'Why are we all marching like some man's army?'

The tide washed on, unstoppable, inexorable.

'We must guard our reputation. We in Germany do not expect anyone – staff, students or guests – to disobey the rules. It is quite unknown.'

Emma, booming with indignation, demanded: 'Any chance I might get an explanation before we finish this marathon?'

The tide stopped, as suddenly as if hitting a sea wall, stalled outside a large iron door. A door, Emma recalled, that was pointed out during their introductory tour, a door leading to the cellars, a door locked and out of bounds.

'This,' Frau Ludwig said, pointing. 'It is expressly forbidden to enter the cellar. I thought I made that clear on your first day.'

Emma shrugged.

Frau Direktor held up a key. 'This is a master key. One of my assistants has brought to my notice that two of your guests have removed the normal cellar key from its place at Reception.'

'News to me.'

'I think in a moment we shall discover that illegal entry has been made.'

Roper arrived at Emma's side and began gently edging her to the front of the crowd. 'When she opens that damned door,' he whispered, 'let's be the first to get inside.'

Frau Direktor made a great indignant show of inserting the master key into the lock. Emma was right behind. She could see a sliver of electric light below the door line. There were strange scuffling noises coming from the other side. Roper was no longer gentle; he was shoving her urgently to the right side of the Direktor's shoulder, the side where the gap would first appear.

Then the door grunted open with a metallic squeal from oil-starved hinges. Before officialdom could react, Emma was inside, standing on the top step, looking down a flight of stairs and into the interior.

No elegant marble here. No fine decorations. Just rough untreated concrete and functional pillars supporting the roof structure. Between these, in a dimly-lit area leading off into shadows and darkness, was a large wooden table, the sort Emma had seen during her visit to the Hofbräuhaus.

But no jolly drinkers sat here. Instead, a cluster of frightened figures was caught in a tableau of panic. She quickly identified them: America, Poland, China and Nagorno.

They came suddenly to life, like marionettes on strings. Laptops were hastily closed, other materials gathered in like lost treasures. She saw calculators, rules, maps and paperwork, highly coloured graphics and large photographs.

'Stop!'

She held out a commanding hand. 'Don't move.'

Emma and Roper were first down the steps. Unlike his friends, Wilkes was at the far end of the big table and had yet to reach his laptop.

Emma got there first.

She snapped it shut and placed it under her arm.

At first stunned, Wilkes erupted into life. 'Hey! You can't do that.' He stepped forward, a clouded, angry face, a threatening pose.

Emma stood her ground, meeting his gaze, daring him to get physical in front of witnesses. 'I'll take that. Evidence.'

'You can't just...'

Frau Direktor was not to be outdone. She stood on the top step and announced: 'You are not permitted in this cellar. You will please remove yourselves and all objects immediately.'

Muzalev was edging away, trying to slip unseen into the gloom in the far recesses of the cellar, but Emma's stare stopped the Nagorno delegate dead, drew him back and sent him with the others in the direction of the conference room.

'We know exactly what you've been doing,' Emma said, back on home territory, 'nothing less than holding an auction for the illegal sale of banned weaponry. It's illegal, against international treaties, against the law of the host nation. What I should be doing right now is calling on my friend, Kommissar Kasper, and having you arrested for illicit arms trading.'

Wilkes was scoffing. 'You can't prove any of that. We were simply discussing modern technology. Sure, we're interested in history... the history of warfare and weapons.'

'Save your fairy stories for the judge. We have the evidence.

Your laptop, incriminating documents and the affidavits of myself and Roper. We've been observing what's being going on... in cafés, taxis, basements and this hotel.'

'Pardon my French, but that's all horseshit. Your evidence!' He snorted in derision.

'Show him.'

Roper rolled out the glossy reproduction of China's Wuhan X5 and a picture of the American Super Nebraska. Then came the now straightened draft contract – still unsigned – for ten American Nebraskas. 'Obviously, we can add to that,' Roper said. 'Surveillance photographs of you lot trying to do a deal, our observations and what we have on your laptop.'

'Where'd you get that?' Wilkes demanded, trying to grab the contract.

'Shouldn't go leaving it about.'

'Horseshit again.' He stepped back, thwarted, then leaned forward. 'Look, lady, you've no idea who or what you're taking on here. You're out of your depth. You're in a dangerous place.'

She leaned an elbow, pointed a finger. 'You may represent some crooked corner of corporate America but you're not the big shot you think you are. Your own President has signed all the pledges to embargo these weapons. And with your fingerprints all over this deal you'll have zero credibility if word gets out.'

Wilkes shook his head. 'You really don't understand, do you? Let me draw the picture. Whatever some politico may have signed up to with the Russians, it can all be undone very quickly. Especially with a change at the White House. There's too much at stake. And besides, the CIA is on my side.'

She laughed. 'Think again, Mr Wilkes. You rate me as some dumb-arsed Brit with no connections, right? Try again. I know what I'm doing. You're going nowhere with the CIA.'

'And how the hell would you know that?'

She was waving that finger again. 'Ways and means. They're jumping off your bandwagon right now, back there in Langley. You're being set up for a fall. There's folks back there, political people, determined you're not going to succeed.'

'You're bullshitting again.'

'Think so?' She was grinning widely at him. 'Want to risk it?'

Another long silence. Then she was at him again. 'You've got two choices. Hop on a plane and clear off. Or stay with me, keep your nose clean, no more arms trading – and do your job.'

'My job?' Uttered with incredulity.

'Yes, your job; to contribute to this conference on the American historical perspective.'

He spluttered.

'The lectern is yours. In two days' time.'

He shot out a hand. 'My laptop!'

'Sorry. Stays with me. My insurance.'

Roper was shaking his head at her. 'I don't think you quite realise what you've taken on here,' he said, looking around, checking they were alone. 'Trying to bully these people... it's a form of madness. Wilkes and his kind, they're a dangerous breed; they're not going to lie down and take it.'

Emma gave him one of her stares. 'They'll have to get up very early to put one over on me.'

'Look,' he said, 'be sensible. Be reasonable. We now know what we've suspected for some time. Half these delegates are bogus. This is a disaster of a conference. Why don't you just pack up and go home? It's going nowhere fast.'

Her face was a thunderstorm. 'Now, you look! When I start something, I don't stop. Not until it's finished.' She expunged from her memory her failings back at Cambridge, her half-hearted dedication to medieval monasteries. 'Don't doubt me, Roper, I'm going to win. I don't care who or what gets in the way, I'm going to win.'

He sighed. He had already spent an uncomfortable twenty minutes mollifying Frau Direktor who had been issuing threats of eviction for the 'English nuisances'. Eventually, she had agreed to move them out of the conference hall and into a side room. Removing an irritant from public view was the least she would agree to.

Roper turned his attention back to Emma: 'How do you expect me to protect you if you go out of your way to look for trouble?' And then he raised a questioning finger. 'And what was with all that guff you gave Wilkes about political opposition back home? The CIA and Langley? As if you'd know!'

'That's what I don't understand about you, Roper, you're so damned credulous.'

'Meaning?'

'With all your years of experience, with all that much-vaunted expertise, you still don't know there's no bigger sucker for a glib line than another huckster.' He began to laugh as she added: 'You'd think they'd see it coming but they don't. One conman outfoxes another every time.'

'Except that, in this instance, for conman read conwoman.'

'Convinced him, didn't I? He's worried. Seriously worried.'

'Still a dangerous man to cross.'

She fixed him with a grin. 'Don't you just crave the thrill? The chill of fear running just below the surface. Lets you know you're alive. Trail your coat, see what happens.'

'Good God, I'm in league with a madwoman.'

~

Emma quite enjoyed shocking Roper. When he asked what she would do if someone came for her – Wilkes or a hired thug, on a dark night in some quiet street, a narrow alley – she flicked open a pouch on her waist belt and showed him her brother's latest piece of self-defence equipment.

'Knuckles!' Roper looked as if he was going to have a fit. 'Strictly illegal. Put 'em away! Get rid of them. Don't you realise you could get arrested simply for possessing those things, let alone using them?'

'Don't worry,' she said, 'I won't get arrested.'

CHAPTER EIGHTEEN

I t was warm, dry and cosy. The waitresses were attentive and the menu was a fantasia of afternoon delights. Pictures along the walls, some grainy photographs but mostly sketches, told of an older, calmer, more elegant Munich: men in top hats and tails with enormous whiskers; ladies in frills and large bows; hansom cabs pulled by white horses with flowers in their halters; bystanders lounging, as if content just to stare. A story, these images seemed to suggest, of privilege and style in a city yet to be sullied by the 20th century, the most destructive century yet.

Emma sat alone at a corner table, the only person with a single cup of coffee and a briefcase. All around her there was a flurry of excitement at the arrival of plates of apple strudel and raspberry cheesecake. No matter how figure-conscious you might be, Rischarts Café announced itself as a venue not to be missed.

She had made the mistake of starting out too early for her appointment and had tried window shopping to kill time, drifting with the crowds along the wide pavements but unable to concentrate. She had assumed the city's renowned drinking culture would be conducted largely underground in smoky cellars. Not so, she discovered, glancing in at the Augustiner beer hall which, like the Hofbräuhaus, was a ground-level emporium with a voluminous menu and a crowded but stately clientele. Should she? No. She was too keyed-up, too eager to open another door in her great quest, to do anything other than plan and plot. The coffee was hot and bitter: just right for the fight. That she would have a fight did not seem much in doubt. She recalled all the warnings; even Professor Chadwick had talked about 'obstacles'. All sorts of predatory ghosts might be expected to emerge from the Gestapo archive, he said, both overt and covert, intent on blocking her, probably with fatal intent.

She thought about the man she was to meet, slipping from her case the preliminary notes she had made on Herr Max Huber. She glanced again through his achievements and publications. Chadwick had broken the dam to fix up this meeting; now it was her task to breach the bureaucratic wall; to defeat all the blocking, parrying, denying and fending off.

You had to know the background, Chadwick had stressed, to appreciate the climate of fear and the distaste in official circles. The archive was incendiary. The Bavarian state hadn't called in Huber lightly; they had closed off the new archive, barring all access as if dealing with a state secret. Most officials privately wished the files had never been found. Many a family was in a state of anxiety about what might be made public. There were even concerns about the likely reaction of certain shadowy groups of former police officers and their modern supporters. Huber himself would be under pressure to find a way to neutralise the toxic nature of any disclosures.

Emma knew she had to be ready to agree to the most stringent conditions to win a tiny window into its contents but the little twirly wheel in her head, that spinning beach ball of the computer world, was running at 110 revolutions a minute to produce a likely pitch to breach the expected wall of obstruction.

'Yes!' she said out loud, banging a fist on the table, making the coffee cup rattle, the teaspoon jump and the people at the next table stare at her. She would defeat all those who thought to thwart her.

Anger welled up. She wanted to do the right thing by her grandfather, to discover what happened to him in those dark days of 1938, however ugly, brutal or murderous it might turn out to be. She would explore, discover and laud his sacrifice.

She pushed the cup away, checked her watch and went out into the crowds on the Kaufinger, heading eastwards toward the Marienplatz and the town hall, steeling herself for the coming struggle.

The man was tall to the point of gangling, had spectacles and a crew-cut hairstyle. But what she really didn't expect was the big smile of welcome and – despite Berkeley being on his CV – the uninhibited transatlantic greeting. And young. Still in his mid-thirties.

'Hi there, Emma, nice to see you; great to meet you; heard all about you; come right in; sit yourself down.'

She couldn't stop smiling at the contrast to Professor Chadwick's cluttered cubbyhole back at Cambridge. Here all was pristine order. The architecture might have looked like a museum but the organisation didn't. Everything was arranged in neatly stacked and shelved boxes. The only things on Max Huber's desk were a single sheet of A4, a desk tidy and a felt pad.

'I've heard about your project,' he said. 'Fascinating stuff. Great idea. I'll be most intrigued to read your final conclusions.'

She beamed back at him. 'You must come over,' she said. 'We're only just across town. Give us a talk. Tell us your role.'

He laughed. 'Don't miss a trick! Don't waste a single opportunity. One of my mottos too.'

They both laughed and Emma couldn't believe her good fortune. Huber was a revelation. She'd anticipated someone of advanced years and unapproachable but this man seemed completely American in tone, descended – according to her notes – from Silesian refugees but international in outlook.

'I'm under instructions to be very strict about access,' he said, waving a dismissive hand. 'You wouldn't believe the number of people who want to put a stop to it all. A lot of old cops are quaking in their boots... or rather, their families are. Big reputations at stake. That's why we have to lock all this stuff in the vaults every night.'

Emma didn't believe in wasting opportunities. 'Tell me how you operate. And why they picked you?'

Huber went into the mechanics of an enormous cataloguing job. 'I guess my lords and masters need someone with the right international credentials to give this job the respectability they crave. But the plan is still the same. Detox the archive. No fallout. No blame.'

'Still, a great opportunity for you.'

'Too good to miss.'

'Pity,' she said. 'I was quite looking forward to a fight with some crusty old bureaucrat.'

He laughed and said something about the complexity of his challenge.

She said: 'Just follow the facts to wherever they lead. Like any good historian.'

'Wish it were that simple.' He sighed, then brightened.

'Look, let's get out of this museum. Somewhere more congenial for a talk.'

They walked out past his unsmiling secretary. 'My gatekeeper,' he said. 'Very efficient, very necessary.'

It wasn't even lunchtime, yet the place had already taken on that unique rowdy atmosphere of a Munich beer hall. The long wooden picnic-style benches were filling with drinkers – mostly tourists but who was objecting? The foot-stomper band was belting out thigh-slapping Bavarian fare and waitresses in dirndl peasant dresses were dashing up the aisles holding high with one hand trays of litre glasses full of amber liquid, froth thick at the top, as required.

Huber leaned over and bellowed in Emma's ear: 'Not so much a beer cellar as a cathedral to the worship of alcohol.'

She nodded. No reply needed. Or possible in the din.

The Hofbräuhaus, entered down stone steps from the street, was enormous; a block across and so deep you couldn't glimpse its end unless you stayed entirely sober. Churchlike arches stretched to a high vaulted roof.

Emma did a double take at the sight of a huge hog's head carried on a wooden tray by a waitress clutching two full glasses in her other hand.

Then she shouted: 'Is this where you bring all your visitors?'

'Always.'

They ordered beers: dunkel, or deep dark brown, for him, white wheat beer for her. Then he cupped his hands again. 'You may have trouble believing this but the Hofbräuhaus is a very historic place. And relevant to your researches.'

'Is there somewhere a bit quieter?'

An alcove furthest from the oompah foot-stompers and the

singing, swaying, roaring benches afforded a modicum of calm sufficient to make normal conversation possible.

'A favourite meeting place for Adolf Hitler,' Huber said. 'The Nazis began life here in Munich. He used the beer halls and cellars in this city to whip up the hysteria of the masses. You've seen his ranting speeches on the newsreels. Well...' He looked around and pointed. 'He perfected them here. In fact, he made his first big speech from a room upstairs. That was the moment he really arrived. From then on, he packed in the crowds.'

Emma put her glass on the table and looked down. 'That rather takes the shine off this place,' she said.

Huber had to return to the town hall and Emma to her afternoon session but they agreed to meet up again at seven in the Jakobs-stübchen restaurant. When she arrived he was anxious to talk about the archive and his work but Emma's focus was not on the big picture. Instead, her interest was centred on just one day, one incident. She hadn't lost the mental image of her grandfather in that cauldron of hostility that was the Führer building – his arrest, the pandemonium of shouting, grabbing and dragging and whatever came next – but she didn't immediately press the point, or reveal her family connection, aware that her timing had to be right.

When the serious conversation began to falter they talked about families – mainly his childhood in a windswept marshland area next to the North Sea where the tradition was to drink a very particular type of tea served up in miniature teacups with huge lumps of sugar. Then they discovered a mutual interest in sports cars. It was a few short steps from the restaurant to where he had parked his Mercedes Kompressor; it was only natural that he would want to demonstrate how well it drove; only natural that he should ask her back to his place to demonstrate the brewing and taking of East Frisian tea.

When they arrived she looked around at the fourth-floor apartment: a one-person-only kitchen, a corridor bathroom, and a living room dominated by a secretaire that looked like a refugee from the Wittelsbachs' palace.

'Yours?'

'I wish. Rented.'

A large textbook tome was out on the coffee table for her inspection and the conversation became serious once more on why Huber's archive was so special. Gestapo headquarters in Munich had been bombed and destroyed by fire, he said. Everyone assumed the records had been consumed by the flames; only a select few knew they had already been removed in expectation of bomb damage and stored in a special place, the Gestapo deluding themselves they had some sort of post-war future. Emma already knew all about the find in the Merkers mine but she resisted the temptation to cut him off, instead waiting for the right moment to slip into the conversation the question that had been gnawing away at her ever since Louise Latimer had revealed her grandfather's gatecrashing of the Munich conference.

She was thumbing through one of his tomes, looking at the chapter headings. He paused for breath. Now, she decided. Now was the moment to put their new-found friendship to the test. 'I've a special reason for asking this,' she said. 'My particular interest is just one day. An incident that happened on September 30, 1938 at the Führer building. Could you trace the case file for that date, do you think?'

'Ah! September 30; what a day! A date to reckon with. The big conference and all that.' He shrugged. 'The archive goes back to 1933. We haven't got anywhere near 1938 yet. But I'll see.'

He smiled back at her and she sighed in relief. She hadn't pushed him too far. He hadn't objected, cited security, ground rules or the need for secrecy. Or gone cool on her.

'I'll let you know,' he said.

She knew then that this could prove a useful relationship.

CHAPTER NINETEEN

Martina had been remiss. No sign of her at the conference for the past few days and an empty channel, as far as Emma was concerned, in her quest for information on her grandfather's hidden history.

Buttons needed to be pushed, and hard. Martina needed to be coaxed, persuaded, if necessary confronted. Initial messages went unanswered and calls were blocked but when she did get through, Emma launched herself into an angry rant: 'Martina, you're holding out on me; I'm getting very disappointed. I thought we had an agreement; you remember, the one we discussed a few days ago... and you've given no apology or reason for your absence.'

There was a stuttering response from the other end of the line, the only clear word being 'problems'.

'What happened to my contact? My resister?'

'It's not as easy as you think.' Pause. 'No one wants to put themselves at risk. I can't find anyone who wants to open up to you.'

Emma had a suspicion. 'Is your father behind this? Is he sheltering someone?'

'We try to shelter everyone.'

'Is he worried about what may come out of the Gestapo archive?'

'What?'

'I'm sorry but there are certain obvious logical possibilities here. Your father may be trying to protect *himself*, rather than others, from accusations emerging from the archive.'

'That's ridiculous! Father is a man of great integrity.' A deep breath, followed by a distinct loss of Martina's habitual diffidence. 'My family is untainted by the past. My grandfather fought as an infantry soldier in the Great War. He was too old for the Second; my father too young, nothing but a boy.'

'Boys went into the Hitler Youth.'

'That's provocative.'

'I'm only pointing out the obvious possibilities.'

'Well, they aren't possibilities, they're lies.'

'If it's not your father then someone else, someone close, an uncle perhaps, or his boss at the university, the vice chancellor, a fellow professor. Don't tell me there's a branch of Munich life without a skeleton rattling around in it somewhere. Gestapo operative, informant, denouncer, supporter, cheerleader, collaborator, Party member...'

'Absurd and mistaken.' Martina was finding her voice. 'The new Germany has thrown off its ghastly past.'

'If you're whiter than white, then prove it! Give me a contact. Open up the channels. Stop hiding. Let the truth come out.'

Next day Emma discovered she had pushed the right buttons. The good name of the family mattered. Its self-image required vindication. Talk of guilty secrets had prized open the clam. She received a terse text giving a time and place: Blumen Strasse 16 at five o'clock.

She was quickly back on the phone. 'Tell me more!'

'Johannes has agreed to speak to you.'

'Who's he?'

'Discretion, please. Don't ask.'

'Johannes who?'

'Just Johannes.'

'What does he know?'

'He's our contact; that's all I can say.'

'What's with all the secrecy? The German Resistance are today's heroes. Remember? The big pitch you gave at the conference?'

'Officially, perhaps, but only on paper. Not really. Not deep down. Not hereabouts.' There was a short silence before Martina issued what sounded like a rehearsed disclaimer. 'It must be stressed, you must take care. Risky for all of us. This is not the friendly city it may seem.'

Emma couldn't help it, couldn't draw back. 'Dark echoes from the past then?' she said.

But the phone was silent. Martina was gone.

Emma found a city map to look up Blumen, a little street way out in the suburbs. Pretty undistinguished territory but at least the name meant flower. At five o'clock, would she come up smelling sweet?

As soon as he heard the news Roper grabbed his coat. 'I'm coming with you,' he said.

'No. I'll do this on my own.'

'Could be dangerous. A trap.'

'Two of us will frighten him off. I sense a great nervousness. I need to be as near invisible as possible.'

Roper shook his head but she insisted. 'You stay,' she said. 'I'll phone you with updates.'

By 4.15 she was at the tram stop just around the corner in Müller Strasse, ignoring the smell of new bread wafting out from the corner bakery that was usually so tempting.

She waited. A threatening afternoon: cloud, a touch chilly but no wind blasting down from the Alps. She got to thinking about Johannes; what sort of information might he have? She let two 17s go and noticed a figure standing on the other side of the street: quite still, clearly with no urgent purpose, dressed in a pork-pie hat and feather, and looking her way.

She'd been in the city long enough to recognise traditional dress for the Bavarian male – fine at weekends, she thought, but a little showy for a weekday. Finally, an 18 ground to a halt with a juddering squeal of brakes, the destination indicator showing Gondrellplatz. She boarded, offering up her strip ticket and cancelling six of the thirteen stripes at the machine for the journey to the church of St Philippus.

The tram took her past the Sendlinger Tor and the main rail terminus, its bell clanging at each junction, accompanied by grinding metallic protestations on tight corners. Emma filled her time by examining the other passengers. It had rained that morning and the woman opposite still emitted the familiar odour of damp clothing. She was in the lead car of a crowded two-car set. A large woman sitting a couple of seats back got up to go to the exit doors, leaving a clear view of the passengers behind. One of them was the man in the pork-pie hat.

Emma was startled. He must surely have bounded across that busy main road to get on board in time.

She began to look at him more closely, a growing sense that there was something familiar about him. Was it the scarred nose? No. The grey jacket with the green collarband?

She thought he was conscious of her presence but trying to disguise it, staring unwaveringly out of a side window.

Emma examined the man's jacket more closely. A row of big brass embossed buttons lined the front. And one was missing.

A chill of recognition came to her. She slipped her hand into her pocket and produced the brass button she had kept from the melee on the Führerbau steps on her first day in the city... and despite the distance between them, it looked remarkably similar to the others on Pork Pie's jacket.

She stared at him. This was the button she had snatched from the front of the angry demonstrator who'd been screaming threats and abuse in the midst of a frightening display of hostility to the presence of English historians, a demo that had almost resulted in their precipitate expulsion. No doubt about it: she was being tailed. Her choice: confront, evade or ignore?

The 18 was already on Westend Strasse and, she noticed, it had started to rain. Passengers were readying umbrellas and donning vast swishy overcoats. The church was two stops up ahead. She made her decision. As soon as the driver announced Flintsbacher as the next halt, using the tinny tannoy that dropped his voice several octaves below the human original, she went to stand by the doorway of the lead car, keeping one eye on Pork Pie.

He had responded by moving back to the trailer car and standing ready by the door. When the doors flapped open Emma stepped down to the street, turning back towards the trailer car, walking in the gutter quickly to catch up to the queue of boarders at the rear. She just managed to join the last of them, stepping back on board before the doors swished shut.

The tram moved off.

Had she fooled her tail?

Emma moved to the window of the rear car and looked back.

Pork Pie was on the pavement, staring at his disappearing

quarry, rain spilling from the brim of his hat, the feather drooping in apparent sympathy.

She grinned and waved.

At the next stop, the church, she got off and walked swiftly past a clock tower and tall blocks of blue-and-white flats, turning down a small suburban street lined with smart, three-storey modern houses sporting immaculate white fronts, dormer windows, balconies and shutters. She cursed herself for not bringing a hat. She passed neatly trimmed shrubs and garages, spotted the sign for Blumen and began counting off the numbers.

Then she checked her pace. Just about where Number 16 should be two police cars and an ambulance were slewed across the road.

She approached cautiously. The building was a small yellowing apartment block with a main door protected by an entry pad. Standard practice for the city. Inside the entrance hall she could see a crowd of people. Outside, there were bystanders.

A postman laden with a big shoulder bag approached, his task to feed the bank of individual resident postboxes that festooned the hallways of all the apartments in the city. He had a pass.

The door creaked open for him, momentarily stalling before the spring mechanism returned it to closed. Emma stepped in behind him.

Outside the ground-floor flat the crowd waited, expectant. The front door was ajar. Emma approached and pushed it open. Before she could put more than one foot across the threshold a voice called 'Stop!'

A familiar voice.

Then she saw him. Kommissar Kasper.

He pointed a finger. 'Emma Drake! What are you doing this

far out of the city? Not your territory. Shouldn't you be at your hotel?'

She shrugged.

'And crossing a police line... Why is that?'

Emma, still momentarily thrown, consulted the piece of paper on which she had scribbled the details. 'I've an appointment,' she said.

'This is a police investigation scene. Do you not understand that? Who is it you're looking for?'

Emma hesitated. Should she say? Was it really so sensitive a matter?

'Don't you know?'

She pursed her lips, scratched her neck. 'Now, why would you be here when I arrive to have a discussion with a fellow historian, I wonder?'

'A fellow historian?' It was almost a sneer. 'And who would that be?'

'Johannes.'

Kasper shook his head. 'No Johannes here.'

'A contact who wanted to discuss the past with me. Your dark past. And now, here *you* are. Any connection?'

'No Johannes here,' he insisted.

'Any ghosts from your past, Herr Kommissar? Now, let me see... The Ettblock... Wasn't that once the home of the SS?'

Kasper's face reddened but the moment passed when an ambulance edged its way close to the doorway of Number 16, doors were thrown open and two paramedics approached. Emma stepped to one side, hoping the distraction would throw Kasper off his guard, that perhaps she could sneak further into the flat to discover the mysterious Johannes, while he dealt with the newcomers.

'You stay there!' Kasper instructed hotly, as he escorted the crew inside, but he managed to position himself so that he could keep her in sight the whole time. 'As I've just told you,' he called, 'there's no Johannes here.'

She drew in a deep breath and put her hands on her hips, making a great show of her frustration and consulting her piece of paper once more.

The two paramedics returned, pushing at a wheeled stretcher. On it lay a figure covered by a thick red blanket. From her position, Emma could see only a tiny white face, male, bald and old.

'Well?' Kasper demanded again. 'How many times?'

'Was that him? Johannes?' she demanded.

'That was Herr Buttner. Herr Herbert Buttner.'

'What–'

'We await official confirmation but off the record, he's dead; satisfied?'

'How did he die?'

'Not that it's any business of yours, but natural causes, I believe. A heart attack.'

The ambulance had its doors shut. It pulled slowly away.

'And now it's time for you to leave. To return to your hotel.'

But Emma was anything but contrite. 'I'm just beginning to wonder why someone of such elevated rank as yourself should be called in to investigate a case involving a heart attack.'

Kasper's habitual studious expression evaporated. 'Miss Drake, I do not intend to discuss my caseload with you. Now go! Or I'll have you arrested.'

Emma's shoulders slumped.

Outside on the pavement it had stopped raining and she shook out her damp hair. Then she produced her phone but all attempts to relay to Martina news of this latest frustration were unsuccessful. Martina was not available to speak, a university receptionist intoned, and there was no one at the university who could help her.

A blank-out. Another roadblock.

It was then that Emma saw him once more – Pork Pie – eyeing her, grinning, from across the street.

It was almost too much. Anger flared briefly as she again felt the big brass button torn from his coat that was still languishing in her pocket. For a moment she considered crossing the street and ripping off all his other buttons, trampling them with a satisfying vengeance into the muddy verge, but then she stopped. The grinning figure was so unsubtle that they – whoever *they* were – could never again use him to tail her. Clearly that could not be the purpose, so perhaps the real aim was to warn her off.

In which case they could go hang.

CHAPTER TWENTY

Max Huber gave her a long, sympathetic look of appraisal, then led her inside the restaurant. He had called her up, all businesslike, and said he would like to 'update her on progress', but when she arrived to meet him outside the Schlesischer Bahnhof her expression must have radiated frustration and fury.

'Clearly, you need some serious soothing,' he said.

'What I need is some good news,' she said. 'To offset my latest disaster.' In answer to a quizzical eyebrow, she added: 'One very dead Resistance contact.'

He sighed. 'Oh dear... but before you tell me all about it, I want you to relax.' He stared at her hard, as if trying to put her in a trance. 'Relax. And embrace the German experience.'

Emma sighed. 'Relaxation? About as likely as sunshine in the middle of a snowstorm.'

It was indeed a chilly evening, so they entered the warm glow of the restaurant just around the corner from the Marienplatz and the town hall. The Schlesischer was named after a terminus in Berlin where once upon a happy time Huber's parents were able to board a train for their home in the far eastern tip of Germany. At least, they could before the war. He made a little gesture of resignation. 'Alas, all gone,' he said. 'Given, by kindly Uncle Joe, to Poland.'

She knew what he was saying. Other people had suffered worse disasters.

Outside, the wind was sharp but on warmer days this place was popular with diners sitting at pavement tables. Inside, a hum of subdued conversation emanated from polished teak tables laid out with embossed red napkins in candlelit corners. Emma did her best to control her angry impulses. She needed this man. *Don't push him*, she told herself. And she had been knowing enough to wear the wrapover dress she had bought down by the Opera House – just around the corner in a pedestrian-and-tram-only street where the windows boasted the names of Otto Kern, Beate Heymann, Kalliste and Coccinelle. Huber was set on lowering the tension, on creating a relaxed atmosphere, introducing her to the delights of quark cakes, yeast dumplings and all manner of strange dishes from Eastern Europe. He was also intent on indigenous pleasure – the Munich kind as well as from his native Silesia. 'You must come over for lunch,' he said, 'but it has to be an early lunch. Before twelve.'

Emma managed an amused look. 'That early?'

'To eat Weisswurst. White sausage. A great local speciality. Boiled in a thin skin. But it's an absolute rule. Must be eaten by midday. Definitely not the afternoon.'

'And if I linger mistakenly into a few minutes after the magic hour?'

'You turn into a frog.'

She wondered if he really had anything of substance to tell her. 'And would the German experience perhaps include any useful little pieces of information, by any chance?'

But he didn't seem to hear. He was into a heartfelt

reminiscence about the involuntary flight of his family given half an hour to pack up and get out of their home in 1945. But there was no bitterness. He was still the tall, friendly, amusing fellow with the loud laugh. She still had him down as her primary source, her best hope of inside information, but knew that Roper was both sceptical and resentful.

'If you get into an emotional entanglement with this man,' Roper told her before she boarded her taxi, 'it'll be a complete distraction and you'll lose focus on your goal.'

'No question of entanglements,' she said hotly. 'He's a prime source, co-operative, beyond what he's supposed to be.'

Roper looked askance, acting, she thought, like some sort of jealous lover, so she told him sharply: 'There's good stuff to come from the archive. He's digging for us; he's on our side.'

'He would say that.'

Emma put this short-tempered spat out of mind as the conversation with Huber roved over the 11th century, the Teutonic Knights, Frederick the Great, native American Indians, various eccentric professors and campuses they had known, then shifted to cars, horses and music. Huber was keen to show off his new music centre, back at his flat. A little warning light lit up in her mind; she'd steered clear of what Roper would have described as 'entanglements'. She was still wary. Still on her guard. Emma had an unhappy history; years of fending off a spurned suitor. But when she looked at Huber again, at this open-hearted man, she decided he was not of the same ilk.

He must have sensed her change of mood because he said: 'Right, you want to know all about Grandfather,' and grinned at her hugely, completely unaffected by her impatience. He seemed the sort never to take offence; a rainwater roof sort of guy, impervious to vagaries of the conversational weather. 'When you told me about the strange people at your conference it rang a bell. Reminded me of some friends in America. One of them is doing a research project on the US in the thirties.'

Emma's eyebrows shot up. 'The thirties? Any links of interest to us? To Wilkes, for instance?'

He nodded. 'A powerful family of special interest to my friend. And especially interesting to you, I think.'

She looked at him keenly. He was grinning. She smiled back. 'Come on, don't be a tease; give!'

He chuckled then produced some sheets of paper, a printout of a message he'd received earlier in the day, and passed them over. She took them eagerly.

Max, here's the stuff you asked for. The Wilkes family was one of three prominent leaders of corporate America who had traded with the Nazis right up to the declaration of war between the US and Germany, dealing in raw materials such as tungsten, oil, currency and banking facilities. They even carried on beyond the opening of hostilities — a point at which 'trading with the enemy' became illegal. They used their contacts inside the US administration to obtain a special presidential dispensation, even though the President himself knew nothing about it.

She looked up. 'That all?'

He took the sheets back, folding them away. 'That's it, so far. If there's any more, I'll pass it on.'

'Stunning,' she said, breathing out. 'What a bunch of

crooks!' She balled a fist. 'Wilkes! A family that still flouts every convention and treaty.'

After this she looked at Huber in a new light. Clearly, she would do well to bring him more into play. It would be foolish not to make the most of his willingness to help.

He was calling for the bill. 'There are so many wonderful things to see in this city,' he said, 'you can't go home without some indulgence.'

'I've a big job on, remember?' she said. 'One dead contact, hostile police... I can't afford to lose focus.'

'I insist,' he said. 'If the weather's better tomorrow, I have a special treat in mind.'

Strollers flowed around them: families, singles, groups, couples, children, dogs, cyclists. All Munich seemed to be here, relaxed and carefree on a day the sun decided to emerge from the clouds and the temperature lifted to spring-like levels.

'This is what makes the city,' Huber said. 'Without the English Garden, it would be only half the place it is.'

Emma looked around. They were seated at a table in a vast tarmac area: dozens of chairs, tables and benches. This was the start of a great park extending for several miles alongside the River Isar; to one side the enormous wooden structure known as the Chinese Tower, focal point for outdoor drinkers by day and by night; close by, kiosks dispensing beer, sausages and pretzels. You could eat around the clock here, from snacks to four-course meals, in between walking the dog, paddling with the children, taking coffee at elegant island cafés admiring the swans, or boating on a lake. A vast city playground of grass, trees, bushes, plants and flowers.

Huber had a litre glass of Doppelbock. Emma was doing the

rounds of all the main Munich beers – Hofbräu, Paulaner, Löwenbräu and Augustiner; this last classified as 'definitely the prince' in her estimation. 'You needed to get away for a bit,' Huber said, 'you were getting far, far too uptight.'

The atmosphere seemed to be working. Emma gazed at those passing by her with a keen eye. There was a man of middle years in a tiny, green, felt hunter's hat dwarfed by a large head and full beard. Mysterious badges festooned the green felt. She grinned. He was 'the Pimple', she decided.

A woman with jeans twenty-four inches too short, an orange jacket and bright-blue floral hairclip sauntered by. 'Fashion plate,' she said.

Next were a tourist in a multicoloured jumper (Cable Stitch), a smoker with huge red-rouged lips (The Kisser) and an old lady with a wide-brimmed black waterproofed hat (Girl Scout). Huber was chortling over Hawkface, Donald Duck and Mr Bean. 'How does your professor fare, back in England?' he wanted to know.

She looked at him solemnly for long moment. 'The Frog? You may yet get the chance to judge for yourself.'

'Aha!'

They returned to his office on the fourth floor of the new town hall, built around 1860, where Huber's 'gatekeeper' drew him aside for an earnest conversation. He was staring hard at some papers on his desk, then looking Emma's way.

He smiled broadly as he said: 'Your lucky day, Emma; I've just been given some good news. About your grandfather.'

CHAPTER TWENTY-ONE

Emma immediately brightened. The gloom that pervaded her since the death of Johannes lifted. So did her eyebrows. A big smile of anticipation – then she saw it in his expression: doubt.

He feared he had raised her expectations too far; had glimpsed, perhaps for the first time, the depth of her expectation. A halfway house of discovery would never be good enough.

'Well,' he said slowly, expression clouding, 'as far as it goes, anyway.'

The eyebrows dropped. The good news was tinged with disappointment, even before its revelation.

'It's significant,' he said in a mollifying voice.

Emma sighed, struggling to contain conflicting emotions: excitement mixed with frustration; that here again, yet again, she was about to crash into another roadblock, another dead end. 'Well?' she said.

'I've just discovered,' he said carefully, 'that ten hours after the initial arrest, Bradley Wilkes was transferred out of police jurisdiction.'

There was a silence while she struggled with the implications.

'Don't you see?' he urged. 'He left police custody. It means he survived. He was still alive after ten hours and he came through the worst they could do to him. Probably the ten worst hours of his life. But he was still fit enough to be shipped out.'

'And what state would he have been in?'

Silence. Then he said: 'You'll have to make the most of what we've got. Stay hopeful.'

Face still bleak, she said: 'And to whose jurisdiction was he sent?'

He shrugged the shrug of a bringer of good tidings who had come up short. 'Sorry. Not clear.'

Still bleak, she said: 'Dachau?'

She was voicing the fear of thousands. Perhaps millions. That they had merely exchanged a fast death for a slow one.

He was silent.

'You must have some clue?'

'Kilometres, Emma. Kilometres of it. Just endless paperwork. We're still digging, still struggling. I've already diverted two researchers on to this.'

But she wouldn't let go. 'When someone is transferred from one jurisdiction to another, there's always a statement about who takes over. About the new destination.' She looked at him hard, willing him, not letting him off the hook. 'There has to be some reference to the proper authority he was released into. They wouldn't let him go without the right authorisation, the right paperwork.' She made him squirm; she didn't care, she was unrelenting.

He sighed and said: 'All we've got are some strange initials.'

'Initials?'

He pulled a scrap of paper from a pocket and consulted it.

'This won't mean anything to you. It doesn't mean anything to us.'

She waited.

He sighed. 'AMTX.' He shrugged again and added: 'A completely anonymous bureaucratic footprint.'

She pursed her lips, pulled out her diary, found a pen at the bottom of her case, made him repeat the letters and made a careful note.

Then she looked at him searchingly. 'Someone, somewhere will know what it means,' she said.

≈

Bradley C Wilkes, The Führerbau, 10am, Friday 30 September, 1938

Survival... that's my goal and my fear. The prospect of it and the price to be paid for it.

It's been six hours of hell in the Führerbau from an angry Müller facing Göring's ten o'clock deadline. No time for clever tricks, elaborate ploys, not even to get me back to his favourite cellar. Just violence and lies, violence and half-truths, violence and names. That's my one advantage: he hasn't had time to check them out.

Finally, when Göring reappears, I'm still tied to the chair, though this time in a concrete cell of a room in the basement, and Müller's report doesn't seem to please him. I begin to tremble. Will the fat man grant him more time? Will I get thrown back into the bear pit?

But then a sour-faced individual in civilian clothing signs a clipboard and waits while they release me. He leads me with scant sign of sympathy to another room where a medic in field grey patches me up. The bill for the ten hours spent under the malign influence of the regime's most infamous secret policeman is probably less than most – but for me, American citizen Bradley Wilkes, it's quite severe enough: a broken nose, a couple of smashed teeth, a dislocated shoulder, a scatter of cigarette burns and bruises too many to count.

I have difficulty walking, so my escort propels me roughly upstairs, out of the front entrance and down the wide staircase to the pavement – the eight steps so familiar to me, the ones on which I have spent many hours waiting for some momentous news announcement. There are no newsmen waiting now; no friends to be seen; instead, I'm expecting some kind of closed prison van.

Surprise! It's a big old open saloon.

I'm bundled into the back seat and my taciturn escort ignores all inquiries as to our destination, but at least he's not violent. And, again to my surprise, I can watch our progress as the car crosses the Brienner Strasse into Meiser, past the giant open space of the Königsplatz and the intimidating Temples of Honour with their parading SS guards, then sedately into Karl Strasse.

Another familiar piece of Third Reich bureaucratic territory. A fairly unremarkable street of five-storey Party offices and for a moment I think they're delivering me into the hands of Putzi Hanfstangl, the international press counsellor who holds court at Number 18 and issues anodyne homilies on the progress of the regime to sceptical members of the press corps.

But no, we pass on by the familiar blue front door and stop instead outside Number 30. I look up. There's a porcelain Madonna set in a tiny alcove on the first-floor frontage and garret-like dormers peer over the tiled roof. A notice announces: NSDAP Legal Office, Treasurer.

I'm ushered up a wide staircase with green tiling and an ornate banister, along a corridor and into a room which brings me up short: the wall cladding is a shade of silky magnolia, topped off at head height with lush leaf-green paintwork. In one corner is a doorway containing golden ochre translucent panels shaped like a mullioned church window.

I'm waved to a seat by a small man sitting at a small desk.

He's wearing civilian clothes and I notice his plain brown pullover. One hand cups his chin. He has tiny eyes, protruding lips and he holds his head slightly to one side like a quizzical bird inspecting a suspect perch.

'I've been doing some digging into your family background,' he says. A quiet voice; no introductions; no explanation, no emblem of office or status. 'I think you could be of use to us,' he says. 'You've made a bad mistake but this is your way out.'

Collaborate with this detestable regime? Unthinkable! But I don't say so. Instead, I mumble through my busted lip and smashed teeth: 'Why should I agree?'

'Think of what you'll get in return.' His hands come together in a little steeple of prayer. 'Your life, reunion with a member of your family. What more could you hope for, given your situation? Of course, I could throw you back into Müller's cellars. Might have to if you don't agree.' He sits back in a relaxed, comfortable pose, eyeing me unhurriedly, and adds: 'Think it over.'

The very idea! I've been writing warning pieces and broadcasting the details of the bullying, imprisoning, confiscating nature of this evil regime since they took over five years ago, trying to warn the rest of Europe what's in store for them. Five years of barbarity, five years of preparation for war. I let the silence stretch. Who is this man? Eventually, I say: 'How could I possibly help you?'

He sits forward and demonstrates a surprising grasp of the mechanics of American international commerce – and, in particular, the part in it played by other members of my family. He lays it all out: the company names, the family tree.

'But I don't speak to them,' I object. 'I know nothing of business.'

He ignores that. 'Here's the deal.' He starts talking fast and my brow furrows. 'A certain task, requiring your skill at persuasion, your many worldwide contacts, your family's expertise...'

I'm shaking my head but he's sitting back again in that comfortable chair. I again protest my ignorance of commerce but he's insistent I must use the web of contacts and connections he's convinced the Wilkes family possesses. The offer of collaboration is a stark one, painful and detestable, but guilt is dragging me ever closer to acceptance; guilt and concern for my friend and fellow resister, Emil Jarek, now suffering the extremes of Müller's vengeance. Emil was mad to take a pistol into the Führer's room – ruining our chances of success – and I'm angry with him – but anger does not extend to rejection and abandonment.

I say to this strange, accommodating little man in brown: 'I want more. I want another life.'

He shakes his head.

'I want Emil Jarek out.'

'No. Müller already has a rope around his neck. Some things are just not possible.'

'Then it's no deal!' I snap back, suddenly full of bravado, ignoring the awful prospect of a return to Müller. 'Throw me back... and lose.'

'Think about it,' the little man insists.

Who is this fox? I wonder – certainly not out of the usual mould of hysterical, flag-waving, arm-jabbing Nazis. What calibre of man? I've heard him conversing in French, I've heard the polite and reasoned tones he uses to others, but does he have real power?

It takes another forty-eight hours of my obstinacy and the smooth efficiency of this unpretentious person before a bargain of sorts is struck: *a specific act of collaboration in exchange for a promise of the eventual release of Emil Jarek.*

'That's the best you're going to get,' he says, and once more I wonder: who is this bland individual who can wrest grudging agreements from a beast like Gestapo Müller?

CHAPTER TWENTY-TWO

Emma pursued Huber all through the evening and the next day, bombarded him with calls about the mysterious initials AMTX. 'What news?' she wanted to know. And later: 'Cracked it yet?'

'Still searching the archive; it's an enormous job but it'll probably be in there somewhere.'

'Too slow! Look, these letters, they must represent someone, some group, some body, even if defunct by now.'

'Almost certainly.'

'What about experts on the period? Ask around.'

'Already have. No one knows.'

That wasn't good enough for Emma. She trawled the internet, playing with the letters, changing the order, adding spaces, inserting full stops, missing fragments out, but all she found were a series of sales sites advertising electronics, TVs, airlines, concerts and computers.

'You must have made a mistake,' she told Huber. 'Go back and check again.'

Late in the evening she was still at it. She was supposed to be working on her notes for the next presentation but the problem kept eating away at her. She was doodling on her pad when a slight noise had her pen poised in mid-air for several moments.

She listened. Nothing. Must be a movement in an adjacent room.

Two minutes later she heard it again. On the third occasion she strode across the room and peered through her spyhole.

She took a step back in surprise. The hunched figure of the Russian delegate, Pavel Komov, presented itself to her, albeit in distortion. She also recognised the distortion of fear. Or was it something else?

'Yes?' she called from her position behind the door, deciding not to open.

The head jerked round to face her and address the spyglass. The expression did not contain cunning, she decided.

There was a vocal hiss, a kind of loud whisper. 'Miss Drake, sorry to disturb; may I have a word?'

She peered through the tiny glass more carefully. As far as she could see, there were no others with him.

'Just a minute.' She slipped the knuckles out of her pouch and over her right hand, pulling down the long sleeve of her top to conceal them. Then she released the door catch.

'So sorry,' Komov said quietly. 'Is it convenient? I would very much like to talk... but I can come back later if that's better for you.'

Either a good actor or a man with no ill intent, she decided, and opened the door wide.

He walked in uncertainly and stood just inside. She clocked the familiar tea-drainer moustache, noticed he was running to fat. 'I realise this may not be the best time for you but I need to say something of importance. And in private.'

She closed the door and motioned him to a chair. Should she call Roper? She hesitated briefly, sensing the need to tread carefully, but came down in favour. She had come to value Roper's judgement.

'Mind if my assistant is in on this?' she asked. 'You can still speak freely.'

Komov made a gesture of agreement and Emma sent a quick summons on her mobile: Come quick, interesting visitor.

She smiled at Komov. 'Coffee?'

'No thank you. I really came to say goodbye.'

That brought her up short. She gave him a big surprised look.

'But we haven't had your latest presentation yet,' she said. 'We all want to hear what you make of all of this. The Russian position. So many unanswered questions–'

Komov cut her short. 'So sorry, Miss Drake; I think you're a wonderful conference leader.'

She shook her head. 'Russia's point of view is important to us.'

'You will, I hope, forgive what I am about to say.' He took a deep breath. 'I am so sorry to let you down, I think you're doing a great job, but there are far more important things at stake here, more important than the truth about the past. What I am fearful of... is the future.'

There was a rap at the door, which she opened quickly for Roper. Introductions were made and Emma said: 'Pavel here is saying goodbye because he's fearful of the future; have I got that right?'

The Russian stared at them for some seconds before saying: 'I wonder if you realise what's really happening here. Much more than a history seminar. Do you have any idea? You're incubating a nest of vipers? And if they're allowed to hatch their evil young, the consequences will be...' He looked pained, as if afflicted by some ailment, then finished: 'Deeply perilous.'

Emma stared back, then said simply: 'You're talking the Super Nebraska SXX2... or the Wuhan X5.'

'You know?'

'For some time. Don't think I condone it. I don't. I'm going to put a stop to it... when I have the necessary ammunition.'

Komov sighed. 'I doubt it. I've been trying ever since I got here. It's all entirely predictable. The Europeans are always trying to exclude us, hem us in, one eye on the main chance, perhaps to grab a bit of Mother Russia for themselves, but we're not going to stand for it. We must try to stop this missile build-up before it goes too far, before it gets too serious, too dangerous, beyond repair.'

'I agree absolutely,' Emma said. 'A diabolical threat to peace. We're on your side.'

Komov looked from Roper to Emma, at their serious faces, then broke into a small grin. 'So, you're not just an academic, after all?' he said to Emma.

She said, straight-faced: 'I'm an academic, just like you.'

His grin widened. 'Of course, how clever! The British! What do the French say, "perfidious Albion"? Yes, very clever. So, what is behind your thinking? What is the British position on missiles in Nagorno?'

Emma said: 'We want historical clarity from the past, and peace and stability for the future.'

'Why?' Komov feigned puzzlement. 'No missile factories in England needing export orders?'

'All our defence is tied in with our European partners.'

'Doesn't stop the French trying to sell it.' She kept silent at this, so he said: 'Okay, we're on the same side, for now, so I'll act like an ally. I can't do anything to stop these people. I've tried reasoning with them, tried warning them but they're quite determined. So, perhaps...'

He shrugged, felt in an inside pocket then produced several

photographs, spreading them on the coffee table. 'My evidence so far, but not enough.'

Emma examined the pictures for some moments, passing them one by one to Roper: America talking to Nagorno at a café table; China talking to Nagorno, America, China and Poland all together, huddled over laptops and papers and deep in conversation at a table cluttered with salt and pepper pots and menus.

'The Café Bavaria,' Komov said. 'Their favourite meeting spot. Their bargaining place. Always the same table.'

Emma nodded. 'We've seen them there.'

Komov said: 'One other thing. Not much for all my efforts.' He grinned. 'Of course, you don't dirty your hands with phone tapping. I know you Brits; always above suspicion.'

He placed a piece of paper on the table. It contained a number and a word. 'Nagorno's private mobile and password. You might find it interesting, if you were of a mind.' He rose from his chair. 'Sorry I can't give you more. Good luck, for both our sakes, but I'm out.'

'Are you quite sure?' Emma asked him, frowning.

He nodded. 'Orders.' He got up, shook hands and went to the door.

But halfway into the corridor he turned back and said: 'Some sound advice for you. I'd be very wary of Mr Wilkes and his friends from now on. If I were you, I wouldn't be seen in public with them.'

CHAPTER TWENTY-THREE

Roper checked the spyhole and the lock on the door then turned to face Emma. 'Don't be seen in public?' He made a sceptical face. 'That sounded like a threat. Or a warning.'

She shrugged. 'He's just fed up he hasn't managed to nail his man.'

Roper folded his arms. 'And something else. What was all that guff you gave him about the British position on Nagorno-Karabakh? About being on the same side... peace and stability?'

She responded with a smile. 'Convincing?'

'Too convincing to be pure invention.'

'What's up with you?' she demanded sharply. 'I thought it worked out well. We've cleaned up, right? You've got a nice little telephone number and password for our trouble. What more could you want?'

'Sounded very much to me,' he said, 'like your line on British policy came straight off some Foreign Office briefing. Like you were spouting the official position.'

She exhaled in a gesture of exasperation. 'That's the trouble with you. Too much cynicism. So much of it you can't see what's right in front of your eyes.'

'Which is?'

'Play these people at their own game. Russia, the Americans, the Chinese, they love conspiracies. So feed them some.'

'Komov... he had his suspicions. So have I.'

'Look!' She pointed an accusing finger. The eyes were large ovals. 'The plain truth is, I'm going to keep this conference free from any taint of corruption, illegal arms dealing or treaty busting. Cleanse it. Purge the poison. No more dirty dealing!' She made a fierce chopping motion with her hands. 'I won't have it exploited. I won't have it under my roof, right? And if I have to tell a few lies along the way, so what? Now do you get it?'

Roper shrugged and nodded. 'Okay, okay,' he said, placating. He thought he could recognise a smokescreen, smell a plausible liar, but you only had to look at her to see this was a performance way up into the stratosphere, way beyond artifice, made of real passion. He recognised the energy, the determination, the sheer force of it. And it carried him back to conviction.

CHAPTER TWENTY-FOUR

Next day there was still no word on AMTX and Emma's mood darkened. Heavy footfalls in the marble-floored corridors of the Führerbau were apt to evoke a host of jackbooted spectres from the past. That morning, when she had arrived at the foot of the main staircase, images of dark days gone by came to frightening life: a succession of black-uniformed figures parading up and down, their footsteps clattering, their cries stentorian, their intentions malign. This was a place hewn large and heavy, an architecture designed to frighten and intimidate; a place where there were no smiles; a place that would never throw off the legacy of the recent past.

As day wore into evening Wilkes ramped up the pressure by pecking away at her. She was working on a new programme during a break between sessions when he said: 'You know, you can't expect this business just to die away; there's too much at stake. Employees are relying on work, companies are putting their futures on the line...'

Emma, who had been effecting deafness, rounded on him. 'Your employees? What company?'

'Just talking export business in general. Companies need

these contracts. There's too much riding on this; we need to do business here.'

When she shrugged indifference, the jibes became more direct. Wilkes wagged a finger. 'You're getting up the noses of some very uptight people; do you realise that? They don't take kindly to this sort of treatment. They're going to kick back.'

'The answer's still no. No arms trading here, absolutely none at all.'

The tone moved from reasonable to threatening. 'Better look out for yourself. If that were me, not sure I'd sleep so well in my bed at night. I wouldn't like to say what some people might be thinking. I'd hate for you to have an accident...'

Emma put both elbows on the table, took a deep breath... and the lights of the whole building went out. It was already dark outside, the windows half-shuttered and draped. At first, she couldn't see a thing.

'Roper?'

'I'm here.'

She felt him come closer.

'What's happening?'

'Someone's blown all the fuses I should think.'

Outside in the hallway there were shouts and calls. Then running footsteps.

'How long are we going to sit here in the dark?'

'Taking their time sorting it,' Roper said.

Emma's eyes began to pick out shapes. 'Someone draw those blinds,' she said. 'Let some ambient light in.'

There were quiet murmurings from others in the room. A match was lit and their faces flickered briefly into view, like some startled tableau, then the match fizzled.

The fire bells started up. A fierce klaxon blotted out all others but cut off as abruptly as it had begun.

'Is it a fire?' An inquiry tinged with fear from the other side of the room.

'The blinds!' Emma said loudly. 'Get them open.'

'Sorry, don't know how; can't see a darned thing,' answered a frustrated voice.

'Roper, is this a genuine technical problem, do you think? Or could it be...' Her words tailed off, some of Wilkes's not-so-veiled threats fresh in her mind. Outside in the hallway more footsteps and shouts echoed around the marble walls.

'A ploy?' she suggested. Her instinct was for self-defence. She felt around for her case, couldn't find it but located a ballpoint pen. She clutched it in one fist, nib arrowed outwards ready to use as a weapon of sorts.

Roper said he was going to feel his way into the hallway and then along to the Direktor's office. 'I'm with you,' she said, moving carefully toward the door, but suddenly, without warning, the lights flickered back on.

Everyone blinked, shielding their eyes. Emma reversed her stab-pen and peered around from under a shielding left hand.

She did a quick head count. No Poland. No Russia. No Nagorno.

But there, still sitting three places away down the table, was a grinning Wilkes.

'Things that go bump in the night,' he said archly.

A messenger arrived from the Direktor's office calling her name. Emma sighed, expecting a tirade, blame for the lighting chaos, more threats of eviction. Instead, when she arrived, there was just a terse statement that someone had called her on the Direktor's phone.

She looked at the desk and saw the receiver was off the cradle. She hesitated. This was her third visit to Room 105 with all its evocative connections to the Führer and her grandfather. She glimpsed again the elaborate chandelier and the oval-topped casement windows, then saw the Direktor's glare. Hurriedly, she took the phone. 'Yes?'

'Emma, is that you?' It was Huber.

'Yes, Max, but why are you phoning on this line?'

'You're not answering your mobile.'

'No, the lights are out... were out. I must have put it down somewhere.'

'Never mind! Got you now. Great news.'

'Have you cracked it?'

'*Have* I?'

Emma clamped the receiver closer to her ear in an involuntary gesture of excitement, listening intently as Huber explained that AMTX stood for Department X, a figment of a certain person's imagination.

'A certain person? Like who?'

Huber went point by point through his latest discovery from the archive. AMTX didn't exist because it was a deliberate stratagem to disguise the activities of a branch of the Nazi state security apparatus, the RSHA. Its proper notation, AMT, was the standard abbreviation for a department, and VIB referred to Department 6, dealing with foreign Intelligence.

'It was run by an unusual character by the name of Schellenberg, who rarely used the official designation of his department, preferring to hide behind the X. Apparently that was typical of the exotic and boyish side of his nature. He definitely wasn't the worst of them.'

'But still the SS,' she broke in. 'Still a terrible peril, a threat to life and limb. Not really much of a release then?'

'More hopeful than that, I'd say. Schellenberg didn't go in for brutality. The B designation was for Intelligence in the

West. So it seems highly likely your grandfather was handed over to him for use in some Intelligence matter.'

Emma was silent. There was hope, perhaps, but a troubling doubt replaced her immediate elation. Had Bradley Wilkes been coerced into some compromising situation, some hateful act of collaboration in order to survive? Was his heroic status now in doubt? Was the story turning bad?

She thanked Huber, replaced the phone, nodded an acknowledgement to Frau Dr Ludwig and walked thoughtfully back to her room, feeling the Direktor's hostility boring into her back. But where, she wondered, would the Grandfather quest lead next? Did she really want to go on with it? Did she still want to know where this darkening trail led?

She found her mobile switched to silent in her briefcase leaning against one of the legs of the big table, having quite forgotten placing it there in the excitement of the blackout.

She cupped her chin and considered again the information she had just received. Should she continue with her search?

Of course she should.

And to prove it she immediately rang Huber back and put pressure on him to chase the lead. More, more, more, she urged.

CHAPTER TWENTY-FIVE

E mma knew she wouldn't sleep, didn't even try getting under the striped bluebell-print quilt, instead sitting by the window of her room, crunching peppermints, looking out over the nocturnal skyline of the city, brooding about her lack of progress. Was there malevolence out there, rising like mists of the night to thwart her? The twinkling lights of menace, the ghosts of this city's dark past plotting to engineer her downfall?

Wilkes and the Russian had made their moves. With warnings and threats, they sought to keep the pressure on. She thought again about the lights-out incident at the Führerbau; clearly, it was meant to intimidate and if she didn't act soon she could expect more of the same.

She flushed angrily, tapping a finger against a bowl of lilac asters, focusing for a few more moments on the 300ft twin towers of the distant cathedral, so much a symbol of the city. These were the bulbous tower cupolas, a guide had told her, that wartime bombs bounced off, exploding at ground level, leaving the cathedral standing but devastation all around.

She looked away, seeing but not registering the watercolours and pencil sketches hung on the hotel wall. Time, she told herself, to hit back, to go on the attack. She rubbed her chin. Problem-solving was her thing so she began a methodical run-through of her list of suspects: the US, France, Czechoslovakia, Germany, Italy, Poland, China; Wilkes, Girolle, Tibor, Lang, Piccini, Zdzislaw, Jihai. One by one, she examined what she knew about each, looking for a vulnerability, searching for a weak link. It was when she came to Muzalev, the man from Nagorno-Karabakh, that enlightening dawned. He was unique. He was distinct from the others in one vital respect. They were all sellers of arms; he was the only buyer.

She thumped the windowsill, leapt up and marched around the room with a new sense of purpose. Muzalev was the weak link; take him out of the equation and the rest were done for. Sunk without trace.

At breakfast she wore a big smile, laying out her plan.

'Please, Emma, no!' Roper erupted, aghast. He almost dropped his croissant, nearly skittled the milk jug. 'I'm supposed to be your protector, remember? How can I do that if we separate, if you strike out on your own? I need to be close by at all times.'

She cut him off. 'Have you noticed how Muzalev always leaves his departure to the very last minute? How many times has he missed the tram and been late?'

'Emma, don't mix it with him,' Roper tried again. 'These people are dangerous. And that little man has got it in for you.'

'Just a little chat. On his own. Away from Wilkes and the others.'

'We've tried that. He won't listen. He ignores you, hides among his friends, won't engage one to one.'

'But today,' she said, 'he will.'

Roper sighed his acquiescence. He wasn't happy with a plan that put him on a No.17 tram bound for the Sendlinger Tor while she stayed back at the Isarhof. He departed grumbling, walking out at the usual time with the other delegates while she sat in an inconspicuous corner of the hotel lobby. And the man from Nagorno did not disappoint, his timekeeping again awry. He arrived at the foot of the stairs well behind the others. She followed him out, observing the portly delegate puffing out his cheeks and stamping impatiently when he reached the tram stop too late for the usual departure just after nine. They were great traffic-beaters, these trams, given priority at junctions and turning up on schedule, almost without fail.

At quarter past the hour Emma was at the opposite end of the shelter, out of his line of sight. He boarded the front car of a four-car set, she in the rear. The 17 swished smoothly along the arrow-straight tracks of the Fraunhofer Strasse then, as it grumbled round a sharp bend and over the switches at the end of the street, she moved a little closer to observe her quarry: an expensively dressed dumpling of a man with grey hair, a large nose and a permanent pout. He seemed to be constantly consulting his wristwatch. Was he worried about time or did he just like admiring the gold?

Her most difficult moment would come when they changed trams at the Tor but she accomplished this by ducking down a concrete underpass leading to the old city while Muzalev waited up top by the pattering fountains for the 27 to take them on to the Führerbau. And there were fewer passengers on the second tram, lost in their own thoughts, conversation abandoned amid the clatter and din. She checked the window; they were getting close to their stop, the big obelisk at the Karolinenplatz.

She got up, clutching a bag. Emma didn't do handbags, usually opting for a shoulder bag, rucksack or belt with pouches, but today she wanted to look like all the other passengers. As she walked forward, she slipped over her right fist the device that Roper had condemned as strictly illegal, pulling the coat sleeve down in concealment. She walked through the bucking concertina couplings that joined the cars together until she was directly behind Muzalev. He was by the doors, his back to her. They were the only passengers waiting to get off.

The tram stopped, the doors flapped open and he stepped down into the roadway. The moment he hit the pavement she was right behind him, dogging his footsteps. One, two three... he turned to glance behind. As he did so, the tram doors closed. They were in the enclosed space of the tram shelter, unobserved, unnoticed. She saw his expression of surprise, then hostility, as she grabbed his collar and swung him round in an arc, pushing him roughly backwards. He stumbled with a resounding, tinny bang as he hit the back of the thin metal panelling of the shelter and slumped in shock. It was easy to manoeuvre him on to a nearby bench seat.

The tram had already swished away.

'Crazy woman!'

'A little chat, just you and me.'

His face contorted and she anticipated the kick he tried to deliver while still in a sitting position. Adroitly, she dodged the lunge and struck back, a quick jab, catching him squarely on the front of the shin bone.

He howled, bending forward, clutching his leg.

Emma glanced about her. They were still alone. It was a shelter on a narrow tram-stop island in the middle of the street. No one was watching, his yelps unheard against the noise of traffic.

A new face of rage announced his response. He began to rise. 'I'll smash your face in.'

She pushed him back. Another tinny reverberation from the almost paper-thin panelling.

She sat next to him.

He reached across to strike at her, then doubled up again as she drove her left elbow into his portly midriff and stamped on his right foot. Muzalev was short and fat, liked his wine and long restaurant dinners – not in the best physical shape.

'Stop struggling and listen!' She had him by the collar with the left hand, the teeth of the knuckleduster showing on her right. 'Got an important message for you,' she said, face up close. 'Need to make sure I've got your full attention.'

'Get off! Nothing to say to a madwoman!' He tried to shake free. 'I'll call the police.'

'You do that!'

He tried to wriggle free once more but her grip tightened and the right hand with its threat came closer into his line of sight. His expression changed to fear. 'You'd use that?'

'Weapon of last resort.' She moved even closer. 'The message is, no more secret deals. Get it? Not at any time for the rest of the conference.'

He said nothing.

'If you carry on with your dirty little trade, I'll have you arrested and chucked out of the country, right?'

Still he said nothing and her attitude changed. She helped him up and brushed down the front of his rumpled clothing. 'Now you and I are going to walk together, all nice and friendly, down to the Führerbau and declare in a joint announcement to all the folks there that the arms selling has got to stop, okay?'

He tried to wriggle free once more and lashed out but her firm grip made it a fresh-air kick and she pushed him out of the shelter, intending to force the pace down to Arcis Strasse, marching together, giving him no choice but to comply. He was unsteady on his feet and she noticed what a mess she had made of his expensive, creaseless Merino wool suit. It certainly had a few creases in it now and one of his shoes, doubtless of the handmade Italian variety, had concertinaed into a quite intriguing new shape.

It was then, as they were slightly apart but still close and out in the open, that it happened.

All at once a whipping rush of air, something snatching at her arm, a whining crack in the air, a sense of shock.

Rather like a very loud smack across the face.

Before she had time to realise what had happened she was down on the pavement. Was it instinct or shock? She didn't know. Her bag was beneath her, the contents spilling over the paving stones.

A car ground past her head, inches away from the tram island.

She shook herself and knelt. The strap of the bag had broken, a scorch mark visible at one frayed end.

She looked up. Muzalev was also grounded.

A shot. It must have been a shot, she told herself, not quite believing the thought.

She got up, took two steps to his body, expecting to see him dead. But he opened his eyes and repeated his most potent phrase in English: 'Crazy woman!'

The word *sniper* flashed into her mind and she looked up and about her. At this point the street was no longer narrow. The building line had widened out. A small fenced-in set of gardens lay to her right in front of apartments forming a semicircle behind some wiry-looking bushes. Cars were parked all around. She looked up. Five storeys of windows stared back at her. The shot could have come from any one of three sides.

'Back here!' she shouted, the danger of their exposed position suddenly clear to her, crabbing urgently to the cover of the tram shelter. 'Come on, move.'

By now the street had come alive to the incident. She saw a figure with a mobile phone clutched to his ear. He was running. She looked in the other direction. The pavements were emptying. Doors banged, windows closed. And in the distance, police sirens.

Then another thought. Get rid of the knuckles. She looked about her, spotting a drain cover. The duster went down between the bars of the grating just as a green-and-cream patrol car sped across the cobbles towards them.

'If you want to keep out of more trouble, you'll say nothing!' she ordered the still prone, sprawling figure. 'Absolutely nothing.'

CHAPTER TWENTY-SIX

K ommissar of Police Franz Kasper had lost his usual languorous calm, to be replaced by a pinched and agitated expression. 'You again!' he said, 'why is it, whenever there's been trouble in this city over the past few days, Emma Drake and her band of English historians are at the bottom of it?'

They were in his office at police headquarters in the Ettblock and he hadn't troubled with the detention room or the interview suite. He'd insisted his officers march her straight into his office and stand behind her while he vented his temper.

Emma gave him her uncomprehending look. 'Trouble?'

Kasper bared his teeth. 'Trouble, yes trouble, like a shooting in the street of this peaceful city.'

In the face of aggression, calm, Emma looked about her. A neat and tidy desk with nothing but a blank computer screen and keyboard; a very old man in a photograph on the wall; some reference books and a spare desk in the corner. She let out a breath and shook her head. 'Sorry, Herr Kommissar, it's all a mistake.'

'A mistake?'

'You're right about one thing. Yes, I thought it was a shot. But that's just a little crazy, isn't it? I realise now.'

'Crazy?'

She nodded vigorously, taking in the absence of paper or pens or bureaucratic clutter of any kind. 'Foolish nonsense, for which I apologise.'

'So, you can apologise away a shooting in one of my streets?'

'Not a shooting,' she said soothingly. 'Clearly, I must have been mistaken. Just a car backfiring.'

Kasper, no longer the man of studied coolness she had encountered before, drew in a deep breath, holding himself in check. 'You must think me a simpleton. A car backfiring! I have three eyewitnesses phoning in to say it was a shot. Three separate people. One man looking out of his window at you sprawling on the ground.'

'Just a bang; we both fell over; a mistake. No harm done.'

'No harm? Have you seen the state of your friend? He's in considerable shock.' He leaned his head across the desk towards her. 'This is a peaceful city, do you hear? I like to keep my streets safe for the citizens and I won't tolerate outbreaks of violence. And you are at the centre of the problem.'

'Problem?'

'My officers are out combing the streets now, looking for more eyewitnesses and physical evidence. Bullet damage, empty cartridge cases...'

'Found any? Found the shooter?'

This was not like any interview he had conducted before. That much was obvious. And he didn't like interviewees who talked back. 'You're coming with me,' he said.

'I am?'

'Back to Arcis Strasse. I want you out of there. And out of Germany for good. The lot of you. Immediately.'

She shook her head and waved a dismissive hand. 'You

can't do that. We've done nothing wrong. And you have no evidence of this *shooting*, as you call it. You've no justification.'

'Plenty of justification and we'll soon have more. We're searching your rooms for weapons.'

'Weapons? What weapons?'

'I'm convinced this is an armed feud you're conducting. That's why someone shot at you. And it can only get worse.'

'No evidence!' she said heatedly.

He opened out one hand and counted off on his fingers. 'First, a provocative procession, breaching our peace, stirring up trouble with the citizens; then four of your people found in a forbidden cellar; then a problem with the lighting; and now this. A shooting on the street of my city. My city! Enough reasons to have you deported four times over. I can get a court order tomorrow to put you all out.'

'What nonsense. You've no grounds.'

'Expulsion as a matter of public policy. Undesirable conduct, disruptive behaviour, persons not conducive to the public good. Been done before. From football hooligans to David Irving.'

'How insulting.'

Kasper was up, shouting for his car to be brought round to the side door. Then he beckoned her up with the sort of instruction that – from a German policeman – you disobey at your peril.

When they arrived back at the Führerbau, Frau Direktor's face was a predictable mask of hostility, Muzalev's face was a mess of criss-cross bandages from his unexpected contact with the cobbles and Roper's an expression of alarm and shock.

'What happened?' he hissed at her as they marched to the conference room.

'Someone tried to shoot me.'

He stopped, shocked, then ran to catch up with her.

'A shot?'

'Just missed. Broke the strap on my bag.'

'Who?'

'Do you need more than one guess?'

He threw up his hands. 'I told you this was getting dangerous.' An exasperated gasp. 'Too much. Too serious. Completely out of hand.'

'We've got an hour to clear out,' she said. 'Kasper's insisting. We're being evicted.'

He shrugged. 'Just as well. I can't protect you against guns and hidden marksmen.'

She crashed through the door of the conference room in a great fury. She'd worked herself up on the car journey. Everything was on the brink of collapse. The conference, her mission, her guests, her ambition.

She crossed the big floor, calling out: 'Pack up your things, ladies and gentlemen, we're leaving with immediate effect.'

There was a stark silence. Someone managed a quiet 'Why?' but she ignored it, striding to the table where Wilkes was tinkering with a new laptop. She slapped her hand down on the desk beside him with a slashing crash.

'Sorry,' he said. 'Just heard...'

'Cut the pretence,' she said. 'I know who's behind this. So now get this. I'm out, the conference is finished and...' She peered over the desk so their faces were close up. 'And so are you.'

'I can see you're upset.'

'Upset is nothing. I'm all out and done. Finished and

washed up. The cops are shutting me down. So I have just one pleasure left to extract from this sorry business.'

'Oh?'

'You. I'm going to get great pleasure in taking you down with me.'

He shrugged and made a puzzled gesture with one hand.

'I know you've been lying to me,' she said, 'pretending you're not still arms trading when I know perfectly well you are.'

He was shaking his head. 'You're making a mistake there.'

'So here goes,' she said. 'Kommissar Kasper is in the office down the corridor right now, arranging for my exit. So when he steps this way, I'm going to feed you to the lion.'

'I told you before–'

'Three easy arrests for Kasper will give him a nice feather in his cap. And Roper here will back it up with worldwide newspaper, TV and radio coverage from the inside. Wilkes, the once great family dynasty, that's now all history, from today onwards. Wilkes, the arms trader feeding illicit missiles to Nagorno-Karabakh in direct violation of his own President's embargo. Wilkes, the olde-worlde family who spent half the last war trading with the Nazis even after America had declared hostilities. What a double story! What a double whammy!'

He drew in his breath. 'I know you've had a shock... but you really should watch what you're saying in public, young lady.'

'No worries. Plenty of backup. Documentary proof from Germany, historical proof from America. My friends in the archive at the town hall; my friends among fellow academics researching the history of illicit trading back in '38.'

There was a long pause while the two of them stared hard, then she hit out again. 'Oh, don't look so gobsmacked. Were you hoping to keep it a secret forever? Your family's enjoyed the luxury of historical obscurity all these years but it had to end sometime. All those damning documents in the archives! Only real question was *when*.'

Wilkes stared at her without speaking for some seconds, then said: 'Mother was right. You're a dangerous dude.'

'Mother was right,' she echoed sourly.

Suddenly, the smirk was back on his face. 'But then, I always knew that. So it was just as well I came prepared.'

Emma sent Roper to attempt to sweet-talk Kasper into giving them another chance. Not at the Führerbau – that was a lost cause, she knew. 'Just tell him I need a week to wrap things up and promise we'll all stay in the hotel the whole time. We'll be on our best behaviour.'

'You're barmy,' he objected. 'Someone's just tried taking you out and you want to carry on with this load of deadly snakes, all shut up tight in the hotel?'

'Do it please. As one ex-cop to another.'

Back at the hotel she waited for Roper's return before tackling Wilkes once more, this time in the foyer.

'I don't see your inspector fellow. Whatever happened to him?' he jeered.

'He'll be here any minute. We have an arrangement.'

'Yeah, yeah, I can recognise a bargaining position when I see one.'

Emma turned to Roper, hovering behind. 'Tell Kasper we're ready for him now.'

'Yeah, yeah,' Wilkes said knowingly. 'Okay, I recognise events have taken a turn for the worse.' He held up two hands in mock surrender. 'So, there's a new balance of advantage to be struck here. So we need to come to an agreement that will benefit both of us. A mutually advantageous arrangement.'

'Mutual advantage?' There was a peel of derisive laughter from Emma. 'Did you hear that? He wants an arrangement. Did you get that? After all that's happened. What arrangement could I possibly want?'

'Not so difficult. I know what you want. You want to know what happened to dear old Grandpa back in '38. You'd love to crack the mystery. Find all the answers. Answer all the questions. It's what's really bugging you. What this whole conference has really been about.'

Emma shrugged and snorted.

'I could provide all the answers,' he said.

'Ridiculous. How would you know?'

'Uniquely placed. It's the barter I always knew I'd have to make – eventually.' Wilkes was brimming with confidence once again. 'I'll give you a tasty titbit, an advance preview. Your grandpa survived the incident at the Führerbau. Hey! See? Knew that would get you.'

Emma scorned him with another burst of derisive laughter. 'Old hat,' she said. 'We've known that for some time. Transferred into the jurisdiction of Department X.' She folded her arms in a 'beat that' kind of gesture. In fact, she'd spent the previous evening chasing down the public record of the man who'd reputedly run this mysterious Department X; a colourful adventurer, by all accounts, more in the mode of a typical English spymaster, whom he admired, rather than following in the repressive footsteps of his murderous colleagues.

Wilkes wasn't in the least deflated by her put-down. 'Sure, the Nazis gave him a hard time – but not for long. Very shortly, he was got out to Switzerland. See, that's your missing link, and I know, know only too well, because my grandfather was waiting for him in Bern.'

Emma drew in a deep breath, entering a state of confusion,

excitement and scepticism all at the same time. Could this be true? 'You're lying!' she accused.

He shook his head. 'Got all the proof you'll ever need,' he said. 'Right here.' He patted his briefcase. 'When you see it, you won't be able to find fault with it. But first of all, the deal is: no hassle; just let me and my friends get on with our business. Right? And you get the full picture.'

She made a rapid decision, already flicking through the numbers on her mobile. 'I'm calling Huber. He can help check on the authenticity of this.'

~

Wilkes was bending over his briefcase. 'Whatever you think you know about my family,' he said, 'there's solid proof here that will establish me as a gold-plated authority on the subject. Convince you I'm really connected.'

Emma said nothing as he rooted about in the case. Eventually, he held up a small medal and turned it over to show the clasp. 'The Congressional Medal of Honour. Go on, read the inscription.'

She read: 'To Wilber Wilkes, for fifty years of unstinting service to the nation.'

'So?' She shrugged, posing unimpressed.

Next out of the case was a miniature picture album. He flicked it open. Tiny photographs of Wilber Wilkes with President Roosevelt, Wilkes with Secretary of War Stimson, Wilkes with Intelligence chief William J Donovan. 'You don't get to pose with those guys unless you're somebody. Unless you're on the inside. That fifty years – that's with the agency, you know, the OSS, then the CIA.'

'How come,' Emma asked, 'you just happened to have all this stuff with you?'

He grinned. 'Anticipation. My fallback position. I'm like one of your boy scouts; what's that motto? Be prepared?'

'So you weren't going to show me any of this unless you absolutely had to?'

'Correct.'

'You're nothing but a deceitful, unprincipled, amoral, avaricious arms trader.'

'That's me, honey, but just add to that, your best damned hope for economic recovery.'

'None of this means you have inside knowledge of Bradley Wilkes.'

'Wilber had fifty years in the agency, starting with Bern, starting with his own brother Bradley. Of course he knew about it. Of course we know about it. Kept it in the family. No archives necessary. Father to son to grandson.'

'Still doesn't mean you have anything of value.'

'I have a name for you. Another piece for your jigsaw. The man who brought out your grandfather.'

'If it's Schellenberg, don't bother, I've already got it.'

'Fine.' Wilkes didn't miss a beat. 'But do you know why?'

Max Huber, summoned urgently to witness this revelation, arrived breathlessly, just in time to join the conversation. He stepped forward. He was too tall, too much a presence for Wilkes to ignore. 'Remember?' Huber asked. 'The Nazi traders of America?'

Emma turned. 'What's that got to do with my grandfather?'

Huber coughed, preliminary to a statement. 'It's becoming very clear,' he said, 'that when this Walter Schellenberg realised he had Bradley Wilkes in custody, and at the same time Bradley's brother was busily doing his bidding in Switzerland, he obviously decided – get these two together! Get them to work in tandem.'

'You've got it,' Wilkes said. 'But there's one thing you have to appreciate about *my* grandfather's role in this story. Okay, you're right, it's true, he started out a businessman yes, but at a certain point he changed. Of course, he kept his cover to fool the Nazis but his primary role switched. He became an agent. Our man in Bern for the OSS...'

'Forerunner of the CIA,' Huber put in.

'I know that,' she said irritably, 'but what happened when Bradley got to Switzerland?'

Wilkes said: 'Your grandfather – with help – escaped the clutches of the Germans once they were over the border and on Swiss soil. Your grandpa... boy oh boy, did he become a great hero? Yessir. For a while anyway. Until he went bad.'

She snorted. 'You don't expect me to take any of this on trust, do you? I'm going to need very convincing proof.'

'First of all,' Wilkes said, 'I wanna know. Do we have a deal?'

CHAPTER TWENTY-SEVEN

Wilkes clearly knew this was an irresistible come-on, that she couldn't say no, and he was right. She couldn't. She had demanded proof and his answer was to open the briefcase again and produce a small semicircular metal object with a frayed edge.

He handed it to her. 'Take a good look. See the serial number stamped on the side? Make a note of it.'

'What is this thing?' Emma was in no mood for riddles.

'It's his German leg tag that he had to wear when he came over the border with his watchdogs. Say what you like about 'em but those guys were way ahead of their time. They had these tags with little transmitters that were linked up to a wireless or the telephone to keep track of people. Years before anyone else. But they weren't that bright. Cos Grandpa Bradley had his sawn off!'

'I want to verify this first,' she said. 'Could be any old lump of iron with a number stamped on it.'

'Check it out,' Wilkes insisted. He pointed. 'Write it down. Check it with that damned archive you're so keen on. That'll settle it... Nope, I gotta better idea...' He took from another compartment of his case a tiny metal disc, oval-shaped, smooth-edged, about the size of a lapel badge. 'There were three numbers stamped on that leg tag, the one you can see and two others. The two that were cut off were made into tokens, keepsakes. Here, have this one...'

A bubble of excitement grew in Emma. She knew it was risky, could still be a trick, that Wilkes could be conning her, that she shouldn't connive at illegal arms trading... but she was never going to refuse.

She nodded.

'Ready?' Wilkes asked. 'Sitting comfortably for this story?'

She gave him a glare. 'Better be good. And complete.'

Wilkes settled himself in his seat. 'This is how it was told to me,' he said. 'When Bradley arrived in Switzerland, he soon lost his sense of gloom. He was on neutral territory. Free! He slipped his German shadows and they had no legal authority to chase or complain because they were on Swiss soil, but they still thought they could keep track of him with this leg tag. Lots of undercover dealing going on, shadowy links between the Swiss and the Nazis, secret collusion and all that, but Bradley had other ideas. Wanted to be shipped back to the States... but his brother had other ideas too.'

Emma was scratching her neck in frustration.

'You see, Wilber was under terrific pressure to provide the Allies with Intelligence on German war intentions – and the Americans, although new in the spying game, were the only ones with a network that counted in Switzerland.'

'Skip the strategy,' Emma snapped. 'Where's your proof for all this? I want more than any old lump of scrap iron.'

'Relentless, aren't you?' Wilkes made a face, fishing in the briefcase once again, this time bringing out another photograph. 'Take a look at that. Recognise anyone?'

Two men standing in a cobbled street outside what looked

like a parade of shops in an arcade; one figure portly, well-fed and commanding; the other pale to the point of haggard, with marks around his mouth and nose.

Emma thought she recognised the unsmiling figure of her grandfather, even though he looked nothing like the confident and exuberant foreign correspondent seen in other photographs.

'Wilber and Bradley,' Wilkes said. 'Note the number behind them. That's Kramgasse 23b, Bern – Wilber's office. See the gold sign outside the door – Wilkes Trading; it's his cover address; one of a thousand financiers in that town.'

Emma examined the picture closely: a city scene of elegant, arcaded shops; next door was a cheese kiosk, a bicycle leaning against some railings around a basement entrance; a fountain and a clock tower could just be made out in the distance.

'Could be anywhere,' she said, stubbornly sceptical, 'you could have faked it.'

More photos: Kramgasse from the left showing cars and motorcycles; Kramgasse from the right showing Number 23b without posing figures.

Wilkes beamed. He was enjoying the telling of this story. 'Can you imagine it? Two brothers who couldn't stand each other, at loggerheads nearly all their lives, at different ends of the political spectrum, and here they were, thrown together by the Germans and told to get on with it, to get working together.'

Emma glowered.

Wilkes grinned. 'Oh, that sure must have been some occasion. I'd have given away half of Granny's art collection just to have been a fly on the wall at that meeting.'

Bradley C Wilkes, Bern, Monday 3 October, 1938

It's been a long train journey from Munich to Bern, feeling like an overdressed fraud dressed up as a German businessman in a new stone-grey checked suit supplied by the SD, but here I am at last, outside my brother's office in The Kramgasse. I'm accompanied by my two unsmiling watchdogs who have delivered me like I'm some parcel containing a bad smell.

There's a gold plaque on the brickwork next to a doorway proclaiming The Wilkes Trading Company which is situated between a sumptuous-looking cheese shop and another selling a multitude of radios.

I'm made to stand outside in the street with Zorner while Schnee goes in and gives Wilber the good news. Time drags.

Somewhat self-consciously, I look down at my new outfit: a camel coat over my arm, dark-brown Homburg and glacé leather gloves, all got up to project the image of a sober and prosperous businessman ready to talk turkey with the financiers of Switzerland. And, I have to admit, it's not out of place. Window boxes are blooming with flowers; bikes and motorbikes are propped against railings; shop windows in stylish arcades offer tantalising choices not seen elsewhere in austerity Europe – shoes, dresses, coats, food and all manner of electrical stuff. You name it, the Swiss have it.

When I'm allowed inside the office I'm struck immediately by Wilber's preference for home sweet home. The furnishings are all expensive: American deco; centre stage being given to a chromed metal table inlaid with Lalique glass panels.

When we come face to face, however, there's to be no warm greeting or brotherly affection. 'This is a surprise,' he says, eyeing me disdainfully, 'and not an altogether welcome one.'

'Didn't have much choice.' I shrug.

'You,' he says, pointing an accusing finger, 'are likely to be very bad for business.'

I didn't expect the welcome mat so I ditch the pleasantries. 'I hear tell that you're a vital cog in supplying war materials to the German war machine.'

After a baleful look, he says: 'We're in business; they're our customers.'

'Making a handsome profit from flogging arms.'

'Not armaments.'

'But in a roundabout way it is. Getting them stuff they couldn't get elsewhere. Materials that if you didn't supply their factories they might not be able to procure elsewhere to create mayhem and murder with the neighbours.'

'Save the sob story, Bradley.' He sighs and shakes his head. 'Hawking your damned conscience around the world, stirring things up, making it awkward for people like me. I don't know how we came to be in the same family, I really don't. Surely some mix-up at the maternity ward.'

Our reunion might have continued along these lines but for the intervention of Zorner and Schnee. I've spent a lifetime holding my nose at the dubious practices of the Wilkes family business, making it my mission to establish a separateness, a distance, a different world view. But at this point the two watchdogs interrupt to check on my leg tag. Oh yes, the little man back in the Karl Strasse wasn't green. He not only sent his sentinels; they were armed with the latest electronic watchers' gear linked up to the telephone landline.

Wilber straightens to his full height, shaking a finger at me. 'I gather things have changed for you. So now, if you're going to be working with me, you'll need a radical change of attitude.'

I look down and shrug. Zorner and Schnee are still within earshot.

'You'll need to show willing,' he says. 'Full commitment. Get a grip if you're going to make commercial connections.'

'Doesn't mean I have to like it.' I stare back at him. 'I want you to know that.'

The watchdogs move to the door. 'We'll know if you vacate these premises,' they say, 'and we'll be waiting just outside.'

We're now on our own and this is marked by a long silence between us. Eventually, he says: 'What is it exactly that those people want from you?'

Direct and to the point from brother dear so I give it to him brief and stark. The Nazis have their eye on an iron ore mine in Portugal where the Brits are trying to negotiate an exclusive contract to buy up all the output of the mine and keep the Germans out. My brother sniffs a commercial opportunity. He's a businessman – and a rich one. He didn't get that houndstooth tweed jacket in the market. What's at stake here, I say, is a rare ore called tungsten, and my unwanted mentor in the Third Reich, whatever his name or status might be, wants me to negotiate a better deal – for him – while posing as an American businessman.

'Why American?'

'That's the pitch. The mine owners don't want to get involved in a tussle between countries about to go to war, so me, I'm American; I'm the safe guy. No taint. No trouble.'

Gradually, the heat haze between us begins to cool. Slowly, Wilber's hostility fades and I begin to sense that maybe his attitude is a front for the benefit of our two friends from over the border who are now on guard outside. Then he starts grinning.

Then comes the real jaw-dropper...

Wilber confesses he's changed sides.

He's now a secret serviceman in the employ of Uncle Sam.

I gape and he grins, but I recover quickly and grab my opportunity. 'Then get me a passport, quick. A visa, whatever's required, and a ride or a flight back Stateside; I want outta here double quick.'

'What about that leg tag?'

'Bust the darned thing off.'

'And your friend back in Germany?'

I sigh deeply. That's more difficult. My conscience is hurting. Hurting real bad. I've pledged to do this crooked deal for the Nazis and go back to get Emil Jarek out of jail – but do I trust them to keep their word? I agonised over this during the long train journey. It's the hardest choice I'm going to have to make. Be realistic, I tell myself, poor Emil's probably dead already. All that bravado on the Karl Strasse has evaporated as I sigh, screw up my face and say: 'Emil can't really expect me to do that. It's a call too far.'

There's another long silence between us and I won't blame Wilber if he decides to fling my earlier accusations back in my face and hiss the word Judas. Instead, he pauses almost interminably before saying: 'Bradley, I have to tell you something. There's a quite different reason why you shouldn't go.'

Wilkes was grinning with self-satisfaction at delivering his killer line. 'So you see, the result of that meeting was quite dramatic.' A pause. 'Bradley, your grandpa, was persuaded to stay and do his patriotic duty and become an agent of the OSS.'

Emma looked at him for some time before saying: 'You could still be making all this up. An agent?'

'Absolutely. A fully paid-up operative for Uncle Sam. Working alongside his brother. You know the kind of stuff: talking to refugees, gleaning information coming out of the Third Reich, running agents on the other side of the border...'

'Proof!' Emma demanded again.

Wilkes said: 'Take my word for it, Bradley came out of Germany a collaborator – to save his skin – but he switched back to being a hero as soon as he could.' He shrugged. 'Let's face it, we all have to make an accommodation with our circumstances.'

Emma didn't like that. There was an uncomfortable resonance with the convenient excuses for compromise at the heart of the Appeasement policy which Bradley had so vehemently opposed – but then, she told herself, he was being brutalised at the time.

'Definitely a hero,' Wilkes said. 'For a while.'

Emma glared at him, curbing a welling desire to give him a sideswipe with the flat edge of her hand, just as her brother had taught her. Instead, she turned and handed the little metal number plate to Huber. 'Can you?' she said.

He nodded.

She switched her attention back to Wilkes: 'Well, what happened next? I want the full story.' There were no compromises, no thanks, and her hand was flexing.

Wilkes's expression took on a sly, arch look. 'First, let's see how well you perform, shall we? How well you keep your promises.'

Her eyes narrowed.

'More tomorrow,' Wilkes said. 'I'm not going to give it to you all at once. Otherwise, what do I get? It's a deal, remember? Something for you and something for me.'

The red mist began to rise and a vinegary taste came to her mouth. She drew in a deep controlling breath and said: 'You can't stop it there... even if I have to wring it out of you!'

'Patience,' Wilkes soothed, unaffected by her hostility. 'Wait for your friend to check on the number on that little plate then you'll know that what I'm trading is 24-carat gold.'

CHAPTER TWENTY-EIGHT

I t felt like the rush-hour at the Marienplatz. Emma, Roper and Max Huber had abandoned the hotel reception area in favour of their office on the mezzanine floor. They were standing, not sitting, jammed into the tiny space, holding an inquest into their day of turmoil – Wilkes's revelations, the shooting, and Kasper's threats of eviction.

Emma was silent, chewing over the new elements of her grandfather's story but still angry with Wilkes for his halfway-house revelations.

The two men, just back from the Ettblock, were more concerned about their exchanges with a furious Kasper. He'd shouted and insisted he had the power to close down the conference and put them all out. Huber, convinced no judge would grant such an order, had finally succeeded in persuading Kasper that, in the interests of fair play, the history conference should be allowed to reach its natural conclusion. Huber knew how to play the system and hit the soft spots, the sensitive areas, the ones that put Kasper on the defensive. An expulsion would look bad, Huber had said, as if the host nation had something to hide.

Now he chuckled at his cheek and his success and Emma managed a smile.

'Congratulations,' she said, 'that was some reprieve.'

But Roper wasn't smiling. 'It's no cause for celebration,' he said, turning away to the tiny table in the corner – just big enough for a kettle and some cups – and opening up a fresh packet of Yorkshire tea. 'All you've done is raise the stakes.' He faced them, wagging a finger. 'We're effectively living under a curfew. We're all stuck in this building together. Up close and personal to a bunch of ruthless arms dealers. It's just a question of time – and which one of them strikes first.'

Emma shrugged. 'Not as bad as that. We've done a deal. Wilkes thinks he's bought us off.'

That afternoon Huber came round again and this time he was holding up the little serial number plate and grinning broadly.

'Success,' he said.

Emma gave him an approving smile. 'Thought it would take ages trawling your archive,' she said.

'Didn't bother with that. Went straight to an authority on the subject.' He brought the plate closer for her inspection, his finger running under the jumble of letters and Roman numerals. She read off aloud: 'AMTIIDOOIII,' but shrugged her shoulders.

'All part of the byzantine nature of the police state,' he said, 'but easy when you know how to read it.'

The first three, AMT, were the standard notation for an official department, in this case within the RSHA, the Reich main security office, followed by other letters guiding you through the labyrinth. So, II denoted the admin department, followed by a D for the technical services bureau, the people who supplied the new leg tag device.

'The rest is easy,' Huber said. 'Two zeros and a Roman three, denoting this was the third one they'd supplied.'

They were silent for a while, eyeing one another. Then she said: 'Is this the proof we've been looking for? Is it a clincher?'

Huber considered. 'It certainly proves this piece of metal is a genuine German-issue leg tag and we know that Wilkes had possession of it.'

'But we only have his word that it came from my grandfather so he might still be lying. I don't trust that man. He might have got it from some other source.'

'On balance of probabilities, I'd say he's probably telling us the truth.'

'But only fifty per cent proof,' she insisted.

Huber nodded. 'We can only hope for the other fifty per cent from a document in the archive. We're already deep into 1938 so... let's hope...'

'So far so good,' she said, 'but still not beyond doubt.'

CHAPTER TWENTY-NINE

Emma prowled the corridors in search of Wilkes, determined despite all opposition to force the pace of revelation, and her mood was not helped when she rounded one of the many corners of the labyrinthine old building and almost fell over The Weasel.

The little man stopped, removed from his mouth one of the matchsticks he constantly chewed and used it as a pointer. 'So now you know,' he said, 'your man got out to Switzerland... and much good may it do you.'

Vincenc Tibor, the Czech delegate, was a man who never smiled. He seemed permanently at odds with the world, but still Emma was puzzled by this sudden eruption.

'Not such a hero after all, eh?' he said. 'Not when you get the full picture; not when the man's exposed. The man turned bad.'

Emma reacted. 'Nonsense! My grandfather was a man of peace. He saved lives.'

'He was a betrayer.' The Weasel was wiping his mouth with one hand, spluttering with anger.

'And how come you profess to know so much about it?' she demanded.

'Why d'you think I'm here? I'm an historian too, remember? This is my special area of interest, putting the Czech story together, piece by piece. New information – that's how I know about your grandfather.'

'Says you!'

'Says me, yes, because I've been digging, because I know. Just how your grand old man ran out on his friend.' Tibor snorted. 'Saving lives? The most important life – the man who helped him get up close to Neville Chamberlain – he ratted on. Left to rot in a Gestapo cell. Never came back. A betrayer.'

Emma was shocked into silence.

'Oh, didn't our American friend mention that bit? Oh dear! What you need to know is the deal. The deal he had with the Germans. They told him: you go to Switzerland, do what we tell you and return. Then you can have Emil Jarek back. Out of jail. But what did Wilkes do? I'll tell you what he did. He got to Bern and did a bunk. He ran away. Never came back. And Emil?'

Here, The Weasel paused briefly for breath. The tirade seemed to have tired him. He shrugged. 'Who knows? Probably the gas chamber. That's your dear great hero for you.'

Emma stopped, motionless. Stared at the wall. A flawed hero? A chameleon? Or was the sacrifice of his Czech friend a necessary price to pay for the greater good?

Suddenly, Tibor was gone, taking with him his smoky breath and matchsticks.

This story, she realised, was becoming more dense and more complex; more elusive, more impenetrable. Would she ever be able to grasp it, give it definition, discover the complete picture?

◈

Such was her anxiety that Emma used a break in proceedings later in the day to check out the dining hall, the sun lounge that had no sun, even the tiny beer stübchen where the old men gathered at lunchtime. But the place was deserted, as was to be expected in the late afternoon. Emma's slim reserves of forbearance were exhausted. She wouldn't play the Wilkes game any longer. She was all through with his drip-drip feed of little portions of the Bradley story.

'Dammit, I want the rest,' she told Roper over strong coffee at lunchtime.

'He won't tell it all,' he said, trying to get her to see the point of it. 'It's the only hold he has over you.'

But she wasn't listening, wasn't in the mood to go lightly, wouldn't play by the Wilkes rules any longer. 'I have to know,' she insisted.

She prowled the ground floor, working herself up for a confrontation, checking all the corners and back rooms in this rustic clutter of a hotel, a place of winding corridors and annexes with parts added and altered over the years to no discernible plan. She checked Reception, even the kitchens, but couldn't locate Wilkes. She started up the stairs. He was probably still in his room, she decided, working on that laptop, the one she now regretted returning to him, or burning up the lines to Washington or wherever it was that he did his crooked business. If necessary she would hammer on his door.

In the event, that wasn't necessary.

When she had reached halfway between the first and second floors a familiar voice approached, descending. He was bellowing into a mobile and didn't yet know she was on his track.

'Give me these new figures, will you? I need them as soon as poss. By this afternoon, latest.'

As he rounded the corner and saw her, Emma thought she

glimpsed a figure, a fleeting shadow higher up the staircase which quickly faded, but not before she thought she'd recognised The Weasel. Then she turned her full attention to Wilkes.

'Time for another talk,' she announced.

He shook his head, waving hands furiously across his face in an exasperated gesture of rejection. 'Not now! Not now! I'm busy.'

Emma stood in his path, feet apart, making herself an immoveable object, stopping his descent. 'I'm busy too, so make time.'

'Later.'

'I won't be rationed like some little kid. I want to know the rest of what you've got and I want to know it now.'

He tried to push past her but she paralleled his descent, matching each downward stride, step for step, repeating her demand.

'All in good time,' he said, putting on a spurt, hoping to outpace her.

'Your time has run out.'

'Didn't anyone teach you the value of patience?'

'Patience is for the bovine and the docile.'

'All the same, I can't just...' By the time they reached the ground floor she had him by the sleeve, steering him towards the stübchen, which she knew to be empty. Maybe it was her words, more likely her uncompromising tone, that had Zuzana, the Polish girl with the pageboy bob who did the early turn on Reception, looking up in alarm, hand hovering in fright over the telephone.

'In here,' Emma insisted, banging open the door of the tiny alcove room; 'you can tell me in here.'

Wilkes flailed his arm and threw off her grip, looking as if he might strike out.

'I insist you honour our agreement,' she said. 'Or all bets are off and I start blowing the whistle, loud and clear, right across the wires, all the way back to Washington and wham bang into the middle of that presidential campaign your family's so hooked on.'

'No time!'

Emma held open the door and pointed.

A noise at Reception had them both looking round to see Zuzana picking up the telephone.

'Want a scene?' she said.

Wilkes growled, then walked through, throwing himself angrily into the first seat.

Emma repressed a smile of satisfaction. No need to avoid the reserved places at this time, she knew. During drinking hours you sat here at your peril; the stámmtisch was the table and seats strictly reserved for the regulars, the locals whose second religion was drinking in this den surrounded by shelves of a hundred mass, and the giant-sized pebble-glass beer mugs.

Now, however, there was no bonhomie, no distraction, no drink, as Emma and Wilkes faced each other across a big wooden bench.

'Well?' She gave him the unremitting stare.

There was a loud bang on the door, which then eased open.

Emma turned to see once again the unwelcome features of The Weasel. 'Everything all right, Mr Wilkes?'

She experienced a momentary pleasure that she had disrupted whatever conspiratorial conclave they had planned, plus silent satisfaction at the idea that Wilkes might be in trouble.

'Fine, just fine,' Wilkes said.

Emma got up. 'Go!' she said, pushing shut the door. Then she resumed her seat and stared at Wilkes.

He looked as if he might attempt further prevarication.

'The agreement,' she said.

He pursed his lips, clearly holding back his temper, finding it difficult to make the transition from implacable dealmaker to family historian.

'Well?'

'I've never met anyone quite as persistent. You're like a terrier digging for a bone.' He shook his head, then shut his eyes in an obvious attempt to achieve the necessary recall. 'Right, off the cuff, this is the best I can do.' There was a moment's further silence before he said: 'Your grandfather spent the first few months of his new role just keeping a low profile.'

'His new role? You mean, as an Intelligence agent?'

'Correct. This was while the Germans were occupying the Sudetenland. But then Hitler went further a few months later and grabbed the rest of Czechoslovakia, so Brad moved up a gear. Landed a job in the rail yards at Prague. He had good Czech as well as German; you know that, don't you?'

Emma nodded. Way back, the Wilkes family had originated in the Sudetenland before immigrating to America. Clearly, still a multilingual household.

At this point Wilkes sighed and opened the laptop he'd been carrying, regarding it thoughtfully for a few moments. Then he fired it up and fiddled with the menu. 'We knew we'd have to keep you going with scraps of information. Keep you on track, so to speak; help you piece the story together.' He screwed up his face in concentration. 'We scoured all the old documents and papers we could lay our hands on and came up with this nugget. From Brad's personal file, I believe.' There was another pause, then: 'Yep! Here it is; this is what I copied over.'

He swivelled the screen round and eased the laptop in front of her so she could read. Emma skimmed down to a heading entitled Surveillance and Intelligence and began to read: *'The mission. In the rail yards he could monitor all the traffic out of the main Skoda arms works, vital information that revealed a massive German arms build-up, prior to the invasions of Poland, Scandinavia, the Low Countries and France. Later, he moved into the factory itself as a workman, obtaining even more detailed information. By 1941 both America and Russia were in the war and Hitler's armies were all over Europe. Bradley resumed his role as an Intelligence officer in Bern. At the same time he became involved with some shadowy resistance groups, the nature of which is unclear...'*

She looked up. 'Where's the rest of it?'

'As far as I got,' he said.

'Is this another half-instalment?'

'Could be.'

Somehow, with great control, she kept her temper.

'Now look,' he said, 'that's quite an advance for you. And maybe, just maybe, I'll trawl some more for your benefit. But right now I must get on. Things to attend to. And we don't want to be late for the history session, now, do we?'

She shook her head in frustration, pointing to the screen. 'But you've just left the story hanging...' A pause. 'That ending. Makes him sound so reasonable, so mundane,' she said. 'So inconclusive. So damned bureaucratic.'

He looked up at her quizzically, giving nothing away.

'His story can't stop there. I need to know. Something more challenging than that must have happened to him.'

'You bet,' he said.

~

Bradley C Wilkes, Bern, 14 April 1943:

Wilber is a salesman. He can fix things. Persuade people. And he persuades me. I'm still agape at the sheer impertinence of him switching sides but I agree to help him run his Intelligence bureau while he continues to pose to Zorner and Schnee – and through them their master in the Karl Strasse – as the collaborative businessman. 'Great cover, don't you think?' he says.

By day I make a show of making telephone calls to business contacts. We pass pieces of paper between desks, talk up bogus contacts, make long-distance calls to no one and post letters to ourselves using false business addresses. When Schnee asks for tangible evidence of progress, we push this great bubble of make-believe further: involve the company's agent in Portugal, negotiate with a metallurgy broker, even make plans to charter a train to collect a non-existent cargo. The Brits are negotiating hard, we say. The twists and turns of this saga could go on and on.

By night I operate from the basement of the flat down by the river in the Herrengasse. More high art deco: the executive suite is all black chrome and red leather, with a novelty aeroplane cigarette lighter. It's here I quiz the more interesting of the refugees who flood over the border from Germany. In the jargon of this new business I'm in, it's the debrief. I learn about one-time pads, dead-letter drops, the brush-pass, bag-switch, cut-outs and all the other paraphernalia associated with Intelligence. What really catches my eye, being an old radio hand, are the miniaturized wireless sets for agents, disguised as a lunch box and fitted with an 80-volt long-life battery.

At times I become uneasy; there's something essentially passive about being a listening post. But we do have some good people; brave souls who don't quit but continue to operate inside the Third Reich to bring out key information. One of our best is a technical salesman for a big chemical company in Germany, supplying laboratories with everything from test tubes to arsenic. It's he who first picks up hints of a dangerous development at a research station deep in Poland. He starts to worry because there's too much poisonous material going into that place to have any innocent explanation. The regime of secrecy, locked inside a security zone, points inexorably to one perilous conclusion: a new poison is being developed for use in war.

Our salesman is a man of conscience. He isn't unpatriotic, but as a chemist and student of history he doesn't much like his country's record in being the first to introduce poison gas to the Western Front. What's more, he doesn't like the brutish regime in Berlin and he won't be the first member of his nation to warn the West of warlike advances in German science. The link to us is through a friend who acts as courier. The courier's job depends on weather, tides and rainfall; he takes messages from the salesman's home in the German-controlled Austrian city of Bregenz and at low tide wades across one of the many lazy loops in the Rhine River to reach Swiss territory.

His information reaches Wilber who naturally sends it up the information chain. Very soon the imperative for action comes winging right back. London and Paris have told Washington they're more than anxious. In a war they expect bombs. They fear gas... but is there worse still to come?

That's when Wilber turns to me and says: 'The top brass are crapping their breeches on this one and we're the only people in the right place to do something about it.'

I can see it coming. And it duly arrives.

Wilber says: 'We need to find out what's going on. I've been told to get someone inside that place.'

I nod. I'm fair sick of debriefing duty – sitting around listening to refugee tales – so I say: 'Brother, this one is for me. I'll do it.'

CHAPTER THIRTY

Roper was trying to get Emma to see sense over breakfast next morning. It was 6.30, a good time to start, well before anyone else showed themselves, part of their routine and an opportunity to iron out the problems of the coming day.

'Look,' he said, 'we're running out of time, don't you see? Only two conference days left; it's just not long enough for any of these elaborate plans of yours.'

She said nothing, concentrating on selecting cereals and fruit drinks from the Isarhof's generous buffet, laid out on a raft of shiny steel benches and loaded with every kind of offering.

Roper was at the hotplates, deciding between eggs fried, poached or scrambled, or a German version of rissoles called frikadelle. 'So little time left,' he said, trailing back to their table, having opted for the cheese and ham, 'there's no way we can set it all up.'

She was about to answer but broke off as a familiar figure entered the dining hall. Kommissar Kasper was striding down the aisle toward them, exuding attitude, wearing the sort of expression that might have announced the start of a crime seminar at the Ettblock.

'Damn that man,' Emma hissed. 'When are we going to be free of him?'

'He's got you on a tight leash.'

Kasper stopped at their table. 'I'm here personally this morning to issue a warning,' he said. 'To make sure you understand the conditions for continuing your discussions here.'

Emma folded her arms.

'I don't want any more trouble spilling out onto the streets,' Kasper said. 'This conference can continue provided it's confined to this hotel. Any problems among yourselves, you settle among yourselves – here, not outside.'

When Emma didn't reply, Kasper wagged a finger. 'And another matter. You would do well to terminate your relationship with Herr Huber.'

This time she couldn't stay silent. 'I didn't realise you had such extensive powers, Herr Kommissar. That you can even choose my friends.'

Sarcasm had no effect. 'I've already reminded Herr Huber of his responsibilities. He's handling confidential state archives. There must be no dealings with people lacking authorised access. Nor must any documents or copies be abstracted from them. No unauthorised communications. And no unauthorised information passed on. Is that clear?'

'What are you afraid of? Something shameful coming out?'

'A police officer has been placed in the state archive office to ensure compliance. Any transgressions will be punished. In such an event, it will go badly for him as well as for you.'

'Your diktat for the day?'

Roper and Emma stared at each other over untouched coffee cups once the Kommissar had departed.

'Looks like Wilkes and Kasper between them have got you in a corner,' he said.

'In their dreams,' she said, unclasping her phone. 'We need

some schedule readjustment.' She scrolled down her contacts. Roper leaned back first in amusement then in admiration. In the ensuing few minutes she located Professor Chadwick, persuaded him to grant her an extension, talked to someone called Lance, gained agreement for extra funding, informed the university of the revised dates and then threw enough money in the faces of Herr and Frau Ostermann to persuade them to offload their bookings to other hotels for the rest of the week.

'But surely the delegates are going to cry off?' Roper objected.

'Certainly not France, Poland, America, China or Nagorno. You can bet on it.'

'Are there any levers you can't pull?' he said.

'Chadwick's arranging for a notable alumni to fly in on Friday. He's coming too for a kind of grand finale. So we've got until then. This new guy's an Appeasement apologist so we should have some fun. At least, that's Chadwick's idea of fun.'

'And your plans?'

'As before.'

CHAPTER THIRTY-ONE

The sign, in cheap signwriter script, said Elektronik-Winkl, set above a single-storey prefabricated structure at the end of a long concrete road out from the shops at Mammendorf. There were fields at one side and fields further on. This was at the end of a straggling satellite town reached from the very limit of the city's Metro system.

Roper paused and took a deep breath. It had been a tiring trek from the station. First, he had passed a most elaborate set of allotment gardens, known as Laubenkolonie, where city folk with no gardens of their own came in the summer to sun themselves on manicured lawns, in freshly painted summerhouses and under miniature loggias reminiscent of the Nymphenburg Palace just across town. He'd trudged on. Next were precise rows of carrots, potatoes, beans and peas, all hemmed in by weed-banishing kerbstones, as if the owners were intent on first prize at next year's Gartenfest. Keeping up with the Schmidts was the motive in this part of town.

Roper turned his attention to Elektronik-Winkl, pushed open the rubber swing doors and entered a gloomy cavern. At its centre, bathed in a fluorescent spotlight, was a wide counter on which lay a huge, overweight ginger cat. The animal was on its side, eyes fixed on its owner, a tall balding man with large spectacles who was holding aloft a feline Dreamies treat between finger and thumb.

Roper ignored them and stared down at the tiers of shelving. There were banks of cameras so miniaturised they could be concealed in almost anything, and then there were the bugs: bog-standard bugs, clever bugs, specialist and expensive bugs.

He nodded to himself. He'd chosen this place for its obscure location, banking on a lack of supervision and an absence of CCTV and he was here because his hopes of listening in to Muzalev's missile auction had proved fruitless. The number and password of the mobile supplied by the Russian had been changed. The Nagorno delegate was a careful man. Regular switching was a mark of his security.

Roper made his choices and laid them on the big counter, presenting his credentials: a letter signed by the Isarhof's owner, Herr Ostermann.

'You're English!' the man exclaimed, delighted. 'Nice to meet a compatriot. Bit tucked away out here but got to make a living somehow, eh?' He thrust out a hand. 'Thomas St John O'Rourke at your service.'

'Bit unusual to find someone like yourself out here,' Roper murmured.

'Had a nice line in holiday homes back in the UK, year before last,' O'Rourke said. 'Of course, in that game you've got to pull a few strokes. One too many as it turned out and well, here I am; ways and means and all that. I always say, where there's a will there's a businessman, eh?'

Roper cut the small talk short. 'Am I okay with these?'

'The stuff on the purple list we're supposed to issue only to people with a special licence. Police, security, chaps like that.' He fingered Roper's letter. 'But hotel security's fine; no worries.

Problems of business, I always say; got to have a wrinkle or two; got to make a living, eh?'

O'Rourke scribbled on a purple form and gave it a hefty thump with an official stamp, causing the cat to leap up and flee the length of the shed.

By afternoon, Roper was back at the Isarhof where he worked the telephones to London, calling up TV contacts from three years back, reminding them of all the co-operation they had enjoyed, even when he'd gone down in the great phone-hacking scandal. At first, he got nowhere with those who had chewed his reputation to pieces but his one stroke of luck was friendship with Robyn Lloyd Hewitt, a newspaper colleague who'd made it across the divide into TV as a political commentator.

Hewitt helped set up a Skype conference with his channel's top executives at which Roper dangled the prospect of a major story – provided they'd play it his way, maintaining secrecy until the very last moment. As he talked he could see on the screen behind the nodding heads a clutter of studio ceiling lights, computer screens, mikes and headphones he remembered so well from that other, uncomfortable day. When he had momentary doubts about what he was doing he reran his last exchange with Emma: 'You're in too deep,' she'd told him, giving him her unblinking stare. 'We're a team, remember?'

Uncompromising as ever, and commanding.

Next morning he was at the airport, having won an exclusive tie-in with Sky and NABC. He'd hired a large minibus for crews and equipment and the two teams were booked in at the Hotel Hofgarten, close to the Isarhof but well out of sight.

The Americans were first out of Baggage Reclaim: big men sporting black baseball caps, brown suede shoes and colourful jackets. Hank, the sound recordist, wore huge specs; Spike and

Jones on the camera were chisel-faced; and Quentin the reporter was keen and pushy. Roper's briefing was friendly but firm: lie low, keep cameras hidden, don't talk about the story, keep everything discreet, surprise and timing being the key.

To help things along, he'd filled the fridge with beers.

Roper's next move was to take his new purchases from the Elektronik-Winkl down to the park by the River Isar. Past experience had taught him to test all new devices. Batteries tended to go flat at the worst possible moments. Satisfied after listening to snatches of park-bench chatter, he'd retrieved his devices and returned to the Isarhof to await his opportunity. The one big advantage was Wilkes's open pursuit of Muzalev, much of the conversation conducted in the hotel lounge. That became Point One: a tiny phone-operated bug under the table.

Sometimes the talk moved to Muzalev's hotel room.

Point Two: a bug buried in the padded headboard of the bed.

Sometimes, when not in conference session, the parleying took place in the dining room. Points Three and Four: a flower pot and a ceiling rose.

Most difficult of all: Wilkes's room. The man was careful. He might even possess sweeping equipment. Roper's solution: a hand drill that bored a hole in a partition wall, inserting the very latest microwave bug. Impossible to detect, even with specialist equipment.

Wherever they talked, Roper was watching, then a simple call from his mobile gave him an ear on the proceedings. And with the more sophisticated Wilkes bug, a short-burst broadcast could deliver a full twenty-four hours of conversation.

Timing was all, Emma had said, and Roper began to marvel at what he heard. The size of Muzalev's 'bung' escalated at every session. Each time Wilkes matched his latest demand, the tariff would rise again. And the principal source talking it up was the TGD company of Marseilles, fronted by the insidious shaven-headed Pole, Teodor Zdzislaw.

Roper relayed all this to Emma. How could she even talk to a man like Zdzislaw, he wanted to know.

But all she said was: 'Keep me updated.'

~

Bradley C Wilkes, Gillowitz, Poland, 6 May 1943

They can ring the place with barbed wire, put policemen on the gate, forbid anyone to leave the plant, impose a total shutdown... but they can't stop people talking. They can't contain fear. Not when there have been so many deaths and injuries.

My journey, using false papers to pass as a foreign worker, has taken several days. A mechanic friend has broken free my leg tag and I've sawn off the numbers for keepsakes. When I arrive at Gillowitz I have elaborate plans to penetrate the plant, perhaps make a switch with an amenable worker, deliver food to their canteen or get a job in the stores.

No chance. They bake their own bread, burn their own dead and the place is protected by a double ring of fences.

I'm attracted to a great stink a couple of kilometres down the road. Any worker willing to endure the nauseating proximity of burning rubber has a chance of employment, from which I glean that a regular supply of protective suits has to be destroyed, such is the corrosive effect of whatever it is they're doing behind that barbed wire. The wearers of these rubber suits get only ten work sessions before the equipment goes to the bonfire.

I stay at the dump long enough to learn all I can – but no longer. The place is an essay in dereliction: mountains of old tyres, haphazard piles of protection suits, mud, ruts, slush, mire, all overlaid with that stink. I cut short my employment, planning to try a funeral parlour, but it seems that fatal accident casualties at the security compound, of which there appear to be many, leave the plant in sealed jars of ashes.

My brother already briefed me on information supplied by Beck, our chemical salesman: ammonia, pressurised air and steam are used for decontamination. Despite this, accidents are frequent, so I try my luck at the hospital at Czechowitz.

Ward orderlies are scarce in this place – good fortune for me, if no one else. At the entrance there are double doors on springs with overlapping rubber surrounds to create a seal to keep out the cold. Inside, a massive vestibule is assigned for coats and hats – which soon leak snow which melts into great puddles on the floor. Mixed with mud and straw tramped in from outside, it's about as clinical and antiseptic as the scrapyard I've just left.

I pose as an itinerant Czech with a comic accent and become an acceptable butt of fun; pushing my trusty trolley, I'm part of the battered hospital furniture. Then my German and Czech and a smattering of Polish lets me in on the whispered horror stories in the corridors and wards. Semi-conscious babbles from the injured have fed the rumours; what happens when you touch the stuff; how long you last when you breathe it in. Talk of blisters, convulsions, paralysis, coma; how it can kill you in a minute. And when those damned Englanders get a dose of it, how we'll have no more trouble from them.

Stealthy observation of the outer perimeter of the plant provides the exact location, and the presence of a Luftwaffe officer going through checks at the guardhouse confirms my stark assessment. Two words have cropped up in whispered conversations – tabun and sarin – which are included in my report.

I work out the co-ordinates and summon Beck with a jaunty postcard from his aunt Vanja on the subject of her birthday trip to beautiful Kraków.

The salesman, who travels to customers all around Germany and the occupied territories, collects my data and returns home to Bregenz. Once again his courier wades chest-high through the shallow loops of the Rhine, this time with precise target information.

A week later, on a moonlit night in calm weather, the United States Air Force turns Germany's chemical warfare research centre at Gillowitz into a scene of fiery destruction.

CHAPTER THIRTY-TWO

Emma stood at the end of the first-floor landing, looking out of the hotel window giving a wide view of the street below. The light was fading, the street lamps in Jahn Strasse already on. She wondered how Huber and Roper were getting along.

She chuckled. She'd sent them out on a boys-only outing to the Hofbräuhaus, counting on Huber's big-hearted sense of humour and a ready flow of alcohol to smooth out Roper's ragbag of jealousies and resentments. She wanted an efficient team, not a pair of sparring partners.

She looked away, turning her thoughts once again to her grandfather and a worrying lack of progress in tracing his history. So far, she'd got no further than discovering he was some kind of efficient spy in neutral Switzerland. Surely it didn't end there?

And then there was The Weasel: he had raised uncomfortable doubts. Had Grandfather Bradley left his friend to die in a Gestapo prison... and what task had the Germans demanded of her grandfather?

She surveyed the street once more for signs of the returning duo and was glad there were none. She could picture the scene in the Hofbräuhaus: Huber, flourishing his wad of fake hyper-inflation currency, starting at 10 million Reichmarks, building through 20, 100, 200 until reaching 500 million, to tell his favourite story of 1920s Munich. 'Enough to buy a loaf of bread!'

Or perhaps the two of them would be upstairs, in the largest hall in the city, made infamous by a certain young agitator known to the crowds as 'the crazy Austrian corporal', standing by a window where he could best make mesmerising eye contact with the audience...

Something out in the street stopped Emma short and she forgot all about her carousing assistants. A street lamp illuminated the unmistakable face and wagging finger of Wilkes. She frowned. Wilkes had been flauntingly open of late, backslapping his associates in the lounge and the sunroom and now here he was talking to someone in the street: a figure dressed in overalls, cap and boots, leaning against a large van. She could just read the sign on the side of the vehicle: Autorent Ulrich with 8965 – the first numerals of a Munich district telephone code. She continued to watch. It did not look like a casual conversation. They weren't discussing the weather, the price of beer or where to get a girl. She sensed this was all about figures. They were cutting some kind of a deal. It was what Wilkes did. What he spent his life doing.

She descended the stairs and when he pushed through the swing doors she emerged from the shadows.

'Friend of yours?' she said, nodding in the direction of the street.

Wilkes blanked her, walking on.

She kept pace. 'Not so fast. You and I have a date with your laptop, remember?' She arrived at the lifts. He screwed up his face, pressed the button and looked up at the floor number, clearly hoping for a quick release.

'You promised more material,' she said. 'Got a printout?'

'No time.'

'Never mind; tell it now.'

Wilkes turned on her then. 'Look, missy, I've just about had enough of this; you'll have to wait till I'm good and ready.'

She stood back and smiled at him. 'That's all right then,' she said.

Wilkes looked surprised – then became wary. There was something about her manner. He grunted and pressed the lift button once more.

'Just before you go up,' she said, 'you might like to take a look at this,' handing him a sheet of typescript.

His brow wrinkled and he plucked the sheet from her, quickly scanning the first few lines:

```
Press release: Shock Revelation at the
Munich Reappraisal Conference: One of
its most prominent members, Cyrus
Wilkes, brother of presidential hopeful
Wendell Wilkes, has just been
exposed as…
```

He looked up, face flushed. 'To hell with this. You're welching on our agreement.'

Just then the lift arrived but she continued to block the doorway. 'I did warn you,' she said. 'No more stringing me along or the deal's off.'

He turned and tossed his briefcase in an angry arc on to the hotel sofa. 'I'll give you five minutes, max!'

'Shoot,' she said.

'You're like a dog with a damned bone.' He turned towards

the window, rubbing his forehead, tongue traversing his lower gum in an evident attempt to change focus and reconnect with his memory. 'Where did we get to?'

'Switzerland.'

'Ah yes, Switzerland.' He tweaked an ear, staring out of the hotel window. 'Yes, as told to me, Brad stayed with his brother in the Intelligence business for quite a while...'

The voice trailed off into silence.

They both stood like statues.

Then he began again. 'He was getting increasingly out of sorts, dissatisfied with himself and with what he was doing, complaining his war effort wasn't good enough. So when something else came up, he leapt at it.'

'And this was?'

'They sent him back into German-occupied territory.'

She walked to the reception area sofa and beckoned him over. 'Come and sit.'

He sighed but stayed upright, hand on the leather backing.

'They sent him back?' she queried. 'Hadn't he done enough?'

'Some war factory.' Wilkes shrugged away the lack of detail. 'Suspected of making something awful. Anyway, here comes the heroic bit. The bit you've been craving. Brad gets over there, finds out all about it, sends back the co-ordinates and hey presto, boom! The bomber boys blow it away.'

Emma relaxed, unable to resist a burgeoning smile of pride, of victory, of discovering this truly heroic role.

Wilkes nodded knowingly. 'Okay? Happy now? Got what you wanted?'

'But what then? What happened to him afterwards?' she demanded.

He sighed the sigh of a frustrated man. At that moment the lift door opened again, disgorging three guests into the reception area chattering loudly and in high spirits, oblivious of the frigid atmosphere around the sofa. Wilkes made a small movement as if he might try to escape.

'More!' she said.

He gave her a sour look. 'The difficult part,' he said. 'A disagreement between Brad and the Intelligence people.'

'About?'

Wilkes sighed. 'He'd found a concentration camp full of thousands of people and wanted the Air Force to hit that too, just like the factory.'

'To bomb a camp full of people?' she asked doubtfully.

'He'd got word. From the partisans. It was a death camp. Most of them were being gassed, the bodies burned. He reckoned bombing was better than allowing the killing to continue.'

She nodded slowly. 'And?'

'Air Force back in England refused. Said they had other things to do. Camp not a priority.'

Wilkes stopped. Clearly, he did not want to continue. This was like tooth extraction, she thought, without the anaesthetic. 'Then?'

'That's enough.' Another long pause, then he said: 'Truly, you'd rather not know.'

She flushed. 'Out with it.'

Wilkes took a deep breath, hesitated some more, then said: 'Brad got mad. Went into a blind fury. So angry he just disappeared off the American Intelligence radar.'

'What do you mean, disappeared?'

'Stalked off. Never heard of again.'

'But someone must have picked up the trail? He must have ended up somewhere.'

He shook his head. 'No one. That was the last we heard of him. Ever. So far as I know, by anybody.'

She put her head in her hands. 'Oh no, not another stray end?'

''Fraid so.' He was nodding furiously, like he was angry with himself for revealing too much. 'And now I've given you every last jot of what I've got.'

CHAPTER THIRTY-THREE

Roper was at the office window, staring down into the main reception area. The Isarhof was chilly. Workmen were in, dismantling the big stove in the far corner. Roper screwed up his face, twisting a pen around his fingers.

Emma, looking at the ceiling while sprawled on the only chair, said: 'I'll go to the market this afternoon and buy you a set of worry beads.'

Roper snorted. Huber was between them. Standing, of course, there was only room to stand, and Roper felt another jolt of irritation at the man's belated inclusion in this close relationship. 'My worry,' he told Emma, taking his gaze from all the activity down below, 'might just save your hide.'

'Oh yes?'

He took two steps, one to pass Huber, the other to confront Emma. 'I need to get you out of this place,' he said. 'And pretty damn quick.'

She gave him one of her sceptical looks but he persisted. 'Wilkes is more dangerous now than ever before. He's told you everything he knows. Nothing left in his locker. He must realise you could welch on him at any time and expose what he's doing. And where there's big money concerned...'

'You think she's in serious jeopardy?' Huber was looking all concerned.

Roper paused, resentful at this display of solicitude. Looking after Emma was his job and a few drinks in the Hofbräuhaus didn't change any of that. He said: 'While there was a deal on the table, it was a fragile peace, but now there's nothing to play fair for.'

Huber made more concerned noises. How was it he was on board, Roper asked himself, considering the hostility of the city police? Didn't he have his own problems?

He looked back down to Emma. She was shaking her head. 'Hang on,' she said, 'I'm still running this show. I'm not hiding myself away.'

Roper stooped to lean closer, almost as if to shut the other man out. 'If you stay, it makes my job of protecting you almost impossible. Best to get you out to somewhere safe.'

'I know just the place,' Huber chipped in.

Roper could guess where – but she was still shaking her head.

'Okay,' Roper said, 'you stay for the daytime sessions but hide out in the evenings. And eat out. Whatever the Kommissar says, he's not your jailer.'

Emma considered and Roper was again insistent: 'Never place yourself in jeopardy, never be caught alone, never be subject to intimidation. These are sharp operators. They're playing for big stakes. Assume a capacity for utter ruthlessness.'

Roper straightened up, standing tall.

There was a long pause, then she nodded in agreement.

～

They had lunch together sitting with exuberant crowds at the picnic benches under the trees in the old market, swilling glasses of Hofbräu, Spaten and Paulaner wheat beer and downing sauerkraut and sausages.

'Did you know?' Huber inquired, not requiring an answer, 'that on a certain day in the spring they serve free beer here? There's a 30,000 litre tank under these flagstones and the beer is simply piped straight into the fountains.'

'I believe you,' Emma said.

'Sure; it's absolutely true.'

'When's this?'

'Ah!' Huber held up a hand. 'The date? That's a little secret I'm keeping all to myself.'

Emma was escorted every minute of the afternoon and they used Huber's Kompressor for the drive to his flat in the evening. But being treated like some highly prized and cosseted piece of horseflesh was never Emma's style and later, when she realised she had left behind a blue ring binder containing her notes for the next day's meeting, she did what she had promised Roper she would not do.

The streets were empty and hardly anyone rode the tram, except for a couple of unsavoury characters in woolly hats and baggy trousers who attempted to give her the glad-eye. It was a direct route so it took only ten minutes to reach the Isarhof. Roper had gone to socialise with the delegates and Huber was out stocking up on supplies of Schneider Flaschenbere and Triumphator DB. They had no need to fret, she told herself; she knew exactly where the file was located and retrieving the background on tomorrow's subject – *Maxim Litvinov, Soviet Foreign Commissar, help or hindrance?* – would be the work of just a few seconds. She walked straight into the hotel, not in the least fearful, confident of her ability to handle herself and thinking Roper's concerns overblown.

Then she stopped. There was a different feel to the place. No one was about. Ghostly and deserted. She glanced briefly into the dining hall and again saw no one. But there was something... something white on one of the tables.

Emma went closer. It was a note, jammed between a teacup and a salt cellar, addressed to Cheung, the Chinese delegate.

'Join us,' it said. 'We're in the basement – if you really think you have anything to bring to the table. But no more skirmishing. This is the real deal.'

She stared at this for some time. Careless of them not to put it in an envelope, she thought, but the urgency was plain. Wilkes and the others were getting close to an agreement. She looked around. Should she contact Roper?

His mobile was on messages and her battery was running low. She grimaced. She wanted incontrovertible evidence for an exposé and two witnesses would have been better than one but she couldn't wait, couldn't miss this opportunity. She climbed rapidly to her hotel room to grab a camera, stopping first to check that no intruder had disturbed her carefully disordered tableau of clothes, towels and papers. Satisfied her room was untouched, she descended rapidly to the steel door leading to the basement.

Hand on the lever, she hesitated.

Should she wait? She shook her head, took a deep breath and hauled open the door.

Concrete steps led down into the gloom.

She fumbled for a switch.

It wasn't until she reached the bottom that she found it.

Another steel door.

She pulled it open, ready to confront another illicit meeting of missile dealers, but there was no one.

She walked inside. A brutal change of scene. From cosy rustic to bleak unpainted walls. It was gloomy and large, running the length of the hotel. Just as stark were the wire mesh cages protecting single light bulbs.

Perhaps they were clever, these missile men; perhaps they had found some far-off recess, some private room at the back of the basement. These old German places were a maze. English houses, she knew, stopped having basements around the dawn of the 20th century. Anything built after that was on a ground-level concrete base. But here the basement was still a standard building component. So much more convenient for storing all that junk you couldn't bear to throw away. She had a brief recall of all her mother's possessions crammed into corners.

By now she had reached the end of the basement and there was no room, no cubbyhole full of smoke and conspiracy.

Frustrated, she turned back and that was when she jumped in surprise. A huge boom rolled like a cannonade around the underground space. Startled, she was momentarily nonplussed.

Then she knew. It was the great steel door slamming shut.

It was several seconds before she realised what it meant. She was shut in, trapped, with no way out. She dashed to the door, found it locked and hammered with her fists. It hurt. So she cried out. 'Come back; I'm in here.'

There was no reply, merely the sound of unheeding footsteps, the sound receding, then the slam of the outer door at the top of the steps.

She shouted again, knowing it was useless.

Hands on hips. Why? Was it some stupid janitor who'd failed to check before shutting the door? Or worse? She shrugged. A deliberate act? Who would do such a thing? Then a dark suspicion came to mind.

She looked around, knowing what an airless dungeon this was. She bashed on the door again, shouting, angry, incredulous.

Nothing.

She began a careful inch-by-inch examination of her new

prison. There had to be a hatch somewhere – a skylight, a trapdoor, a basement entrance.

But she had gone no more than ten steps when there was another explosion of noise. This time, water.

Her frown increased and the noise led her down to the lowest point. Two monster taps. And both gushing water. Pouring out as if from some angry flooded river.

Why? The truth began to dawn. Yes, a deliberate act and with only one likely culprit: Wilkes had slammed the door, Wilkes had turned the taps, and Wilkes intended her to drown.

She reached down to turn off the water supply, knowing it wouldn't be that easy. They didn't move; they were jammed wide open.

She directed all her strength to turning, first with one, then with both hands, to no avail. Surely they must turn? She looked closer, supposing the maintenance men used these taps for scrubbing the floor. Then she recognised the locking mechanism which should have closed off the supply – except that it was locked in the open position, with the key removed.

She turned away, jogging back, searching desperately for a toolbox or some object to grip and use as a lever.

Nothing.

The water continued to pour.

She was furious at being so easily tricked. She stamped a foot and it made a squelchy splash. Surely it wouldn't end like this? She had never cared much for water. Swimming wasn't on her sport CV.

Could she kick her way out? She only had to look at the steel door to know there was no chance. Like a bank vault, fitting absolutely flush and locked from the outside. This basement was a tomb. Her tomb.

She gripped her mobile to summon Roper but could get no signal. The thing was dead. Useless! She threw it angrily into a spreading puddle. The only way was noise. Kick up such a stink someone would come. But the prospects were not good. No one came this way, through an outer door and down some steep concrete steps, unless they wanted to park their old fridge, store unwanted Christmas presents or tuck away a sun umbrella for the winter.

The water was in her shoes, cold, threatening and numbing her feet. She decided to make another search to see what useful tools she might find before they were all submerged but all she discovered were four wire-encased booths locked and bulging with old bikes and boxes. Further back were tables, chairs, furniture, deckchairs and other hotel equipment.

By now the water was creeping higher and higher, paralysing her legs with a stinging cold, its tendrils reaching for her upper body, the temperature not much above freezing. The inrush of water was so great that the tide was rising with shocking rapidity. Soon it would be at waist level. There was a crash as an old cupboard started to float, tilting over. Inside, she could hear the tumble of falling crockery and the jingle of loose cutlery. Several chairs were already bobbing about on the rising tide, crashing into one another, making it difficult to move.

She swallowed. This was one problem she had not anticipated. Her usual confidence that she could meet any challenge began to wilt. There were splashes in her face as she moved and the fright of an early childhood mishap returned to haunt her: a ducking at the swimming baths; the only time she had been the victim of a prank. The experience of that day – water in her nose, a sense of blind panic, thrashing wildly about, arms flailing for lack of something to grip; the memory of it returned to her now and she shouted all the louder.

She swished about in renewed desperation, on the edge of panic, still in search of a tool, a manhole, a crowbar, something. The engulfing flood was over her thighs then above her waist as she began opening wall cupboards, the ones high up, and noticed some wires leading to a black box. By this time she was in a state of confusion. The cold seemed to have paralysed her thought processes and the idea came to her quite slowly: water and electricity don't mix... *There's going to be an awfully loud bang when the tide reaches this point.*

It was then that she had her first really useful thought. She recalled the episode with the lights going out at the Führerbau and Roper's mention of a fuse box. She looked again at the black box above her. Was this the hotel's fuse box? The one that controlled all the power and the lights? She studied it, then began to reach for it.

Some blokes acted like overgrown babies. Roper was grumbling to himself about the rump of delegates still attending the conference and their inability to amuse themselves in the evenings. He'd just spent an hour organising a card school, buying drinks at the bar in Fraunhofer Strasse. Did they want their sandwiches buttered in the mornings?

He shook his head in annoyance as he walked back to the Isarhof. He still had plenty to attend to and didn't feel himself to be under any kind of a threat. Carefully, he sidestepped Frau Ostermann, once again – probably for the third time that day – on her knees washing, brushing and polishing the hotel entrance. He eased his way past her to the lift door. As he did so he was conscious of a strange smell: a damp watery sort of odour with a hint of drains.

Roper shook his head and pressed the button for the second floor but before the door opened the head cook appeared, puzzled, wiping his hands on his apron, making for Reception.

'Herr Ostermann!'

The cook had to repeat his address. The hotelier was deep into his crossword.

'Herr Ostermann, we have a problem in the kitchens.'

The lift door opened but the chef's worried tone caused Roper to delay. He lingered long enough to overhear the next exchange.

'The water pressure's right down. Something's not right. The taps are hardly running at all. Taking us far too long to fill our pans and kettles.'

Roper took a few steps back and sniffed again. The smell seemed stronger than ever. The old hotelier looked blank. Just then the lights flickered and went out.

'My screen!' the old man said. Even he had mastered a hotel booking programme but it was no more. The lights were off, the power was off, his screen blank – but then, just as suddenly, the lights came back on. Then off again. Then on.

The hotelier and the cook were gaping at each other in complete confusion.

'It's a signal!' Roper said. 'Someone is trying to raise the alarm.'

'Alarm? Alarm? What for?' Ostermann said.

'Someone is using the power supply, turning it on and off to make us aware.' There was an immediate sense of foreboding in Roper. The situation had an unfortunate resonance with what had happened at the Führerbau.

'But why?'

'Let's find out. Where's the mains switch?'

Ostermann looked perplexed for a moment, then jerked upright. 'On the fuse box.'

Roper sighed. 'And where's that?'

More wrinkles to the brow, then: 'In the basement.'

Roper strode to the outer basement door, tried it, wrenched at it and stepped back. 'Locked!'

'The key is in the door.'

'No it isn't!' He sniffed. 'There's water down there. That's where that curious smell is coming from.'

Ostermann was in a fluster, didn't know what to do.

'I think your water supply is draining off into the basement,' Roper said. 'Where's the stopcock?'

At last, the cook had something useful to contribute. 'In the kitchens. There was some workmen fiddling with it this morning...'

'Then turn it off!' Roper was getting angry – partly because of their inertia but also because of an even greater sense of foreboding: where was Emma? He tried her phone without result. Some instinct told him she was not at the flat. His suspicions mounted that her carefree attitude had led her into trouble. The same instinct warned him that the alarm signal might be hers. 'Find the key!' he shouted to Ostermann over his shoulder as he dashed two at a time up the stairs to the second floor.

Panting, out of breath, he made it to her room, knocking loudly, calling her name.

No response.

The lights flicked on and off again.

He went back down the stairs five at a time, sliding down on the handrails, his feet just kissing the edges of the risers.

'The key! The key!' he yelled at the old man.

Ostermann was flustered, bumbling about among pigeonholes and drawers.

Roper ignored him, jumping behind the counter, pulling out drawers, emptying them on to the floor, the old man spluttering, the old woman making a belated appearance. The chaos and affront to her ordered world would probably bring on a heart attack. Roper didn't care. He could smell danger.

Finally, a bunch of keys clattered to the floor. Roper held them up. 'Which one?'

'So long since I–'

'Which one?'

But Ostermann was in a fluster. In his present state he wouldn't remember his own name.

Roper didn't wait, ran to the basement door and looked at the huge cluster in his hand. *Must be keys here to open every damned door in the hotel*, he thought. He looked at the lock and decided two large brass keys seemed the most likely, tried one, then the other. He knew he should keep cool but fumbled and dropped the second one before he could get it into the lock. He cursed loudly but succeeded in turning it at the second attempt.

He pulled open the door and looked down the concrete steps in shock. The place was completely flooded. The water was well up the stairway, not far off the roof of the basement. A second steel door at basement floor level was just visible, the handle well below water.

'Emma!' he yelled, the voice loud and distorted as it carried around what little space that remained.

From behind the basement door, sounding as if from afar, came a strangulated, indistinct response.

Roper splashed down the steps. The water was black and oily. All kinds of rubbish bobbed around the surface. He took a very deep breath, pinched his nose and slid painfully into the dense, cold, wavering mass, clawing his way down the rim of the lower door until he felt the handle.

He heaved.

All he achieved was to swing his body round in an arc in the water. He struggled, freezing, lungs tight, forcing himself to stay in control, lashing out with his feet for something to grip. When he found purchase, he heaved at the handle again.

Nothing. His resistance was gone. The cold was killing him.

He kicked upwards, broke the surface, panting, gasping, spitting rubbish, scrabbling for the stairs. He forced himself to climb to the top, his clothes sopping and heavy, water draining down his legs. He grabbed the key cluster from the outer door and descended once more.

Which one?

Momentarily, he hesitated, hung up by distaste for the idea of going in again. Then he heard another sound from below. That settled it. He selected the most likely of the big brass keys and slid painfully back into the uninviting tide, searching for a keyhole. When he found it, he brought his key hand towards the right position, but the water seemed determined to wash him away.

He felt his arm floating. He struggled. By an act of supreme willpower he got the key into the lock. Turning was never so difficult. Still jammed, still immobile.

Roper broke surface once more to gulp air. Then, steeling his resolve, knowing he was close to his limit, he switched keys and slid back to try again.

Another struggle. How much longer could he last? He forced a new desperate strength into his thumb and twisted. The pain in his arm and shoulders screamed but the key turned.

The door still wouldn't move. He tugged and tugged and when he thought he couldn't hold his breath any longer the door gave a sudden boom and jerked open. At the same moment a dark shape brushed across his head. He felt a foot on his shoulder, then another.

Roper jack-knifed upwards and broke the surface in a swirl of spray and splashes.

When his vision cleared, he saw her, half in and half out of the water, hanging on to the chef's outstretched arm, panting, gasping, at the edge of exhaustion. Then she turned, looked at him and blew water from her mouth.

Water stung Roper's eyes, there was nausea in his stomach and breathing was still painful.

He saw her blank white expression change, recognising elation and exhaustion combining in a heaving chest. She swallowed and said in a barely audible whisper: 'You took your time.'

Roper shook a wet head. 'Can't leave you on your own for five minutes, can I?'

They stared at each other, a long bedraggled examination, then began to smile. The smiles turned into laughs. Loud laughs of shock, pain and relief.

The chef was looking from one to the other.

Ostermann was behind him.

'Are they mad?' the hotelier asked.

CHAPTER THIRTY-FOUR

They wrapped themselves in blankets and drank coffee with rum to drive away the cold and sense of exhaustion. She had a deathly white pallor and a headache, he a pain in the chest.

'Any longer than ten minutes in there and we'd have had it,' he said, after changing into dry clothes. But with Emma, rest was out of the question.

They joined a crowd on the pavement outside the hotel to watch firemen pump out the basement. Roper knew she was in a dangerous frame of mind: light on her feet, poised like a boxer waiting for the bell to signal the next round. She wanted to confront certain persons whom she regarded as clearly responsible, a guilt demonstrated by their absence and lack of curiosity.

'They're scared to come near us. Proves it!' she said.

'But we don't really know,' he objected.

'Before, I just wanted to defeat him,' she said. 'But now it's a matter of annihilation.'

He shook his head, looking at her closely. She had a tremor in her right hand, one eye was swollen and she had a slight limp.

Anyone else would have taken to their bed but she was all for storming into Wilkes's bedroom and holding his head under a sink full of cold water. On another day, her strength fully restored and pumped up with the adrenaline of fury, she might have attempted it. She had the wildness and the temper.

Eventually the slow progress of the pumping operation calmed her. Single acts of physical vengeance were pointless, Roper told her, and led only to more violence, more injury and a police cell.

'You know what they say. Don't get angry...'

'Get even,' she completed, sounding unconvinced.

'The best revenge,' he said, 'is to hurt Wilkes where it hurts the most. In his pocket.'

When she said nothing, he pressed the point. 'Defeat in the eyes of his family. Humiliation back in Boston. Can you imagine it? The reaction of the old lady? That's what he'll fear most.'

Mention of another outbreak of difficulty with the town, the Music School Direktor and the likely appearance of Kommissar Kasper had the required effect. Emma consented to retreat to Huber's flat. But even there Roper was nervous. He knew that every time Wilkes and she came within shouting distance there was the prospect of an uncontrolled outburst.

'Don't be tempted into any meaningless revenge,' he told her. 'You have no proof. He'll only deny it and put you in the wrong. You have to be cleverer than that.'

She sat on Huber's massive sofa and glowered.

Roper, feeling uncomfortable on another man's turf, stood watching her, resentment building. He knew he had no right, no proprietorial claim to her. His reaction against her holing up with Huber was foolish but he resented the man all the same. He hated Huber's friendship with Emma, his status as an academic and his youth.

Then he sighed and got a grip.

'Take stock,' he told Emma. 'Consider progress. Think where we are on the trail of your grandfather.'

Defeat, humiliation, annihilation – all the words Emma had in mind for Wilkes. She still had the tang of that disgusting water in her nose, her eyes were sore, fatigue was setting in. It was easy for Roper to talk of being clever. Grateful though she was for rescue, his immersion had been much briefer than hers and the prospect of death by drowning was not something she felt neutral about. She knew she had been badly shaken. Hostility, anger, revenge – they all shored up her defences, preventing disintegration.

She needed a change of subject. Grandpa. She clenched a fist and tore her mind free of the oily blackness of the encroaching tide, the diminishing airspace of a flooded basement and the imminent prospect of a watery extinction, and focused instead on a man rejecting his role in Intelligence. Here was Grandfather Bradley, another angry human being – a parallel personality to her own, she was quite certain. Out of the same mould, her mother always said, a carbon copy; it was a wonder she didn't have his red hair, and so on. Emma remembered thumbing through family albums and lingering over one particular photograph: Bradley beaming next to his fast twenties tourer, a six-cylinder Mercedes SS Super Sport, all gleaming bodywork in cream and brown, huge mudguards and a bonnet held down with a leather strap. 'Ditto my love of cars,' she mumbled, and began inserting herself into his place in that other time, in that other location. Several other locations, in fact: Switzerland, Poland, and a concentration camp. Anger, so much anger, that he had walked away. But to where?

Where would she have gone?

She reran in her head the sound of Bradley's voice. The rich timbre, the confidence, the authority. She and Roper had spent hours listening to the NABC recordings and the more she listened the stronger the kinship she felt. They shared the same thought patterns, diction, attitudes; it was a tragedy they had never met. His distaste for the Nazis was clear but what of other things, other places? She cast her mind back. Should she trawl through the discs again? Then memory worked for her. Reports he had sent from other countries, like Czechoslovakia; his fondness for Prague and sympathy for its people.

She went to her briefcase and retrieved the brown plastic case with the NABC logo. Then she spent more time replaying and reliving the incredible tension of the pre-invasion days of September 1938 when war clouds threatened the city. She listened intently as Bradley Wilkes told how its citizens went about their daily business while fearing for the future. They knew what to expect: German bombs, tanks and police.

It was then she had it. Bradley's admiration for their preparations. The Czechs would fight, he said, but in the event of defeat several groups were preparing for the worst, travelling to the forest regions where they could wage a partisan war. The recordings spelled out the broad outlines: underground tunnels, caves and forest hides stocked with weapons, ammunition, food; put in place for a long war of resistance.

'That's it,' she told Huber forcefully. 'That's the answer. Definitely. You can tell from his tone. His admiration for the partisans. That's where he would have headed.'

She had Huber put out an internet appeal in the Czech language. It specified the forest regions and sought news of 'an

American escapee last seen in the area around 1943 onwards and who might have been in contact with Resistance groups'.

'A long shot,' she said.

Huber, all solicitous, assured her: 'Don't worry, something will turn up. It always does.'

Had she got a hero grandfather – or not?

She was still smarting from the Wilkes put-down of her grandfather: 'The man turned bad.' And The Weasel's accusation of betrayal. She pushed from her mind warning words from Roper: 'A man can only take so much. Even this man. Perhaps he'd just had enough.'

No! Despite all the doubts, she wanted to treasure Bradley Wilkes's memory as an implacable pursuer of truth and justice. She wanted him vindicated.

She prowled around the apartment, trawling through her messages without result and found it impossible to sit still. Huber was in his Lilliputian kitchen, banging pots and pans and cooking some family speciality called a Königsberger Klopse. 'Sounds like an elephant in the zoo,' she said.

'Succulent meatballs in a fantastic sauce,' he replied. 'Another of my extensive repertoire of Silesian cuisine.'

She lightened a little when he fiddled with his music centre. He was a Vivaldi freak, just like her. Strains of Nigel Kennedy's 'Four Seasons' filled the flat. He was wearing a Carla Bruni T-shirt. He'd already tried to invite her to one of the singer's concerts, to be staged at the Gasteig on Rosenheimer Strasse, but she wasn't feeling in the least social.

She saw him looking at the sofa and drew in a long breath. How far was she going with this? She had avoided emotional entanglements since her long-ago nightmare relationship. The name of Charles Nash should have been consigned to the past but it still made her boil, in particular the day he turned up demanding to trace his child. Memories of this had her flexing the fingers of her right hand. There was recall of her brother teaching her the techniques of self-defence; recall of a final confrontation with bad penny Nash; recall of her prowess with the knuckles.

She sighed. However generous and supportive Max Huber might be, he was sleeping on his own couch this night. Alone.

In the morning it was good to get out of the flat, outside in the fresh air, with a sense of freedom restored, bad thoughts banished. Huber thought it too dangerous to go to the Isarhof after the events of the previous day but Roper went anyway and Emma hailed a taxi to take her to the city centre.

She got out just before the Karlstor, walked under the old archway that once guarded the city, making for the big Oberpollinger department store. The crowds filled the wide pedestrian thoroughfare but she resisted the temptation to linger and went directly to the third floor, choosing the most nondescript and instantly forgettable plain-blue overcoat she could find.

She didn't enjoy it. This was Roper's idea; items of disguise for a fast getaway from the Isarhof. 'Our hotel could become a trap,' he'd told her; 'we could be ambushed, holed up or imprisoned if things go badly.' He'd even insisted they remove passports, credit cards and other essentials to Huber's flat.

Emma shrugged, refusing to take all these precautions quite as seriously as he, and descended to the basement to try on hairpieces. She looked in the mirror and recalled a teenage prank – invading her mother's room when she was out, trying on her wigs and hooting with laughter. She wasn't laughing now.

Last on her list was a pair of hideously large off-the-peg spectacles. Finally, there had to be some form of compensation for all these painful purchases. She searched out the big black boots with the silver buckle she had spotted several days earlier, then added a patterned scarf, arranging it in a circular fashion in the German style.

As soon as she stepped back into Huber's flat she was caught up in an atmosphere of excitement. 'Told you,' he said. 'It's come good.' He motioned her urgently to the desk. 'Come and look at the screen.' He scrolled through his emails before settling on one using the Czech language. 'It's from an amateur historian in a little town in the mountains. His special interest is Resistance groups of the last war.'

'And?'

'He wants to speak with us.'

'What's wrong with this?' She pointed to the screen.

'He wants a face-to-face. To check and exchange documents and information. We should have photographs and identifying objects.'

'Put all that on the system.'

'Look, this is a very old man operating from a remote village. The web's probably new to him. Probably doesn't trust it. He'll say, safer one to one.'

She considered. 'Huge distance to travel. Could be someone else entirely. Our message was pretty vague.'

'An American Resistance fighter? Couldn't be many of those around at that time.'

Emma nodded. She would follow every trail, explore every possibility. 'But I can't absent myself from the final conference sessions,' she said.

'Problem,' conceded Huber. 'Nor me! Sorry, I'm tied to my archive.'

'Then I'll send Roper,' she said.

CHAPTER THIRTY-FIVE

The car was stuck frustratingly in slow-moving traffic over the river bridge outside the Deutsches Museum and then, again, waiting for the trams to cross at the Max-Weber-Platz, but once on the autobahn ring the Porsche came into its own, the ideal vehicle for an 800-kilometre dash.

Roper grinned to himself and savoured once again the car's sleek interior, the velvet pile carpet, the leatherette upholstery, the graphic navigation display and the souped-up music system. Spotless, like it was on exhibition. She probably had a valet job after every trip. Couldn't be many university researchers who could afford it but then he knew her secret. Her brother specialised in rebuilding wrecks.

Roper aimed to reach his elusive contact – an old man with an unpronounceable name who called himself Rabbit – in seven hours, most of the way on the limit-free autobahn, using a thermos for refreshment, but once across the Czech frontier the forest roads slowed his progress. The Beskid, located along the border between the Czech Republic and Slovakia, was all mountains and trees interspersed at the edges with dilapidated and rotting relics of industry. Some of the trees, he noticed, showed signs of pollution from the mines and factories; a legacy of the communist years.

Roper struggled with his Hofer map. The tracks all looked the same and in the deep forest it was almost impossible to retain a sense of direction. It took four wrong turns before he spotted the shack. Was this it? Then, as he drew closer, an old man came into view, white-bearded, his right arm raised and lowered in a rhythmical chopping motion, hard at work cleaving firewood. Roper stopped the motor and switched his attention to the shack. Lines of rabbit skins hung from the eaves, a window was cracked, another was missing, and lichen crept up the walls. He clocked a meadow, some sheep, chickens, a horse, a dog and several stacks of logs.

In the silence he could hear the old man grunting, his breathing heavy, with the occasional curse. Then the chopping stopped.

The man looked up and spotted Roper.

Was this Rabbit? And what kind of reception would there be when he unwrapped Emma's package... inside that shack?

The old man was flicking through the pictures, laid out over the warm bonnet of the Porsche, and with each rapid dismissal Roper's spirits began to fall. It had started well, the introduction successful. This was indeed Rabbit, the forest resister, and he agreed to approach the car. But there the good news ended. Emma had put together a memorabilia package – newspaper cuttings, photographs from seventy years past, Bradley's passport picture, even stuff from his boyhood, and Roper was armed with a list of written questions in the Czech language requiring yes or no answers but the old man had enough German to make himself understood.

Next day, back in Munich, Roper gave Emma the gist of it.

'It was him, all right. Amazing old bloke. At ninety, as fit as ever; lived in that forest all his life, keeps sheep and shoots rabbits, has no electricity, his nearest neighbour across the hill, contactable only by horse.'

Impressive as all this was, the result was disappointing. The old man had failed to provide the desired confirmation. 'Apparently, Rabbit didn't have much to do with the mystery man, so he's not sure. Says his friend had most contact with him. He would know for certain.'

Emma tugged at a hair and massaged with some force the birthmark on her neck.

'But I did get something,' Roper said, hoping to mollify her. 'Their strange American fighter was known among the Resistance as The Brakeman.'

She frowned.

'He had an obsession. One he pursued relentlessly. A kind of mania they couldn't understand.'

'Like?'

'Shooting up trains.'

There was a long silence as Emma considered. 'Does this help us?'

Roper shrugged. 'Another thing. He didn't destroy them. Didn't derail them or blow them up, as you might expect a partisan to do. He only shot at the locomotive. At the crews. He wanted only to target the driver and the fireman.'

She spread her hands. 'Bizarre! And why the strange name?'

'The real brakeman on a train has a lookout tower and a brake, but this man...'

'Used a rifle?'

'Right.' Roper looked down at his notes. 'There were three of them,' he said, 'old Resistance fighters from the war, keen to keep the legend alive and known only by their roles: Rabbit, Logs and The Cobbler.'

'Sounds like a stage turn.'

'They've been looking for years to trace their mysterious American. Refused to give his name. Spoke fluent German and Czech.'

'Fits,' she said.

'Rabbit has kept your package. Says they'll call a meeting of the old fighters and go over the photos and give us a definite answer in a couple of days.'

~

Bradley C Wilkes, Beskid Forest, Occupied Czechoslovakia, 13 November 1943

This man Rabbit is a fool. He never was much good – a lousy shot and a poor tactician. His only expertise is filching cigarettes from the principal black marketeer in the town, the butcher Novacek, but I have to concede, in reluctant fairness, plundered cigarettes are the main currency. I first encounter Rabbit in the Moravka market. I've ditched Wilber and his hamstrung Intelligence operation. I'm furious beyond words at his powerlessness, at his inability to prevent a great tragedy. I won't accept it; I won't shrug shoulders; I won't accept orders are orders.

So here I am, quitting Switzerland and setting up in the market of this poor Czech town, offering to sell a good quality coat (off my back), a woolly jumper (from my rucksack) and a beautifully crafted pair of brown leather boots with high instep, size 43 (off my feet).

'How much?' The man goes by the name of Jan Fronek but is known to all as Rabbit. Having got his attention I carefully enunciate what I have been advised: 'Two crowns and an

introduction to the friends of the anemone.' An absurd price tag: seventy-five would be nearer the mark but I know the flower of the Beskid is the appropriate phrase of significance.

This is how I meet Jaroslav Urbanovsky, known as The Cobbler, leader of the group. He wants to know why I want to join. Suspicious, naturally, so I explain why I'm furious at the Allies, how I've abandoned the role of spy and now wish to fight in another way. I get a trial and pass the test: raiding a military store and busting a bank. And it's during frequent scavenging sweeps that I get to know the railway line, ten miles down the valley on the wooded plains of the Beskid, a cross-country route leading into Poland. All sorts of useful things fall off trains, mainly coal – a highly prized commodity for heating but also for the baking of black bread. Then I stumble on my big idea. I lie hidden, studying the traffic and soon recognise it for what it is. I have seen these long trains of cattle wagons before, seen them arrive in that other terrible place, and I know their cargoes are not cattle but human.

Soon I discover that the trains begin their journey in Brno, a city once boasting a Jewish population of 12,000, now rapidly diminishing through Nazi persecution. Other trains start from the ghetto town of Theresienstadt. They enter the Beskid region at Frýdek-Místek, the boundary between Moravia and Silesia, continuing on through our forest to Teschen, then over the Polish border to Oświęcim. An old railwayman tells me this while out walking his dog. The Germans, he says, have another name for the destination.

With the passing of each line of wagons my determination grows. In the forest hide, they say my easy manner has gone, my expression permanently grim.

So be it. This is what I have come for. This is my war.

～

The three of them were having lunchtime snacks in their mezzanine office. Emma had hardly touched her frikadellen sandwich. She was smiling, studying her messages, Roper's bugs giving her a ringside seat on the missile auction. Apparently Wilkes was finding it hard-going, she said. Every time he thought he'd clinched a deal with Muzalev someone came in with a lower contract price and the size of the Nagorno delegate's bribe rose even higher.

'You've got a spy!' Huber said through a forest of tomato and lettuce. 'Someone on the inside.'

She smiled and tapped her nose. 'And now they're talking about having a final session all together to decide who gets the order.' She raised a triumphant fist. 'And his bribe has just hit four million!'

'Impressive Intelligence, I'll give you that.'

'It's definite! The three of them are going to fight it out and settle it. China, America, France, all together with Nagorno.'

Roper looked up, his mouth full of currywurst. 'What's the odds on the meet? A 500 euro note says it's the Café Bavaria.'

She took her first bite of frikadellen. 'And we'll be on hand for the big exposé,' she said.

CHAPTER THIRTY-SIX

They arrived with Emma in a big Mercedes taxi. It seemed to Roper, as she ushered the VIPs and the promised alumni across the Isarhof forecourt and into the lobby, to resemble a tour of inspection by some minor royalty. His first job for the conference grand finalé had been to line up the reception committee: three of the more presentable delegates for unctuous handshakes.

Before the arrival, the three of them had stood about in the lobby, shuffling their feet, sucking in their breath, a stiff gait of uncomfortable impatience. It reminded Roper of his earlier days awaiting a general's inspection.

Then the arrival, the smiles and the handshakes. Had he chosen right? There was the ever-amenable Carlo, the formal Jean-Francois Girolle and the always-dressy Mimi Aschemeyer. Definitely the glamour number of the line-up.

A rotund figure with an egg-shaped head, a fluffy red tie and cord trousers going bald at the knee was first to burst free from Mimi's clutches. Professor Chadwick, without a doubt. Roper, matching the man to the picture painted for him by Emma, stepped forward and felt under no obligation to be obsequious.

He'd been bottled up at the Isarhof for days. 'The Great Conductor making his appearance at the gala performance,' he said, clutching the proffered hand.

Emma looked at him as if he had just uttered an unspeakable obscenity but Chadwick merely chuckled. 'And here, I presume, we have the Big Bassoon.'

Roper did a mock bow. 'Unfortunately blowing a few wrong notes along the way.'

'Ah! But I have every confidence. Everything will be all right on the night.'

The other professor was quite different. Roper recognised him: Terence Copperthwaite, TV commentator, author of five heavyweight tomes and the holder of the Benjamin Boyd chair of history at Oklahoma. He was tall, wore a black leather jacket, tailored jeans and high brown boots. Pursed lips suggested disapproval of Roper's levity.

The socialising continued over drinks in the hotel bar. Roper looked across a crowd of talking heads to find Emma. She was engaging the attention of Chadwick and Copperthwaite. He considered the possibility that he was mistaken; perhaps *she* was the real conductor. He felt a movement at his sleeve. It was Jean-Francois Girolle, edging him gently away from the general conversation into a conspiratorial corner. 'Monsieur Roper, our distinguished visitors, they're staying at the Hilton Hotel, yes?'

Roper nodded, sighing inwardly. 'What of it?'

'Tell me this, why are they getting international-style luxury while we are stuck in this awful place?' He swept a dismissive hand around him to indicate the Isarhof.

'Just an overnight stay,' Roper said.

Emma arrived at his elbow in time to prevent more protests. 'Ready for your session, Jean-Francois?'

'Madame Drake, I must tell you something. This conference

is getting far too Anglo-Saxon. The French point of view is being strangled.'

She faced him directly. 'Good. If you want to say the funk-ridden English bullied the French out of standing up to Hitler, that's fine; I happen to agree with you.'

'You do?'

'Only, present it with style.'

Girolle looked taken aback. 'Style?'

'Try something different. Use the newsreels Professor Chadwick's downloaded from the archive. Pathé News – plenty to get your teeth into there. Look forward to it.'

She was off, back to her guests, leaving Girolle blinking in astonishment and Roper grinning. He knew the real reason the visitors were at the Hilton: to shield them from the fraught atmosphere of conflict and threat hanging over the Isarhof. No one wanted the likes of Wilkes or his cronies to cast a shadow over the scene.

The thought of what his quarries might be up to had Roper hurrying from the room to check. As he did so, he had to stop himself yawning. After all, he had been up since five that morning setting up an elaborate and highly complex trap.

It had begun two days before with Roper throwing silly money at Umberto Borghesi, the Italian owner of the Café Bavaria. It had been obvious from the beginning that expenses were on a generous scale. Emma carried with her a wad of twenties and fifties for everyday requirements, but Roper was shocked at the amount of euros it took to persuade Borghesi that Emma's plan did not represent notoriety and a threat to the good name of the restaurant but a unique business opportunity. Coachloads of tourists would be stopping in Schelling Strasse to see the location of The Great Sting, she promised. People from Beijing to San Francisco would sit at his tables to sample the atmosphere. The Bavaria would be on the signposts of all the city bus tours.

To make this work, Roper and NABC's Hank, a tall man with a plaid shirt and monster specs, had been hard at work from the early hours installing devices at all the tables. They were under the chairs, in the magnolia table lights, in the gap between table and wall, and under the fading red wallpaper. Spike, the ferret-faced cameraman, was equally ingenious with his miniaturised devices: in the candelabra and fixed atop the wooden partitions which separated the seating alcoves.

It wouldn't matter where the targets decided to sit. Roper, hunched in his kitchen cubbyhole with a spyglass through to the dining area, could dial up any table to listen in, and Spike could activate the nearest camera eye.

'Hey, Roper!' Hank was testing the devices at the third table, the one next to the wide picture window. 'Are you sure this thing's going to work? What if these guys decide to go someplace else? We'd look a right bunch of lamebrains.'

'No worries! They won't shift.'

But this reply was all bravado. Wilkes was no fool. Roper, knowing his adversary could well have second-guessed them, bit down hard on a sausage sandwich supplied by the kitchens and nearly lost a tooth.

At Emma's prompting, Herr Ostermann roused himself from his obsessional crosswords long enough to set aside a room at the Isarhof as a projector room. It made a strange cinema. There were long curtains and rows of seats but around the edges of the room in alcoves and corners were examples of the old-fashioned

Bavarian farm art known as *bauernmalerei* – cupboards and wardrobes painted by the farmers themselves with flowers and bright colours. It was to this room that the delegates trooped at the behest of their French colleague.

Jean-Francois Girolle had taken Emma's advice. The Pathé newsreels ran not to the accompaniment of the smooth Anglo-Saxon commentary of Bob Danvers-Walker but to a more fractious French discourse. It began with the iconic cock symbol and the usual flashing numbers. But Girolle had a new line on the familiar scenes of prime ministerial arrivals, VIP limousines and po-faced pictures posed on the negotiating couch: the Führer, staring stony-faced and mad-eyed directly into the camera; Chamberlain, like an ageing refugee from a care home; Mussolini, a jaunty day tripper; and Daladier, a man about to jump off the Eiffel Tower.

All this was pictorial ammunition: the French government, indeed the whole French nation, Girolle said, had been bullied out of their desire to stand up to Hitler. Prime Minister Daladier was in despair. France could not confront Hitler alone without Britain's support, and Chamberlain was signed up to surrender. Daladier wanted to declare war rather than allow the Germans to attack the Czechs but in the end had to follow Britain.

The result was to wreck all France's careful plans for security – her eastern alliances exposed as worthless and Russia turned away to make its own peace with the Nazi dictator. Daladier, even though he signed at Munich, knew it was a disaster. Of the cheering crowds, he said: 'The blind fools.'

And so it proved.

Roper was never still, keeping a sharp watch on the activities of his target delegates. He could see Nagorno's Muzalev lounging on the hotel terrace enjoying an early celebratory lunch of poached turbot in champagne sauce. Already, he was on a third refill of Château d'Astros. A man awash with gold bracelets, medallions and watches. Soon there would be a new Rolls at the door.

Phone calls had been monitored but still no word of the secret meet. Roper switched his attention to the other big player, Wilkes. Where was he? On instinct, he dialled the bug in the hotel bedroom and picked up his man making an encrypted call to his Washington office. Wilkes was preparing his pitch for the final meet. Five o'clock was the deadline, he told his unknown listener. The deal had to be signed by then. The world's intelligence agencies were on constant alert for meetings like theirs. If they continued after the conclusion of the conference their pose as historians would be exposed as bogus. The afternoon conference session at the Isarhof would be the final opportunity to complete the missile deal, shielded from the prospect of surveillance. They would be safe until five.

The conversation, to his company office contact, was all about bottom lines, protecting commissions and, most important of all, a substantially increased inducement for Muzalev. He felt confident the details would pass unnoticed. This was, after all, an encrypted conversation.

Roper knew all this because the words going into the secure phone in Wilkes's bedroom were being picked up in their unencrypted form by the splendid little microwave bug snug in its hole in the partition wall. All Roper had done was dial the relevant number on his mobile.

But of the vital information he sought – the precise when and where of the meeting – there was no mention.

There was a coffee break in the hall. Two mob-capped girls in long blue dresses weaved between the chattering delegates to refresh supplies of crisps, biscuits, a variety of dips and coffee. Carlo Piccini was talking to Mimi Aschemeyer, Girolle to Tibor, and Zdzislaw to Nyek. Frau Ostermann was arranging vases of flowers. The coffee, of course, was the city's own speciality brand, Dallmayr Prodomo.

When the cups had been cleared away Professor Copperthwaite began the next session and his line on the Great Appeasement issue mirrored Roper's own; that it was unfair to blame Chamberlain for the misdeeds of the Nazis. The Prime Minister, he said, was a man of peace, committed to avoiding the horrors of war; a man who did what the vast majority of the country wanted – keep Britain out of another conflict.

Roper gazed across at the chairs and studied the expressions. The man from Hungary was doodling on his pad, drawing squares and funny faces and other strange patterns that might interest a shrink but no one else. Mimi Aschemeyer had her eyes closed.

Unfortunately for Copperthwaite, the professor hadn't anticipated the cinematic style of the day and had to make do with some old front pages from the thirties and copies of *Picture Post*, but they held the message right enough: fear of war and fear of the bomber were on everyone's mind in pre-war Britain.

Copperthwaite continued pumping what Emma would decry as the apologist line: the much-maligned British Prime Minister had bought valuable time for the RAF to deploy its latest fighter, the Spitfire, the plane that kept the Germans on the other side of the Channel.

Roper was intrigued: how was Emma going to answer this powerful defence? He glanced across at her and saw her punching away at her pad. He noted the tight jawline – clearly planning her response. He was wrong.

She looked up, caught his eye and signalled her mobile.

Seconds later there was a text waiting for him.

It said: Wilkes on move; let's go.

CHAPTER THIRTY-SEVEN

Copperthwaite's lecture suffered a ripple of audience distraction as Mimi Aschemeyer took the chair, and Emma and Roper strode through the kitchens to the loading bay where Huber was waiting in his Kompressor.

The next moments had been planned with precision. Huber turned his car north-east through the less congested streets to reach Schelling Strasse on the far side of the old city. They knew Wilkes and his friends would be following their satnavs and battling through the usual midday snarl-ups at the Karlsplatz. Huber, by contrast, was an expert at beating the jams.

The plan was for Emma, Huber and Roper to arrive first at the Café Bavaria.

The little room at the back of the kitchen where they'd set up their control consul was crowded with bodies and equipment: cameramen and reporters as well as Emma and Roper. A couple of wicker chairs were jammed in a corner. Hank had one leg over the arm of his, while smoking a cheroot; Quentin chewed gum and perched on a rickety stool. The bulky hand-held TV cameras were stowed on a bench. There was spilt black coffee on a ledge and brown mug rings on a table.

The atmosphere resembled a hospital smoking room, Emma decided. Her eyes began to water but she would not complain. She needed these men and she knew they were getting impatient with the long stake-out.

She glanced at Roper, noticed his pensive expression, the wandering tongue, the flicker of the eyelids; clearly fearful the ambush would turn into a fiasco, that Wilkes wouldn't show, worried he had chosen another location.

'Quit fretting,' she told him. 'You're making everyone nervous.'

'Why so sure?'

'He'll come,' she said.

'Admirable confidence. From where does such certainty spring?'

'Know your history, Roper. Every good general needs a Trojan Horse.'

In the kitchens, all decked out in stainless steel, four big men in white hats and blue-and-white patterned overalls worked at a mountainous pile of onions. Another was at the sink. Yet another at a deeply recessed window that gave a clear view of Schelling Strasse.

Emma watched a postman busy on the opposite pavement. His equipment looked genuine, right down to the hunting horn symbol on the yellow bike, but was he for real? Or a Wilkes lookout? The postman vanished inside a big block and she began to wonder why Wilkes had chosen this place: Schelling Strasse, a name synonymous with the rise of the Nazis. Number 50 was once the Party's Honour Hall and nearby was the studio of the Führer's personal photographer. But then, of course, you could hardly avoid these locations. Hitler had put his stamp on this city from his early days. Even the Café Bavaria had been touched by him – touched being the operative word. They'd once refused him credit and he had never cleared his tab.

Just then three cars nosed their way down the street in convoy followed by a taxi. Her window watcher called: 'All stopped. Doors opening.'

Emma, now back with Roper in the control cupboard, called out: 'How many?'

'Four persons. About to enter now.'

Two men marched imperiously through the front door and made for the largest alcove with the biggest table situated by the picture window.

Roper recognised Wilkes and Muzalev immediately as they pulled chairs back at their favourite table. Behind them trailed two men, disconsolate and uncertain. One was the duplicitous Polish delegate Zdzislaw and behind him, the Chinese Cheung Jihai.

They approached, lingered, did not sit.

Wilkes was all smiles, stripping off his Harris tweed overcoat, hanging it over a chair, rolling up the sleeves of his bright-blue shirt and flashing his gold Rolex. Then he banged a bulging black briefcase onto the table, almost skittling salt and pepper pots and menu card, making himself centre stage, announcing himself as open for business.

No one spoke. Not his rivals, not Muzalev. All eyes were fixed on this display.

Wilkes fired up his laptop and turned in the direction of the Nagorno delegate. 'This is a real clincher,' he said, and his words were heard with perfect clarity in the kitchen. 'Just watch and listen. We've factored in the performance details of all the missiles on offer to see how they compare.' He chuckled as a video played out a virtual missile war, lining up three systems on the Nagorno border and launching them all against the Russian frontier several hundred miles to the north. What was clearly understood – but unstated – was that all the weapons on show were breaking the Non-Proliferation Treaty, whose permitted limit was set at a maximum of 187 miles. Total distance from Nagorno's capital city Stepanakert to target Moscow: 800 miles.

All the variables of the technology – speed, height, payload, enemy radar – were fed into the mix. Wilkes's virtual reality aimed to demonstrate that while the French and Chinese came up short against a vastly superior system operated by the Russians, only the American missile, with multiple warheads, radar-defeatable capability and a range of nearly 2,000 miles, managed to penetrate the defences successfully.

Wilkes shut down his display with a grin of triumph. Part of the video had included close-ups of the Nebraska's control panels; clearly visible was a large red key to open up the system, and with it a smiling, welcoming crew chief calling himself Captain Nebraska. The only factors missing from this virtual war scenario were devastated cities and destroyed human beings.

However, Polish Zdzislaw was quickly on his feet, crowding the table, ready to argue. 'I'm still in this...'

'Big talk!' Wilkes was dismissive. 'You can't deliver. Just wreckage in the sky.'

'On the contrary,' Zdzislaw said, opening his briefcase.

'Put it away!' Wilkes said. 'Second-hand Nato junk. You won't get clearance, you can't get your hands on it and, anyway, it's already out of date.'

Cheung edged forward. 'I'm offering you the very latest. Technology to match anyone's.'

Muzalev didn't speak, contenting himself with an apologetic smile – a smile that said: '*Not enough zeros in my bank account.*' All this time, the Italian restaurateur had been waiting patiently, a bundle of menus in his arm. 'May I recommend–'

'Later!' Wilkes said. 'First to business, then we celebrate.' And with that, he had one more piece of theatre to perform. He fiddled with his mobile and within a few minutes he pointed out of the window. Outside in the street a large covered lorry had drawn up.

'Just watch this,' Wilkes commanded.

Slowly at first, then with increasing speed, the sides of the truck folded away, revealing a quarter-sized mock-up of the Nebraska rocket strapped in an upright position, nose cone pointing skywards.

Muzalev stared hard, intrigued as a panel in the rocket opened and a camouflaged figure in peaked cap stepped out. The broad grin of Captain Nebraska was instantly recognisable. Muzalev convulsed with laughter, shouting several 'bravos' as the captain advanced across the pavement, red control key in hand, thrusting it through the half-opened window.

'For you, Mr Muzalev; welcome aboard!'

Wilkes's laptop went back in the case and out came a large parchment-like document on pink paper vellum. The heading was in blue – The Blue Star Corporation – and the decorative initial letters looked like refugees from a Tudor scroll. Wilkes was arranging pens. 'Now, Mr Muzalev, Blue Star is very pleased to do business with you and I think I can say we've managed to meet all your requirements. Price right, goods right, commission right, eh? Best deal you could hope for; you won't regret signing today, I can assure you.'

Muzalev steepled his fingers and looked non-committal.

'You won't better it. A hundred million for a battery of ten Super Nebraska SXX2s. Vastly below normal rates. A quite fantastic deal.'

Muzalev, negotiating for his tiny, mineral-rich state, nodded slowly.

'And 5.5 million for your private account in Zurich.' Wilkes spread his hands in a gesture that said he was giving all his goodies away, that Father Christmas couldn't have done better.

Muzalev was still looking distant, then he fixed Wilkes with a stare. 'Just one outstanding detail, Mr Wilkes. I think I need another million. For my grandchildren, you understand. Here are the bank details for your transfer.'

For the first time Wilkes was silent. 'Another million?' A long pause. Much rubbing of chin. 'I don't think we can cover that. We've met all your requests for cash. I'm at my limit right now. Perhaps instead we could talk gifts. Another car?'

'I already have the Aston.'

'Who said you only need one? A Ferrari or a Chevy Cruz perhaps?'

Muzalev shook his head.

'Visits to the States. Book yourself in at Vegas.'

Silence.

'Jobs for your family with our most prestigious institutions; university places for your sons and daughters.'

Silence.

'Places at the top schools. Those special places – Eton, Harrow?'

Silence.

'Half a million, Mr Muzalev; that's the most I can manage at this late stage.'

'Three quarters.'

Silence. Then, 'You squeeze me... Very well, three quarters

it is, and now I think the time has come to finalise our arrangement. Are you ready to sign?'

'First, the cheque, please, Mr Wilkes, made out in these names.'

Wilkes took a deep breath and wrote.

Muzalev smiled.

Wilkes lifted a large black fountain pen and offered it. 'A corporate gift to mark the occasion; a Montblanc Meisterstück with gold nib. For you.'

Muzalev obliged.

'And at the bottom of each page, if you please.'

Several watermarked pages later, the deed was done. Wilkes's relief was palpable. 'And now,' he said, 'for that very big bottle of champagne. No, goddammit, make that a dozen.'

It was the magic moment for Emma: the signing, seen clearly on the monitor screens in the little room at the back of the kitchen and fed into the can for all the world to see on their TV screens in a few days' time. The words, the pictures, all the damning evidence she needed that would go out over the air on Sky's foreign news documentary slot *WorldView* and NABC's *Around The Globe Tonight*. Her main event.

'Let's go!'

She beamed at Roper, turned and gave the thumbs up to the others. 'Bring your kit,' she said, heading for the door to the restaurant, all fired up for the big confrontation, eager to savour the moment Wilkes knew he was exposed before the television cameras for all the world to see.

But Hank, the tallest of the three Americans, shook his head, staying just where he was.

Her smile froze. 'Why ever not?'

'That's not the way we do things.'

'But we can expose him right now, at the very moment of his guilt.'

Hank shook his head. 'Doesn't work like that,' he said.

'Then, how does it work?' Her hands were on her hips, eyes ablaze.

'First, the prog has to be got ready – timeslot agreed, edited, voiceover worked out, lawyers consulted, all the other angles covered, *then* we confront the subject at the very last moment, giving him no time to obfuscate, apply for writs or issue injunctions. His only option is a straight reply. Don't worry, you'll see him squirming on the hook.'

But that wasn't good enough for Emma. 'I want to skewer him now,' she said.

'You can't; it'd spoil the whole thing – give him time to wriggle.' Hank took a deep breath. 'Look, we've played ball with you, now it's your turn.'

'I can just happen to bump into him. On my own.'

'But you can't mention us. No way. Not yet.'

❧

She was waiting for Wilkes on the pavement as he emerged from the café. Arms folded, a taunting expression in place, Roper at her side.

Wilkes did a double take. 'Dammit, Drake, can't I escape you anywhere?' He slammed the door of the café behind him rather too strenuously and it bounced open again with a whine and a crack, hitting something hard. There was a snap and the glass crazed. But Wilkes didn't notice. 'You're like some clammy octopus that won't let go. Who told you we... I... was here?'

'I have eyes everywhere,' she said.

'Anyway, this was a private meeting. Nothing to do with you.'

'I know what you've been doing. What you've just done.'

Wilkes snorted. 'Nonsense.'

'I want to ask you a question. I'd really like to know the answer. How do you justify to yourself selling millions of dollars' worth of missiles to a tiny republic on the Russian border when your own President has signed up to a non-proliferation treaty? Why are you breaking the agreement?'

'Missiles? What missiles?'

'Don't lie to me, not again.'

Wilkes glared, then poked an accusing finger. 'If you must know, not that it's any of your damned business, we've been discussing machinery. Precision tools, laser technology, for civil engineering. Tractors, and so on.'

'Tractors, my foot! Dishing out millions to this dodgy businessman...' She waved an arm in the direction of Muzalev who had taken several paces away and was trying to look inconspicuous standing next to a parked car, rummaging in his pockets as if he were looking for a set of car keys. 'Sooner or later, you'll have to justify this flagrant act of corruption before the great American public.'

Wilkes moved closer and wagged a finger. Roper closed in, ever the protector, but that didn't stop the American. 'Now look, you, you're out of your depth, you don't know what you're getting into, so just keep out of it. My deal *has* to go through. We're talking about efficient machinery here. Right on the nose. It's an essential part of our economy. We need the trade, we need the jobs, the cash, the currency. And you can forget all about politics – it'll all be changed after the election anyway. But if we don't get the order it'll mean laying off workers back home, maybe closing the factory, ruining the firm, ruining the family; what's the good of that? We're supposed to be climbing out of recession, for God's sake!'

'And?'

'And if I don't supply them, the damned French will anyway.'

Zdzislaw, who had been pitching strongly for the French weapon system, appeared slowly from the restaurant doorway, careful to avoid the cracked glass. He coughed loudly and said: 'Must put you right there, Mr Wilkes.'

There was a silence while Wilkes, Muzalev, Roper and Emma turned to look at him.

Zdzislaw coughed again and said: 'That was a scam. The French company knows nothing about it. I bid without them ever having a clue. Got it down from 120 million. Cost you a bomb, hasn't it?'

Wilkes's face was puce. He turned wordlessly on his heel and re-entered the café, crunching glass, hitting the keys on his mobile.

Roper stared after him. 'But I thought...'

Emma grinned.

'That duplicitous bastard,' Roper said, ignoring Zdzislaw, still standing on the pavement wearing a sheepish grin. 'That nasty little turncoat... He was your spy?'

'Always have an inside source,' she said. 'Right, I think that concludes our business here.'

CHAPTER THIRTY-EIGHT

Emma was shamelessly playing to the gallery. She knew Chadwick and Copperthwaite were keen to hear her final analysis. This was the last session. It was her show; the moment she could make her name. Any young historian would relish the opportunity to challenge the conventional narrative of the period. And no one was going to doze through this session. She had the fire stoked, the blinds drawn, the lights dimmed and she stood in a spotlight close to the projector screen.

Theatrical, Roper thought, *definitely stagy. Was this how the academics did it in Cambridge?*

'We've already heard,' she said, 'how Chamberlain and the British public of 1938 were in a blue funk at the idea of being bombed. We saw those terrible images of Guernica, we saw the worried faces back home; we've heard how Chamberlain was horrified when he saw all the little houses of London down below him when he took his first flight in a plane, fearing how they would all be destroyed.' She paused. Not a sound. 'This, then, was the impetus for the surrender at Munich – fear – but the big question is: what was the reality behind that fear?'

Another pause, then the spotlight was switched off and her

laptop projector switched on and the wall screen lit up with images of aircraft with black crosses bumping over grass fields and lumbering into the air.

'This is what they were afraid of...'

The image changed to a room looking remarkably similar to a school classroom. Staring into the camera was a large man with a shock of white hair, a red face and a red shirt to match, standing next to a display board. In his hand was a pointer.

Emma's voice came from somewhere in the darkness: 'This is Herr Dr Feissler from the Munich aircraft museum at Schleissheim, just outside this city, an expert on military aircraft of the Third Reich. I recorded his talk last week.'

Feissler's image on the wall sprang into moving life. Using his pointer, he explained in only slightly accented English that the Dornier Flying Pencil, a principal component of Hitler's bomber force, flew at 217 miles an hour and had a range of 410 miles carrying a full bomb load.

At this, he flipped over the picture of the Dornier to reveal another image, this time of the main fighter aircraft of the day, the Messerschmitt 109: speed 398, range 528. This was followed by more statistics for the Heinkel and the Junkers.

Another chart, this time a diagram showing the North Sea coast. The pointer moved up from the bottom: here was Calais in France, then Belgium, then Holland and finally Germany. Feissler had helpfully drawn a circle from the closest point in German territory to the United Kingdom. The circle represented the outer limit of the range of each bomber type flying from German airfields with a full load.

The circle's outer limit, just about 400 miles for a return flight, finished in the middle of the North Sea.

The screen went blank, the spotlight sprang back to life, and there was Emma. 'Simple, isn't it? They couldn't even reach us. Now, why didn't Chamberlain know that?'

She paused. 'And now, I would like to introduce another friend from the museum. He's an expert on the German Wochenschau newsreel archive and has kindly brought along some to show us.'

The wall projector was working again, showing several of the flickering black-and-white stripes that were photographic preliminaries typical of the period. Then a crowd scene in a street.

Emma's voice, again from the darkness: 'This is the Wilhelm Strasse in Berlin a year before Chamberlain went to meet Hitler. The crowd is outside the air ministry building and the smart man in the light-blue uniform stepping up the steps is Hellmuth Felmy, commander of the Luftwaffe group on the North Sea coast.'

The smart man mounted the steps to be met at the top by a beefy figure in an even more flamboyant uniform – all gold braid and medals. Smiles of welcome, handshakes and backslapping.

'This is Felmy meeting his boss Hermann Göring, we think to discuss future operations. Now we cut to when he leaves the building.'

Down the steps went the smart man. No farewells. And a glum expression.

'What did they discuss? Well, of course, we weren't there, but shortly afterwards Felmy wrote a memo to his boss. After the war it was unearthed from Luftwaffe records.'

The screen filled with a page of typewritten script, all in German and on Luftwaffe headed notepaper. Helpfully, the next frame was an English translation, which read:

```
I regret to inform you that, with the
means now at our disposal, a war of
annihilation against England is out of
the question. The range from our bases
```

```
in the Reich is too great. We cannot
guarantee success for such a venture.
```

The lights went on and there was Emma launching into her conclusion: 'To attack Britain from the air, the Luftwaffe would have needed bases much nearer Britain, along the coasts of Belgium and France. The truth is, the Germans were no more ready for war at the time of Munich than Britain or France. No military analyst would have given them a chance of successfully invading Belgium or France in 1938 – and when they did invade, when they were much stronger, it came two years later. The point is, Chamberlain didn't need to play for time in 1938. Hitler needed time too – just like his adversaries. And a tough response by Britain and France at the time of Munich might...' She paused. 'Might have stopped him.' Another pause. 'And changed the course of history.'

She turned towards the switches to restore the lights but was stopped by a strong American voice issuing from the darkness. 'But the German bombers did arrive over Britain.' It was the professor, raising a voluble objection. 'Remember? Something called the Blitz?'

Emma snorted. 'Only because it was launched from France, not Germany. Only because Chamberlain gave Hitler Czechoslovakia on a plate... so he could plunder the vast armaments at the Skoda factory. And where did most of the tanks come from for the great German blitzkrieg that sliced into France? From Prague.'

The lights came on and a ripple of applause broke from the tiny audience. Chadwick was clapping wildly, bouncing up and down in his seat, beaming and clearly enthralled by her performance.

Roper glanced at Copperthwaite. He was shaking his head.

However, a finalé is a finalé and the curtain had run down.

CHAPTER THIRTY-NINE

There were frankfurters on sticks, cheese hedgehogs, quark and garlic dips, and butter pretzels, but the social session to top off the formal ending of Emma's conference had a distinct air of anticlimax. Now that the talking was all done, history had taken a back seat and the general impulse was for a rapid departure. Luggage was stacking up in the foyer of the Isarhof.

Roper did his best, a glass of Triumphator in hand, thanking all the participants. Professor Chadwick joined in the effusive farewells, first in the hotel foyer and then spilling outside on to the pavement when a fleet of taxis drew up in Jahn Strasse.

Emma and Roper walked their guests to the kerbside for final goodbyes. He shivered in a fresh wind whipping up the canyon-like gulley between the tall blocks but Emma seemed not to notice, still on a high over the success at the Café Bavaria and at her performance in the final presentation.

Copperthwaite, however, was not smiling. He looked as if he wanted to continue the argument, even through the open window of his cab, but Roper's attention had suddenly become fixed elsewhere. A large white Ford van had arrived on the opposite side of the road and with it came the sound of several sliding doors being opened all at once.

He began to tug at her sleeve.

Familiar figures were gathering on the cobbles. When the last of the guests had been driven away, Wilkes, Muzalev and several others Roper did not recognise began appearing like lapping floodwater in the gaps between parked vehicles. Then they advanced as one toward the front entrance of the Isarhof.

'Let's get out of here,' he insisted, pulling Emma after him. 'Upstairs, while we still can.'

Inside the lift to the second floor, she shrugged and said: 'I'm not bothered. What can they do? The film will be out of Germany and on the TV screens before they know it. Tomorrow at the latest, nine o'clock.'

The lift door opened and he ushered her out. 'Did you see their faces?' He hurried down the corridor, demanding her keypad.

There was a figure outside her room: Cheung Jihai. He had a phone in his hand, punching buttons.

Roper walked directly at him, staring, challenging. The Chinese delegate turned and backed away.

'Inside and lock the door,' Roper told Emma.

Her hands were on her hips. 'I can handle this. I'll warn them off.'

He guided her in. 'Emma, there are at least six of them and two of us. No good appealing to the Ostermanns. Or do you want to call out your favourite Kommissar? The guy who's already told you to sort out your own troubles?'

'We'll barricade the room. Demand police protection.'

'That's what the mob outside expects us to do. Gives them the time they need.'

'But they're finished,' she protested, spreading her hands.

'So will we be – if we're not quick. Vengeance is top of their list.' He too was hitting buttons. 'One of their messages sounds like an instruction from Boston.'

'And?'

'Prevent by all means possible.'

'God, that awful old woman. She really is poison...' Her words tailed off at a sharp rap at the door, followed by a pounding with a fist. Or possibly several fists.

'Call out to them,' Roper said. 'Some excuse.'

'I'm in the shower,' she shouted, close up to the door, looking through the peephole. 'Give me five minutes.'

She stood waiting, as if expecting a reasoned reply.

Roper called to her from the other side of the room. He had the tall glass balcony door open, beckoning her through. 'Get your gear!'

Emma gave him a stare. She didn't like taking orders but another pounding at the door settled it. She snatched from the wardrobe the long tawny hairpiece, jamming it on without the benefit of a mirror, grabbing the cleaning smock with the hotel's IH insignia above the left breast and fumbling hurriedly at the buttons.

More banging on the door.

Roper picked up his kit – a small toolbox – and coughed.

Emma, flashing him another irritated glance, snatched up the pile of clean sheets, white embossed towels and a mop he had positioned there. Into a yellow bucket went the new coat – pleated, belted and in anonymous beige. She stuffed it hurriedly to the bottom, concealing it with a rumpled sheet, spurred on by more pounding and shouting from the corridor.

Outside, on the narrow balcony, there was barely room for both to stand. She said: 'There's three of them waiting in the corridor.'

Roper reversed the key, shut the door and locked it from the outside.

'What now? This is freezing.'

He was across the waist-high party wall and on to the balcony of the next room. He beckoned her over and tapped on the window. 'It's an old couple,' he said.

Emma was behind him, clambering awkwardly with her load of linen but just in time to see alarm register on the face of the woman, concern on the man's.

The old lady, bundled up in a top-to-toe white dressing gown and wearing an enormous pair of red-and-purple spectacles, reached for the telephone. Roper shook his head vigorously, mouthing: 'No.' He spread his arms. 'Please, no.'

The old man who, by contrast, looked all set to go out in a grey charcoal suit, advanced to the window, hesitated when the woman said something, shrugged and unlatched the door.

'Are you for real?' he said in the cadences of New England.

'Thank goodness, an American,' Roper said. 'Sir, I do most sincerely beg your pardon for this intrusion but there's no need to telephone.'

'And why the devil not?'

'We're maintenance and room service,' he said. 'Unfortunately, the door in the next room jammed shut so we can't get out that way, but everything's okay now; if we could just trouble you briefly to come through, we'll soon have the problem sorted. No need to alert Reception and get them all bothered about it, eh?'

A knowing smile aimed at the old man begged for his indulgence but the old lady was not quite the credulous tourist Roper hoped for.

'Very odd, I must say; thought you must be part of these carnival capers.'

Roper shook his head. 'No, no, carnival's not till February. It's just that we've got a small mechanical problem.'

'But you're English,' the old lady objected. 'I recognise the accent.'

'We're a very international bunch at this hotel. Now, if you would be so kind...'

Emma, reacting to Roper's promptings, made it into the room and across to the door. 'Rendezvous Hugendubel, seven o'clock,' Roper whispered as he let her out into the corridor.

Then he closed the door quietly and turned back to the old couple.

'Aren't you going too?' But at that moment a gust of wind blew through the open window, distracting the old lady from her inquisition. She turned to her husband: 'Close that, will you, Gilbert? This is all very well but we don't want any more strange people clambering through our room.'

Roper needed to play for time. How long would it take Emma to dump the sheets and bucket, put on the long coat and clear the hotel foyer? He put down his toolbox, adopted his most beguiling manner and went into a long explanation of the problem of door locks and hotel keypads and their frustrating tendency to jam. He even added something about the carnival, spinning out the minutes until, standing by the window, he saw Emma bobbing into a cab.

As it drew away, his relief was cancelled out by a pummelling on the balcony windows of the room they had just fled.

He looked around. The corridor was an unlikely exit. The men out there had been fooled by the cleaner's disguise but would be fully alert to Roper's plight. And how long before Wilkes and co were through the glass door and on this balcony too?

'This is outrageous,' the old lady grumbled. 'I'm going to complain. And why are you just standing there?'

Roper went back to the balcony. 'Sorry, in all the hubbub, I quite forgot. Have to check the facia, sills and soffits – from the outside,' he said. 'Won't be a moment.'

~

Emma went down one floor, found the lower corridor empty and dumped her towels on a ledge. Then she took the stairs down to the ground level, pulling on the coat as she went, anxious that it should cover the cleaner's overall. There was one other person in the foyer but Herr Ostermann didn't look up as she crossed to the door. She was relieved to reach the safety of a cab outside.

'Marienplatz,' she told the driver.

'Sorry, pedestrian zone,' was the reply.

She sighed. 'Then Karlsplatz,' she said testily.

There had been a man in the foyer who'd eyed her suspiciously. She'd wondered if he would make a fuss but he hadn't reacted. As the cab pulled away, she looked through the rear window.

And there he was, the staring man, looking after her on the pavement and beckoning another cab.

Damn, she thought. *Now I shall have to put into practice all those tricks Roper talked about.*

At the Karlsplatz she had the driver drop her close to the subway entrance. She went down the steps in a hurry. Thousands swirled around this underground labyrinth, looking for trains or trams or the many subterranean temptations on offer: cafés, bakeries, tailors, grocers, jewellers, internet booths. It was a thriving heartbeat of the city, all below street level. So what next? Duck into a photo booth? Possibly. A bookshop? Then she spotted gold: a café kiosk in a far corner peopled by a crowd dressed in outrageous costumes. What better place to hide?

She sat on a bar stool next to a female clown in an enormous red wig, silently thankful for the bizarre showiness of the city. The carnival parade might not be until February but there was always a procession, a street orchestra or a juggling act to entertain passers-by. Dressing up was a way of life. She ordered a coffee, put on the dreadful spectacles Roper had insisted she buy, reversed the long coat so that the brown lining was on the outside, and joined in the merriment without ever knowing the point of the joke. After a lapse of ten minutes she felt confident she'd outwitted her tail.

Her goal was Hugendubel, the best bookshop in town, which stayed open for late-night shoppers. She looked at her watch: two hours to rendezvous. She tried calling Roper, without success, then Huber. His gatekeeper intoned that he was 'engaged in a meeting'.

Would Roper make it out? And what about her luggage? A suitcase containing her new dress and shoes were in the porter's room at the Isarhof.

Roper went back to the balcony and looked down. Too far to drop. Instead, he studied the frontage. Like many of the big blocks in this city, there were ridges right along the facia that were level with each floor. Most were several inches wide. He'd gotten the idea on a rare sunny day when walking in the street. Office girls were at the open windows, their legs dangling over the sills, some with heels perched on the ridges.

Roper swallowed, ignored the open-mouthed couple and went over the balcony wall. He edged out slowly, face to the wall, better to see the handholds, his fingers probing crevices in the mortar between the blocks. As he did so, a vision of himself flashed into mind: the ten-year-old scout going hand over hand on a rope to win a badge. Remember the cardinal rule, he told himself: don't look down, and ignore all sounds from ground level.

He stopped, running out of obvious places to grip. Would he feel it if he fell? He stayed stationary for a couple of minutes, trying to keep calm, but his heart was pumping and there was a foul taste in his mouth.

Then he began again, inching along, his right shoe testing the masonry for imperfections in the ridge that might send him plummeting. His fingers clawed, nails blasted, seeking out precious holds, toes digging painfully into the wall. There was a pain in his lower stomach and he feared for his self-control.

He swallowed again, conscious of noises, whistles, horns, tyres, motors, even background chatter.

Ignore it! They probably can't see you. Who looks up when you're hurrying along the street?

What seemed, when viewed from the safety of the balcony, to be a short distance stretched agonisingly before him. Who would really care if he didn't make it? He doubted his ex-wife would raise more than a derisive eyebrow; Emma might be annoyed, but the person in whom he invested his most serious hopes was her mother. *Do this for Agnes,* he told himself; *do this for both of us.*

After an interminable spell of slow progress, he stopped to consider: had he made the wrong choice? Perhaps he should go back and face whatever torture Wilkes had planned. A smashed nose, broken limbs, incarceration... they all seemed better options.

But a sideways glance revealed his predicament: he had passed the halfway mark. He had to go on. Then something in the distance, a slash of blackness, caught his eye. Trying not to panic, he carried on until his hand, outstretched and clawing, touched metal.

Relief. Two adjacent black drainpipes running down from the gutters on the roof.

It was like he was a boy again. Like the time he shinned up drainpipes to impress his friends and appal his mother. With two pipes to cling on to, Roper reached out, tested for rigidity and then clutched each one like a wall ladder. Then he crabbed down the front of the building, past the windows of the first floor, then the windows on the ground floor until finally his feet touched the pavement.

He stayed there, facing the wall, not letting go, heart still thumping, allowing tension to drain away.

His relief was interrupted by a presence behind.

A raucous voice close to his left ear said: 'Mr Wilkes would like a word.'

CHAPTER FORTY

Emma tried calling Huber again, without result. She knew that trying to meet up with him would be a mistake. The historian's office was too obvious a bolthole and she had to assume Wilkes or his associates were staking it out. Her only option: wait until seven at the Hugendubel.

She checked the bookshop in case he was early. He wasn't, so she tried window shopping for shoes and clothes at The Hirmer but couldn't find any distraction in it. She looked again at her watch. The slow passage of time was driving her crazy. She lingered under the arches to listen to a five-piece street orchestra grouped around a grand piano playing 'The Four Seasons'. She knew she should keep moving, that it was dangerous to stay in one place, but couldn't wrench herself away. The violin player could have been a double for Nigel Kennedy. Further on, another crowd was listening to a man on a xylophone. Emma floated, adopting the lazy gait of the window-gazers, drawing close to the bookshop.

That was when she spotted him. The droopy moustache and the constantly chewed matchsticks gave him a presence in the crowd.

'Not clever, Weasel,' she said under her breath.

He hadn't seen her but it was a warning signal. The rendezvous was being staked out. Their meeting was blown.

Her brow furrowed. How could that be? How did they know?

~

Whistles blew and a crowd gathered. The green and brown of a police uniform came into view.

Roper seized his one advantage. He spoke German. Wilkes did not.

'Who's the idiot who's just climbed down this wall?' the policeman wanted to know. 'Is there property missing?'

Roper pointed. 'Him,' he said. 'The thief.'

Wilkes argued vigorously but couldn't make himself understood. Several in the crowd shook their head and became voluble eyewitnesses. The cops – two of them now – told them to shut up. Roper kept pointing, advising several times: 'Check his pockets.'

The scene became chaotic. One of the officers had his cuffs out, ready to slip on to Wilkes's wrists. Wilkes was arguing and squirming and trying to avoid detention. All eyes were on the struggle.

Roper gently eased out of the crowd and into the next-door grocery shop. He made a show of studying the potatoes, slipping off his jacket and putting on his reading glasses before returning to the street.

The police were still patting down Wilkes, looking for loot.

Roper slid sinuously between two parked vans, crossed the street and made it to an alleyway which removed him from view. He set off at a fast pace, feeling in his pocket for his mobile to check that Emma had made it away successfully – then stopped dead. A woman walking behind cannoned into him. He didn't apologise. He was too stunned.

No mobile. But why? He remembered most distinctly picking it up from the hotel room. He carefully went through all his pockets. Still no trace. There could only be one explanation: it must have slipped out and dropped into the street during his crab-like shuffle across the front of the building. He sighed. Now the rendezvous he had fixed with Emma would be their only point of contact.

Ten minutes later he was in the Fraunhofer underground station, thinking he was in the clear. Not so. He might have cheated the police but one of the opposition, little Muzalev, had kept him in view. Roper, lingering by the ticket machines, spotted him crossing the street.

He narrowed his gaze and drew on his stock of past techniques. One thing all old cops knew was that a single tail had little chance against a quarry who knew he was being followed.

He took the escalator down to the train platforms, then switched to the up. He passed Muzalev in the middle and grinned at him. Just before he reached street level, however, he had a worrying thought: would they have another man waiting at the top?

He studied the faces. No loiterers, no one reading newspapers in shop doorways, no one eyeballing him.

Reassured, he crossed the street to a tram stop, sheltering in a pharmacy until a tram bound for Amalienburg ground to a stop, masking the view from the station.

He hopped on and sat low. As soon as the tram turned the corner into Müller Strasse he was off again, using his local knowledge to pick up another tram heading in the opposite direction, alighting three stops further on within a few hundred yards of the Marienplatz.

'Why?' he asked himself furiously, 'why did I tell Emma seven o'clock?'

It was the one detail of the escape plan he hadn't thought through. Ad-libbing was a mistake. Now he had to kill two hours. His first move was to join the queue at a sausage kiosk. No sign of Muzalev, but could his least favourite Eastern European have been part of a team? Roper studied the faces, clothing and behaviour of those around him but by the time he reached the server he was satisfied: there were no singles loitering or faking nonchalance. All around him were couples. They were genuine marketgoers. And genuine sausage eaters.

Emma's focus was on the faces around the Hugendubel. In the street, by the entrance, in doorways opposite, far off in the square. She had to stop Roper before he went into the bookshop; head him off before he could walk into the trap.

But as the hour approached there was no sign.

Perhaps he'd already been taken. She waited until three minutes past seven then decided she had to risk entering herself. She went straight to the map department on the first floor which she knew to be his favourite place. No sign. She moved to a likely shelf and pulled out a green Hofer map, studying the back cover as if planning a mountain walk. There was a constant movement of figures all around.

After a couple of minutes she retreated to the English-language section, opened a volume on German history and pretended to read while still checking faces.

How long dare she stay?

A few minutes at most.

She glanced at her watch again. She had used up five.

No sign of him. No sign of them. Time to abort.

She moved casually to the escalator, down and out of the front door. It was a high-risk manoeuvre, she knew, and she paid the price.

This time, as she passed the exit, she spotted The Weasel. And Vincenc Tibor, the Czech, clocked her.

This time she had to assume there would be more than one on her tail, so she headed straight for the Kaufhaus, the biggest store in town, a mecca for late shoppers. She felt an initial chill, then confidence grew. It seemed that half the female population of the city thronged these floors. The constant stream up and down the escalators reminded her of rush-hour on the London Tube.

She smiled. She knew there was danger but, in a way, action was a relief to the tension of the last few hours. She was going to enjoy herself leading The Weasel or Wilkes or whoever was in his team into a labyrinth they couldn't possibly know.

First she went to the basement (hosiery), then to ground floor (perfume, leather), next to the fourth (household) and finally settled on hats and coats (first). The sense of mischief appealed to her. Making this a game added an edge.

She browsed among the coats, vowing to come back sometime for an elegant navy short coat from the house of Cinzia Rocca. It had a slip-on collar using concealed press studs and there was a matching hat. Just then, doubt began to dent her exuberance. They couldn't take her here, could they? With some concealed weapon – a poison-tipped needle perhaps?

She shook her head. Of course not! They weren't that well prepared.

Moving away from the cash desk, she went to the underwear department, assuming any male tail would feel conspicuous. Finally, having given them time to stake her out, she carried the Cinzia Rocca into the fitting rooms and hung it on a peg in the corridor next to a dowdy grey overcoat. The owner of the grey was doubtless in a cubicle trying something smarter. Emma decided to relieve her of the old garment. In a pocket there was a multicoloured tea-cosy hat that almost covered her eyes. Somewhat regretfully, she left the Cinzia on a peg as she mingled with a group of laughing women who used an exit by the fire escape. There was an up escalator in the centre of the floor but the down escalator was much closer. It took less than a minute to use a dress display to mask her exit route. She arrived on the ground floor by the umbrella department and went through a glass exit door which led to the Galeria Kaufhof luggage centre. She strode through a passage to a terrace café with the extraordinary name of Guglhupf, along another passage and out on to a small street running at right angles to the main shopping mall.

It was a short and uneventful taxi journey to Huber's flat. She would wait there for further contact.

Roper took his cardboard plate, the dollop of mustard and the big fat Nürnberger and joined the flow, wandering around the kiosks, careful to keep to the thickest part of the crowd. Normally he loved the big sausages, there was a huge variety to choose from, but somehow this one didn't taste quite as scrumptious as before. Stress, after all, never did anything for the taste buds.

The market was a feast of smells, if only he had been in a mood to appreciate them: bakeries, a barbecue stacked high with steaks, precisely displayed flowers, tiers of vegetables and fruit. One kiosk sold nothing but pretzels, another a hundred varieties of rolls, another a multitude of cheesecakes. On any other occasion he would have savoured the aroma of jasmine and lilac.

But Roper, through killing time and staying hidden, couldn't relax. They – Wilkes and his followers – could check all the cafés, beer halls and stations they liked; he hoped they would be wasting their time surveying the shopping crowds on the Kaufinger. They surely couldn't touch him here.

He sat on a bench, ordered a beer, chewed without enthusiasm another sausage and worried. Rain would be a problem. Rain would clear the crowds.

He had eaten but was becoming hungry again. He thought about a steak or a hamburger but shook his head. He couldn't relax, couldn't enjoy. He looked down into his beer and frowned.

'Mr Roper? Mr Gerald Roper?'

He jerked up. Opposite his table was a tall man with a black brush moustache.

Roper feigned surrender, sighed and slumped. 'Police?'

The tall man nodded, then Roper knew. A plain-clothes man would have identified himself, produced his badge.

Roper sprang up and bolted into the crowds behind him, weaving a zigzag pattern between stalls, kiosks, generators, store tents and parked vans. He had every chance, he reasoned, unless there was a team – but he must not break free of the market. Out on the street he would be seen. Instead, he found another sausage stall. Behind was a tent. He stepped inside. On a peg hung a chef's blue checked smock and white hat. He put them on, edging slowly out into the servery, hoping to look busy.

'Oy! Who are you?' demanded a perspiring cook.

'Replacement from the agency. I'm the relief.'

'Get lost! And take that damned coat off before I baste you

with this!' A large sausage pinioned on two sharp prongs weaved in his direction.

Roper stepped back out of range. 'Fine! Sorry. My mistake.'

'Bloody chancers!' said the cook, following up with the menacing hook.

'Okay, I'm going; terribly sorry...'

Roper was whipping off his unsuccessful disguise.

But not quick enough.

He had the smock half over his head when he felt rough hands grasp his shoulders and pinion his arms to his sides.

'Got you, Roper,' said a familiar voice through the thin blue shroud. It was Wilkes. 'Didn't really think you could get away a second time, did you?'

CHAPTER FORTY-ONE

Emma and Huber sat on opposite sides of the dining room table, looking at one another, saying nothing. Helpless, wondering, waiting. Would Roper show?

There was no point in cruising around. They had no idea where to look. The minutes passed in silence.

Could anyone help? The only realistic possibility was the police but Emma didn't trust them, didn't like Kasper and didn't want to call attention to herself. How had the bookshop rendezvous been blown? Had the old lady at the Isarhof overheard Roper's instructions and talked? And if Roper's long silence meant he was taken, why had The Weasel bothered staking out the bookshop?

She smacked a thigh in frustration. Of course, even if Roper had been taken they would still be after her.

The clock on the window ledge seemed stuck, hadn't moved. She checked her watch. She tried to force herself to relax, imagining the TV people back in London and New York, writing scripts, editing film, holding endless conferences. Tomorrow would come the big exposé. Wilkes would be powerless after that. It was the gap before the nine o'clock deadline that was Roper's great peril.

Why wouldn't the phone ring? Why wasn't Roper knocking on the door? Imprisoned, pursued, trapped, attacked... Could they have gone as far as murder? After the drowning episode, she didn't doubt Wilkes's capacity for violence.

She could no longer sit still, wandering around the flat while Huber fiddled with the controls of his music centre. She ignored him, flicked some dust off a shelf, found a dead fly that hadn't made it through a window and stared angrily out across the city skyline. The great sound that was Tchaikovsky's 'Piano Concerto No. 1' issued through some well-placed loudspeakers. Huber was doing his best.

She nodded vaguely. He was a patient man. He hadn't pushed their friendship. She'd been wary, treading a fine line and was grateful for the space he allowed her. It had not been necessary to go all the way to get the information she sought. This had been volunteered freely. The closest he'd come to a proposition was the remark made softly late one night as she headed for the door: 'Don't feel you have to go... if you don't want to.'

It was tempting... very tempting, but she was still treading her delicate line. Then she thought of Roper and felt a confusion of emotions: concern, guilt, a sense of debt... and something else. She knew Roper was jealous of Huber's presence; perhaps he was a little in love with her. That, despite the hard time she'd given him over the past few days. She permitted herself a tiny smile, enjoying being the point of focus for two attentive males. Such a shame to disappoint one or possibly both. Perhaps, soon, she would have to make a choice but she would put off the moment of decision for as long as possible. She wasn't ready for anything serious, she told herself; there was ambition and a bright future to serve.

She drummed her fingers on the kitchen table.

And that's when the call came.

The voice on the phone changed everything.

The situation was instantly transformed.

And now she was asking herself an agonised question: Why would she do this? Risk everything when she was so close to reaching her goal? Now, on the very cusp of success, she might have to give it all away. The voice on the phone had flung her a stark challenge: Wilkes had Roper with a gun at his head and the choice was – him or her?

She had taken the call on her mobile. It was from Roper and he sounded strange. 'They want you to come to the tower.'

'Tower? What tower? What do you mean, they?'

He didn't answer. Instead, there was a scuffling noise then a voice she recognised instantly as that of Wilkes. 'The Alter Hof, the old tower in Burg Strasse; it's his head or yours. If you want him, you'd better come. If not...'

She heard Roper, from a distance, shout 'Stay away' – an impressive sentiment of self-sacrifice she simply had to match. The strange thing was, she hadn't even liked Roper when they'd first met, but that had all changed. She would have achieved little without him. A hero, she decided, is not betrayed by his friends. A hero's friends stay loyal.

On the phone she had raged at Wilkes: 'You've got no hope. When I show up with the police, you're prison fodder.'

Then the voice, the one she had come to loathe, had jeered: 'You're out of your depth, Drake, you always were. The cops are already here. The cops are in my pocket.'

She put that down to bluster. She didn't have time to call the police anyway, he'd given her a deadline of ten minutes, and she didn't fancy trying to persuade Kommissar Kasper that this time she really did need his help. He'd argue and there would be a long inquisition, comments and delays.

She raced to the front door and paused long enough to remember her brother's first rule of self-defence: always have a distraction, a misleading point of focus with which to sell your opponent a dummy. She glanced down at Huber's fancy leather driving gloves on the umbrella stand and snatched them up, then grabbed the overcoat which she had worn to escape from the Galeria Kaufhof.

She sprinted to the Porsche, which was parked a hundred yards distant, an hour still on the parking meter. Out on the ring road, she jiggled the car around a slow-moving truck and breathed in deeply, knowing she was placing herself and her whole project in peril. She asked herself again: Why do this? The answer involved acknowledging some uncomfortable truths. She knew she was manipulative and exploitative and yet she could not walk in the footsteps of her grandfather without acquiring a sense of moral purpose. And now the man who had saved her neck in the flooded cellar deserved his own special lifeline.

She glanced quickly at her watch: twelve hours to go. Twelve long hours before Quentin and Hank had promised her top slot for the Wilkes exposé on NABC's special investigations programme *World in Focus* and nearly eighteen hours before Sky had their programme ready.

She went fast down the Strauss Ring, knowing the choice was stark. Could she hang it out long enough? She was almost there, squeezing past another truck and shooting some red lights before giving silent thanks to her brother for all his training and preparation. She slipped out of a side panel the sap glove that had served her so well in the past. One hand still on the wheel, she felt the reassuring strength of the material and the protective steel bands on the inside. Then she leaned forward, reached behind her, tucked the glove into the waistband of her jeans and covered it with her jumper.

Once off The Tal she tunnelled like a madwoman down the tiny street and zoomed under the old tower, swerving to a stop on the cobbles in the quadrangle beyond, pressing the number on her pad.

The loathsome voice was instantly in her ear.

'So you do value him. How very noble.'

'Send him down,' she said. 'When Roper walks, I'll come up.'

CHAPTER FORTY-TWO

E mma opened the car's secret panel once more and extracted a tube. One of her many precautions. 'For the Purpose of Defence Against Animals', it said on the label. 'So you see, Roper,' she said aloud to the empty passenger seat, 'it's perfectly legal in this country.'

She pulled on Huber's fancy driving gloves, hauled out the grey overcoat, got out of the car and looked about her.

An enclosed square. Tall buildings all around. And directly in front was the towering old court, known to the locals as the Monkey Tower after the legend of a pet monkey which supposedly grabbed a baby prince and took him to the top, threatening to throw him off.

Emma didn't care for that story.

She scanned the windows for familiar faces, right up to the steeply-roofed gate tower and turrets, but saw nothing. The tourists loved this place, she knew, an impoverished Hitler having painted picture postcards of the blue-and-white rhombic facade. You simply couldn't get away from the man's poisonous legacy. It was everywhere.

Her gaze dropped to the central archway she'd just driven

through. Set into the arch was a wooden door with enormous black hinges. It looked as if it hadn't been used since the last king of Bavaria fled this way to escape a republican mob.

On the far right-hand side of the courtyard, some distance from the archway, another door swung open. A man in a black leather bomber jacket held it ajar, looking in her direction.

The mobile buzzed again.

'Well?' the voice said.

'Don't take me for a mug,' she said. 'I want to see him out first. You're not getting two for the price of one.'

'He'll be released from the doorway inside the arch.'

She snorted. 'Proof of the pudding,' she said, and didn't give him a chance to argue. She snapped shut the phone. Wilkes wasn't going to dictate all the terms.

She waited. There were no other people about. All was silent. The only other vehicle was an old East German Trabby bearing the insignia of the town museum. Perhaps they'd changed their minds. Perhaps they'd try and grab her, blocking both exits from the quad. Was this a trap?

Finally, movement. With a protesting judder of warped and aged timber, the door under the arch boomed, then gaped open and she saw Roper there, held fast by his arms.

At that moment he saw her. 'Don't!' It was a yell of desperation. 'Get away while you still can. Go!'

She shook her head.

'Are you crazy?!' he yelled.

She laughed. 'Kind of,' she said in a loud voice that seemed to echo and bounce off the walls, then in an even louder tone, added: 'Let him go... And, Roper... get right away, right away, now.'

Roper took two paces forward. Two free paces.

There was a loud cough. The man in the bomber jacket

beckoned to her from the far corner of the courtyard and advanced across the cobbles.

Emma started forward to meet him, the grey overcoat she'd taken from the Galeria Kaufhof folded neatly over her left arm. As she drew closer, she smiled at him. 'No problem,' she said evenly, 'but take my coat, would you?'

His expression changed from hostile to wary but he shrugged and took the coat, thereby occupying one of his arms. With the other he leaned over and grasped her shoulder.

She didn't react, didn't shrug him off. Her voice was velvet, soothing, non-combative. 'Looking forward to this meeting,' she said, 'and I hope you've been treating my friend well.' She knew he probably didn't understand. He had a small black moustache. She turned to face him, and he to her. She smiled again as her right hand came up. There was a short squirting sound, rather like a perfume spray, and he closed his eyes, shook his head and let go of her shoulder.

Emma stepped back, feigning puzzlement, as the man, bent forward clutching his face, began to cough and suffer body spasms. Finally, he collapsed onto the cobbles.

Another man, this one in an olive-green parka, appeared in the far-right doorway.

She pulled away, looking puzzled, acting distraught. Her hands displayed signals of fright; her expression was an appeal for help. 'Oh dear,' she said, the tone all sympathy, 'what's the matter with him?'

The second man left the doorway and hurried forward but he hadn't reached his stricken colleague before the pepper spray in her right hand was in action again. The would-be rescuer took a full squirt in the face and in seconds both men were clutching their eyes and coughing, falling about like drunks. The first was trying to get to his knees.

Emma's sympathy ceased abruptly. She stepped through the

unattended doorway, closed it behind her, found a bolt and shot it.

She looked around. She was alone in a tiny lobby at the foot of a flight of steep wooden steps. Stacked in a corner were brooms and cleaning equipment. She was immediately conscious of the musty odour of neglect and confinement, of dust and old blankets, but topping it was another smell, one that struck her as familiar. She sniffed – then got it. They had the decorators in; the smell was linseed oil. She had a brief flashback to childhood, of working with putty while helping her brother fix a broken window.

A voice called out from somewhere up above. Indistinct, but clearly an instruction to hurry. In front were some steep stairs and she began climbing.

The staircase was unpainted, the handrail rubbed smooth. Chicken wire hemmed her in. It was gloomy but she could just make out recesses behind the wire, full of ladders, paint pots, trestles and benches cluttered with tools – hammers, saws, and the like. She came to a small landing, half-filled with more painters' debris.

The next flight was metal, rusty and brown, with the steps set at a steep angle.

Staking all on a bluff, she bounded up as fast as possible, her feet ringing like bells on the rungs, emerging on to another landing and looking straight into the baleful gaze of Police Kommissar Franz Kasper.

She recovered quickly and snorted in derision.

'I always knew you were a crook,' she said.

Roper was still a little shaken. There had been menacing words in his ear as he was propelled by a hostile boot into the freedom of the cobbles of the Alter Hof: 'Shoot your mouth off and you'll be putting a garrotte around her neck.'

He didn't take it lightly. His ordeal in the tower had made him quite certain: these people were desperate. He hadn't been harmed but there had been unsubtle hints about 'a procedure' and prominently displayed was a stout tall-backed wooden chair fitted with straps and restraints. Next to it on a table was a tray containing a syringe and a rack of unidentified phials. Roper shivered at the thought of it, rubbed his upper arm and wondered again: Why had Emma volunteered to take his place?

He'd tried to warn her off. It was ridiculous to place herself in their power, putting the future of her project in jeopardy. He was on the outside now, looking up at the windows but seeing nothing, shaking his head. He knew what Wilkes and Kasper wanted. They wanted her to pull the story. Ridiculous! No journalist would agree to that to save their own skin. Or would they?

Would she?

He thought again about her action. Brave to the point of idiocy. He felt flattered, amazed and mystified. Why would she do that? He hadn't seen her as a highly principled person. In the circumstances he had expected her to regard him as expendable. Should he call the police? That was a joke. Kasper was in their pocket. And the threats were more than convincing. Emma had shouted at him to get right away. Instead, he lingered in the courtyard, wondering what he could possibly do to help her.

Kasper's normal calm seemed to have deserted him as he peered at Emma. No longer the studied languor of the professional police officer. Now the lower jaw worked repeatedly in agitation. 'You're like some virulent pestilence. Wherever you go, you spread contagion.' He bared his teeth in a rictus grin of hate. 'But you've gone too far. Did you really think we'd leave you free to mire us in controversy? To ruin us all?'

'Us?' she queried. 'Thrown your lot in with a bunch of rogue traders, have you? Now why would that be?'

He ignored her and approached.

She tensed.

'A pat-down,' he said. 'We know you're a tricky one. Don't want any concealed weapons. Then you'll be cuffed and taken upstairs. Mr Wilkes has a proposition for you.'

'Should I be interested?'

'First,' he said, holding out his right hand, 'the gloves.'

She looked him the eye, defiant, then slowly, very slowly, began to remove the left hand of Huber's pride and joy. Without averting her gaze, she held it out to him.

'Get a move on,' he snapped. 'Don't hang it out. Both of them!' He was pointing at the right glove.

'What's the big hurry? Getting nervous? An attack of the jitters?'

He made another agitated gesture, urging speed with his forefinger and she let the left glove fall to the floor. He registered mild surprise at this then pointed at her right hand.

That glove, too, went on the floor.

'Turn around,' he said, bringing out a set of handcuffs from a pocket.

She didn't move, simply held out her hands. 'In the front,' she said. 'I'll need my fingers to grip the ladder.'

He hesitated, then moved closer and stooped slightly to manoeuvre the cuffs over her left wrist, clicking it shut and switching attention to her right.

That was when she moved. Wrists still together, she brought them up in a sharp movement, catching the metal ridge of the handcuffs on the underside of his nose.

He staggered back, blood spurting from the wound.

She followed that with a sharp kick to the crotch. Just like her brother had taught her. 'Kick-box Emma' the boys had called her and no one asked her on a night out.

Kasper went down groaning.

He was in a foetal position. She rolled him over. On his belt were some keys. One, two, three... None of them fitted. Finally, a fourth fitted the cuffs and released her left wrist.

'Kasper!'

It was a distant shout from above – and she recognised the voice. She glanced up. She was hidden from observation by the gloom and curvature of the staircase. She bent over Kasper once more, clicked one claw of the handcuffs over his right wrist and attached the other to a metal stanchion on the staircase rim.

Any minute now he would recover from the shock and agony and yell an alarm. She grabbed her gloves, tucked them in her waistband and looked about her. More chicken wire, then a panel door. She pulled it open. Lots of painters' gear. She rifled in haste through pots, brushes, trowels, spatulas and knifes before holding up an item in a gesture of silent triumph: gaffer tape used for masking edges.

She snapped off a length, then moved back to Kasper. He had his eyes shut, still stricken by pain to both nose and groin. She knelt on his shoulder. His eyes opened and registered surprise, hostility, fear. She put all her weight on his shoulder to bring him on his back, then planted the gaffer tape over his mouth, pressing down hard.

'Kasper!'

The shout from above was repeated.

She leapt for the stairs, counting once again on the power of surprise, climbing noisily – just as, she hoped, he would expect from his faithful lapdog. At the top she flung back the partially open trapdoor, heaving herself fast on to wooden floorboards. A rapid glance told her this was the top of the building, the jutting, outwardly picturesque oriel turret.

Wilkes stood motionless, staring back at her.

'You!'

She glared her defiance.

'Where's Kasper? Why aren't you cuffed?'

She said: 'Never trust a bent cop. So unreliable.'

He made to go to the trapdoor but she slammed it shut with her foot. 'Never mind him, you answer me this. What are you doing up here? Why fight a lost cause? You're beaten. Time to run away. Time to hide.'

He began to move closer but she stood on the balls of her feet, poised, adopting a boxer's gait. 'Don't you get it? Still?' she demanded. 'The secret's out, it's all over, you can't do a thing about it.'

He stopped then, folded his arms, a smug smile. 'But it isn't! We've been monitoring all the screens; there's still time.'

'For what?'

'You to retract.'

'A pathetic delusion.'

'Just at this moment you're in serious peril of your life.'

'Serious, yes, for you.'

He pointed, angry, brow darkening: 'If you want to save yourself you'd better stop those TV people.'

'Too late. I couldn't stop it even if I wanted to. It's in the hands of the studio. I have no control. None at all since they left here.'

'Your one and only chance.'

'Impossible.'

'Make them listen. Plead for your life.'

'No way.'

He pointed to a chair with leather straps for hands and feet. 'I'll knock that bravado out of you.'

She said, in an even tone, deadpan, matter of fact: 'A major criminal act, a life sentence in jail, maybe the death penalty, and what for? Just to please the old crone? Do you always do what Mother tells you? A bit too old to be a mummy's boy, aren't you?'

His answer was a sneer. 'You'll lose some sensitive parts. Organs, maybe teeth, very, very painfully. Then over the side with you. A fatal fall. No surviving that. An unfortunate accident.'

She shook her head, pointing to the trapdoor. 'They've all deserted you. Kasper, the others, they've seen the light and fled. The name of Wilkes is slime, the crooked arms dealer, trader with an enemy, a kidnapper.'

Just then there was a call, a shout, a strange voice, and not Kasper's. 'Mr Wilkes!'

Wilkes beamed. 'Deserted, my foot! One of my associates come to work you over...'

There was the noise of climbing, then the hatch flew open and over the grating stepped the man with the brush moustache and the black bomber jacket.

Emma repressed a curse. The effects of the pepper spray were supposed to last longer than that.

Wilkes turned to his assistant. 'Ready? You know what to do.'

His mistake. In those few seconds, he took his eyes off her. He didn't see her reaching behind her back, releasing the sap glove from the waistband of her jeans and slipping it over her right hand.

But something of the movement caught his attention. He turned back to her. Too late. She leapt across the two paces between them and landed a stinging right hook on his jaw. She put everything she had into that punch, every last ounce of venom that represented payback for the injustice meted out to her grandfather, the duplicity and mendacity of Wilkes and his dishonourable branch of the family, and every last punch power to avenge Roper's ordeal.

There was a dull thud like a hammer hitting a sandbag.

Wilkes went down and she kicked him hard as he went.

The man with the moustache wasn't looking so eager anymore. He stood still, immobilised by shock.

Emma leapt over the prone body and ran at him, fist drawn back.

He turned, bolted for the ladder, swinging himself down so his feet were scrabbling for a grip on a lower rung. But he still needed to keep a handhold on the top rung. She stamped hard on his fingers.

He yelled.

Then she crashed down the trapdoor. The screaming got louder.

Emma turned. Wilkes was trying to struggle to his feet, groggy, holding his jaw.

Somewhere a phone was trilling.

He lurched to a corner where a jacket hung from a hook, pulled out a mobile and grunted a response. There was a pause, then his eyes focused on her. 'Comment?' he said into the phone, shaking his head, fighting to focus. 'Ridiculous! Broadcast any of that stuff and I'll sue, I'll break you...'

The voice was weak, carried no conviction; the ritual threats of a man who knows his time is gone. He let the phone fall. Clearly the pre-broadcast quote call. Quentin and Hank had kept their promise.

Emma held up her right hand, flexing the fingers of the sap glove and giving him one of her special stares. 'Just in case they didn't get around to giving you the timetable,' she said, 'they're broadcasting in...' She consulted her wristwatch. 'About twenty minutes.' The lie came with a smooth conviction. 'I should bury yourself before then or risk arrest. The name of Wilkes is going to stink the world over. People will be holding their noses in Washington. And as for vengeance, simply to please the old crone, that was a really stupid idea.'

Her right fist opened and closed in a clenching motion.

'And not very likely,' she said.

Wilkes's eyes had changed. There was no arrogance there, not a trace of the earlier bombast. They had become globes of fright. Without a sound he hoisted himself up, adopting a strange expression she had not seen before, then loped across the room straight toward the open turret window. It had a low rail and he didn't stop. The momentum of his run carried him forwards, somersaulting his body over the railing and out into space.

There was no sound.

She went to the window and looked out.

The body lay inert on the cobbles below.

A crowd was gathering.

She spotted Roper at the back of the crowd, signalled to him to move to one side, and took off the glove, pulling the other from her waistband. She waved them at him.

He nodded.

She let them drop to the cobbles.

He would dispose of the gloves. There would be no evidence for the police to find, nothing that could be construed as incriminating.

CHAPTER FORTY-THREE

R oper knew what to do. He whisked the gloves away before anyone in the crowd noticed them falling. Their attention was on the body. But he was worried: had she pushed the plummeting figure to his death? Punched him over the barrier? And who was it? Roper desperately wanted to know: Wilkes? Kasper? Or someone else?

He walked slowly out of the quad, adopting the aimless gait of someone with no considered purpose, but his mind was working. Where to dispose of the gloves? A bin would be dangerous. Someone would retrieve it and contact the police; burning would attract attention; burial in the park invited some rooting dog to dig them up.

He entered a private courtyard and spotted a stack of bricks and roof tiles by a line of garages. The gloves went well down the pile. Some bricklayer might stumble on these strange objects, hopefully months or years hence, when the incident at the Tower was but a memory.

When he returned to the Alter Hof, an ambulance was leaving the courtyard. From lingering, chattering bystanders he gleaned the information that police had also left with a young woman. She had seemed shocked, they said, and the police solicitous.

Roper made his way to the Ettblock, marvelling at her aplomb. Clearly she was acting the role of the shocked innocent. Where did this woman come from?

∾

The Ettblock was a busy place. The big gates were open and police vehicles formed a constant stream. Roper stood behind the railings in the street, anxiously examining the faces of the occupants.

His mind kept returning to the plummeting figure and the body on the cobbles of the Alter Hof. It was a horrible way to end a life. He earnestly hoped Emma wasn't responsible, that the autopsy wouldn't discover telltale bruises on some vulnerable part of the torso. Such a discovery would send the police and lawyers into a frenzy of activity. Emma had brushed aside his objections to the knuckles and gloves and now he could see this ending very badly.

More cars, more faces but no sign of Emma. As he waited, his thoughts centred on her. She had risked everything for him, including her job. But what exactly was her job? Uncovering historical truth, discovering her grandfather's fate, the prevention of missile proliferation? Or what? She was an enigma, her role a mystery.

For the first time since he'd arrived in Munich he was beginning to feel out of his depth. Overtaken by events. Beset by unanswered questions. He sighed. Still no sign of her. And then there was Huber... Another factor, another mystery.

He hesitated at the kerbside for several more anxious minutes. Should he continue to doorstep, waiting outside to see how events developed, or should he barge in, insisting on being by her side? He'd rescued Emma from the clutches of Kommissar Kasper once before but now the danger had gone sky high. If Kasper was the victim on the cobbles, the police would be hyperactive, looking for a culprit. And if Kasper wasn't the victim? If he were still alive...

Roper scratched his head as he wondered why Kasper had thrown in his lot with a bunch of arms dealers. Was he party to the deal, receiving a kickback? Roper was sure of one thing: if still alive, Kasper would bluff it out, knowing Emma and Roper could report his complicity, and be more than ready to destroy them as credible witnesses. Arrest on a false charge was an obvious tactic. A desperate man, fearful of public exposure, was capable of any act.

Roper would be of no use to Emma dumped in a police cell, he decided, so he kept his vigil on the pavement.

In the police interview room Emma turned on the charm to the two young officers. They had their notebooks laid out on the table while she went carefully and slowly through her version of complete innocence: a visit to the Tower with friends for a grandstand view of the city and an appreciation of the refurbishment work being carried out on a wonderful old building.

But her mind was racing. What had happened to Kasper? When she had descended the stairs at the Alter Hof he was gone. No trace of the handcuffs either, only a splintered door lock. What of the man with the moustache whose fingers she had crushed? Had he released Kasper?

At the foot of the stairs she had greeted a police squad. She had made the required noises of shock and sorrow, eager to co-operate with their inquiries into a tragic accident. She could not understand how the man had fallen and could furnish no explanation.

On the way to the Ettblock she glanced at her messages. One from Roper, one from Huber. The latter read: Be careful; there's something you should know...

One of the officers insisted she switch off her phone. She acted out the innocent. 'Messages of support,' she said, glancing at the rest of Huber's brief message. A complete stunner, she thought, and one that explained a lot. Then she smiled, adding: 'Just one more, to my friend Lance...'

They took her to an interview room: metal chairs and a wide desk. An anonymous place, a room that could have been in any police station or army barracks the world over; two tones of green and cream. She worked tirelessly at her pose of willing co-operation and complete innocence. The man must have slipped, she said; she saw nothing.

Some way into this, however, they were interrupted when the door opened and the unsmiling figure of Franz Kasper beckoned her out. She looked at his patched-up nose and bruised mouth and could tell by his eyes that he was acting calm but raging inside.

Out in the corridor, he was silent, pointing ahead. She wondered what excuses he'd made to his colleagues to explain all the cuts and bruises. As well as the nose plaster there was a cut above his eyebrow and a bluish tint around one eye. He walked gingerly.

She said loudly: 'Goodness, Kommissar, whatever's happened to your face? Looks like you walked into a tram.'

He opened a door. The same door, she noticed, passing through, where she had professed innocence after the street shooting, and he closed it rather too quickly behind them.

She was ready.

He came at her, teeth bared, eyes afire, reaching out a hand to close around her throat. There were no wasted words, just an animal growl. He had her backed up against the wall. The back of her head hit the hard surface, turning her face to one side, and she felt a ringing sensation around the top of her skull.

There was a fleeting moment when he had her stunned, then all her fury and prepared responses kicked in. With a slashing blow she brought her right arm down, striking Kasper's wrist – the one that was doing all the damage. At the same moment, she heaved herself off the wall, lunging forward with her right knee, jerking upwards into his groin.

He grunted, folded and released his grip all in one movement, like the sigh of a collapsing balloon.

'Twice in one day!' she spat, towering over his crouching figure. 'Must be getting pretty hot down there.'

He was hugging himself. She stood massaging her throat, her head still hurting.

'Maybe I should call for assistance,' she said, 'make a complaint of assault.'

Kasper lurched painfully around his desk and slumped into his chair. He exhaled a desperate gulp. 'You attacked me. Another black mark against you. On your way to the cells and a murder charge.'

She laughed a bitter, ironic laugh. 'Digging another hole for yourself? I can still yell blue murder, show them these red marks on my neck before they fade – evidence of an assault by a senior officer. A corrupt senior officer.'

There were footsteps outside, evidence perhaps of concern at the noise of the scuffle. She went to the door, opened it and beckoned inside one of the young officers from the interview room. 'Herr Kommissar's not feeling so good just now. A bad headache. Could you arrange for a coffee and some aspirin?'

The officer looked confused, uncertain.

Kasper looked up and gave a pale nod.

When they were alone once more, she took a seat in front of the desk as if they were about to conduct a routine interview. He pointed an accusing finger. 'You're worse than any criminal I've met in the last ten years. Slippery as an eel and twice as dangerous. But I don't forgive easily. Forgiveness is not in my nature.'

'Comes of mixing in poor company.'

'You'll be looking at the inside of a prison cell for a very long time.'

'Pure fantasy.'

'You may think you have some kind of an advantage – but you don't. I'm holding you on suspicion of murder. You'll go before a judge this afternoon. No bail, and I have every confidence that come the morning I'll be charging you with the murder of Cyrus Wilkes.'

She threw up an exasperated hand. 'I've already explained, it was a complete accident.'

He tried to wave this away with a contemptuous gesture but the effort caught him with a painful jolt. He massaged his wrists. 'We're looking for the murder weapon right now. I'm confident the autopsy will show that Mr Wilkes was dead before he fell. Murdered by you.'

She stared back at him. 'Should this foolishness ever get as far as the courtroom, I shall have to reveal the full extent of your complicity with a group of illegal arms traders.'

'Which I will deny.'

'And insist on an investigation into your connection with Wilkes. I have to say, one very crooked family.'

'Mr Wilkes will be seen as an innocent victim. Your murder victim. The family will be furious. Looking at you for vengeance.'

'I think not. Not after tonight's *World in Focus* on North American TV, they won't. And then there'll be some very serious questions for you to answer. A suspension from duty, I shouldn't wonder. And, of course, there's also your family thing.'

She saw the merest quiver in tortured eyes.

'Son of Obersturmbannführer Kasper, and all that.' She paused. 'Oh yes, we know all about your disreputable family history and the motive it provides. All this irregular activity. Old Nazis, new Nazis, protecting the family name. Kidnap, threatening behaviour, false imprisonment, physical assault, criminal conspiracy–'

'No proof!'

She grinned back at him.

Then he demanded: 'Who's *we?*' Confusion clouded his pained features.

Just then the phone rang.

She saw him hesitate then pick it up. He answered, followed by a long pause. He seemed to do a great deal of listening before replacing the receiver.

He stared at her hard, examining her closely as if for the first time.

'Who are you?' he demanded eventually. 'That you've got so much damned clout?'

CHAPTER FORTY-FOUR

Two big four-by-fours, a BMW seven-seater SUV and a Range Rover Evoque drew up outside the front entrance. No other vehicles used that space, Roper noted; patrol cars, vans, tow trucks – they all went in at the service ramp. You surely had to have some front to loiter in a no-parking zone at the main entrance to police HQ.

He moved closer. Two people were in the lead car. Ten steps closer, he pulled up short. Was that Huber in the Evoque? Sitting up, bold as you like, chatting to the driver?

Roper took a couple of paces closer. Their window was open. He could hear their voices – not the words but the accents. And the driver had the most definite transatlantic intonation.

Suddenly, the big entrance doors of the HQ sighed opened and there was Emma tripping down the steps. Standing back, on the top step, was a bruised Franz Kasper, his expression at once incredulous, perplexed and resentful.

Emma's gaze had a frantic quality, searching this way and that. When she spotted Roper she beckoned urgently.

He stepped forward.

'Get in,' she commanded. 'Get in, we're off; don't get left behind.'

Roper hauled open the passenger door of the rear car and climbed in beside her. The floor level was high. Before he could say anything, he was forced back in his seat. The drivers, whoever they were, took off at some unseen signal and swished out of the Ettblock driveway like some presidential motorcade, racing without stopping to a junction, taking the tiny streets at unbelievable speed. When they had finally settled into the main stream of traffic on the ring road Roper looked across at her.

She grinned back.

'May I know what the bloody hell is going on?' he said.

The interior was all dark veneer and deep velvet. The seats were enveloping, the floor space huge. Emma was opening a tiny fridge, pulling out a shelf, setting out some glasses and opening a bottle of the best malt. 'Glenlivet,' she announced. 'Twelve years old. You take ice with yours, right?'

Roper sighed and accepted. By now he knew her tone. This one said she wasn't going to be rushed into an explanation – if at all. Since it was useless to try and pump her, he contented himself by looking around the vehicle. And what he saw only increased his puzzlement: a television monitor, a radio, a set of paperbacks, a spread of that day's papers – *The New York Times*, the *Herald Tribune*, even the London *Times*, *Newsweek*, *Time* and the *New Statesman*.

She fiddled with some buttons. 'Let's have some music,' she said. 'What's your favourite – ah, here it is, Pavarotti himself; will that soothe the fevered brow?'

When she was settled back with her glass, and strains of 'Nessun dorma' eased from hidden speakers, he looked out of the window and adopted her air of studied unconcern. 'Okay,' he said, 'don't tell me who these people are or where we're going or what it's all about... but there is one question you do have to answer.' He turned then and fixed her with a demanding stare. 'Who the hell was it who hit the cobbles back at the old court?'

'Couldn't you guess? Wilkes, of course.'

'Come on! Tell me! What happened up there in the tower? Did you give him a push?'

'Of course not!' It was the first time she was at all animated. 'Would I do a thing like that?' His sceptical look provoked more. 'He simply decided to do the decent thing; took his own life because he had nowhere else to go.'

'You didn't help him on his way?'

'I simply pointed out the cul-de-sac into which he and his family had driven themselves. A phone call from the TV people seemed to clinch it.'

'Did you land a punch?'

'Initially, yes, to prevent him from doing what he had in mind with a tray of some evil-looking substances.'

'You mean, the big chair and the syringe?'

She nodded. 'Those and the Bunsen burner, yes. No doubt some sadist was on hand with a drill or the thumb screws; no thank you very much.'

'But if you landed a punch and he took a dive they'll find marks on the body. Who's to say whether he was dead before he went over?'

'That's for the forensic people to decide, by which time we shall be out of the country.'

'I'm amazed they let you go. I saw Kasper on the steps. Surely you're a suspect?'

'Some foolish talk about a murder charge.'

Roper exclaimed: 'Thought so! What stopped him?'

'Friends.'

'Would you like to help me here? Really, you should. Who are these people? Why is our friend Huber in the front car? Where are we headed? Who's the Yank up front? And what sort of friends can spring you like a jailbreak from a murder charge and organise all this?'

She gave him one of her rare sweet smiles. 'Let's just say, your work is done. In fact, your job is very well done and I'm extremely grateful, but now you can relax and enjoy the ride.'

'What about your Porsche?'

'Taken care of.'

'The luggage? You were frantic, I seem to remember, to get your luggage out. Clothes, papers, all your records and notes.'

'Been collected for us. In the front car. Don't worry, yours is there too.'

His frown was a Nile delta of anxiety.

'Look,' she said, 'I know you were organisation man back there at the Isarhof but this is where your role ends, this is where your final task is done; now it's time for you to relax. Everything is fine. Everything has been resolved.'

'One more thing,' he said.

She frowned.

Then he leaned over and kissed her. She didn't protest.

'That's for saving my skin back there,' he said. 'A truly magnificent but foolish gesture. A crazy thing to do.'

～

It was true. He had been at the centre of activity for many days but now that everything had been taken out of his hands he had a distinctly helpless feeling, washed up like a piece of flotsam on a great tide of events he did not control or understand.

He also knew that when Emma wanted to be uncommunicative no amount of probing would open her up. He would have to wait for the right occasion. Perhaps when they arrived at their destination, wherever that might be. She owed him that much at the very least.

He glanced at her and shook his head. Her fearlessness was amazing. What had happened at the tower would have plunged most people into a state of shock but for her there were no shakes, shouts or craving for litres of alcohol. She could put it all behind her with no apparent reaction. Truly, she was a chameleon.

He sank back into his comfortable chair and watched the signposts whizzing by – Salzburg, Linz, Vienna, Bratislava – and began to ask himself: Was age creeping up on him? His doubts continued. Could he possibly expect to keep up with her?

They had crossed the frontier into Austria and pulled up at a service station for fuel and a break where, during a conversation on a picnic lawn between Huber and Emma, it quickly became obvious that their destination was the Czech Republic.

'Our forest friends are getting quite excited,' Huber said, reading off an email on his laptop. 'Now we've told them we're on our way they can't wait. They like our pictures and they're quite sure.'

'Sure of what precisely?' she queried.

'Don't say.'

'So ask 'em.'

'Look, these are three old guys. Grandsons have bought them this computer, like I said before. They're all into history, to telling everyone their story, but they don't really trust this machine. It's new-fangled. Like a tractor. Put your trust in a horse, man! Face to face is their way. We can't bully them by email.'

Emma shrugged and looked at Roper with a grin. 'I'd really like to be sure, to have a definitive answer, to know exactly what we can expect at the end of another 800 kilometres, but hey-ho, why worry?' She shrugged again. 'Never mind, Lance and Max are driving.'

Roper butted in. 'Lance?'

But she only smiled.

'Look,' Roper insisted, 'it's time you let on. How the devil did you get sprung back there in Munich?'

'Friends,' she said. 'Friends who persuaded the Ettblock that a murder charge was out of the question. Any half-decent lawyer could get it knocked down to GBH and what would be the point of that? A trial would be an open sore... Ghosts from the past... The Gestapo archive. You know how sensitive they are about that. Plus, of course, the Kasper family tree. Not an edifying sight.'

Roper snorted. 'I'd like to meet your friends. Useful people. Seem to be able to fix anything. How about a medal for you and a pension for me?'

'Okay,' she said lightly, 'I'll speak to the head man. About the medal.'

Huber began acting the shepherd dog. 'Right, folks, time to get going again.'

During the next part of the journey Roper occupied himself with her laptop, scrolling down the news channels until he found what he hoped to see: Breaking News... *World in Focus* Shock Exposé: Wilkes Family Named in Illicit Arms Trading Scandal; and a little later, Calls for Senate Investigation into

Arms Affair; later still, Wilkes Presidential Campaign Under a Cloud; and finally, Wilkes Family Hit by Bereavement.

'It's broken,' he said, passing back the laptop.

Emma shook a triumphant fist but her enthusiasm was muted. The defeat of her No.1 adversary was something to celebrate; his demise was not.

Later still, Roper managed to extract a few more facts. Huber, who naturally fell into the role of translator, came back to the second car to fill in some of the details. They were visiting the three old Czech fighters who had signalled their certainty that they could solve the Bradley Wilkes mystery. They had unpronounceable names but that didn't matter; they went by their roles. Roper had already met Rabbit; then there was Logs, clearly the most lavishly equipped of the trio – he had a quad bike for towing timber. He was also the one with the message machine. Today, however, they were bound for the home of the third member of the trio: The Cobbler.

'From what I can gather,' Huber said, 'The Cobbler was the only member of the group who really understood our mystery fighter, who really talked to him, so let's hope we strike lucky with him.'

CHAPTER FORTY-FIVE

T he approach was slow and bumpy, the place well off the patchy network of tarmacked roads. Access was via a gravel track, winding and rutted. They passed an unfamiliar wooden building set back in the trees. It had a vast planked roof reaching almost to the ground and was topped by two turrets supporting tiny domes.

'Sweet little hut,' Emma said.

'That was the church,' Huber said.

There were other small log-like structures set back off the road but during the whole of their journey into the forest they had seen no one. No pedestrians, no workers, no traffic.

Finally their cars stopped outside another wooden building, this one slightly larger than the rest and with a tiny window facing the road. Huber vanished around the side, returning minutes later to indicate that they had, indeed, arrived.

The Cobbler's workroom was at the back of the house, he explained, and they had to troop through the living room to get to it. The house was surprisingly warm and in the main room Emma noticed a vast tiled object reaching almost to the ceiling.

It was arranged in ascending tiers and covered in bright-blue glazing with elaborate decoration.

Huber caught her gaze. 'The kachelöfen,' he said. 'The masonry heater. You can feed it with wood or straw or even grass and it retains the heat for hours,' he said.

'Absurdly elaborate,' Emma said.

'Signals his status.'

Leather dominated the pungent smells of the workroom but there was also the tang of steel from tools and nails, mixed with sweat, the mustiness of the old man's apron and a faint aroma of coffee wafting in from the kitchen. He was a little man, perched on a stool, permanently hunched from his work, balding and bespectacled. His tiny bench was crowded with old soles, broken shoes and a big last – no machinery here, just wizened hands and the craft of centuries. A sad man, she thought, not given to sudden impulses, still able to make a living since the nearest competitor was an expensive thirty miles away.

Huber charmed, Emma smiled and Roper nodded their thanks and their interest. The little man listened, cleared away the forlorn piece of footwear he had been working on and produced a sheaf of photographs. Their pictures, it transpired, the ones sent to Rabbit. Emma watched closely as The Cobbler turned each photograph over, his fingers bent into oddly crooked shapes. This, she assumed, was the result of years of work with needle and thread.

'He says these photos are of a very young man, different from the one they knew, but he's still sure it's him,' Huber supplied.

Emma nodded with enthusiasm and relief.

A little black dog, aged like its master, sprawled by the man's stool, its tail making a strange scratchy noise as it wagged against a threadbare rug. Huber was doing a useful job at translation, giving a rounded picture rather than a literal one.

'He's semi-retired; still does all the repairs for family and friends. His wife says he'll never give it up, never put away the hammer or the last.'

They all smiled their approval.

'Not many people are left in the village, most have moved on, bad times and all that, but he'll never go, never desert his village; loyal to his beloved forest.'

Emma recalled passing several overgrown ruins on the way in. The old man began a monologue. They had been waiting a long time, he said, to discover the true identity of their mystery fighter. He had been secretive, closely guarding all detail of his past, and would only say that he was American – but they hadn't believed him. His German and Czech were too good. He had to be a native.

'Partly correct,' Emma said. 'The family came from the Sudetenland some years back. Obviously, they continued to speak both languages. That's why he got the radio job. He knew the lingo, the terrain, all the old wrinkles of central Europe. Perfect for a foreign correspondent.'

The old man was talking again. His group reckoned the fighter's family would come looking one day – and they were right. He nodded at them, smiled slightly and eased himself off his stool. He went to a drawer, returning with a small cloth bag tied at the neck with string.

All eyes were on the bag as he undid the knot.

He held it upside down and several items fell out, spilling on to the bench. Emma drew in a deep breath, held back for a moment, then put her hand forward, attracted by a small badge-sized oval disc with stamped markings. She held it to the light and read off the letters and numbers: AMTIIDOOIII.

She nodded at Roper and Huber and slipped the companion disc from a pouch on her belt. The one that Cyrus

Wilkes had given her at the Isarhof, the one taken from Bradley Wilkes's German leg tag.

She laid the two together: AMTIIDOOIII.

'Matches exactly,' Roper said gently, looking at Emma.

She nodded slowly, letting out a long breath, all three recalling the explanation given at the Isarhof: markings that reflected the byzantine nature of the Nazi police state and its apparatus, the Reich Central Security Office.

'This has to be the ultimate confirmation,' she said. 'Has to be him.'

Huber gave the thumbs up and Emma beamed hugely, nodding her thanks at the old man.

But Roper's expression remained serious. 'Next, we have to ask him about the trains,' he said. 'Why he kept attacking them. Why he was called The Brakeman.'

∿

Bradley C Wilkes, Moravka, Occupied Czechoslovakia, 13 November 1943

They won't listen. They don't want to know, however many times I explain. They just can't see. All they desire is to attack the police armoury and steal the rifles, rob the town bank and put a stop to collaborators. It's parish pump stuff; they can't understand the bigger picture, the wider significance.

But these village fighters are not the only wooden-heads. Take the air strategists back in London. Happy to bomb the sarin factory when I gave them the co-ordinates but refused to target a camp that kills thousands on arrival and works the rest to death. I could not continue working for people so bereft of humanity and common sense.

My new friends here in the forest complain I have too much to say, so I resign myself to silence and – at the risk of sounding preachy – consider it my humanitarian duty to act, and to act alone.

Today I'm trekking the forest line, planning my sixth ambush. Each one requires a change of tactic. I've seen steel helmets guarding bridges and crossings. They know I will strike but don't know from where. Last week my position was a bridge; the week before, a tree. I rely on their predictability. Monday is their chosen day; always the same, at the same time, with the same pair of ancient locomotives.

A shot from the side is impossible when the train is in motion. Too fast, too fleeting. The best way is from directly ahead of the locomotive when the driver, and often the fireman, look over the sides of the cab in the direction of travel. These days they learn to keep their heads inside and peer through the porthole windows. This is what they expect and what they fear – the shot from directly ahead.

How many more times, I ask myself, will the men of the footplate agree to do the occupier's bidding? How much longer before the Czech train crews save their own lives and refuse to work these journeys? How much longer before they recognise these actions have but one purpose – to stop all death transports to Oświęcim, the place the Germans call Auschwitz-Birkenau, just a couple of hours away over the Polish border?

Tomorrow I plan a surprise.

Emma, Huber and Roper were still clustered around the old man's workbench. The mystery of the disc and Bradley Wilkes's identity had been solved but Emma's attention remained focused on the other items that had fallen out when The Cobbler had emptied his cloth bag.

She picked up a ring. Plain to see were the engraved letters BCW, her grandfather's initials. A watch, once a prized object that told not only the time but the date and the temperature, was similarly marked, then another tiny object, a grey-green leather pouch fastened with a miniature silver button. Gently, she prized it open. For a long minute she studied the tiny photograph inside: a woman's face, a serious expression, wide mouth, clear gaze. It was one of those long-ago studio shots in which the subject was not allowed to smile. There was a deep fringe and the fingers of the right hand were steepled in a theatrical prop against her cheek. A thirties photograph but redolent of the decade before.

Huber, Roper and the old man awaited her verdict in silence. At last she looked up. 'My grandmother,' she said.

'Can you be sure?' Roper peered over her shoulder. 'It's very faded.'

'I have the self-same photograph at home,' she said.

Then, with great solemnity, she turned to The Cobbler, clasped his hand in both of hers and, with Huber translating, thanked him profusely for the safekeeping of these treasures. 'All my fondest hopes have been fulfilled here today,' she said. 'Thanks to you. Everything I had hoped for. An heroic story for my grandfather. The final chapter revealed.'

She gave him her warmest and most generous smile. The old man beamed back. A landmark for him too.

But then her smile faded, brows knitting. 'But there is one aspect of all this that needs to be resolved,' she said, taking up Roper's earlier question. 'Just why was he called The Brakeman?'

The old man's expression went blank.

'Why,' she persisted, 'did he attack trains? And all alone? That's the last piece of the jigsaw I really don't get.'

All trace of pleasure disappeared. The old man was quite

still. An inscrutable mask, as if this was a question he'd hoped she would never ask.

~

Bradley C Wilkes, the morning of 14 November

For the fifth time in the last few minutes I check my watch, trying to suppress the worry that's building like a black fog, trying to keep my breathing even, trying to keep stress from my body. They're late.

I'm lying in a nest of pine needles in a hide on the treeline 350 metres back from the track, my headgear festooned with twigs and branches. Today I am at right angles to the railway, my position camouflaged along the edge of a line of trees and commanding a wide arc of fire across open ground. The location is a curve restricting the view of the locomotive crew and around this curve is a farm crossing.

This is my sixth and most risky ambush but this time I have a unique advantage: I have help. Several hundred metres to the rear is my friend, perhaps my only true friend in this forest. Radek Vasko has his loaded farm cart and his horse at the ready and he's waiting for my signal. His nerves, I know, are on a cliff edge even steeper than mine.

Attention to detail! Once again I check the tool of my adopted trade, a trusty Karabiner 98k, paid for with a boxload of plundered cigarettes, and one of the best sniper rifles of the war when you add the Zeiss ZF39 telescopic sight. I didn't inquire about its provenance, nor the fate of its former owner.

Peering through the scope I again check out the far distance, the point at which the railway track disappears from view, willing myself to detect smoke or steam or to hear the faintest of sounds that will herald the approach of the train.

Nothing. The forest is quiet, its rich wildlife of deer, boar, foxes, wolves and brown bears reserving their strength for the night. Have the Germans done the unthinkable and changed their routine? My whole plan is based on their abhorrence of breaking a schedule. Every Monday around this hour the transport passes this place. Where are they today?

I run through the possibilities: shortage of coal, bomb damage on the main line or a mechanical malfunction on one of their ancient locomotives. God knows they must be working wonders to keep those museum pieces going.

My tactics are high-risk. I'm not taking a distant shot from far ahead. Today I'm going side-on and at much closer range. One factor is my eyesight. It's been getting worse these past few weeks and I'm relying on my right eye to do all the work. Another factor is that I can't move further back because of the narrow channel through the forest carved out by the railway. And, lastly, I can't afford a single miss. I must get close enough to ensure each shot strikes home.

To stay calm, I do more breathing exercises to depress the heart rate. Pine needles make an acceptable base but lying still and prone for long periods turns muscles stiff, a fatal condition militating against fast flight. I long to move and stretch and exercise but I cannot jeopardise my camouflage. Instead, I watch a sparrowhawk in the distance, a common species. My farmer friend insists there are corncrakes, woodpeckers and even golden eagles in the Beskid but so far they have eluded me.

I watch a snail on a nearby leaf leaving his slimy trail. Thirst is a problem but a full bladder an even greater one. After a while something tickles the right leg and I brush away a tiny insect. There are other irritants: sores on my face and body; a multitude of cuts and bruises; and a churning stomach. I haven't eaten well these past few weeks, supplies being scarce, but is this nerves? Or just the constant gut problem of the forest fugitive? None of us can shake off the gaunt and ragged look that comes with living in a cave. I touch the tissue-thin paper pack in which I've wrapped my food: the leg from a scrawny chicken; black bread that tastes like the sweepings of the barn; and an insipid cheese.

Images of my past life spring to mind. A golden past: a heated swimming pool; holidays on a Florida beach; and learning to stalk deer and elk on the Snake River with Grandpa and the proficiency with his .270 bolt-action Winchester. I ask myself if I am justified in what I do. Before the war I would have been in turmoil at the thought of taking a life but too much bestiality has crossed my path since then: lines of Jews behind the wire and the stink of the chimneys that signals mass murder at Auschwitz-Birkenau. I breathe deeply to control a rage. I would happily take out any number of soldiers but it is the expertise of the locomen that keeps this monstrous death machine rolling.

Waiting is the true ordeal but, at long last, the enemy does not disappoint. Faint at first but growing louder, I hear the steady blast of exhaust steam and the crashing rhythm of the cranks. I glance at the farmer; he too is alert. I draw a bead on my chosen spot. I work the bolt of my rifle. Five in the magazine. Make them count!

Then it comes into view, the long snake wriggling around the bend.

Action is about to commence.

～

The tension in The Cobbler's workshop was broken by a sudden explosion of noise outside the cottage. Rabbit and Logs had arrived by quad bike. This was followed by excited exchanges between the families. The newcomers were keen to witness the unravelling of the mystery.

However, Emma was not distracted. 'What I want to know

is, how could all these personal items have been saved all this time? I mean, wouldn't the Germans have confiscated them?'

The Cobbler's expression lifted. He even managed a small smile. The American's left leg, he explained, was shorter than his right. His left shoe had been built up to compensate. He knew this because he had repaired the shoe. And discovered a small hiding place in the built-up section, a secret compartment to keep the locket and the disc.

The Cobbler's wife, wearing a white apron over a calf-length blue dress with black banding at the hem, was handing round drinks, a strong white liquid worked from a home still. It was potent stuff. The Czechs were noisy and pleased, Huber was beaming and Emma reflective.

She heard Roper's whispered warning. 'Careful. This stuff will scramble your brain.'

There were snacks too, peppery from some forest herb inside an insipid doughy casing, creating a garlic-like fug reminiscent of travelling on the Paris Metro.

Emma glanced out of the window. From nowhere, it seemed, a knot of boys had appeared to inspect the vehicles, peering in at the windows of the SUV. Then she looked again at the woman of the house, much younger and more exuberant than her husband and clearly pleased with the occasion as one on which to dress up in her newest acquisition, a pair of high lace-up boots in black leather complete with a silver buckle.

A roomful of smiling faces. Except one. The Cobbler wasn't in a joyous mood. There seemed to be a deep sadness about this man. Yes, Emma was welcome; yes, he wanted to solve the puzzle of the mystery fighter; yes, he was giving her answers... and yet she was conscious of a reserve. She wondered if it could be resentment at this cavalcade of strangers in their smart city clothes and extravagant vehicles. Or an underlying hostility to displays of luxury from a world he did not wish to ape or enter.

She studied him again. Did those haunted old eyes convey more than resentful stoicism? Something shameful perhaps... Guilt or even betrayal?

She put down her glass. She was determined to extract the whole truth but it wouldn't emerge from an inebriated party. Instead, she walked The Cobbler back to his workshop and encouraged him to give her a demonstration of his craft. She made a show of fascination for his dexterity with leather, thread and nail. Then gradually, with Huber's assistance, she began to probe, query and push. The Cobbler, at first evasive, eventually gave ground on The Brakeman's one-man war.

'It was his thing,' he conceded, 'but we didn't want any part of it. We feared the consequences. Bringing refugees to our camp. Drawing attention, bringing the enemy down on us.'

The old man shook his head and the details dribbled out: targeting the crews, stopping the trains, the impossibility of releasing the people on board. 'If we'd let him bring them to the forest,' The Cobbler said, 'it could have been the end for all of us.' He shrugged again. 'Besides, it made no sense to us. We weren't interested in his trains; we had more urgent concerns. We didn't want any part of his strange war.'

Emma's earlier elation subsided at this tale of loss and disappointment. Her admiration for the old man deflated. He hung his head. Emma, Roper and Huber stared down at the little collection of artefacts on the bench. A long silence hung heavily.

The old man made another attempt to justify. 'The occupier knew we were hereabouts. Sent several search parties. We had to keep moving. It was just one cave after another. Damp, dark, cold, no change of clothing, no hygiene, bad food. It's no fun being the hunter – or the hunted.'

Huber seemed anxious to be understanding. 'A terrible time.'

'What would have happened,' the old man continued, 'if a whole crowd of people had been camped out on us? How would we have managed? How long would we have lasted?'

Huber nodded again, Emma said nothing but Roper addressed the old man. 'There's one part of this story we still don't know,' he said gently. 'How it ended.'

Huber looked at The Cobbler and asked the question. The man hesitated, took off his apron, hung it behind the door, beckoned them towards the road and spoke his one word of English. 'Come,' he said.

~

Bradley C Wilkes, the morning of 14 November

As the train steams closer I give my farmer friend the signal, the waving of a leafy stick, and Radek Vasko kicks his horse violently into motion. A smart start is necessary to allow time for the deed; time also for the man's escape.

I can see approaching the familiar rake of a double-header train, two ancient tank engines plucked from retirement and pressed into wartime service. Due to curvature and forest, they can't see Vasko as his cart grumbles into life, halting at the crossing.

Will this ruse work? In his panic I worry that the man will blunder into an error and deliver his load to the wrong place. I can see him atop his burden, kicking off the first log, then the second, then the third, until the whole load has rolled directly across the track. I silently applaud the man. The dust cloud of his urgent escape has just descended as numbers 84 Deggendorf and 83 Bayerwald cruise slowly into the curve.

From my position, I have a good view and count the trucks: thirty-one cattle cars in all, just like last week, all bolted shut with long metal levers on the outside. On the inside, I know, as yet unheard and certainly unseen, are hundreds of victims – men, women and children, the physically active among them bound for work details, the weak for the ovens.

I feel a rage at yet another atrocity in the making but I must concentrate. I'm not a natural warrior; a hunter, yes, in childhood, but not a military man. Stay cool, stay clinical, I tell myself and take deep slow breaths to lower pulse rate, blood pressure, reduce perspiration and relax tense muscles. I inhale through the nose, allowing the belly to move, breathing out through the nose, each breath a little deeper and a little slower.

But my gaze does not leave the train. In the middle is the passenger car containing the guard detail: my biggest threat. On the footplate of Deggendorf are the Czech crew and a military policeman. You can't miss him, even at a distance: a field-grey figure with a luminous half-moon metal gorget hanging on a chain from his neck and Schmeisser submachine gun slung at the ready.

Why are the crew so slow-witted this morning? Then, at last, the sound of brakes. Late but not too late, they spot the obstruction and bring the train to a halt a few yards short of the logpile.

Close by is a pole to which I earlier fixed a notice.

The Feldgendarmerie soldier jumps down from the footplate and advances at the crouch, peering ahead. Slowly, expecting a shot from his front, he inches towards my notice.

More field-grey figures from the guard wagon are running, also keeping low, alongside the train. The Germans congregate hesitantly at the buffer beam, expecting a shot. When it doesn't come, they go forward to the notice. They read:

Take this train back. Do not deliver these people to their deaths and servitude. Be warned, railway crews who collaborate will be executed. Do not

collaborate with mass murder; do not collaborate with the evil occupier.

Angrily, they begin to tear it down. Next they will manhandle the logs or use the locomotives as a battering ram to clear a passage. By now I can hear another sound: the wailing of female voices, high-pitched childish calls and some form of male-voice chanting. The lead cattle car has an air vent high up near the roof; briefly, I spot a row of fingers clutching wood and my scope picks out eyes, fearful eyes.

The cabs of the stalled locomotives are side-on to me. The train crew from Deggendorf, after some hesitation, climb gingerly down from the footplate to witness this spectacle at the logpile, banking on the lee of the cab to protect them from danger. Like their masters, they expect danger ahead.

I breathe slowly and deeply and focus my good eye, lining up the sight at the end of the long barrel of the Karabiner, holding her rock steady on a prepared plinth of stones and brick, and take up the slack of the trigger. The fireman is fatally motionless. I ease gently against the tautness of the trigger pressure and the big killing machine barks an echoing blast around the forest clearing.

Without waiting to check the result, I work the bolt fast for a second shot and get off another as the driver clambers in panic up his footholds, scrambling for the protection of the bunker, the footplate, anywhere.

Too late.

Three rounds left, but I decide to spare the crew of the Bayerwald.

Now it is my turn to flee. I am acquainted with the forest and the ways of wildlife, thanks to my partisan friends. A hare runs fast uphill in a straight line. A pursuing predator, be it fox or dog, chases in the same direction not knowing that behind the ridge the hare has changed direction. I aim to encourage a similar ruse;

specifically, several well-planted footprints in a muddy pool leading in a wrong direction.

Panting, heaving under the weight of the big rifle, I am on my second leg heading parallel and towards the rear of the stalled train when something gives me pause. The noises of confusion below are familiar: shouts, screams, steam, commotion. But this noise is different: the rasping gasp for breath, the striving for flight.

I peer through the bushes and see a figure struggling to reach the edge of the trees, intent, like myself, on escape. A balding middle-aged figure in tattered clothing, gasping from unaccustomed exertion. Clearly not crew, nor guard. This I cannot understand. No one before has succeeded in escaping a locked wagon.

I stay still and allow him to approach.

He starts and halts when he sees me, aghast at the prospect of recapture.

My rifle is across my chest, easily to be swung into the firing position if required. I must look menacing.

He begins to back away.

'Stop!' I say in Czech, then repeat in German.

Fear on his face. 'Are you...?' he says, pointing downhill.

'No. Partisan.'

'Ah!'

I sling the rifle into the carry position and grab him by the arm. 'Run!'

But not fast enough. We've been spotted. A field-grey by the track is crouching in the fire position. A shot thwacks into a tree above my head, then another in quick succession, and the third finds its mark. It feels like a hammer has just taken off my right leg. No pain, simply numbness.

My new friend holds on to my arm.

'Move!' I yell, and somehow we hobble into the trees.

'Keep going,' I urge, surprised I can still travel, amazed I feel nothing. 'Fast, until they give up.'

'Will they?'

'They have to deliver that train,' I pant between breaths, 'that's their imperative.'

He nods. I already know from his voice, his diction, that I have met an educated man.

He is my crutch; I am his guide.

After a while we stop and listen but there are no sounds of pursuit. The consequences of not delivering his human cargo, as stipulated in his orders, will be the urgent concern of the train commander.

I take a moment to look over the stranger: a sledgehammer chin, wide mouth, alert eyes and a prominent mole on the left cheek. And he's demonstrating a high degree of self-possession by ripping off his shirt, tearing it into strips and winding it round my wound. Not a neat job, given the haste of the moment, but we stumble on.

'How did you get out?' Questions distract me from the struggle of motion.

'Worked loose some planks, managed to scramble out, but the others were too frightened to follow,' he says.

I have a brutal response. 'Most of them will be dead before nightfall.'

He's shocked. 'Worse than I imagined.'

His name, he says, is Vaclav Chladek, lecturer in psychology at the University of Brno, corralled into a ghetto and rounded up at dawn. We crab along and I feel the need to explain to someone who will listen and has the wit to understand. Thousands are being taken, I tell him. 'And I'm alone. I have no help. My associates will not join me. I do not have the means for more elaborate forms of sabotage.' I sigh deeply. 'Regretfully, I have no means of effecting an escape.'

'Why?' he wants to know. 'Why are they so unsympathetic?'

'They rate only forest people. They've listened to the occupiers' propaganda. They believe your people to be gypsies, criminals, the socially undeserving.'

He is silent, perhaps fearing a hostile reception from my friends in the forest, but I need to talk. 'When this war is finally done, I'm ready to justify, to answer for my actions.'

'Seems a long way off.'

In truth I'm thinking with pain of my failings, the greatest of which was to leave my compatriot, my fellow resister, Emil Jarek, abandoned to his fate in a Gestapo cell. My tribute to him, my conscience clause, is to keep faith with all these unfortunate souls consigned in cattle trucks to Auschwitz-Birkenau. Souls like Vaclav Chladek.

'Look,' I say, feeling a sudden urgency, 'don't get caught. Your survival is my justification. I may not have much of a future...' I look down at my dragging leg and a bloody trail. Medical help in the middle of a remote forest? Not a great hope.

'But you,' I insist, 'you must live to see the peace. For me, to justify me, for my sake.'

Emma, Roper and Huber were in an annex to the village churchyard, hardly more than a clearing in the forest, but encroaching nature had been kept at bay, the grass cut short, and a simple wooden cross stood apart, solitary and alone.

And without a name.

The Brakeman's war against the German trains had run for six months, The Cobbler said, then railway crews found reasons to go absent and the transports were thrown into chaos. However, his one-man war couldn't continue. The sixth ambush was his last. Despite the gunshot wound, he made it back to the forest hide with his one trophy man – the only survivor of the transports – but died soon after.

'He wouldn't hear of calling a doctor,' The Cobbler said, 'that would have put us all in peril, but when he got so bad we called one anyway.' The Cobbler sighed. 'Too late. Septicaemia had set in.'

Emma stood for a long time looking at the little cross.

She drew in a deep breath. 'Anonymous and unrecognised no longer. Time for the world to know. What we need now is to put a name to this cross: Bradley C Wilkes, The Brakeman.'

CHAPTER FORTY-SIX

Roper lugged his case out of the boot of the big car and humped it into the station yard. Emma was behind him, for the first time beyond the hearing of the others.

He stopped at the entrance to the concourse and turned to her. 'So, you're not going to introduce me?'

'To?'

'The man up front. Mr Mystery. The man with the American accent.'

'No.'

He raised an eyebrow. 'Not even to say "nice to meet you and farewell"?'

'Lance...' she sighed, 'is a shadow man. He's stayed out of our little drama at Czecho. And he stays out of us, completely.'

'At least give me some inkling. The curiosity is killing me.'

'You don't need to know.'

He snorted. 'You're already talking like one of them.'

'I am one of them. You must have guessed.'

He nodded. 'All makes perfect sense. The high-powered motorcade. The big clout with the German police. You and missiles and non-proliferation. How the hell would a normal academic know all that stuff? History takes a back seat, I guess. The CIA – they pay well, do they?'

She gave him one of her enigmatic smiles.

'What?' he demanded.

'That's what you were intended to think.'

He exploded. 'Oh now, come on, Emma!'

She looked around in alarm, but he persisted: 'You can't play those games with me right to the last moment, right to the point where I get on this train. For once, please, be straight with me.'

She glanced behind, then to the side, leaning close. 'For an ex-cop and investigative reporter, you aren't very good, are you?' Her mouth gave a little amused twitch. 'Lance Scranton is no more American than you or I. Hails from Toronto, if that little nugget calms your itch to know.'

Now it was Roper's turn to chuckle. 'Canadian? I see, I get it. Canadian! I know enough about the espionage game to know the Ruskies always pretend to be Canadians to disguise their terrible American accents. So, the man is from Toronto... And what does that make you?'

She was serious, more serious than he had seen for days. Her tone was just above a whisper but just as forceful as if she had been shouting. 'Lance is not a Russian. Not, not, not! Okay? And if you think I...'

He made calming motions with his hands.

'Why on earth would I?' she demanded. 'No connection with Mother Russia. No family, no ideology, nothing.'

'Okay,' he said, 'calm down.' He sighed and looked about him, satisfied no one was earwigging. The place was deserted. Must be between trains. 'So,' he said, 'if you're not CIA, if you're not Moscow, what the devil are you?'

Her smile was back. The unknowable smile. 'At times,' she said, 'you can be unbelievably dense.'

The sound of a klaxon broke the spell of their exchange. She turned briefly to look back at the cars, parked out on the street. Huber was standing by an open door, staring in their direction.

'And what about him?' Roper demanded. 'What's his role? Another Intelligence asset? Or lover?'

'He's too good to spend the rest of his working life digging in dusty archives. He's a natural.'

Roper repressed the bitter taste of resentment, recognising the illogicality of it. Emma and he – theirs was an affair that didn't happen, couldn't happen. Age, youth, her mother and Emma's own chameleon-like personality made it an impossibility. It was ridiculous to be jealous of Huber, he knew that. What was it she had once asked him? Did he fancy a younger woman? He grunted and wished he was as certain of the answer as the negative he had given her. He swallowed before returning to his role as protector. What was he going to tell Agnes Drake about her daughter's prospects and future?

'Is this all for the best?' he demanded. 'I hope you know what you're getting into.'

There was another toot on the klaxon.

'A better life,' she said quickly. 'Easier; better than being a professor. More exciting; easier on the feet and the head. Farewell, academia.' Then she lunged forward and grabbed him in a great bear hug. 'And this is goodbye us,' she said. 'Thanks is a completely inadequate word...' She pulled apart and laid a finger on his chest. 'But you must keep all of this well and truly under that wise old hat.'

The toot was longer and louder this time. She turned without another word and dashed across the yard, got in the open door of the car and didn't look back.

Roper stood there like a spurned lover, staring after the dust cloud left by the four-by-fours. When they had disappeared from sight he trudged into the station to book his ticket for the long way round and obscure route home. His train would be skirting German territory – 'Just to make sure,' she'd said – and there was time enough for inquests.

He took a window seat. There was a menu on the table. He looked at it but didn't read. She'd called him a dimwit – so who else would she be working for?

Suddenly, to the consternation of his fellow passengers, he slammed his hand down hard on the table. 'You're SIS,' he said out loud, then looked out of the window, adding silently to himself: *Emma, I've tabbed you. You're Vauxhall Cross... You've even recruited a German asset to bring through London's front door. Some prize to start your spook career!*

He laughed some then, amused by the revelation but slightly shamefaced that he had not glimpsed the truth before. Then he worked through the politics of the arms auction in Munich: the CIA might or might not look with approval on a maverick American selling arms to the Nagorno-Karabakh Republic, though not now, given the scandal that was breaking over the pond; the French would have been keen to flog Nato's latest weaponry, never ones to worry about the rules – if they had known about it; and China was always in for an arms export order. Others – Iran, North Korea, Pakistan – could well have been sniffing around the edges of the auction to see if there was a chance. It was only in the interests of British foreign policy to obey the Non-Proliferation Treaty, to play the good guy who upheld all the international protocols.

We, Roper surmised, had nothing suitable to sell.

It also made good sense to get on the right side of Russia, perhaps brokering a new détente with Moscow; good policy to wreck the presidential prospects of the dreadful Wendell Wilkes, the danger man of international politics; and it would feel good in Whitehall to scupper the American arms industry.

Roper brushed aside the question of whether this whole

episode had been a British Intelligence operation from start to finish. Almost certainly, from the moment Professor Chadwick entertained a certain gentleman from across the Atlantic... but what did it matter? Instead, his thoughts returned to Emma: enigma, chameleon, a young woman who could be so many different people all at once.

Then he addressed her, as if she were sitting in the seat right across from him: *You'll be good at it, Emma; you'll take to the duplicitous life with talent, panache and ease.*

And to her mother, when he finally reached home at No.24 Orchard Street, he would answer the question he himself had posed on his first day out of Wormwood Scrubs: How is your clever daughter doing?

Answer: Just fine. She's found her natural home.

EPILOGUE
EDINBURGH, 2003

My name was Vaclav Chladek. I am retired now, retired from my chair of psychiatry at the city's university, and I am writing this to put on record for posterity that I have done as I was bid.

I have survived.

For the rest of my life, from that day on the train and in the forest, I have strived to make my life a worthwhile testimony and a fitting tribute to my rescuer. To achieve much and live the good life.

My speciality has been to study the effects of late-developing trauma, particularly among survivors of the Holocaust, many of whom have suffered depression and ended their lives by their own hand. I considered myself suitably qualified, having been born a Czech and begun my medical studies at the Masaryk University in Brno. This institution was closed by the Nazis. Most of our professors were executed. I remained in hiding, only to be caught in a round-up.

My fate should have been labour and death.

Instead, I escaped – thanks to a brave man of the forest – and *have continued my career in a land of freedom dedicated to the concept of high achievement.*

In the course of this I have been privileged to live a normal life – a happy marriage with a son; a wonderful son – intelligent, inquiring, bent on an academic career like myself. Forgive a father's pride.

This is the testimony of the former Vaclav Chladek, subsequently reborn as Victor Chadwick, father of Cedric Chadwick, professor of history at St James's College, Cambridge.

A high achiever winning many laurels; a marvellous son. What greater gift could be bestowed on a survivor such as myself? Again, forgive an old man's pride.

For all this I give thanks and pay tribute to The Brakeman of the Beskid forest.

THE END

ACKNOWLEDGEMENTS

I'm indebted to a great teacher, Jill Dawson, and all those on the University of East Anglia writing course and to my equally talented mentor, Jim Kelly.

A NOTE FROM THE PUBLISHER

Thank you for reading this book. If you enjoyed it please do consider leaving a review on Amazon to help others find it too.

We hate typos. All of our books have been rigorously edited and proofread, but sometimes mistakes do slip through. If you have spotted a typo, please do let us know and we can get it amended within hours.

info@bloodhoundbooks.com

Printed in Great Britain
by Amazon